www.davidficklingbooks.com

Other titles by Emma Shevah

Dream on, Amber
Dara Palmer's Major Drama
What Lexie Did
Hello, Baby Mo
How to Save the World with a Chicken and an Egg
Ping and the Missing Ring
Time Travel at Puddle Lane

EMMA SHEVAH

MY NAME IS JODIE JONES

David Fickling Books

My Name is Jodie Jones
is a
DAVID FICKLING BOOK

First published in Great Britain in 2025 by
David Fickling Books,
31 Beaumont Street,
Oxford, OX1 2NP

EU Rep: Authorised Rep Compliance Ltd., Ground Floor,
71 Lower Baggot Street, Dublin, D02 P593, Ireland.
www.arccompliance.com

Text © Emma Shevah, 2025

978-1-78845-351-6

1 3 5 7 9 10 8 6 4 2

The right of Emma Shevah to be identified as the
author of this work has been asserted in accordance with
the Copyright, Designs and Patents Act 1988.

All rights reserved. No part of this publication may be reproduced,
stored in a retrieval system, or transmitted in any form or by
any means, electronic, mechanical, photocopying, recording or
otherwise, without the prior permission of the publishers.

Papers used by David Fickling Books are from
well-managed forests and other responsible sources.

DAVID FICKLING BOOKS Reg. No. 8340307

A CIP catalogue record for this book is available from the British Library.

Typeset in 10/14.75 pt Sabon by Falcon Oast Graphic Art Ltd
Printed and bound in Great Britain by Clays Ltd, Elcograf S.p.A.

To me, the greatest pleasure of writing is not what it's about, but the inner music that words make.
Truman Capote

I am a free human being with an independent will.
Charlotte Brontë, *Jane Eyre*

1

I don't know. Maybe bubble or fluff.
Maybe elixir or hotchpotch.
Or murmur or piffle or shade.
Mmm. Shade. I like shade.
Actually, I can't choose.
I really like 'actually', actually.

It's definitely not hatchet.
Or vomit or mucus or snack.

2

Dr Kumar is still waiting for me to answer but I can't, so I sit looking at him, kicking my legs. I don't have a favourite word. Why do I have to choose one when I like so many?

'Five, then,' he says. 'Five you especially like.'

I kick my legs some more until my mother puts her hand near my knees to indicate that I should stop. I desist for a minute because the gesture is so arresting, and she returns her small hand to her lap. When they revive their kicking, she lifts her chin, looks at Dr Kumar and shakes her head almost imperceptibly, but not imperceptibly enough for me not to notice.

Dr Kumar is tall and thin, as if he's shot up overnight, like boys do when they hit thirteen, and although he's an adult, he hasn't grown adult-shaped yet, which is when you grow sideways and puff up. His shoes are suede and beige with rubber heels worn at the edges. It's hard to get over the hairiness of his arms. He has long, flat hands with short, clean fingernails. Thick, spidery lashes surround his bushbaby eyes.

'Lash,' I say, and stop kicking.

'Oh, yes. Lash is a lovely word. I like that one, too. Not if it's a lash from a whip, though.' He laughs, but then frowns and folds his lips inwards. He is no doubt contemplating the appropriateness of this comment. Mental-health professionals are exceptionally concerned with correctness. He's quite young – not that much older than Becca's sister, Amaryllis – and he's more like a woman than a man. I can picture him in a dress and make-up, which you can't say about all men. It's something about the way he moves, in a gentle gliding drift, and the way he blinks and crosses his legs.

'Lash,' I say.

'Yes, you've said "lash". Any others?'

'Lash.'

His head docks and his gaze fixes on me more closely. My legs kick again. I'm not sure why; they just fire up, and off they go. My mother shifts position and pinches the bone on her nose, so I know she is bothered by my behaviour. She grips and un-grips her fingers, then flattens the furrows on her skirt. Her hands are astonishingly talkative, but then so are Dr Kumar's.

'This,' she says to him in a tone I can clearly hear. 'This is what she does.' She smiles demurely and gives him a telling look, as if they've discussed my misdemeanours already.

'If you wouldn't mind, Mrs Jones,' Dr Kumar murmurs, reminding her that he isn't talking to her now, he's talking to me. Then he smiles expectantly, hoping for more of my favourite words. I don't submit any further offerings. Telling him four more isn't going to make him get it. It isn't about choosing five, or having a favourite – it's about the way they sound, and the way they feel in your mouth and in your mind, and if they don't know that by their age, I'm not sure they ever will.

'Health-wise?' he asks, when my legs take a rest, and the seconds of silence become minutes. 'Do you eat well?'

'Depends what you mean by "well". I don't feast on life's delights like some rambunctious king, if that's what you mean.'

'Mmm. Rambunctious.' He nods, keenly. 'That would be one of mine, I think. No, I suppose by "well" I mean "healthily".'

'I eat food that has been chosen for me, like everything else in my life,' I tell him.

My mother's sigh is an irritated one. More a fractious sniff followed by a brisk downhill nostril sweep. I'm clearly being disrespectful and ungrateful, and she is not happy about either of those things. I *am* being honest, though, and she should be pleased about that, at least. Parents are exceptionally concerned with how honest their children are, even though they lie to our faces from birth about tooth fairies, Father Christmas and how babies arrive in bellies.

Dr Kumar considers his notes with a 'Hmm'. He hmms a lot. It must be a psychiatrist thing. I wonder which book he'd give me for my birthday. Something by Oliver Sacks, at a guess, about the uncanny mysteries of the brain. He isn't getting very far with this line of questioning, so he presses his fingertips together and does some doctorly digging. He's trying to work something out. I can tell by the tone of his eyebrows. 'I . . . er . . . I understand you menstruated for a year, from . . . age eleven to twelve, but you haven't had a period for the last . . . For nearly two years. Is that correct?'

I nod nonchalantly. It's awkward talking to a man and a doctor about the period I now don't have. I'm embarrassed, when there's no need to be. I didn't choose to be a female or to menstruate. The word 'menstruate' is misleading – 'struate' sounds like you're forcing something out in a constipated way, when it flows freely regardless of effort or consent. And why does it have 'men' in it at all?

'Menstruation can often stop after a shock or an ordeal,' Dr Kumar explains, never having menstruated himself and therefore not being the world's leading expert. I don't ask him about his bodily functions so I find it unfair that he can ask about mine.

'What's slightly unusual, though, is that your menstrual cycle began as normal when you were eleven, which was a year after the . . . er . . . incident, you had it regularly for a year, and *then* it stopped.' He pauses, his forehead furrowed. 'Which might suggest . . .'

He doesn't suggest what it might suggest, leaving it open for suggestion. As it's not officially a question, I don't officially have to answer, but he looks at me all the same.

To mask my discomfort, I gaze around his office. It's furnished with two unexciting blue sofas at right angles and a yellow felt armchair, which is slightly more exciting but still somewhat disappointing, on which Dr Kumar is seated. My mother and I are sitting on an unexciting sofa each. Behind him is a scuffed white desk, a grey net-backed swivel chair, and a computer monitor facing the opposite way so we can't see the secrets on the screen. My mother's unnecessary gift to him – a green ceramic bowl of pointy, plumy and orbicular plants, the names of which I don't yet know – sits uneasily on the edge of his desk. The only books on the shelves are on psychological disorders, childhood development and trauma – no novels, travelogues or biographies – with some titles stacked horizontally across the line of upright spines, which rattles and clatters rowdily in my brain. I feel sad for him and his forlorn bookcase. I hope this is merely a work bookcase, and he has a more satisfying and orderly one at home.

My mother is uncomfortable, I note. On the other hand, Dr Kumar doesn't seem to mind these awkward, wordless pauses. In fact, he creates them. That's also a psychiatrist thing. He goes extensively quiet in the hope I'll elaborate, which I have no intention of doing. As he waits for me to tell him more, I watch rain descend in cold slants onto the asphalt path and think about sentences instead.

The first time I cried over a sentence was when Champ was in the toilet. A book he was reading lay open on the table as I skipped past to get some staples. No one was looking so I leaned over and sneaked a peek. Actually, there were two sentences. I only had time to read those two (I heard the toilet flush) but they were the most beautiful sentences I'd ever read. They made me cry. Not just pooling, welling, eye drops, either. It was as if they squeezed something deep inside me that ruptured my eyes and my lungs to lift and waft into the air above my head.

Waft. Some words you just have to say again and again.

I heard Champ close the toilet door and walked away so he wouldn't see my crumpled face.

I didn't see the name of the book, but I realized then that it wasn't just words that made me feel that way. Words are a sky full of snowflakes, individual and free. But sentences are ribbons tied to a pole, flapping and dancing in the breeze.

From then on, I collected sentences like other people collect keyrings. I searched for them everywhere and wrote them down. Words as well.

See?

'Words as well' sounds so nice. I need to write it down so I don't forget.

*

Later, I'd asked Champ what he'd been reading.

'Gatsby, Twit Face,' he said.

I paused, unsure. 'Is that what it's called? "Gatsby Twit Face"?'

His laugh flicked out like a forked tongue. 'Seriously, how stupid are you?'

I didn't know the answer. Was it a measurement or a number? If someone asks, 'How heavy are you?', you answer in stones or kilos. If they ask, 'How tall are you?', you say it in centimetres or feet. If they say, 'How clever are you?', the answer might be 'Very clever', 'Quite clever' or 'Not very'. But if you say, 'I'm not very stupid', it means you still are a bit. Does anyone know how stupid they are? Is there a stupid scale? I gawked at Champ trying to work out what to say.

'Ex-actly,' he said, and walked off.

I'm not stupid. If he'd asked, 'Are you stupid, yes or no?' the answer would have been no. But 'How stupid are you?' is an entirely different question.

He's the one who's stupid, because he thought the novel was boring.

I remembered that the sentences were at the beginning of Chapter III, so the next time he left the book lying around, I picked it up and memorized them. Then I wrote them down in my new journal, the one I'd started especially for sentences.

They went like this.

There was music from my neighbour's house through the summer nights. In his blue gardens, men and girls came and went like moths among the whisperings and the champagne and the stars.

I read it over and over. Slowly. Each time changing the rhythm, and pausing momentarily at a different word. The best places to pause were after 'gardens' and 'moths', but any way you read it, it was beautiful. Summer nights. Blue gardens. Whisperings. Stars.

I longed to take the book to my wardrobe, but Champ was working on it for a controlled assessment and would have gone ballistic, which has to do with the way things fly so I don't know why it means angry.

I wanted to read the words repeatedly and learn a better life from them.

It's called *The Great Gatsby* by the way.

There's no 'Twit Face' in the title.

Just in case you wondered.

3

Dr Kumar is looking at me. I've clearly missed a question when I was thinking about moth people, so he asks it again.

It's about my name.

I have grown to dislike this question.

I can't avoid answering it, though. It's very direct and my choices, as usual, are zero. So I relay the facts. 'My name is Jiāyì Jones but everyone calls me my English name, Jodie Jones. My brother's name is Cheng Jones, but he's known as Champ.' I hesitate, and add, 'Jones.'

'Right. Got the Jones part.'

'My dad's half Scottish and half Chinese, and my mother is English and Welsh. Hence, "Jones".'

Dr Kumar squints. 'And . . . you and Champ use your mother's surname?'

I nod. 'Dad's surname is "Zhang", which might *sound* like it starts with a J, but it starts with a Z. My mother thinks life is complicated enough without having a surname no one can pronounce, so she gave us hers.'

'Ah, I see,' Dr Kumar says, smiling professionally but not tenderly at my mother, which is the acceptable smile under the circumstances, but it tickles me to see that smiles have a language all their own. My mother – her Caucasian hair brown and blow-dried, her make-up discreet and impeccably applied, attired today in a navy dress with gold buttons and white, kitten heels – smiles back. If you think about it, and I do, kittens look like nothing like those heels. And they don't wear them, as far as I'm aware. Are they made of them? I glare at my mother's shoes, my baffled brain aboil.

Dr Kumar's gaze returns to me. He takes in my marginally kempt hair, my Asian-esque yet hazel eyes, and my style-crushing, soul-crushing, imagination-crushing school uniform. He says, 'You don't look especially alike.'

Everyone says my mother is stylish, glamorous and attractive, so I wonder if this comment is an insult. Unsure of the subtext, I reply, 'People say I'm the spit of my dad.' It's a gross phrase; I only say it because the thought of Dr Kumar writing 'spit' down once we've left amuses me. Mind you, it's difficult to know what might really come out of his pen. Perhaps he's got zero interest in psychiatry, and once we're gone he'll practise sketches of tribal tattoos for his arty side job.

I want to tell him it's Grandma Tara I most want to look like. And be like. Dad's mother was spectacular. Amber chignon. Firework freckles. Blazing blue eyes. Easy, infectious laugh. Fly and floaty clothes. A wit-sharp, whip-smart mind. 'I've done astonishing things in this "one wild and precious life" of mine,' she said once after reading me 'The Summer Day' by Mary Oliver, 'but having you as my granddaughter has been my greatest joy.'

My mind considers saying this to Dr Kumar, but my mouth chooses not to comply.

'So, you turned fifteen innn . . .' Dr Kumar scans the paperwork, 'November. And Cheng is . . . sixteen.'

'Champ. No one calls him Cheng. He'll be seventeen innn June.'

Dr Kumar doesn't find it as funny as I think he should. 'You were telling me about your name,' he says.

He's wrong. I wasn't. But now I suppose I have to, seeing that, as usual, my freedoms are scant. 'Dad and Grandma Tara wanted us to have Chinese names. My mother chose Jiāyì.'

'I see.'

He doesn't see, but I don't argue the point. I avoid eye contact with my mother as it feels unusually triumphant to have the liberty to speak about her while she's in the room, and I don't want to spoil that by noting her expression.

'What does Jiāyì mean?' Dr Kumar asks me. I consider whether he really wants to listen for 21.69 seconds while I relate all the meanings of Jiāyì. I decide he probably doesn't so I tell him what I tell everyone else who asks, which is, 'Morning lotus petals opening outwards, like words unfurling from a book.' That only takes 6.39 seconds to say so it's easier for everyone.

'Oh, please. It does not!' My mother laughs, her cheeks displaying the dimples people say are charming; but they're just small, involuntary facial hollows so what does 'charming' really mean, then? 'Jodie, stop. She's toying with you,' my mother says to Dr Kumar. 'It's auspicious. Her father wrote a list of Chinese names, and I chose the best of the bunch, believe me.'

'And "Cheng"? What does that mean?' Dr Kumar asks me, effectively silencing my mother without directly silencing her, which I find impressive and intend to remember for future occasions when it might prove a necessary tactic.

'Success,' I reply. 'Hence "Champ".'

Dr Kumar nods. He hasn't met Champ so he can't picture what I picture: floppy-haired heartthrob; tall, muscly sportsman; cello-playing music scholar; popular, confident socialite; academic wunderkind; perfect son. At least, that's what the world sees. I see other traits as well. 'It may also mean "noxious rectum boil",' I add. 'But I have no confirmation as yet.'

Dr Kumar titters, then composes himself because my mother's head-turn in his direction is not complimentary. It's astonishing that a head-turn can convey so much disdain. To help him out, I distract her by kicking my legs even higher and saying, 'It's discriminatory that my name means whatever it means, and he gets to be a winner.'

Dr Kumar blinks in what I think is affirmation, but it's hard to tell.

My mother, meanwhile, is getting agitated. I must be being disagreeable again. She clenches her hands and tenses her lips. Her fingers tap a frenzied ditty on her thigh, then pick irritably at an invisible speck of fluff on her dress. Her shoes shunt forward on the carpet so she's balancing on the heels, making the kittens inside more restless, or at least they would be if they were still alive rather than squashed to smithereens and lathered in leather.

'Can I . . . Let me ask you something else, then, if you don't mind,' Dr Kumar says. I do mind but he doesn't offer me the opportunity to say so. This is also a psychiatrist thing, but to be fair, other people do it, too – ask questions that aren't questions. They're not rhetorical, either – as in, used to fortify one's oratory – they're purposeless questions that fill the air with reverberations of no consequence. 'Let me ask you something, if you don't mind,' is one of them. 'Might I just add. . . ?' is another, and, 'If it's alright with you . . .' Sad, really.

'Why do you want to be called "Jodie Jones" and not just "Jodie"?'

I pause. Surely the answer is obvious. I insist people call me by my full name, even teachers, even *parents*, because I don't like the names 'Jodie' or 'Jones' on their own. It's been a few months of this now, so they're getting used to it. My mother doesn't enjoy calling me by my full name every time she speaks to me, but I don't answer her unless she does. She is not happy about this. She's not happy about a lot of things. Namely the suitcase. Sometimes a suitcase is just a suitcase and sometimes it's an act of war.

I wasn't happy about the suitcase, either. I needed to take action, so a couple of months ago, just after Christmas, I dropped hints about the usefulness of my former psychiatrist, Dr Haliki. She was youngish, perfectly nice and probably a decent psychiatrist, but I wanted to see a different one. I had to do it in a way that made my mother think it was her idea. She was annoyed about the Jodie Jones thing, my behaviour at school and my other so-called 'peculiarities'. She said she'd find someone else.

She had to go through Dr Woolf, the consultant overseeing my case, but I'd already asked him to write down the names of two doctors and give them to my mother at their next meeting. My mother stuck the Post-it with their names on under the Lake Como fridge magnet at home. One was a Dr Lopez, whom I didn't want to see but wouldn't have minded if it came to it, and one was a Dr Kumar, whom I very much did.

I like 'whom'. It sounds like ghostly for reasons I can't express.

To help manoeuvre things, I stood facing the fridge door and said, 'Lo-pez,' lengthening the 'o' and emphasizing the downward descent of the second syllable. 'I like that name.' I said it a few more times. 'Lohhh-pezzzz—'

It worked. She called Dr Kumar.

The only available appointments were during school hours – it was another month to see him after school – so despite her reluctance to take me out of lessons, she booked it. My mother is irked that a child of hers needs to see psychiatrists and psychologists at all, but for the last four years they've been assigned to me continuously. She couldn't argue then, and she can't now. She is more recently exasperated that I collect sentences, repeat words again and again, refuse to replace my red Converse with more formal footwear in a public setting, refuse to preoccupy myself with hair care or make-up – refuse to do anything, in fact, that she wants me to do – and I'm not top of my classes any more.

'Exasperated' sounds like 'raspberries', which I often want to blow at her.

I don't see what the big deal is, asking to be called Jodie Jones. No one questions it when you're five. You can answer 'Jodie Jones' every single time you're asked your name, and no one takes umbrage. In fact, they seem to enjoy it. They even join in. 'Hello, Jodie Jones. And how is Jodie Jones today? Would Jodie Jones like an ice cream? Oh, Jodie Jones would? Splendid. What flavour would Jodie Jones like?' Why the sudden change because I'm a teen?

Dr Kumar is still waiting, so I roll my eyes and say, 'Oh e oh.'

He says, 'Sorry?'

I say, 'Juh juh.'

Dr Kumar and my mother look at each other and her face contorts, like she's won a debate.

'Could you explain?' he asks, his long hands drifting to his knees, where they rest like butterflies on a flower.

I say, 'Dee.'

My mother lifts and crosses her arms, so she's squeezing her boobs. There's no good word for boobs. 'Breasts' is terrible. 'Bazookas' is ridiculous. 'Bosom' is old fashioned. There's a shorter, perkier word, but that's even worse. We need a better one, and we need it soon. Why are nouns for the female physique so objectionably named? Penis is no better. Pee nibs might work.

'Jodie Jones?' Dr Kumar asks, his head listing to one side like a ship in trouble. I'm embarrassed that he's caught me thinking about pee nibs, and I redden. All I want to do is carry on reading *Rebecca*, but he's already asked me to return it to my bag. It's a titillatingly tense part, and that's the only acceptable use of the first syllable of that word. Mrs Danvers is creepily compelling and uncomfortably unnerving. 'You haven't answered my question. Why "Jodie Jones" and not just "Jodie".'

My mother stiffens and I shrug.

I have answered. Can he not see?

The vowel sounds in my name are 'oh e oh'.

'Juh' and 'juh' are the sounds of my initials.

'Dee' is the central spring in 'Jodie' where the tone falls down and bounces back up again.

And they all belong in a sound family together.

I'm not going to explain what is plainly obvious.

Then I realize that perchance he knows the answer to my current conundrum, so I ask, 'Dr Kumar? Do you know how stupid you are?'

My mother jumps. 'Jodie! Jesus. What's the matter with you?'

I ignore her because she calls me Jodie Jesus and not Jodie Jones, which makes her all of these things: unhinged, fuming, irate, deranged and a number of other words that mean angry. I don't really like the word 'irate'. Unhinged is lovely, though.

From the peculiar sound she makes with her mouth, I gather my mother is less than delighted with the way this session is progressing. I've clearly bothered her, but not quite enough. I'll have to do better next time.

Dr Kumar hasn't told me how to measure how stupid you are, so I still don't know how to answer that question.

He says we need to book another appointment.

4

At school, I'm faced with a piffling but nevertheless precious decision to make: do I walk in late to History and explain where I've been? Or do I wait for the next lesson so I don't have to?

Easy. I duck into the toilets and read *Rebecca* till the bell.

Becca meets me at lunch, which, being a Thursday, means fish and chips. After she gets us each a plate and we eat it in the designated classroom, we sit under the stairs in our usual spot. She's miffed with me for my academic nosediving, but it's hard to take her seriously right now. Her orthodontist has designed a Perspex retainer shaped to fit Becca's particular dental configuration. It has a thick, hard platform that slots over the roof of her mouth, which transforms her 'sses' in the most spectacular fashion. When she pulls it out to show me, her spit stretches from the frame like strands of mozzarella on pizza, which I find objectionable, foul and repugnant, but her stretched sputum is also amusing. She clicks the retainer back in and, intrigued by the new sounds her mouth is making, I test it out.

'Say "sandwich bags".'

'Schanwisssshhhh bagsssss.'

'Say "sausages".'

'Scchhoshhhagesss.'

'Say "supercalifragilisticexpialidocious".'

'Schheriouschly, schtop it. Guessch what you misched.'

She doesn't let me guess, which is a shame because all manner of possibilities manifest like mushrooms in my mind. The Head dropped dead. A classroom went kaboom. Everyone over the age of fifteen vanished in a synchronized puff. Becca removes her fingers from her mouth and ties back her wild cascade of curls, no doubt making them a bit saliva-y, which doesn't bother her but would absolutely bother me.

'Mr Clementssch did the asschembly thissch morning. On fearlesschnessch.'

I tug at her sleeve. 'Say that again.'

'No. Sschussch. He sschaid he bet no one had the gutssch to sschtand up and ssching in front of the whole asschembly. Guessch who sschtood up – bam – right away and sschang "Where is the Love"?'

'You.'

She laughs a *ccchhh*, as if she's clearing a hair from the back of her throat. 'No way on earth. Guessch again.'

I name three random people, all wrong. 'How about you just tell me, Becca?'

'Moschesch Calvet.'

Moses. Warm fluid fills my every cell. Course he did. My insides smile but not my lips. I don't want Becca to see how much that pleases me. Only Moses could sing songs with relevant lyrics in front of two hundred cripplingly self-conscious, snide and sneering teens.

She then tells me just how unimpressive (her word is 'sschucky') she finds my current attitude to school, which is all I seem to hear at the moment. 'Sscho? Did you missch me?' she asks.

'I was gone two hours, Becca.'

'Yeah, but did the world scheem schtrange and dull and crappy?'

'No more than usual.'

'Fine. Don't admit it. Schuit yourschelf.'

While the world did once sscheem sschtrange and dull and crappy, now things have sschomewhat changed, so it's sschort of interesting again. Only sort of – I mean, I still have to go to school.

Thursday afternoons, we have PSHE, a subject annoyingly mandatory in all schools in the UK. The only positive of this enforced lesson is that at our school, we're matched with other year groups and this year, we're paired with Champ's. I wish I could say that the positive is the joy of being with my big brother, but it isn't. It might have been when I was in Year 7 when he used to pass me in the corridor and mouth, 'You OK?' and I'd nod even though I spent most of my lessons dreaming up scenarios where he'd storm over and beat people up for me if I needed it. Not that I ever needed it. At lunch, he'd come and find me in the Year 7 base to give me jam sandwiches and mini packets of Lotus biscuits from his friends because we weren't allowed sugary stuff, and at home in the evenings, I'd seek his sage counsel.

'Champ, when you put your hand up in lessons, do you ask to go to the toilet or the loo? Because I say loo but no one else does.' And, 'Champ, should I wear my hair in a high pony or a low one? Is a high one cooler or is it a comfort thing?' He wasn't the world's greatest guide to navigating secondary school, but who else did I have to ask?

These days he goes out of his way to ignore me. So, no. The sole positive in this hybrid-year-group arrangement is that I get to sit with Moses, Champ's friend.

That Champ has friends at all is mystifying. His other friends are Tavish and Bear, which are their given names, unlike Champ, who doesn't have 'Champ' on his passport. Tavish has floppy hair and green eyes and half the school are 'literally in love' with him; the other half are 'literally in love' with Champ. Bear is short and thin with glasses. He is utterly un-bearlike, which is why parents should avoid opting for certain names if they have a particular genetic make-up, or at least wait until they see the span and breadth of their babies before deciding. I don't think anyone is 'literally in love' with Bear, or even figuratively, except maybe his mother. I might be wrong.

I'm equally not sure who's 'literally in love' with Moses. They don't know what to make of him. He's tall and plays electric guitar. He has a candy-floss flume of curly hair and wears clothing that should be compulsory menswear worldwide: orange T-shirts with burgundy jeans, sky blue T-shirts with navy jeans, and pale green T-shirts with dark green jeans. He sings aloud when walking around school (instant pariah behaviour) and gets exasperated when anyone leaves lights on or puts their rubbish and recycling in the wrong bins, because he's the Sustainability Ambassador. Everyone else pretends to care about the planet and climate change, but they buy fast fashion by the parcel-load, eat burger after burger after burger, leave litter lying around and use planes like buses.

'Hey,' Moses says, not turning his head as I arrive at the double desk.

'Hey, yourself.' I wipe the surface with my sleeve and dump my bag on the floor.

'You good?' He's still not looking at me.

'Passable. "Good" is a bit of a stretch.'

We only really get to talk to each other in these lessons and then it's mostly to discuss the topic of the day, but it's my favourite hour of the week. Moses's presence is inexplicably comforting. Most boys act tough and cool. Mansplain. Manspread. Manscorn. Not him.

Miss Slavin shares the PowerPoint to the screen. The first slide indicates the direction this session will take, and today's topic is Our Lives Online. Moses buries his head in his hands with a groan.

'Yessss, you, too, Moses!' Miss Slavin trills. 'Off you go in your pairs, please.' Her tone is one of relentless optimism, even if the subject matter is dire. Moses sighs, cracks his knuckles and reads, in an amusing deadpan monotone, 'Question one. We can feel pressured by social media to change our look online. Do you add filters to your selfies?'

'Don't take them,' I say. 'My phone gets confiscated all the time. I tend to send people brown circles and robot-arm emojis, so it's probably for the best.'

He turns to me then. 'When do you ever need to send a brown circle?'

'But a robot arm you wouldn't question?'

He considers that, as well he should.

'Someone has to send the weird ones,' I explain. 'They'll feel left out otherwise. Have you *seen* the options on the emoji menu?'

He grins. 'Have actually.'

'Sent them all?'

He shakes his head, giving his curls a mini fiesta.

'Exactly. No one needs two thirds of those. So,' I point to the screen, 'in answer to this: I take selfies of my elbows, known as "elbies". And I don't use filters because my elbows are stunning without them.'

He eyes the arms of my jumper, which is an interesting phrase because he'd never arm the eyes of my jumper, and says, 'I'll remember to look next time you're in short sleeves.'

I ask him question one in return. He says he adds fairies and sparkles to his selfies. I relish the thought and read on. 'Question two. Online profiles stay forever. Do you post photos of yourself on social media in swimwear or underwear?'

'Only when I've bought a new bikini,' he replies. 'You?'

'Every day. I strap on my leotard, bend like a banana and hold two fingers up like this.' I demonstrate with my digits. 'I think it's a Japanese thing.'

'Me too. Except I'd do it like this.' He holds two fingers up the swearing way, and we hear, 'Mosessss! Jodieeee!'

Miss Slavin loves choosing us for whole-class feedback. The first time we were paired, we talked about frogs (my fault: their little suckery fingers were on my mind), and which book she might give us for our birthdays ('Pollyanna' is my guess; 'Pride and Prejudice' says Moses). The only reason we bother to answer the prescribed questions now is that we know she'll choose us to share our answers with the class, so we'd better have something to say.

Moses repeats his line about the bikini, making everyone laugh.

'And Jodie? How about you?'

She doesn't say my full name, so I don't respond.

'Er . . . Jo-die?' Her tone turns stern. 'I'm talking to you.'

'Got to call her "Jodie Jones",' Lucy Lee shouts. 'Or she won't answer. She's a Very. Special. Case.'

The class laughs again and Mira Volvek high-fives Lucy Lee.

'The hell?' Moses yells. 'That's totally out. Not gonna let her get away with that, are you?' he asks Miss Slavin.

Miss Slavin snaps, 'Lucy, Mira, that's enough. Let's move on.'

I stand up, pushing my chair back with a screech.

'Ignore them,' Moses says, looking up at me. 'Bunch of a-holes. Don't let them get to you.'

I walk out anyway.

Miss Slavin can't leave the room unattended – the last time she did, someone unplugged the tech and the next class had to be re-roomed until someone from IT plugged plugs back into the right plugholes. Instead, she runs to the door and shouts, 'Straight to Mr Fowler's office!'

I hear a loud, 'OOOOOHHH!' and the raucous laugh of most of the class, and over the top of them, Moses shout, 'What's the matter with you? You lot should be ashamed of yourselves.'

5

Mr Fowler isn't there, so I sit on a plastic chair in the company of Mrs Danvers, Maxim de Winter and the unnamed narrator who is forging fake news about Rebecca in the furrows of her own fragile head. Du Maurier's lyrical sentences slip and burble like brooks through the heathered glen of my inner ear, but the comfort I draw from the sounds is short-lived.

Mr Fowler walks as if he's being yanked by an invisible string tied around his chest. 'Morning, Jodie Jones. Reading, are we? My, my.' He nods with his bearded mouth downturned, as if impressed, as if it's remarkable to be carrying a book in an educational establishment when surely shouldn't everyone be reading? Including him. Especially him – he's a teacher. Role model and so forth. Educational Influencer, as it were. Not that he'd have many followers.

He turns up the volume of his greeting. 'I said, "Morning, Jodie".'

I don't answer because a) I don't want to, and b) the 'Jones' has suddenly disappeared, which can't be accidental. He follows it up with, 'This is where you reply, "Good morning, Mr Fowler". Otherwise, it's rude.'

'Who *decided* it was rude, though?' I ask, as innocently, lightly and politely as I can because I'm genuinely curious.

He rolls his eyes. 'Society, Jodie. That's who.' And the chest-string pulls him in to his office. 'Enlighten me. Why are you here this time?'

At least he's self-aware: if anyone needs enlightening, it's him. I stand at the door. His office smells of wet trainers, withered dreams and pickled sarcasm. From his throne behind the desk, he waves an offhand arm at an unexciting bench. 'Come in. Sit.'

It's more a command than an invitation, but I don't sit. It's my micro-choice not to and I micro-choose it.

'Well?'

'I walked out of PSHE.'

He smirks unappealingly. 'Course you did.' He must know the way he speaks and acts is objectionable, but what I can't work out is why anyone would choose to be that way. 'Why this time, hmm?'

I don't have a single answer that covers the many reasons, so I say, 'I needed to.'

He sits back hard on his swivel chair. His shirt is smeared with a dribble of ketchup and it pleases me. 'And why did you need to?'

'Just did.'

The knuckles on his right hand tap the desktop. He has no rhythm. There's a hole in his earlobe where an earring once sat, and his ears are unusually pointy. The birthday book he'd give you, if he bought you anything at all, is *How to Make Friends and Influence People* (which I've seen on the shelf at Becca's house) and he'd want it back after you'd read it. 'Not good enough. Getting a tad tired of seeing you in here, Jones.'

I like that 'tad' means 'a small amount' and it has a small number of letters. It seems apt. I don't like being called 'Jones', though. I don't call him 'Fowler' so why is it acceptable for him to call me 'Jones'?

'My name is Jod—'

'Not now.'

What an odd comment. I want to say, yes now. Always. My name is always Jodie Jones, not just sometimes. He is glancing at his computer screen, which has been pinging with emails since he walked in, and no doubt long before. The pinging puts me off, even though this is a cause worth fighting for. His fur-lined mouth mutters something and then his eyes dart disapprovingly back to me. He smirks again, but this time it's even more unfriendly.

'Right. Listen to me, and listen good. I've got a hundred-and-twenty pupils in my year group and you take up fifty per cent of my time. I know you've had serious issues, and they're ongoing, clearly, but your attitude and behaviour recently have been unacceptable. You're not doing any work. You're messing around in lessons. You've been in detention at least twice each week this term and on report for a month. You're literally throwing your future away. What's going on with you, eh?'

My eyes rise above his blind to the pale, frail, frangible sunshine outside. What's going on with me? Lots of things. As if you care. You'd be the last person I'd tell.

'Is seeing the psychiatrist not enough? Do you need more counselling at school?'

My many rapid blinks are a 'no', but perhaps he isn't fluent in Blink.

He sighs. Slightly overdramatically, if I was rating his sigh, which I'm not. 'How's your weaker head?' he asks.

I frown. I wasn't aware I had more than one. My expression must convey the precipitous cavern of confusion I've plummeted into headlong. 'How's my . . . weaker head?

'Your week, Jones. How is next week looking?'

'Ohh. My week *ahead*.' I laugh. A lot. Which seems to annoy him.

'Fine. Looks like we need another meeting with your parents,' he growls. 'Unless we see some major improvements, your time here is running out. Hear me?'

I don't blink. Surely, he'll get it this time.

'Nothing to say for yourself, as usual. Well, that's just peachy. How can I help you if you don't talk to me?'

There isn't an easy way to answer that question. I don't want to talk to him, I don't want his help, and I don't know what peaches have to do with anything.

'You might have a ton of concessions in place because of your pastoral issues, but the same rules apply to you as to everyone else. That's the deal we made with your parents. Makes my heart bleed to see a clever kid like you tossing it all down the drain. Pull your socks up, or it won't just be detention you're getting. Understand?'

I pause, perplexed. Deals. Bleeding hearts. Drains. Socks. There's a lot to take in. Which part does he want me to understand?

He waves a dismissive hand at me as if I'm a bluebottle dowsed in dog poop. 'Detention, this afternoon. Out of my sight.' As I turn to leave, he adds, 'Er . . . forgetting something, are we?'

I scan the floor with a frown. I didn't bring anything in with me.

He says, '*Thank you*, sir?'

My lips fuse firm. I object to being forced to say something I don't want to say. Because of school, I have to dress in a way I don't want to dress, learn subjects I don't want to study, and spend eight hours a day with people who, on the whole, I don't want to be with. At home, I have no say at all. At least what comes out of my mouth should be my decision.

'Still waiting,' he says, tapping his knuckles arrhythmically on his desk. If I were him, I'd sign up for some thumb-drumming lessons.

'What am I thanking you for? You just gave me another detention.'

He sniffs, issues a sarky snort, and points at me theatrically. 'And that backchat's just earned you another one tomorrow.'

I run 'that backchat' over in my mind, and leave without thanking him.

Despite the Friday detention on top of the Thursday detention, it feels like a triumph.

6

Our cleaner, Daniela, has almost finished making our clean house cleaner, but she's on edge. She's vacuumed, mopped, polished, sprayed, wiped, ironed, folded, and put away, yet her eyes flit fretfully over the fixtures, fittings and furniture as she folds the cleaning cloths and squirrels them away under the sink.

Dad doesn't notice Daniela's discomfort. He and I sit in our spotless, spotlit kitchen, perching on barstools. We don't possess a bar, but the name 'counter stool', I'm told, is not an acceptable alternative. He's distracted. His eyes are equally as flitty, when he is not usually one to fret with his eyeballs or with any other body part. He turned his phone off quickly when I came into the kitchen – universally suspicious behaviour – and he's now fiddling with the corner of a cardboard folder lying idly on the countertop. I pretend not to notice and invite him to join me in some light entertainment.

'Parma ham and melon,' I begin.

'Cheese and pineapple,' Dad says after a long pause and a nudge.

'Watermelon with feta.'

'Um. Pineapple on pizza,' he says. 'Pineapple with anything.'

'Peanut butter and sriracha on toast.'

'Thought they had to be well known.'

'It's a thing,' I tell him, but I get his point. It's not in the Parma ham and melon league. He's distracted by a car alarm as he knows alarms alarm me, but I'm indoors and this one doesn't as much, so I give him a verbal nudge. 'Your go.'

'Hmm? Oh. Er . . . baked camembert and sticky jam,' he says. 'Lots involve cheese, actually. Can we stop this now?'

Dad doesn't always enjoy playing 'Weird' with me. He liked it when we played 'Weird Fashion Trends', 'Weird Place Names', 'Weird Habits', 'Weird National Dishes', and 'Weird Proverbs and Sayings' but he's clearly not in the mood for 'Weird Food Combos'.

'Only if you tell me what's in the folder.'

'What?' he says, placing a protective hand on it. 'Oh. Insurance papers.' His eyes dart from the folder to the window. I would typically lose interest at the word 'insurance' because that has to be the most boring collection of papers imaginable, but his eyes tell me he's lying and that's intriguing.

'OK. Why is it on the table?'

'I'm just checking the . . . umm . . . when we need to renew our contents insurance.'

I study the lines on his face and the greeny-blue earthwormy vein across his temple. This can't be true. You must be able to check this stuff online. 'And?'

'And what?'

'When does it need renewing?'

Dad scratches his neck. 'December.'

I'm riveted as to why he would hide whatever he was doing on his phone and then lie to me about folders and insurance. My mind jumps to all manner of wild conclusions. Dad is an agent for MI5 and the crappy cardboard folder is to throw enemy spies off the scent. Dad is the prime minister of Micronesia and is reading the latest cabinet notes, which can't be extensive because surely Micronesia is small. Dad has a secret wife, and the folder holds the sum of her many letters pleading for him to come home and father his twelve other children. Dad has a Mongolian mistress and he's changing his will to leave everything to her, except his secret collection of rubber ducks, which he'll leave to me.

My mother will be back soon, which is why Daniela is apprehensive about the impeccability of the house, Dad is removing whatever is in that folder to an un-spotable spot, and Champ has already snuck up snacks and whatever else he sneaks up to the snuck-up snack stash he stores in his room. I don't care any more: I will not hide or pretend, and this makes her more rather than less strict, which is curious.

Daniela takes a last look around, glances at her watch, and smiles uneasily at us as she puts her arms through the sleeves of her startlingly red down jacket.

'It's look OK?' she asks, putting the s in the wrong place as usual.

'Perfect. Thank you, Daniela,' Dad says. 'As always.'

'You wellcam. See you tomorrow.' Her eyes furniture-flit some more as she turns to leave.

'Does it? Look OK?' Dad asks me. He could stand in a room full of rubble and not notice the mess. In stark contrast, my mother's standards of cleanliness are unreasonably high. I cast my eyes over the gleaming glass, the lickable surfaces, the magazines with articles on tech billionaires that my mother leaves on the coffee table to motivate us in our career choices and makes Daniela spread into a perfect magazine fan. 'She'll find something wrong.'

I very much want to open that folder and see what's inside, but Dad tries to deflect the direction of my gaze by ramming it under his armpit and asking about Dr Kumar.

'How was it this morning?' He faces me squarely, his eyes meeting mine, his ten, solemn fingers spread flat on the counter. He is doing what is known as 'active listening'. When you see as many counsellors, psychologists and psychiatrists as I've seen over the past four years, you recognize it. 'Is it . . . you know . . . helping?'

I wince. 'Helping?' The term is contentious, but he's Dad and he doesn't mean anything by it. Still, I sniff and say, 'Helping me become cured and normal?'

Dad's eyebrows wibble and warp. He turns his hands over so that his palms are facing the ceiling. It's an unspoken invitation to place mine inside his, so reluctantly I do. I'm hoping the folder will fall from his arm and I wiggle my hands to help it along, but it's wedged. 'Not what I mean,' he says gently. 'Stop jiggling. Tell me how it went.'

'OK. But . . .' I make a face and pull my hands away, because although it's a caring gesture, Dad's hands are warm and clammy. He's fine about it. He knows I can't bear hot hands or wet sleeves or wet hands or hot lots of things.

I say, 'Dr Kumar has kind eyes with long lashes, and butterfly hands. In his office, he has a yellow Wes Anderson-esque armchair. He hmms a lot.'

'Nothing wrong with a hmmer. Notorious hmmer myself.'

'You are.' I tell him about my mother's enforced silence and my not being able to adequately supply five words that I like best of all in the whole of the English language.

To his credit, Dad says, 'That's a serious challenge for any wordsmith.'

I consider telling him I called Champ a noxious rectum boil, but decide against it.

There are details I could add about our session today, but I need some space and time to think. There aren't enough spaces or times to think in this world. If I were in charge, there definitely would be.

Dad needs time and space to think as well, so I offer him some as an unspoken gift. When he talks to my mother these days, their conversations brew into bursts and bellows. They roar and crash over each other, then ricochet and zigzag from wall to wall, up and down, roof to floor, back and forth until static sizzles through the house and it hisses with hostility.

This is because two days after Christmas, I saw Dad carrying his dressing gown and memory-foam pillow to the study. He hasn't been sleeping well since Grandma Tara died, but I doubt it was because of that. I asked him where he was placing his pillow henceforth and he pointed at the Chesterfield, where his duvet was already folded on one end. 'Till I buy a sofa bed,' he said, which made it sound more long-term than I'd first assumed.

Then, last month, I passed the study and the door was slightly ajar. The large blue suitcase stood upright near the chest of drawers. The shock of it winded me as if someone had kicked a football hard into my stomach.

He was leaving.

I lurched to the bathroom.

It was only bile I brought up, but still.

The move and the suitcase did not please my mother. They were arguing more, anyway: about how hard it is for her with Dad's ongoing downward dip; how no one cares about her well-being or how hard she works for this family; about the success of Bannermans' competition and Bannermans' subsequent loss of business; Champ and me. Especially me.

But the suitcase detonated a domestic mine. Tense silences went on for days. Snippy comments followed. Then crying. Then shouting. Their interactions became heated. The fighting and the sofa-sleeping have continued into the middle of the spring term. The folder has something to do with these new developments, but I don't know what exactly.

'Are you . . . OK, Jodie Jones?' Dad asks.

I want to say, 'Not really, Dad.' But there isn't much point. I also want to ask, 'Are you OK, Elliot Zhang?' but he'll tell me he's fine, even if he isn't.

Dad rises, the folder still under his arm and likely a little damp and odorous by now, rubs my back with his unclamped hand and walks in the direction of his study.

I say to his parting form, 'Gherkins in burgers.'

He pauses and says, 'Katsu sushi.'

I say, 'Vanilla ice cream with soy sauce.'

'No one eats vanilla ice cream with soy sauce,' Dad says as he turns the corner.

But he's wrong. Becca does.

*

I haven't told anyone about the developments at home. Not my teachers, who love to know information of this kind. Not Becca, who would be compelled to say something to someone because that's what Becca is like. And not my dad, because he must know Champ and I can hear their arguments, but that doesn't stop them happening.

Presumably because of this, my nightmares are more graphic. I try to run, but my body can't move. My mouth strains to scream but no sound comes out. Aware I have to propel myself somehow, anyhow, I haul my inert body by lying facedown and pulling as hard as I can on the weeds growing between the paving slabs, getting nowhere. Horror engulfs me. I wake up retching, sweating. My heart takes full minutes to return to a regular rhythm.

The dreams stay with me all day.

The only way I can manage this current situation is knowing that one way or another it will end soon.

7

I hear my mother before I see her. She's chatting and laughing with the neighbours in the driveway. Within minutes of meeting people, she's their best friend: she knows all about their family sagas, their children's graduate jobs and how they got them, their to-die-for salad recipes, their top-ten reads, their job woes, allergies, stabled horses, burgeoning hernias, and trips to Galway, Copenhagen and Kyoto. She remembers who likes panettone and who prefers medjool dates, and buys them some for Christmas; buys others flower seeds and wine of their preferred grape variety and gives big tips, making her a very popular client and diner.

Bertie, our neighbours' son, broke his leg last week on a school skiing trip, so their current topic of conversation is skiing accidents. My mother says that one raucous night post-uni, ten of them fell down a piste in San Moritz, tied together, and three in the tangle ended up with broken bones. 'Not me!' she laughs. 'I rolled over Polly James just in time. Great cushion, it turns out, but she broke her tibia and had to be airlifted away. And it was only day two of the trip.' They laugh, even though I'm not sure how funny that is. 'Top tip,' my mother says, 'if you tie yourself to someone on a mountain, make sure it's someone plump!' Her voice and her laugh are loud, and they laugh loudly to match it. I wonder if we turn up the volume of our laughs depending on the decibel level of the current conversation. I decide to pay more attention to this in future.

'Hilarious,' Minty says. 'You never fail to cheer me up. We're so lucky to have such wonderful neighbours, aren't we, James?'

'Absolutely. You must come over again, Monica,' James says. 'Not tied to anyone, preferably. Except maybe Elliot.' They laugh again.

When my mother walks though the door saying, 'Hello? Hellooo? Where are you all?' we greet her in the hallway and then I'm exiled upstairs to study. Tonight, though, I decide not to. Instead, I put noise-cancelling headphones on and hunker down in my wardrobe to finish *Rebecca*. Black journal in hand, I note my favourite phrases and wonder why the narrator doesn't ever just ask for information, which would be the obvious and most simple course of action. Half the time you want to strangle her. Then there's the line I like best: '*But what goes on in the twisted tortuous minds of women would baffle anyone.*' And not just because 'baffle' is a bodacious word.

Along with Daphne du Maurier, Emily Brontë is also in the wardrobe. Well, not Emily Brontë herself, although that would be fun. I imagine for a moment having a succession of authors visit me in my wardrobe. They would tell me stories about how things were when they were alive, insist that pies are not what they once were, and gripe about rainy carriage travel on muddy roads for morning calls, which, as the decorum of the day denoted, lasted an hour exactly and it was unfitting to remove their bonnets or shawls. In turn, I'd ask why they were so obsessed with the decorum of the day and marrying rich, boring husbands, whether winters were dull or actually much more fun before the days of electricity, and why they wore countless long skirts and petticoats when they didn't have washing machines and servants had a dire old time washing them all by hand.

Talking to them would be like time travel. Mind you, by reading their novels, isn't that more or less what's happening anyway?

I sit facing Emily Brontë. Her novel, *Wuthering Heights*, is filled with people talking spitefully to each other in-between bouts of searing passion. I tell her this, seeing as she's visiting me in my wardrobe today. I have read three quarters of it and liked not very much. Heathcliff is heinous and Cathy is a cow. Dad thinks I'll feel differently with age and a reread. Only time will tell.

With Emily, I soften the sting of my criticism (authors are sensitive creatures) by adding that despite the clear and cruel abuse, there's a line I'm remarkably fond of: '*I love the ground under his feet, and the air over his head, and everything he touches and every word he says. I love all his looks, and all his actions and him entirely and altogether.*'

I wonder whether I'll ever feel that way about someone.

Emily Brontë reckons I will.

I explain to her, once she's calmed down about the feedback, that Moses comes close, but I don't know him well enough to know whether every word he says is worth loving. The ground under his feet, yes. The air over his head, yes. The things he touches, yes. His looks. His actions. The way he moves. Him entirely and altogether I'm not certain about just yet.

Emily Brontë says that's normal.

I tell her that's the first time anyone's used that word around me for a very long time.

I finish reading *Wuthering Heights* so I can give her a full and comprehensive disclosure of my thoughts. It seems unfair to pass judgement without reading it all. Once I do, Emily wants to hit me on the head with one of my hiking boots, which tells you a lot about her characters and their behaviour.

I put Emily down (which sounds strange), pick up my black journal and start writing. I make notes about Dr Kumar's hands, about my choosing to not to choose five words in my visit today, about my dislike of the word 'feedback'; about my near altercation with Emily Brontë.

'Unbelievable!' my mother shouts. I can hear her easily from upstairs. 'Would you look at this?' Other people might exclaim phrases like this when reading the newspaper, but she doesn't read newspapers so I rule that one out. Perhaps she's spotted a speck of dust on a surface or a smudge on a wall, but my guess is she's holding my phone up to Dad. She knows my password because she set it, allegedly so she can supervise the murky quagmire of my mind. And I can guess what she's showing him. An email from Mr Fowler. One he's sent to me.

I dive out of the wardrobe and scramble to my bed as her feet clap up the stairs.

My mother, attired in her home clothing of silk pyjamas, or maybe they're satin, is now standing in my room. She walks in without knocking. She is not a knocker. I notice she's not particularly relaxed at the moment, despite wearing lounge clothes, and one of her lower buttons is undone. I don't tell her there's an imperfection about her person. I just enjoy it.

By this point, I'm writing in my red journal – the one I leave lying around and know she reads. She thinks I don't know, but she's not exactly subtle. I only write random words in it, which I hope drives her batty. This type of writing doesn't count as schoolwork, so she is not overly pleased.

'What the—? What are you doing? Why aren't you studying? I told you to— *Tsk*. Put that bloody thing away, will you. You have a ton to catch up on and you know it. You're so far behind. God. Do I have to watch you night and day?'

As I slot the journal under my pillow, mind my plays with: 'You're so far behind God', which is no surprise to anyone, and, 'God, do I have to watch you night and day?' I wonder how God would answer that. Depends who's asking, I suppose.

My mother, her hand angry, her fingers jabby, holds up my phone. 'Two more detentions. What's wrong with you? Fail at school and you have nothing. Don't you understand?'

I wince. The timing is terrible. But then it always is.

She walks out with it, leaving my bedroom door open.

I don't mind that she's taken my phone. I do mind that she's left the door open. Obviously, I like looking up fun facts and cast info when I'm watching films, doing the world geography quizzes Becca tries to beat me at and never does, checking the definitions of 'meretricious', 'ribald', 'timorous', 'wizened' and 'limpid' when I come across them and feeling like a modern human being who's connected even vaguely to the rest of the planet. But phones don't provide me with the things I prize most highly. Yes, I can read free samples of books when I'm waiting for the bus, and communicate with Dad or Becca, but I always carry a book in my bag, and I see Dad and Becca every day. There's nothing so urgent it can't wait.

Now, though, with the suitcase situation, things do feel significantly more urgent. I may need that phone after all.

Champ's shaking, judgemental head appears in the open door space. 'Asking for it,' he says.

'Definitely not.'

'Not very smart, are you? What did you think would happen?' he asks. 'Obvious.' And he goes back to his room. I'm not sure if he's being supportive or snide. Maybe both.

I would kick myself for this phone blunder, but why bother when a big brother will do it for you?

When my mother returns, she holds my phone out in front of my face again. I dutifully read the email that she's sent from *my* school email account to Mr Fowler. I have apologized, it appears, for 'acting like a small child and being annoying, rude and lazy', and she's added, 'because I'm clearly the brightest in my class, I will be diligent and conscientious and get As in every subject from now on.'

Diligent and conscientious are basically synonyms. I wouldn't use both in one sentence, but I don't say so. My mother wedges my phone under her arm, picks up my blazer and checks the pockets. When she doesn't find whatever it is she expects to find, she says, 'And clear up this mess.' The mess consists of two homework handouts on my desk, a jumper slung on the chair – and my slippers, which instead of being parallel under the chest of drawers, are a fraction misaligned. Otherwise, my room is immaculate.

At least he'll know the email's not from me.

8

My plan isn't working fast enough. I don't know what else to do. It's infuriating having a plan with no power to implement it. Unlike me, adults have choices and options. But even with all the power in the universe, how do you stop someone you love from leaving?

I try to think of a back-up plan at school the next day, but other things keep happening. School is not the best place to think, which is ironic. Surely an educational establishment should be exactly that place.

The lowlight of my day is hearing Champ in the lunch queue laughing with Bear about Greg Trân. I'm waiting in the corridor for Becca to get my lunch and I'd storm over and yell at them if the dining room wasn't so terrifying. Greg Trân is a genius. He arrived in the UK from Vietnam, aged thirteen, did fifteen GCSEs in one year, aged fourteen, and is now doing five A levels, aged fifteen. He already has a place at Oxford. As he's so young, they've recommended a gap year, so he'll start his degree at seventeen. In an article written by the young reporters for our school newspaper, Greg said that in his gap year he'll study Japanese and Astrophysics and write a book about nebulae. He didn't say if the book would be in Japanese, but no one except me seems to wonder about this. I don't know him well enough to ask. He also has a stammer and is not great at queues.

Greg is shuffling from foot to foot, staring at the floor, a few feet in front of my brother and his friend with the ill-fitting name. I hear Bear say, 'I'm n-n-n-n-n-not sure, Champ. B-b-b-b-urger or st-st-st-st-stir fry t-t-t-today?'

Instead of calling him out, Champ laughs.

Enraged, I swing on my heels and storm away.

Champ is whatever the largest measure of stupid is.

The highlight of my day is finding another sentence for my collection. Someone has left a book on a table in the hall, so as I pass I pick it up. I'm not immediately drawn to reading it because the title is the opposite of scintillating, but I slip it in my bag, nonetheless. I can look at it properly in Private Study but only because Becca has the orthodontist and can't make me revise with her.

In the booth in the study hall, I remove the book from my bag. The cover is deathly dull, and I wonder if the writing is, too. But after I read the first sentence, I blink a few times, stunned. Then I read it again, and sigh one of those rare, long, shuddering sighs of contentment and peace. I sense a replete feeling deep inside me, like something small and magical has crept into a hollow and is nestling in the sanctum of my chest.

How will I ever get through this book if each sentence deserves to be read multiple times? It could take months. Years. That excites me, too. Imagine a book so beautiful you have to read each sentence again and again before you move on to the next. I don't know of any books like that, but I hope they exist. Perhaps this is one of them.

The sentence goes like this.

When he woke in the woods in the dark and the cold of the night, he'd reach out to touch the child sleeping beside him.

I read it again and again, five times, maybe six. The beat seems to bounce from 'woke' to 'woods' to 'dark' to 'cold' to 'night' like stones skipping over the surface of the sea.

I'm not sure why, but 'the dark and the cold' sounds better than 'the cold and the dark'. It must be that the 'd' at the end of 'cold' feels more final, more threatening, or maybe cold is a colder word. The stretched vowels in 'he'd reach out' resemble an arm extending in the darkness, and the 'would' in 'he'd' gives the impression it isn't a one-off act – he reaches out often, and repeatedly. 'To touch' sounds soft as ballet steps; 'child' is weightless, and the long rhyming 'e's add to the overall softness before it comes to rest on a gentle, sinking 'm'.

A man. A child. A simple, wordless gesture of love and protection and care.

The nestling creature squeezes my insides, making my face tighten and contort. I wipe away tears and close my eyes to the silence of that moment. Waking in woods. Dark and cold. A child asleep. A loving, caring arm reaching out to touch him. Anguish, suffering, fear, affection and enduring protection, and all in twenty-five words.

The magical creature leaves my chest, and the hollow expands into an ache.

Some parents love their children more than anything.

The following sentence is even better, because even though

the words are in the wrong grammatical order, they're in the right order, really. The one after that takes my breath away, too. And the next. There are hardly any commas or speech marks. I didn't know that was allowed.

The book is *The Road* by Cormac McCarthy.

It's the most beautiful novel opening I've ever read but it makes me cry more than I can explain.

I'd like to find a sentence that makes me smile next.

9

Becca arrives late with adjusted retainers and asks me what she's missed. It's sweet of her to think she's missed anything when this is the most boring place in the universe, so to humour her, I tell her I found *The Road* on the table, which is a strange sentence unless you know that *The Road* is the title of a book.

I recite the first line to her, which I've memorized, having read it over and over. Becca isn't as captivated as I am by it, but at least she has no objection to my interest in words and sentences. She has her own 'weird little obsessions' as she calls them – or hobbies, as I call them. I'm not saying hers are pointless, but the world only needs so many crocheted animals. I support her endeavours, nonetheless, by convincing Dad to give me money and using it to buy her wool and hooks. To further encourage her, I download patterns for quirky crochet creatures and sit decoding them with her, so a mammoth looks like a mammoth and not a fat and wonky horse.

'Isssch that it?' Becca asks, checking nothing else important has happened in her absence.

'More or less.' I don't mention that instead of focusing in

lessons, I've been attempting to create sentences in my head like the one that opens *The Road*: ones with a pulse and bounce and beat leading to an outstretched elongation, then a featherlight touch of softness and a gentle sloping fall. It's not an easy task. Plus, thinking about this in Geography instead of completing the worksheet on global migration, has earned me another detention, which Becca doesn't need to know as she's worried enough about me already.

In English, Miss McLaughlin hands us a poem printed on a piece of paper. I don't expect my skin to burst open on a Friday afternoon in an English lesson, but burst open it does.

'A Birthday'
Christina Rossetti

My heart is like a singing bird
    Whose nest is in a water'd shoot;
My heart is like an apple-tree
    Whose boughs are bent with thickset fruit;
My heart is like a rainbow shell
    That paddles in a halcyon sea;
My heart is gladder than all these
    Because my love is come to me.

Raise me a dais of silk and down;
    Hang it with vair and purple dyes;
Carve it in doves and pomegranates,
    And peacocks with a hundred eyes;
Work it in gold and silver grapes,
    In leaves and silver fleurs-de-lys;

Because the birthday of my life
Is come, my love is come to me.

I want to leave the room and be alone with it, but lessons in secondary schools do not allow for being alone with a poem to savour the rapturous beauty of the sounds and rhythms, and the giddy, uplifting lavishness of how being in love must feel. Miss McLaughlin asks us what it's about, and Lyra Lewis says, 'Getting a birthday present?' but then Lyra Lewis resides in the land of the obvious. It's not about a birthday or a present. Rossetti's love has come. It's better than any birthday. It's the birthday of her life.

I try to mend my ruptured skin by gazing at the thin winter sky beyond the window. I wonder whether love will ever turn my heart to a singing bird. To stem the tears welling up, I run, '*Raise me a dias of silk and down*'; '*Whose boughs are bent with thickset fruit*' and '*leaves and silver fleurs-de-lys*' through my mind. I only turn my focus back when Becca says, in answer to Miss McLaughlin's next question, 'It'ssch sschtructured in two sschtansschzas of eight linessch,' and I grin and wonder what the world would be like if everyone's 'esses' were as pronounced and impressive. Sschlightly sschtrange, I sschould think. But alsscho sschomewhat sschplendid.

Miss McLaughlin must have put her foundation on blindfold, because she has an uneven line under her jaw where the orange foundation stops and her white neck begins. She mustn't realize, or maybe she doesn't care, that when she stands at the front, we have a perfect view of the underside of her chin and the starkly unblended foundation line. Today, she has her hair tied back, which means she hasn't washed it, which is perfectly acceptable, obviously, but it would look better tied back when she has washed it because then you wouldn't be able to see the greasiness that this style seems to accentuate. But these are not suggestions you can suggest to teachers.

We chew through the poem in a puerile, pithy and pedestrian way. It is utterly, entirely and wholly unsatisfactory. Rossetti deserves better.

At the end of the lesson, Miss McLaughlin announces that next week an author is visiting us for World Book Week.

It's the best announcement I've heard in a while. You don't hear many great announcements.

Parents announce updated screen rules, social arrangements you're compelled to attend, and time limits for showers. Teachers announce room changes, modifications to online safety policies, punishments for earring infringements, and skirt-length outrages. Friends announce when someone at another school has had a fringe cut, when someone someone knows has broken up with some other someone someone else knows that they've been seeing for two weeks, or when Taylor Swift has posted something minorly significant.

If the government announced that the word 'crotch' has been permanently removed from the English language, that would be a very welcome announcement, but ones like those are sadly lacking. An announcement of an author visit is the next best alternative.

'Is the visiting author F. Scott Fitzgerald who wrote *The Great Gatsby*?' I ask, knowing it can't be, but stalling for time. She's going to collect our work in any second now and I haven't done it.

Miss McLaughlin says, 'F. Scott Fitzgerald is dead, and anyway he was American.'

I'm not sure which she's more disappointed about. After hacking the poem into slivers of similes, dental alliteration and iambic tetrameters, I ponder that somehow literature is even more beautiful when the author is dead. It's as though they're talking to us from yonder about a world that has disappeared, using language they inherited, used and left behind, and now it's our turn to use it to describe our world. Which is no walk in the park, let me tell you.

'Walk in the park' isn't a pleasing phrase. It doesn't capture the earthy scent of the wet soil. The dank, cold stones. The green, unseeing leaves in the tall, unspeaking trees. The flop of a toad or eddying float of a boat on a mossy pond. The chitter, cheep and caw of the birds. The bounteous blades of bold green grass. The frenzied dogs galloping across it with flapping, lolling, flopping tongues. It's also a cliché and no one likes a cliché, as Miss McLaughlin reminds us at frequent if not daily intervals. I'd imagine F. Scott Fitzgerald didn't use it, so I'm not going to, either. I draw an X on my hand and write the words 'walk' and 'park' to remind me to write it down when I get home.

'Miss McLaughlin,' I say in a semi-questioning tone when she comes around to collect our homework.

'Yes, Jodie.' I look at her and wait. She rolls her eyes and adds, 'Jones.'

'When I read sentences phrased in ways I'd never phrase them myself, I write them down so I can learn to say things differently. I think that's what authors do, but I've never actually met one.'

'Possibly.' She puts her hand out. 'Where's your essay?'

'I didn't do it.'

'Jo-die.' Her tone is one of deep and desperate disappointment. 'That's a detention.'

'My name is Jodie Jones,' I remind her, matching well her tone of deep and desperate disappointment. 'Isn't your sister an author?'

'She writes about Djiboutian politics. Amy, where's yours? Becca? Homework? Thanks. Bit short, Becca. Should be two sides at least. Ben?'

'Dji— What does that mean?'

'The politics of Djibouti. You know, the country in Africa?'

I *don't* know. How is this possible when I've done so many geography quizzes? 'Djibouti? Never heard of i—'

'Jodie! This can't carry on. Why haven't you done the homework?'

'My name is Jodie Jones. You know, I also learn how *not* to phrase things by paying attention to *ugly* sentences. And there're more than you think, even in bestsellers, which—'

Miss McLaughlin doesn't look attractive when she scowls. She's losing control and we know it: the rest of the class is chatting, plaiting hair or stabbing their books or each other with their pens. 'You're falling behind and you don't even care,' she says to me with hurricane eyes. 'You won't be able to do anything without English GCSE – you're aware of that, I assume?'

That's clearly not true and I say so. 'I'll be able to water ski. Read. Repot plants in plant pots—'

'Enough!' Miss McLaughlin snaps. 'Don't push me, Jodie.'

I want to repeat, yet again, what my name is, but behind her, Becca, distraught, is gesturing unfathomable gesticulations at me, so I don't. Becca was under the impression I had done this piece of homework, but only because she kept telling me to do it. I didn't say I would.

I'm the one who should be niggled because she keeps getting

my name wrong, but Miss McLaughlin seems much more niggled than I am. It's only homework. I don't know what the big deal is.

'She's collecting sentences,' Becca quips. 'And words. That's English-y, isn't it? It sort of counts as homework. Will you find some for her? Please, Miss McLaughlin?'

'I want it Monday at nine,' Miss McLaughlin says to me. 'You still have detention.'

'It'll have to be next week,' I helpfully inform her. 'I already have detention today.'

'And I'm emailing home. I'm not having this.'

Oh, good. I'm pleased. This will displease my mother. Yes, please. Please do displease my mother. 'If I do it, will you share your favourite sentences with me?'

'Monday. I'm serious.'

I used to think Miss McLaughlin would give you a literary classic or a Women's Fiction Prize winner as a birthday gift, but now I think she'd give you her sister's book on Djiboutian politics. Miss McLaughlin, her face less attractive with the squally demeanour, returns to the front of the classroom and says, 'The author's called Ambrosia Benedictine. She'll be here on Wednesday afternoon so go to the hall for Period 7 instead of Enrichment.'

Ambrosia Benedictine.

I like her already.

10

As we leave the classroom, Becca is picking at her split ends with her thumb and forefinger, scowling. I wonder how successful a business called 'The Scowling Hairdressers' would be. Maybe wildly, because of the gimmick. Maybe not.

'Whyyyyy-yuh?' she yells, dropping her hair like it's angered her. 'Why didn't you do the homework?'

A phoney frown furrows my forrid (which is my preferred pronunciation of 'forehead'). Surely the answer is obvious. 'Didn't want to.'

'You said you wou—'

'Definitely didn't.'

'Ugh. You're annoying me now.' She grabs me and hugs me. I mock-cringe and pull away saying, 'Ew, get off.' We wave at each other and head in different directions: she has Drama; I have French. I'm not a fan of Drama, but even so, I wasn't allowed to do it for GCSE. Surely my GCSE and career choices should be mine, seeing as it's my life, but then when have I ever been given the freedom to choose anything?

Except now. I'm making micro-choices until I can make whatever the opposite of micro is. I think it's 'macro' but that sounds even smaller. I must look it up. At present, my micro-choices are trying to proceed with a plan that's proving problematic to implement, and choosing to learn what I wish to learn in this learning establishment. In the subsequent French lesson, this is not revising irregular verb conjugations for the forthcoming test along with the rest of the class, but looking up some beautiful words. *Coquillage. Chuchoter. Saperlipopette. Étoile.*

My micro-choices also include using the English language in a way I find pleasing, such as 'proceed with a plan that's proving problematic to implement' instead of 'getting absolutely fricking nowhere', and this plosive patterning, somewhat predictably, pleases me plenty.

When I return home, I decide not to mention the author visit and instead keep the information in the cool vestibule of my mind, where my mother, happily, has no access. Her shopping bags clutter the foot of the stairs. I count five this evening. As I pass her shoes and coat in the hall, keeping a broad berth of both, her voice lassoes me from the kitchen. 'You're ten minutes late.'

The vocal rope jerks me by the neck. I stand to attention at the kitchen door. Our kitchen is speckless, shiny, stark. Surgeons could operate in here, but I'd much prefer bouquets of herbs awaiting a scalpel instead. If only our kitchen buzzed with the sizzle, hiss and clatter of culinary commotion. Gastrophilanthropy is neither alive nor kicking in our house. Becca's kitchen has delectable smells, steaming windows and simmering pots. The Hitchin kitchen walls are adorned with gadgets, contraptions and well-worn recipe books, and there is always a little something on a plate to nibble on while you marvel at the opera flowing from the speaker and the sorcerous performance of her parents cooking dinner.

In our food-less, aroma-less, music-less version of a cooking space, my mother slams her laptop closed. 'You finish at four, it's a five-minute walk to the bus stop and a journey of twenty minutes.' Her timings allow no room for toilet breaks, cat stroking, bookshop browsing, answering which-direction questions from lost-looking suitcase-wheelers, or any other random acts of benevolence, disorder or insurrection causing a deviation from the norm.

'Accident,' I explain. 'They rerouted the bus.'

She narrows her eyes and picks up her phone to check.

'What reason would I have to lie?'

Still looking at her phone screen, she says, 'Like I'd trust anything you say. You're probably only saying "accident" because you like the word.'

She's wrong. I like 'rerouted' but it doesn't mean I'm lying. She puts her phone down with a tut and runs a harried hand through her hair. 'Must you cause me endless stress?' I like the sounds of 'endless stress' but I can't focus on them because she adds, 'Go upstairs, clean your room and study. No reading. Understand? Study all evening. You were top of the class and now you're bottom in everything. I swear, if you're not top again by the summer . . .'

She doesn't finish her sentence, so I'll never know what the upshot will be. I'll spontaneously combust? The mountains will dissolve? Dinosaurs will roar once more?

'And . . .' she adds, '*and* . . . because of those detentions, you're not going anywhere except to school for the next two weeks. Hear me?'

I nod to confirm I can hear her, although surely it's obvious when she's this close to my ears. Being imprisoned isn't the biggest deal because places to hang out are limited when you're a teen. Parks in the summer, if you're allowed. Shopping centres, if you're allowed. Each other's houses, if you're allowed. That's about it. But it's not summer. I hate shopping centres. I only ever really go to Becca's. And I'm usually not allowed.

More words spout from her mouth, but my mind drifts. Her nails are painted Poo Gloss Brown. I swear she's had Botox. Will the school really kick me out? Moses moseys into my mind but I mosey him on out.

I see my phone on the counter, but I know I won't be getting it back. I know the drill.

Apparently, there's a thing called a 'Friday feeling'. My mother does not embody or embrace it, but I choose to all the same. She can't decide for me how I desire to feel, and I desire to feel Fridayish. Whatever that means.

Dad comes out of his study looking rough. Tired. Baggy-eyed. I turn to face her, so I'm in front of him, which we orchestrate whenever possible, and hold two fingers behind my back (in the victory direction, not the sweary direction) to demonstrate to Dad the current level of my mother's annoyance. He does a low-down squeeze of my other hand. We have codes. Hand-signal number one signifies her mood: she's relatively irritable (one finger) or incensed (five). Hand-signal two means that regardless of her mood, squeeze, I'm here and I love you. This language of hands makes me happy.

'She's grounded for two weeks, Elliot. She doesn't realize she has the world's greatest mother, just as you don't realize you have the world's greatest wife. But you'll figure it out one day. Go and do your chores.'

I assume the final sentence is directed at me, so I swing 180 on my heels, smile at Dad, and go and chore do.

Being grounded is nothing new, but it might impede my plans. I consider this as I perform my duties as a lady's maid. Hanging damp socks in lines, according to colour rather than size, I wonder why it enrages her that I read so much. I've read every novel in the school library and most of the ones in the local library. I don't like the word 'local' – it's ugly if you say it lots of times.

Once, she was proud of how much I read. She loved that I read books for much older readers, because that made me better than other children, which made her better than other mothers. But now it narks her. Maybe because I used to be a model student and do three hours of homework a night on top of whatever workbooks she placed in front of me. Now I refuse to do any, but I much prefer my evenings. I read, search for sentences, make hair clips by lacquering sweets and toy food on to plain clip bases, and write down words that make me smile. 'Lacquering' is not one of them, but 'clip' most definitely is.

My mother's maddened that I don't play an instrument at conservatoire level, I'm not a championship tennis player and haven't mastered Maths. Apparently, parents sit around and compare their children's accomplishments. It's a constant game of parental competition and of course she'd like to win. She links other mothers' arms and coos, 'So tell me, Helly. What's the secret? How did you get Arlo into Oxford?' She giggles with them at parties and gets the intel on who we need to beat next to be the best and who she can ask to give us work experience.

Winning doesn't, for some reason, involve having children

who lacquer sweets and toy food on to hair clips. I don't know why. I'd be extremely proud of my child if they did that.

Dad used to agree with her about her expectations of us. He agreed with most things my mother said because, if I'm going to use a euphemism, she's persuasive. Becca calls her 'The Dictator', but not to her face.

Dad is in his green-walled study, reading the paper on his viridescent armchair. Watching him from a foot away must be disconcerting because he lifts his giant eyes and says, 'What?'

'Are you busy?'

He lowers the paper. 'Never too busy for you.'

I sit on the deep, dark green Chesterfield and fiddle with the leather buttons. Dad looks tired. A little old, a little grey, a little slumped. His tufty hair is still quite thick, but he cuts it short round the sides with the front sweeping back so it shows off his forehead and frames his face with a flourish. His wiry eyebrows have two lone hairs, one on each side, that seem to have a life and length of their own. His reading glasses enlarge his brown eyes, so I make him look up at me often, just for the goldfish-bowl effect of it and to laugh at their enormity. Grey and black chest hairs peep out from under his T-shirt and the skin on his hands is leathery as he turns the pages, like he's an old salty sea dog rather than an economist with minimal interest in the economy who would rather be visiting National Trust sites or playing squash. When he's well. He hasn't done either for ages.

There are many things I love about him, but one of them is his Asianness. He has interesting ingredients inside: a cup of Confucius, a glass and a half of Great Wall, 50g of faraway and fascinating, and a teaspoon of typhoon. Other things I love are that when I was small, he'd cut my food so it looked like a face on my plate. He would evenly button my uneven buttons. He tried to teach me chess, but I kept sitting the bishops bareback on the knights and galloping them through the line of pawns. He took Champ and me to Bodiam Castle, Sutton Hoo and stately homes in half-terms and holidays, trying to teach us their history while we ran around the gardens firing Nerf guns at each other. Then we'd have a picnic of spring rolls, sticky chicken, and cheese and pickle sandwiches, usually in the car because it always seemed to be raining. On the way home, we'd insist on stopping at a service station pretending we needed the toilet when we really just wanted Krispy Kremes and to check if any Toblerones had our names on the front. They never did.

In the green study, accompanying my father and me, are all the things we're not saying. They hang in the room like spectres, which is my preferred synonym for ghosts. 'Ghouls' sounds horrible. 'Apparition' because of 'apparatus', I suppose, reminds me of Bunsen burners. 'Ghosts' sound like empty vests for reasons I can't explain. 'Spectre' looks better than it sounds. How often do you see 'ctre' together in a word?

The spectres in the room with us are these: what's going on with Dad and my mother. Why he works partly from home, but there seems to be more 'at home' than 'working' going on. Why he's moved to the study. Why he's leaving me. If he knows what this will do to me. Why he doesn't seem to care.

'Sourced a suitable sofa bed?' I ask him.

His eyes drop back down to his paper. 'Not yet.'

'Need help? I have splendiferous searching skills when it comes to sourcing suitable sofa beds.'

'You've been practising that.'

I nod. 'All afternoon.'

He grins. That I practised saying it in Maths instead of bracketing equations might rankle him so I keep that minor detail to myself.

'How was school?' He thinks I haven't noticed that he's changed the subject. It's been nearly three months. He needs to buy a sofa bed because that means he's not leaving. And he hasn't bought a sofa bed.

'I learned things I will never need to know in my lifetime,' I reply.

'Like how to speak only with words starting with "s"?'

'That's useful. I'm talking about science stuff.'

'Science stuff is useful,' he says.

'Really? When was the last time "mitochondria" came up in your daily conversation?'

'Comes up in the office all the time.' He grins but his grin is sad. 'Schoolwork is important, Jodie Jones. It's the key to everything.'

I disagree. There is no single key to everything, and if there was, it would not be schoolwork-shaped.

'Sofa bed,' I say to Dad. 'Tomorrow you will buy one. That is the law.'

'Getting bossy in your old age, aren't you?'

I kiss him on the head and go upstairs to shower.

11

The air feels different on a Saturday. I haven't worked out why. This one feels like a day I'll find a new sentence. I haven't established how I know that, either. Despite being held captive, I choose another micro-freedom and slip out of my house via the patio doors and side gate, and head to Becca's. The Hitchin house is not poor in books, so if it's going to happen, it's going to happen there.

My mother is doing one of the many time-consuming self-care activities she does with regularity at weekends. Maybe she's at the gym, having her hair or her nails done, having a facial, clothes shopping or drinking a goji and acai shake with rhino horn or whatever. On the plus side, this means she isn't monitoring the exit routes. I skip along the path wearing lemon-yellow pyjama bottoms and the lime-green beanie Becca gave me for my birthday that I took out of the bin after my mother decided no child of hers was entering a public domain in a hat like that.

I like the rhythm of 'regularity'. Like a ballerina bending, then leaping skittishly across the stage in a flurry of fragile footsteps.

I also like it at Becca's house. Her father, Clyde, is cooking breakfast. He has interesting slippers. They aren't furry or fluffy; they're striped, made of canvas and say 'Toms' on the back. I'm not sure they're even slippers, but I don't know the correct definition: I think if you slip them on, it counts, and these are definitely slip-ons.

Clyde is tall and has hands the size of frying pans. He's Jamaican and speaks gently, like someone has put a lid on his sentences and only the steam of them escapes. He makes phenomenal eggs: poached, perched on hot, buttered muffins, peppered with pepper, chilli flakes, pink rock salt, and pizzazzed with a dash of green Tabasco. Becca's mum, Francine, is nowhere to be seen. That's a rhyme they say often in their family, usually in a Jamaican lilt. 'Me wife Francine is nowhere to be seen. Me mudda Francine is nowhere to be seen.' I wonder what they'd say if her name was Angela.

Becca's brother, Ambrose, is drinking tea from a bucket-sized mug and reading the paper, his Afro spectacular this morning. He is eighteen, but still: reading newspapers is such a parent thing to do. I've yet to find a single beautiful sentence in a newspaper, so I don't bother reading them myself. He's genuinely interested in politics and economics, and I am genuinely not interested in either of those topics, so that may be another reason I'm not a newspaper reader.

Becca's sister, Amaryllis, is lying on the sofa scrolling on her phone with a hot water bottle on her stomach. She has bad period cramps, which I no longer suffer from because I no longer have periods. She's tall with small, gingery ringlets, speckled freckles and the longest arms I've ever seen. Francine is a redhead, but Amaryllis is the only one of their children to have been bequeathed the ginger hair.

Becca inherited the short genes in the family, but she's not as short as I am, even though I've inherited the tall ones in mine. Clyde is six-foot-four, so anything shorter than that is short in comparison, and my mother is five-foot-one, so anything taller than that is tall. It's funny that height is relative. I'm five-foot-five and Becca is five-foot-seven, but tall and short don't mean anything unless you compare them to something else.

Clyde has dub on this morning. I wonder if opera is just for evenings or whether the cooking soundtrack relates to the type of meal they're preparing. Or maybe dub is a Saturday or even a March thing.

So many questions.

Lyra lurks, eager for scraps. Becca is setting the table and shouting at her siblings to help. 'Siblings' is not a pleasing word. The hard 'b' and much too close 'l' make you pause abruptly mid-word, added to the assonant 'i', the letter combination just doesn't work in those two staccato syllables. 'Podlings' would be better, but it's not like you can just change it.

One of the many things I love about the Hitchin home is that they have separate and disconnected conversations. They supposedly speak to each other, but no one seems to be listening to anyone else so they're essentially all talking to themselves. It's so much fun.

'Are these chillis even hot?' Clyde says, facing the open fridge with a packet of red ones in his hand.

'Huh,' Ambrose begins. 'A head in Newcastle is getting rid of exams in her school. Scrapping GCSEs and A levels completely.'

'Can sschomeone pleassche tell me why I'm the only one sschetting the table?' Becca yells.

From her scroll spot on the sofa, Amaryllis shrieks, 'No way! Little Simz is touring in June!'

'They're basically just peppers,' Clyde adds.

'I do everything in thissch houssche. I'm the backbone of thissch family.'

'It's mainly festivals. Why isn't she playing at— Uch! Hurry up and load.'

'Wait. No A levels at all? How's that going to work?'

'Supermarket chillis are useless. Why do we keep buying them?'

'I'd better be your favourite child, Dad. I am, aren't I? Admit it.'

'She *is* playing at Party in the Park! Sick! How much are tickets?'

'Oh, three EPQs a year for both years of sixth form. Don't you think that's weird? That's so weird.'

'Nope. Nothing. No kick to them at all. Whatever that is, that's not a chilli.'

'Dad, you'd better leave me everything in your will. I'm the only one who helpssch you. Jodie Jones, what colour?' She holds up a blue and a green glass and she says, 'Acsschually, I want the green one. Blue it issch.' She squirts honey from a squeezy tube on to her finger and sucks it, then says even louder, 'Ambrossche and Amaryllissch can't have a glassch because they're not helping me sschet the table. They can die of thirsscht for all I care.'

'A hundred-and-fifty pounds! Oh my God. Why? Don't they know we're students?'

'I wouldn't want to do three EPQs. Would unis even accept that?'

'Tut. Going to have to be chilli flakes today.'

'Clyde?' I ask as he spoons out the poached eggs. 'Can you recommend a beautiful sentence?'

Clyde's face clouds over. 'Beautiful, meaning profound? Butter your muffins before they go cole.'

I pick up a knife, wanting to ask why he says 'cole' and not 'cold' but this is not the time, and start buttering. 'Beautiful, meaning sounding nice.'

'Depends how you define "nice". Can't recall one offhand. Ambrose, slide more muffins in the toaster. This one's for you, Jodie Jones. Parsley? Chilli flakes?'

I nod. Ambrose, still reading, unplugs his charger from the wall with one hand and drinks tea with the other – an admirable multitask move.

'Hitchins, move it,' says Clyde in a firm but gentle tone, and Ambrose and Amaryllis jump up.

'Wow. You lisschten to Dad, but do you lisschten to me? Nooo,' Becca yells, as feet shuffle and slap, chairs are pulled back, muffins are sliced, and arms whip left and right laying down coffee cups and water jugs and condiments and seasonings and serviettes and juice. There's so much action in this room, it's like a scene from a film. Smells wafting, plates clacking, toasters popping, taps gushing, knives scraping, shoulders flexing and, at the same time, hips swaying and fingers clicking at the change in the beat. Thin spring light filters through the windows, birds chirrup and chinwag outside, car music blares, dub bass thumps. Despite the sensory overload, I revel in every second.

The eggs are excellent. And that's an eggsellent phrase if you say it correctly.

12

After we collectively wash and dry up, the Hitchens singing 'Coming in from the Cold' loudly and dancing around the kitchen, I spend an industrious hour or two by their bookshelves searching for sentences to add to my collection. Phrases and words to snack on will do. Becca basks on a beanbag wearing her strap-on beard, which she says makes her feel more artistic. She's bought one for me, too, but the urge has not hit me to wear it. As she crochets a bee the size of a rugby ball, I open twenty-two books, one after the other. It's startlingly hard to find a fitting sentence, but after period of dogged disillusionment, I finally find one I like and note it down. It's near the start of a novel called *Cold Mountain* by Charles Frazier. *He flapped the flies away with his hands and looked across the foot of the bed to an open triple-hung window.*

There's lots to like. The fricative f. The skip-a-long, half a pound of tuppeny rice rhythm until 'bed'. The 'open triple-hung window' jingle at the end. I'm not sure about 'across' and would prefer a synonym, but it's hard to think of an alternative.

The book has other potential sentences to note down, so I go to ask Clyde if I can borrow it. He's tidying the sitting room, folding blankets, moving cushions, stacking books in neater piles on the coffee table. A breeze billows through the net curtains and frolics with the leaves of the fern in a pot by the window.

'Clyde?'

'Jodie Jones.'

The unwavering kindness of Clyde and the fact he now calls me 'Jodie Jones' every time he says my name brings tears to my eyes. I blink them away, and not for the first time wish he was my dad, too. I love mine, but a second dad in another house would be a very pleasing thing.

'May I borrow this if I absolutely give it back?' I ask, holding the novel straight so he can see which one.

'You always absolutely give them back,' he says, 'so yes.'

'Clyde?'

'Jodie Jones?'

'What does . . . "necessity is nothing but existence" mean?'

'What?'

I say it in the same way, not faster or slower. It seems only fair. He stops shaking the soft seating accoutrements and holds a pale blue cushion in his sizeable hand. 'No idea.'

'It's from a line in one of your books.'

'I'm not familiar with all of the lines in all of my books. I'll need some context. Read me the sentence, please.'

I'm grateful he's said that because it's the sentence I understand least of all the sentences I have ever read in my life. In their study, I'd read it again and again before writing it in my journal, but still I was baffled. There are myriad incomprehensible sentences in that book, one after the other, forming incomprehensible paragraphs, pages and chapters. Reading it makes my brain feel like it's in a cerebral washing machine.

I pick up the journal and read him the line slowly.

'Thus totality is nothing else but plurality contemplated as unity; limitation is merely reality conjoined with negation; community is the causality of a substance, reciprocally determining, and determined by other substances; and finally, necessity is nothing but existence, which is given through the possibility itself.'

I pause.

Clyde is laughing quietly. He then makes a noise like a pressure cooker and says, 'Which book is that?'

'"*The Critique of Pure Reason*" by Immanuel Kant.'

Clyde says, 'You want to understand Kant? Good luck. I tried for three years, and I still can't understand a thing.'

He says 'tree', 'c'yan' and 'ting'. I'm aware that he speaks in a Jamaican accent only in certain situations and typically for comic effect, so I feel honoured that this is one of them.

'It's not one I wish to borrow,' I say. 'Thanks all the same.'

'Noted.' He puts the cushion down, smiling to himself. I'm not sure what he's smiling about, but Clyde's smiles are never hostile.

'Clyde,' I say, my eyes resting on his reassuring face like they've come home after a long and tiring trip. I wonder what it is about Clyde that makes me feel safe. 'If I ever needed to, could I stay with you a while?'

His gaze is a long one, a deep one, a thoughtful one. It has a concerned undercurrent and an overt fatherliness that makes my heart hurt. 'Maybe we can talk about why you might ever need to.'

Words don't, won't, can't form in my mouth, so after a beat

or two, he adds, 'You know you're always welcome here.'

I swallow hard and blink a thanks, and then before I cry, I take the book back to its rightful place and slot it in next to his other philosophy titles. I don't know which book Clyde would give me for my birthday. His shelves are so eclectic, I just can't work it out. It bothers me and I let the bothering bother me a while.

Becca has finished her bee. She's stuck two googly eyes on and sewn in pipe-cleaner antennae. 'Your mum rang,' she says. 'Rang *me*. From *your* phone, which is just rude. When's she giving it back to you?'

'Dunno. Don't care.'

'Why not? That's so weird. She said you have to go home, but like now. She ain't happy you broke your curfew, girlfrien'.' Becca hasn't got her retainer in, clearly. 'Do you think Champ'll like Bee-atrice?' she asks, waving the fat, knitted bee in the air.

My stomach hardens. No, I do not think Champ will like it, but more concerningly, I'm uncomfortable that she's made it for Champ, and that she has any other thought about Champ than as my brother.

'Doubt it, Becca.' The disappointment would be better coming from me.

'Course he will,' Becca says.

'Seriously? A crocheted bee? For a sixth former? How old are you?'

'That's the main problem in this world. No one gives teenage boys soft animals. Made by hand.' Her wide eyes shine as she waves Bee-atrice at me.

'Really. That's the main problem in this world?'

'Sure. They love this stuff. Let's go to yours and I'll give it to him.'

'My mother will not be in the best mood.'

'I know. I was the one who talked to her, remember?'

'So coming home with me, especially today, is not a good idea.'

'Your mum doesn't scare me.'

Becca smooths her hair down with both hands and flicks her eyes wide open. 'She petrifies me.' Becca laughs loudly. 'But we FIERCE. We BRAVE. We stand up to The Dictator because we have Bee-atrice to give to Champ. Let's go.'

As usual on the walk to my house, men and boys look at us, but Becca is oblivious, and I try to be, but I can't help it if I notice everything. To distract myself, I make her play 'Weird Brand Names' with me as we coat our fingertips in the sharp spuddy crumbs of her salt-and-vinegar crisps.

I don't know why the male of the species looks at us. Is it because we're young, or unselfconscious, or mixed race of two different mixes, or an unlikely combo of friends? When I asked Dad once, he said, 'All of the above, I'd imagine. And you're fabulously beautiful, the pair of you.'

This is nonsense. Dads are notoriously biased: we could look like blowfish and he'd still say that. That's dads for you.

I'd further imagine that Becca screeching 'Banana Republic', 'Sweaty Betty', 'Moonpig' and 'Lululemon' as we lick our vinegary fingers might have something to do with it. I won't ever know for sure.

Males are even more baffling than females.

13

'Hi, Daniela,' I say, walking in with Becca, my eyes scanning my home as if for mines. Daniela waves at us as she washes the kitchen floor; she wants to smile but Becca's presence, we both know, is contentious. Daniela watches me de-shoeing without de-lacing and this is de-no-no but I de-do it anyway. Becca never unties her shoes so for her it's normal practice.

'D'you like Bee-atrissche?' Becca asks Daniela.

'Oh, is great,' she replies. 'You make it for Jodie Jonns?'

'It'ssch for Champ,' Becca whispers and then giggles.

Daniela opens her eyes wide, winks conspiratorially and nods. She's very tactful. She doesn't say Champ is a rectum boil, even though she must see it for herself, and she hasn't mentioned the duvet on the Chesterfield. She's the kind of person to give you a cake-baking book for your birthday, and I know this from experience. She hadn't been working here long and mustn't have realized that back when I was twelve, my mother would never let me bake in our kitchen because it would make a mess, make our house feel cosy, and there'd be cake in the house, none of which is allowed. Daniela realizes it now. I wonder if she regrets her choice. I know I would.

Daniela tells me there's grilled chicken and yellow rice in the fridge, and when we ask where Champ is, she tells us he's at a debating tournament, except she calls it a 'debit competition'.

Becca is deflated. 'Shall I leave it on his bed?' she asks me.

'He would hate that.'

She decides to do it anyway.

My mother, weirdly, doesn't appear. We creep up the stairs and I stand guard as Becca smuggles the bee into the forbidden fort. We're tiptoeing back to the top of the stairs, when my mother comes out of my room, my phone in her hand. She's either been looking through my drawers or taking my most valued things again. Probably both.

She is icy. Seething. She glares at Becca and says, 'Why are you here? You know I'm annoyed with Jodie. You also know she's grounded, yet when she sneaked to your house you didn't send her back. So, I'm also annoyed with you.'

'I came to borrow some notes,' Becca lies.

'And she couldn't give them to you at school?'

'I need them today. For prep. Forgot mine in my locker.'

My mother displays facial disdain and launches into a tirade about sneaking out. Then, casting a glance at my pyjama bottoms that double up as loungewear, says, 'You wore those out?'

I look down at them. An inner narrative weaves through the viaducts of my mind. *Er. Yes. What do you mean? I was lounging so who cares?*

'You're telling me you actually walked down the street in those?'

In actuality, I wasn't telling her anything, but I keep schtum about that. Becca is silent beside me. I don't mention I also wore the lime-green beanie, which I've accidently left at Becca's house.

'What the hell, Jodie!' my mother cries. 'The state of you. People will think I let you walk round like that. Get those bloody things off – I'm throwing them out. Why have you got toy food stuck to your hair. What are you, five?'

When she sees it's having no effect, she stops and eyes me slyly. She has a different weapon up her sleeve, I can tell. She shakes her head, holds up my phone and shows me an email Mr Fowler has sent to her and Dad about my attitude, being on report again – this being the final time before 'other action is regrettably taken' – and my current and critical level of educational malfunction. Predictably, it is not complimentary.

'As you're still failing abysmally, I've taken matters into my own hands. You have an online Maths module from four till six today,' she says.

'Module,' I repeat because it's such a gratifyingly word.

'Don't you DARE!' she thwacks in slow monosyllabic punches. She turns to Becca with a saccharine, sardonic smile and adds, 'Do you think she is grateful for these extra efforts I make for her?'

Becca is trying not to fidget but her jiggling knees are giving her away. 'I'm ... sure she is,' she replies, blinking lots and moving her mass of hair to one side with her hands.

'No. She isn't.' My mother's tone is terse. 'Jodie can't have friends around. You know this. And she's not going anywhere, either. Time to go home, Becca,' she says to my friend. She should have no authority over Becca but then this is her house, I suppose. Clyde would never, ever tell me to leave. He wouldn't even ask me to. Nor would Francine. Something crushes in me and hardens.

'Oh. Sure. OK,' Becca says widening her eyes at me good-naturedly because she knows my mother is like this. I follow Becca downstairs and she says to both of us, 'Bye, then.' She removes her brown furry jacket from the hook and gives me a hug. 'Tell him it's from me,' she whispers in my ear.

My mother stands watching from the kitchen door, her mask-face blank but somehow also leering. Her eyes are malicious. Triumphant. I have no choice with these Maths modules, and I know it. Being an adult is about having choices. When I'm an adult she won't have the power to make me do anything I don't want to do, but that's a way off. The additional felicity is that 'do you think she's grateful?' is one of her codes. It means that I will spend the next event I might like to attend – a Christmas party, a friend's birthday, a school play performance – in my room in disgrace.

'Additional Felicity' could be the name of a band. Not sure I'd like their music, though.

When I close the front door and swivel whimsically on my heels, I see my mother looking at me intently, her arms folded. She's sporting new highlights, I notice, and her lips look slightly puffy, as if she's recently had dental work on her front teeth or she's been deservedly smacked in the mouth but I'm guessing it's some kind of toxic filler.

'One reason you're failing so magnificently,' she says, 'is because you hang around someone who's living proof that humans can survive without a brain. She's put on weight, as well. Don't her parents care about her?'

I grit my teeth and try to walk past her. I need to oust myself from her environs, but she stands blocking the way. 'That's the last time you go to her house. Hello? I'm talking to you. Stand up straight. You look like a sack of carrots. You could do with some exercise yourself.'

'I need the toilet.'

'Four o'clock,' she says. 'Go and study until then. And you're not getting your phone back. Carry on like this and you'll have no phone and no friends.'

As I walk past her, she adds, 'You will not flunk school because you've chosen to check out. I care about your future, even if you don't. No child of mine is going to be a loser. Have I made myself clear?'

I don't rise to her insults, and I don't protest about friends or phones or futures. That's what she wants me to do – it would fill her with the satisfaction of dominion, and I've decided to remove her dominion over me. I walk on, knowing this will anger her further. Hoping it will.

As I pass by, I peep into the study. Despite not being called Francine, Dad is nowhere to be seen. His bedding is still there, and his clothes, and the suitcase. Seeing it somersaults my insides. This time I manage to keep my food down, but only because I haven't eaten since Clyde's eggs this morning.

14

'Anyone seen my hairbrush?'

I'm halfway down the stairs in a noncommittal choice of floors. It's a useful spot: neither close nor far from anyone, yet right in the middle of the house. Dad can hear me from the study, Champ can hear me from his room and my mother can hear me from the hallway, where she is in tight black Lycra, tying her laces.

My hairbrush is my latest possession to go missing. My mother is doing it to mess with me, I'm certain. It's a shrewd ruse. She takes something I like or need, exerting her authority over me, and I spend my free time scanning the house for it, under things, over things, thinking, where *is* it?, so she gets inside my head at the same time: a double whammy of control.

'Is that why your hair looks like a scarecrow?' she replies, clopping a cap on her head.

Make that triple whammy.

If anything, my hair looks like a scare*crow's*, but I don't argue the grammar point. My other unsaid sentence is, 'Maybe it's because I don't buy the planet's most expensive shampoo, and if I did have that much money to spare, I'd donate it to people who needed it.'

'Disorganized,' she says, checking her appearance in the mirror before going on her run, which, arguably, is the one time it really doesn't matter. We have so many mirrors in this house. I don't need to see myself quite that often, and it surprises me that some people do. 'Be more careful with your stuff.'

'I am careful with my stuff.'

'Really. So why do you keep losing things?'

I don't say, 'Because someone keeps taking them?'

'Use a comb,' she adds, 'so you don't . . .' she waggles a dismissive finger at my head, 'look like this.' She glares at me, her eyes half obscured the long curved shade of the baseball cap. 'No child of mine is walking around like that.' And she goes out closing the door behind her.

The 'no child of mine' line is wearing thin. If lines can wear thin. Which they can't.

Rooted to the stair, my mind reminds me of a time she used to brush my hair. She'd stroke my head and tell me I was her lovely girl, and I liked it because I wanted so much to be her lovely girl, but then she'd snap minutes later because I'd left a lid off a bottle or a wet towel on the floor and she'd hiss that I was 'Lazy, messy. Pick it up. You never think of anyone but yourself. Tsk. Go to bed.'

I dislike my mind's reminders. They should develop AI that lets me filter them into the ones I'd like my mind to remind me of and the ones I wouldn't. I'd invent it, but being a tech whizz would make her happy, and making her happy would make me unhappy so peradventure I will not.

She's left my phone on the radiator shelf by the door, next to the prospectuses and leaflets for the world's best universities, so I move off the stair, retrieve my phone and spend the rest of Sunday morning searching for my lost belongings while methodically ministering to the mindlessly menial chores she has administered to me today.

I don't find my hairbrush.

I also don't use a comb.

Sharing with Becca that my phone is temporarily in my possession is a mistake. She jumps at the chance to send me endless messages. The only other messages I ever receive are from Dad (when he knows I have my phone), my network offering me upgrades, and my mother asking what time I'll be home or about tests, then inevitably telling me a reason she's offended by my behaviour, which is always her real motive in contacting me.

Becca wants me to 'report back'. I ask about what. She says, 'You know what. Stop being annoying. Tell me what Champ thinks of my love gift.'

She actually calls it that.

I knew she'd harass me for this, so I did in fact do some espionage. When Champ returned from debating, I waited behind the door in the spare room and listened. He shouted, 'What's this bucking ugly thing doing on my bed?' and threw it through his open bedroom door onto the landing.

I believe, from this research, that Champ found it all of these things: repugnant, disturbing, pointless, creepy, puerile and girlish. I find the spelling of 'puerile' unsightly, but it sounds OK, I suppose. The meaning is not what you'd think. And I like that repugnant has 'pug' in it, because I find pugs ugly. But that's just me.

This morning, I placed the bee in the corner of the landing, in case Champ does secretly like it and comes to retrieve it. Then I positioned myself on my bed with my legs crossed and my red journal open, writing 'puerile' and 'repugnant'.

The bee is still there. Pugs remain ugly. The status is still quo.

Becca sends a gif of a women in a red dress with her hands out to the sides and the words 'WELL . . .??!!' in white underneath.

'Well what?' I type. Just to mess with her. But also to stall for time. because I'm not sure what to say.

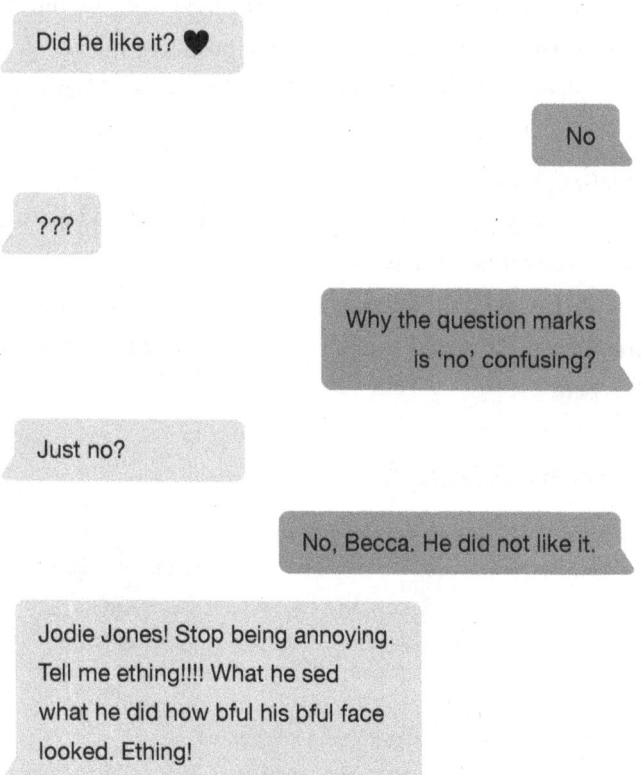

> Bful? How do you manage to turn a word like 'beautiful' that somehow even *looks* beautiful into one that looks and sounds ugly? And 'ething'? I should just stop interacting with you at all.

Meanwhile, what do I tell her? There are lots of words in the English language for this. Conundrum. Dilemma. Quandary. Predicament. Imbroglio. Embranglement. Pickle. Jam. Fix. Some are better than others. Curiously, three have 'em' or 'im' and two have to do with preserved food products in jars. I like 'embranglement' best, but it doesn't help me know what to do.

My eyes dip to my journal. I don't have a smorgasbord of superlative sentences in my highly selective word-and-sentence assortment as yet, but Becca is my sole and cherished associate so this situation needs assessing precisely.

I wish I could ask Becca to say that sentence, because with her retainer in, it would sound tremendous, but I can't because she's typed:

> Waiting 😒 😊 😊 😊 😒

> He's not enamoured by the bee, Becca. But he's an atrocious person – you don't want anything to do with him.

> I want to marry him and have his babies
> Who uses 'enamoured' and 'atrocious' in a message? Only you, Jodie Jones.

Becca is too impatient to wait for typed replies, so she calls me instead. Normal people say 'Hello'; she says, 'Scchhould have made him a cat,' so I know she has her retainer in.

Champ might secretly like the love gift because having someone think fondly of you must be comforting and uplifting, even if you do brutally lob their crocheted bee gift through a doorway.

I wonder why Becca likes my brother. Why Moses likes my brother. Why anyone likes my brother.

'Wouldn't have swung it,' I say about the cat, but Becca disagrees. I consider telling her about her bee being flung furiously through the door frame, but I refrain.

'Bet he doessch like it. Bet he took photossch of it for the sschecret Becca love album on his phone. Bet he tellssch all his friendssch about it. Bet he'll sschleep with it toni—'

'Secret what-album?'

Becca laughs. 'Sschpy on him sschome more for me.'

I tell her I have to go.

I try to list in my journal words that sound resplendent when said with a retainer, but my brain repeatedly presents me with images of Moses. To combat this, I try to imagine my mind as a bus stop, like we did in Mindfulness. The thoughts are buses that I don't need to get on – I can just sit on the bench at the bus stop and watch them pass by. But trying to picture a bus stop and passing buses makes me think of Moses on a double-decker, playing his electric guitar in his orange and red clothes, which I think is my favourite combo (or maybe the green), and all I want to do is get on board and sit upstairs with him as he plays.

If I gave Moses a crocheted bee, I would feel all of these things: embarrassed, fretful, awkward, vulnerable and schmaltzy.

'Schmaltzy' is a fun word, even though 'schmaltz' is the Yiddish word for chicken fat. It used to mystify me why 'chicken fat' had anything to do with being cloying and sentimental, but then one day Clyde was frying chicken, and I mentioned the conundrum aloud. He told me that 'schmaltz' means 'melty' and then, he presumed, 'melty' and 'overly sentimental' seemed more logically linked. I licked my chicken-fatty fingers and nodded in agreement. But I like 'schmaltzy' for another reason now: it belongs to the sschnazzy, sschplendid sschphere of words that sschound great with retainers.

I'm writing 'schmaltzy' when my bedroom door swings open and Champ barges in. He never knocks, and my mother won't allow me to have a lock installed. I find this lack of privacy objectionable.

'Tell your idiot mate I don't want her bucking toys,' he snarls, using the f version of the word, and throws it at me. He misses, which wouldn't please my mother. She likes our aims and targets to be attained.

'You're the idiot,' I say, although not because he missed. Unattained targets are fine by me.

'You are, freak.'

'Really. Which one of us is incensed by a crocheted bee? Rectum boil.'

'Shut it, mental case.'

He knows I hate that one, so I hit low, too. 'You shut it, Mummy's boy. Get out of my room.'

He sneers and slams the door.

He'll get me back for that.

15

As it's a Monday, Champ and I enter the kitchen at 6.45 p.m. and settle on our usual counter stools. We do this every Monday, Wednesday and Thursday, as on those days, we are obliged to eat together in the kitchen. The other nights, Champ has co-curriculars or my mother either has commitments with clients she's trying to influence, or social engagements with the few friends that meet her high standard of human being.

Those nights, I prefer.

My mother uses health as a missile. Sugar is an addictive poison, so we have nothing sweet in the cupboards. Everything desirable and tasty is full of saturated fat. She doesn't have time to cook and Dad isn't allowed to cook: she doesn't like him clattering around the kitchen making 'stinking, godawful food', washing things up shoddily, or putting them away in the wrong place. So, when she's out, we get surreptitious takeaways, or heat up whatever she leaves on the countertop. This might be something 'homemade' (by a chef) that she's ordered at a high-end delivery company, or if she's out, dim sum, kung pao chicken, duck, and congee from Chai Wu, our favourite Chinese restaurant. Takeaway does not make up for Dad's Chinese friends and relatives being banned from the house. No one should get their cultural connection from a Deliveroo driver.

Tonight, though, my mother has a new weapon.

Near the sink sits a brown paper bag from the overpriced organic deli supermarket on the high street. Inside the brown bag are brown cardboard boxes. Presumably, these sustainable food containers contain tonight's edible delights, which may or may not be brown, but at this point I'm presuming they will be.

'What's this?' Champ asks, reaching a rebel hand towards the bag.

'Don't . . . touch,' my mother snaps, taking out glasses and a bottle of water. She's the one who has to orchestrate the meal, even if it's from a brown paper bag. 'Bad enough that this one embarrasses me,' she says to Champ about me, 'but now you join in?'

She's fuming – because it rained today and made her hair a little wavy when she likes it straight, because she called Dad earlier and he didn't answer and, mainly, because Champ didn't get chosen to play cello in the spring concert.

'Never been so mortified in my life,' she begins. We both know this is the start of a tirade. It's also not true. I'm sure there are many more mortifying mortifications than this, and in her life she's been mortified by them much more. 'You play in that every year.'

Champ says, 'Exactly – they have to give other kids a chance.'

'Don't you dare lie to me! It's a snub. What did you do?'

'Nothing! Mum, it's not a punishment,' he yells.

'Of course it is! Now everyone will sit watching other people's children in the spotlight because my son prefers to disgrace his mother.' Her voice wavers and tears fill her eyes. 'My son would prefer to embarrass me than show those other parents how much better he is than everyone else.'

'Mum, that's not—'

'Or did you not practise enough? If you were top of your game, they'd want you to play.'

'It's not tha—'

'AND NOW YOU ARGUE WITH ME?'

Champ shuts up. He looks sheepish. Sheep don't look sheepish. Cows look more sheepish than sheep, but we don't say people look 'cowish'. In fact, 'to cow' means to intimidate someone into doing something. I'm no farmer, but a cow has never pinned me to a wall, taken my lunch money and told me to do its Maths homework or else.

Champ's not usually in her line of fire, but when he is, the consequences are weighty. He has to be the perfect son at all times: flawless at cello, top in all classes, and shiny and beautiful when we're being displayed in public. If he makes a mistake, comes second, gets less than a nine or makes her look or feel bad, she insults and berates him. When he was thirteen, she took the new Xbox he got for his birthday and threw it in a skip because he got a B in Biology. He'd only played on it once.

I'd rather just disappoint her all the time and not have her switch like that. I used to do my best to make her love me, but she only loved me if I won a prize, came first in the class, danced well in ballet or made her look good. If I came second, made a mistake or made her look bad, she'd snap her love into a briefcase and take it away again, locked.

But it's my love for her that's locked away now. And it has been for a while.

She used to say to me, 'Why can't you be like Champ?' but she doesn't this evening, so that's one positive. He and I sit with our hands in our laps and wait for whatever is inside those cardboard boxes. I dream of Grandma Tara's creamy fish pie. Or fried rice noodles with crispy tofu, gyoza and dipping sauce, and papaya salad, followed by sticky toffee pudding and ice cream.

Champ and I side-eye the 'super salad' box, side-eye our forks and side-eye each other, bonding as podlings, seeing as we share the commonality of this particular parent and her particular method of parenting. Meaning we are both used to character assassinations.

I like the word 'assassination'. I like the suspicious and sinister hiss of all those sibilant 's's. The dictionary defines it as the political killing of someone important, which only heightens the accuracy of the sibilance: the sullen dissatisfaction; the suppressed disappointment and surreptitious scheming; the hushed conspiracy; the clandestine whispers in shadowy corridors; the sly, sneering, duplicitous disloyalty, and the sudden, ferocious assault all sheltering in those resonating 's' sounds. A-ss-ass-ination. So snakelike.

My mother is still talking. She talks a lot: it's one of the ways she controls the room. Most of it washes over me, but then she says to Champ, 'I should send you upstairs with no supper at all,' and this amuses me: he might as well have no supper considering how much this will fill him up.

We're still waiting for her permission to start eating. She knows we're hungry. Win for her.

'I'm calling the Head tomorrow,' she says, getting over her emotional outburst and wiping her eyes with a serviette (brown).

'I'm not having this. First your A levels, then UCAS, now the bloody spring concert.'

I roll my inner eyes. Last year, she insisted he took Chemistry, Maths, Further Maths, Physics and Economics A levels for 'PPE at Oxford and then an MBA'. He had no interest in three out of four of those and categorically did not want to do five. When he reminded her he wanted to be an architect, she laughed. 'You think I'd let a child make important decisions about the future? Who knows more about the adult world, you or me?'

Champ is good at arguing: he does debating. But she shut him down. 'I pay for everything. You do as I say. Easy. PPE at Oxford. Forget about architecture at Edinburgh. Not happening. I keep telling you, Oxbridge opens doors. Only a moron chooses not to go to the best university,' said the woman who didn't go to Oxbridge herself.

He did four of them in the end. He has to apply for university in the autumn and he still wants to read architecture at Edinburgh. I, for one, am not looking forward to those arguments. Our house is a war zone with more than one war taking place. Our future is one. Theirs is another. The spring concert has just added an additional volley of fire.

My stomach rumbles.

Outside, I hear the whine of a scooter and glimpse a food delivery driver with a big square bag pull up and park. I get excited – maybe this boxed delight is just the side salad – until I realize it's for Dasha and Maxim next door. They're the unacceptable neighbours on the other side. I believe they're unacceptable because they sold their company for millions and that really narks my mother. We don't socialize with them, even though Maxim helped my mother change a tyre when she had a puncture, and Dasha takes parcels in for us and always offers me cookies and juice when I'm dispatched to pick them up.

My mother is still gibbering. Champ sits slumped, his shoulders hunched, his nostrils flared, his teeth grinding. I make a small, mouth movement that shows I sympathize. As usual, I'm on edge. Alert for danger. In my own home. Which shouldn't be a thing.

Champ ignores my friendly mouth-twist.

After what Dr Kumar calls 'the incident', I was mute for months. Champ tried to talk to me, make me laugh and persuade me to play board games with him, but I folded inside myself, like protective organ origami. Then during lockdown, we spent more time in our rooms, me reading, mainly, increasingly disconnected by global circumstances as well as personal ones. I talked to Becca, psychiatrists and school counsellors on Champ's old iPad, but the world shrank, and Champ was online in his room with his studies and his friends.

Now he's embarrassed by me. Who wants a sister who gets eleven per cent in tests, is on the detention list almost daily, repeats 'gibberellins', 'fractious' and 'truncated spur' aloud in lessons and wonders publicly whether Polly Peptide is a good name for a chemical superhero? A sister who is out of school all the time for psychiatrist and psychologist appointments, is so nervous of commotion and disorder, she can't even eat in the dining room, and has the highest pastoral measures in place. Word gets around. Kids are notoriously mean. I know because Becca told me, because Ambrose told her, that Bear taunts Champ about me all the time. And he's not the only one.

If 'cool' means one predetermined, mutually accepted set of attributes, I definitely lower Champ's cool ranking. If 'cool' means what I think it should mean, I raise them considerably. Depends who's doing the defining, I suppose.

My mother, talking, still, gets up to open the window. It's cold and my arms goose-bump. I resist the impulse to ask if I can go and get a jumper because she'd say no and anyway, I'm still practising invisibility.

'Start,' she says, handing us the boxes. 'And don't you dare complain. No one thanks me for keeping you all fit and healthy. All these idiots eating poisonous food. Well, it's not happening in my family.'

I open my box. Green leaves, beans, brown quinoa. Smells of citrus. As we eat the leafy delights, my mother catalogues the many negative aspects of Champ's personality, most of them untrue. I manoeuvre the fork from the box to my mouth as slowly and carefully as I can so as not to attract attention. I don't care that she's directing her ire at Champ because he's an infected pus wart these days and he deserves it. 'Can you not?' my mother says to him. 'Tsk. I've told you about picking your teeth.'

There's something zingy in the salad dressing I'm not overly fond of. Lemongrass? I can't tell. I want to know so I can avoid it in future, but I eat it without asking because I just know the focus will turn to me at some stage, and I'm right.

She stabs at her salad with her fork and snaps, 'This is all your fault!'

I don't think eating in a bad mood is healthy, no matter how expensive the superfood is.

'You stress me out so much – don't you think I have enough hassle? I run the business, run this house, pay the bills, make all the decisions for this family because your father's lost the plot, and this is how you repay me? I GAVE UP MY WHOLE LIFE

FOR YOU AND YOU ONLY CARE ABOUT YOURSELF!' She stands suddenly, making the stool screech on the marble floor, and bangs on the counter with her palms.

I jump, wondering if she'll hit a five-finger rage: fling open cupboards, smash crockery, tip up empty stools, flip her box up so her salad detonates all over the table and us, and threaten me, but she bangs on the table repeatedly and shrieks, 'AND NOW YOU'VE TURNED YOUR FATHER AGAINST ME! I HOPE YOU'RE HAPPY.'

I lower my eyes and run tongue-twisters through my head. If two witches were watching two watches, which watch would which witch watch? Many an anemone has an enemy anemone as enemy anemones eat many an anemone. To sit in solemn silence in a dull, dark dock—

Her phone rings, making me jump again. She grabs it, marches to the sitting room window and stabs at it with her finger. 'What, Beth? What? What is it this time?'

Champ slumps, relieved.

'May I leave the table?' I ask. Ever the opportunist. She's swearing at Beth, but she must hear me because she turns her head and says, 'Finish your salad! I paid good money for that.'

I've eaten most of it. All that's left is rocket. Rocket tastes like three-day-old socks, but I eat it because she's watching me with eyes of savagery. When she turns around, I pull a strand out of my mouth. Why is it called 'rocket'? Who would fly to space on a green stringy leaf that tastes of socks?

'Finished,' I say. I hold my box sideways so she can check it from over there, which she does, of course. She doesn't say anything else to me, which I take to mean, 'Go, dammit', although I could be wrong. She's listening to Beth with an attitude they would not appreciate at school, but she still manages to point at Champ and say, 'Stay right there. I'm not finished with you yet.'

As I pass him on my way to the sink, I stick a stalk of rocket on his back. The words 'stringy' and 'socks' and the sight of my half-chewed rocket leaf on Champ's back as I leave the room are small consolations.

'You didn't give up anything for me,' I mumble to the air. She doesn't hear me because she's berating Beth in a tone that is cuttingly abrupt.

Poor Beth. Beth is around the fifth assistant my mother has hired, and my guess is that she'll resign soon, too. Employees quitting does not sit well with my mother: she takes it personally, yells, has a meltdown, and, once she's recovered enough to become vindictive, she slates them to anyone that will listen, refuses to write them a reference and gets revenge by leaving their parents' restaurants scathing one-star reviews or calling up the florist they've booked to do the flowers at their forthcoming wedding to say the wedding is off.

'Just leave it!' she yells to Beth. 'Christ. Can't you do anything right? I'll do it myself. I'll be there in ten minutes.' And she hangs up.

I know business is bad. My mother runs Bannermans – no apostrophe because it relates to the family members in a plural fashion, although I still find this grammatically incorrect – the company established by my Scottish great grandfather. She fired Jessica, the excellent, experienced manager who'd been running Bannermans for years, and – never having run an interiors business or indeed any business before – became the big boss. She'd worked in finance so she thought it would be easy.

But Bannermans is not what it was. My mother blames Brexit,

oil prices, the cost-of-living crisis, copycat competition, Dad not helping her enough, even though she says she knows what she's doing, and the fact that she thinks everyone she works with is an idiot.

Relief and relaxation flow through me at the unexpectedly good news that she is now going out, and I leave the kitchen before she changes her mind and makes me stay as well for more berating.

A tongue-twisty ditty comes to mind: Poor Beth is doing her best but Beth's best isn't the best Beth can do – Beth must do better.

I'm mildly happy with that one.

16

Passing the study, I see Dad on the sofa engrossed in something on his laptop. He's rubbing his chin with his thumb and forefinger, and he has a deep furrow in his brow. I wonder what has captivated his attention so, and hope to catch him in the act of doing something surreptitious.

As I enter the study, he hands the laptop to me, so it can't be that surreptitious.

He's ordering dinner on Deliveroo. He wasn't included in the super-salad purchase because he didn't answer the phone when my mother called him earlier. He didn't miss anything with tonight's dinner choice, and I tell him so. I add pad thai, crispy tofu, and spring rolls to the basket, then hear the front door slam. After a minute, Champ sticks his head in and says, 'Satay and duck pancakes,' so I know Dad has messaged him. Dad orders extra dishes for leftovers, and offers his lap as a footrest. 'What was that about?' he asks, meaning the kitchen shouting.

'Nothing. As usual.' I take his laptop off him and google UFO sightings. 'Doesn't take much to work her up.'

I show Dad the screen. There are a surprising number of results, some very official. Although he's as inquisitive as I am about this information, Dad is also perturbed. 'I'd have rescued you, but it's not always the best course of action.'

My glare challenges that. 'Sometimes it is the best course of action.'

Dad raises my glare and does whatever betting people do to throw more money on the table. 'Would have made it worse,' he says. Which is true. Now that Dad's standing up to my mother, she's even more unpredictable and volatile, which causes him to stand up to her more, so she's even more unpredictable and volatile – et cetera, et cetera, et cetera. The words she shouts are not melodious to the ear. More like metal ringing against metal in the crash and clang of battle. Jet black spikes of sound that puncture a quiet Sunday afternoon. Along with the bellowing, she flies into rages five-fingers wide and ferocious. I hear the smash of hurled objects. Dull thuds. Sharp shouts. Riled cries.

'Stop clicking on UFO stuff.' He takes the laptop from my hands. 'What was she angry about?'

'You didn't answer the phone. Tut-tut, Dad. How dare you not be at her beck and call.'

'Right. How dare I have a shower and how dare I not ring her back as soon as I turn the water off.'

'How dare Champ embarrass her. How dare he desire his own path in life.'

'How dare it rain and ruin her hair.'

'How dare I turn you against her.'

Dad's nostrils flare. 'She's managed that herself.'

I sink my head into his memory-foam pillow. Dad has never confessed the inner workings of their relationship to me before.

Although I feel we're more of a team now (Team Anti-Monica!), it also reminds me he's planning to leave. The suitcase glows supernaturally. It whispers from the corner, 'Look at me. Look at me. I am leaving with him, and soon.' I try not to look at it, but I can't defy its mesmerism.

The suitcase wins.

I wonder whether blue luggage will distress me forevermore.

While we're waiting for the food, and to take my mind off the mind-controlling suitcase, I ask Dad about his work. Champ is back from the toilet by then and for some reason is allowed to pick up the laptop, which is all kinds of unfair.

'Tell me about your work,' I say to Dad. Because that's the kind of question you ask when you ask someone about their work.

'What about my work?' he replies, which is not the kind of answer you answer when someone asks you about your work.

'What you spend your day doing interests me.'

'I'm glad it interests someone.'

As Dad finds this concept hard to understand, I tell him I'm not interested in the role of 'analyst', which is the subject matter of his interactions and the lexical set of his working vocabulary.

'What are you interested in then?'

'More . . . the times you have to focus, and what on. The elements of your day that give you a knotted forehead. The conversations you have over tea breaks. The sounds and smells and workiverse of your office.'

Dad says, 'Workiverse?'

'I feel sorry for you, Dad,' Champ mutters, looking up from the screen. 'I really do.'

He's closed the UFO page when he could easily have left the tab open, and is researching the websites of architectural companies. I have to admit, they do look interesting. I ignore Champ and add, 'How fast or slow your colleagues move. What they wear. Who you smile to, and why. Whether you have one computer monitor or more. How long it takes for the coffee to brew in the machine and what the options are. The details interest me.'

Champ snorts and says, 'Jesus H. Christ.'

Dad looks flummoxed. Maybe it's because he's also wondering about that middle name. Herbert? Horatio? Hank?

Dad is not a man for detail. 'I have a normal desk in a normal office, Jodie.'

I don't mind that on this occasion he says Jodie and not Jodie Jones, because we are all in his study escaping the wrath of my mother, even though she's out, and it feels almost like we're a family again.

'I don't know what normal is when it comes to offices,' I remind him.

'Or anything else,' Champ quips, and Dad says, 'Champ,' in a way that makes Champ stop laughing. The rocket has fallen off his back, but I know my saliva has touched his shirt, so I feel strangely elated. It's not often 'saliva' and 'elated' find themselves in the same sentence.

After we eat a scrumptious, flavourful, moreish, toothsome, ambrosial meal that actually fills us up, I leave Champ's tabs open, because that's what considerate people do, and show Dad my favourite outfit. Mainly to ask him to buy it for me. Admittedly, there are myriad colours and textures: the floor-length checked skirt has many a loop and pocket; the orange top is unashamedly fluffy; the tartan waistcoat sports a scattering of red sequins; the leg warmers really do glow a rather immodest yellow; the bag and hat are clearly creatively crocheted and cleverly covered with fey and floppy flowers. Champ glances at the screen over the book he's now reading and says, 'Looks like someone ate a craft shop and chucked up on her.'

I'm thinking 'chucked up' sounds like 'chuck tup' but realize swiftly that means nothing at all. Unless it's a man's name. Which would be unfortunate. 'What do you know?' I retort.

'I know if you wear that, you'll look like a clown that entertains sick kids.'

'Least I'd make them happy. If they saw your face and clothes they'd never get better.'

Champ reaches over Dad, grabs my sleeve and hisses, 'Watch it, freak.'

'Hey, hey, you two – be nice,' Dad snaps, yanking Champ's arm off me while belching a noodle-smelling burp. 'Oh, ex*cuse* me. I think it's . . . I think she looks glorious, Jodie Jones. Bit like a children's TV presenter.'

Champ laughs. I try to kick his shin across the Chesterfield, but Dad pulls us apart, which is understandable as he's in the middle.

When Champ leaves to do his homework, I pick the laptop up again. 'I'm finding you a sofa bed,' I tell Dad. 'You're really bad at this.'

'Not now.' I hide the fact that this shatters my heart into a trillion shards. 'Put the laptop down and tell me about your day.'

I put down the laptop and pretend I'm fine with the postponement of the sofa-bed purchase. I'm not. To be clear. I am so very not that I feel sick.

I don't tell him about my Beth tongue-twister, because he'll be annoyed that Beth is being treated so badly and the business is dive-bombing.

I don't tell him about finding *The Road* on the table because I've already told Becca that and words lose their vigour if you say them too often.

I do tell him about Becca's retainer. He pretends to be interested. I know he isn't as thrilled as I am at the thought of the entire human race speaking with retainer-accentuated sounds, or that someone who spoke with retainer-accentuated sounds would have trouble saying 'retainer-accentuated sounds', but he listens anyway.

When my conversation comes to a natural end, Dad leaves a space like an empty room in case I need to step in and add something else. I like that my dad does this. He doesn't interrupt. He lets my answer unwind like a spool as far as the thread can go, and then waits to see if there's any more. If I don't have anything to add, then he will, eventually, ask me another question.

Apart from psychologists, who are professional silence-offerers and therefore don't count, I don't know anyone else who does this. My mother interrupts after a tenth of a sentence, and Champ laughs or walks away when I speak, so my words wonder whether to follow him or stop and hang in the air, unheeded.

Dad's listening feels all of these things: restful, sedate, unrushed, phlegmatic. Of these words, 'phlegmatic' is the most unattractive. It means unemotional and calm, from the Greek word, 'phlegma', or 'inflammation'. How inflammation and calm are linked is another etymological mystery. I'd like to ask Dr Kumar about it, seeing as he's in the medical profession, but in some interactions, one person's questions take precedence, and when we go to see him, his do.

I don't like the word 'precedence'. It doesn't feel nice in the mouth.

'How's the sentence-collection going?' Dad asks, adjusting the toes on his fluffy socks, which have twisted to one side. 'Twisted' is a mangled word, as if the letters are knotted together. So is 'mangled'. And 'knotted'. I'm not sure why. Something about those letter combinations. Maybe because there's no space between the 's' and the 't' of 'twisted', the 't' and the 't' of 'knotted' and the 'g' and the 'l' of 'mangled' – even if you try your hardest to prise them apart.

'Could be better,' I reply. 'The kind I like aren't easy to find.' The buttony indents on a Chesterfield are fun to fiddle with, but I'm not convinced they're the world's most comfortable sofas.

'Happy to help,' he says. 'Stop doing that – they'll come off. Tell me the kind of sentences you like and I'll keep my eyes peeled.'

'Ew.' I wince. 'Disgusting.'

He laughs and tells me where it originates from, which involves policemen and a man called Robert Peel. In turn, I supply him with examples of sentences I enjoy, explaining it largely has to do with rhythm and sound. 'If you find any, will you write them down for me?' I ask. His socks are still a little askew and this makes me love him even more. I can't say why.

'Course. And school?' he says, pushing his glasses up his nose. 'Friends? I'm worried about your . . . you know.'

I spin my legs sofawards and slap my feet back on to his lap. 'I don't know. Tell me.'

'You need to cut your toenails.'

'You're worried about my toenails?'

'Among other things.' He's hesitant, awkward. He sniff-snorts and clears his throat more than is usual. 'I'm worried about your . . . er . . . social development. Your . . . you know, future. It's not like . . . I mean, you can't drop everything except English and then just do what suits you.'

He's not as good at sitting in a metaphorical empty room as he used to be. 'Going,' I tell him, removing my feet and standing up. There are other things I could furnish the empty room with, but I'd rather leave it unfurnished for a while.

'Boring you, am I?' He grins sadly. 'Don't go,' he says, pulling at my jumper. 'Stay.'

'One condition. I really do want to know the details of your day.'

He pats the sofa, so I sit and re-slap his lap with my legs. He lets me fiddle with the buttons as he outlines the various options offered by his workplace coffee machine and how long, more or less, the two he usually chooses take to brew. I learn that an Americano is a longer drink than an espresso as it has hot water in it, but because one of the dispensing nozzles is blocked, if you press that option, it sprays sideways and most of it misses your mug. I learn that the women wear colourful patterned dresses to the knee and the men wear grey or blue suits. I ask if the men ever wear colourful patterned suits to the knee and the women grey and blue dresses, and he says no but he isn't sure why. He smiles predominantly at his boss and at a new colleague called Andy.

'Why those two?'

'My boss is my boss.'

'Do you have to smile at your boss?'

'It's wise to. And Andy seems unsure of himself. I don't really smile at anyone else; it's a nod or a blink, if anything.'

'And Andy' sounds interesting, a little like 'Ann Dandy'. I play with that while Dad continues. I like the fact that going around my mind is something he doesn't know about; he's assuming I'm listening to him, but I have an interior world that's mine and mine alone, and there I'm free to do and think and be whatever I want, and no one will ever know unless I tell them.

Dad says that almost everyone in his office moves quickly, whether they are walking, doing a presentation, photocopying or stirring their tea. He finds that as disturbing as I do, once he thinks about it, and I do make him think about it. He agrees that there's no poise or grace in being speedy.

Today, he spoke to Andy about his cat, which Dad knows is called Huxley because it walked across the desk, and therefore the webcam, when Andy had his job interview on Zoom. He also talked to someone called Shivani about her upcoming maternity leave. I need a mental picture of her before he can go on, so he says, 'Tall. Thick, dark hair. Large eyes. Wears satin shirts in vivid colours.'

I can see her better now, so I say, 'Go on.'

'Talking to her is mainly what made my forehead knot, because she's proactive, methodical and systematic, and now I have to find a replacement for her.'

I tell him that 'proactive', 'methodical' and 'systematic' are adjectives that no human aspires to being. He puts forward a compelling case to the contrary.

I sit and listen, letting him walk into an empty room because when I'm talking, he lets me, and I appreciate it. But also because he's talking about his work, for once, and I'm learning all kinds of fascinating things.

He only has one computer monitor. I think that's the only disappointing information of the evening. I expected two, at least. Everything else is captivating. Once his spool has completely unravelled and he has nothing left to place in the empty room, I tell him that.

He replies, 'I promise you, captivating is the very last thing my office is.'

Then I kiss him on the cheek and leave his study happy. Well, as happy as I can be knowing he only has one computer monitor, that tonight he's sleeping on a bumpy Chesterfield after no doubt watching a dark and broody Scandi crime drama on his laptop, and that at some point soon, he's leaving me, and that is something I will not survive.

17

The inside of my wardrobe is sacrosanct. A secret, sacred space.

As I write my newfound sentences, I pause to chew my pen. I like sitting here. On the inner panels are photos of colourful insects from *National Geographic* magazines, which I can see if I move the long clothes to one side. No one knows this because they don't enter my wardrobe, move the shoes to one side, sit down and peer behind the dresses and rain macs my mother buys and expects me to wear, and why would they?

My room, on the other hand, is a space I dislike. Being a child and therefore ignorant of the dogma of interior design, I had no input.

'Input' is another horrible word. 'Choice' isn't much better: it sounds brash and insolent. I rarely have choices. Must be a teen thing. So many freedoms denied us. To put it another way, no one asked me how I would like my room to be furnished.

'Furnished' is a word I like much more. Nice sounds at the end.

My low bed has a dark wooden frame. I'd prefer a high one

with a red velvet headboard. The duvet cover and pillowcases are white with tiny blue flowers; I'd like brushed cotton sheets in soft burnished oranges. The walls are white and the window blind is blue. I'd have chosen one with clouds, at least, so I could come into my room and say, 'nice sky', because it tickles me that it sounds like 'nice guy' and you can't really tell which someone is saying. I'd also have low-level lamps, rugs with red ripples, supersoft fleeces for warmth when reading, Oswald, my cuddly toy owl, which has suspiciously gone missing, a yellow felt chair, and shelves and shelves of books. I'm only allowed one shelf, so I can't display the Fimo creatures Champ made at Grandma Tara's to cheer me up when he was eight and I was six and I had measles, nor house the rest of my books. Instead, I wrap books in jumpers, hide them in drawers and in my locker at school and, along with the Fimo cats and snails, store them in the empty suitcase under my bed. I have classmates who hide food, alcohol and tobacco from their mothers. I hide books.

In the depths of my wardrobe, my phone beeps. It's Becca. Of course.

> Forgot to tell you. Clyde's got a sentance for your collection.

That Becca calls her father 'Clyde' used to feel odd to me, but it's better in some ways than 'Dad' as there are plenty of Dads but there's only one Clyde.

I've told Becca countless times that 'sentence' is only spelled with 'e's. The 'a' grates on my insides, but some things in life are more important than spelling (admittedly, not much), so I accentuate the 'e' so she'll get the message.

> My journal is open. What's the sEntEncE?

> why u using random capitals?
> Thiought u were god at spelling

> god = good

> 😂😂😂

She doesn't correct the 'i' in thought. I ignore it and send her a poll.

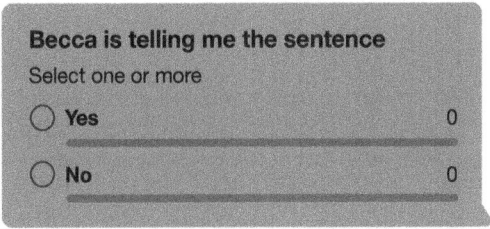

She ticks yes, then types

> So it's the first line of this book called *Madame Bovary* by Gustave Flaubert.

> OK, I've written that down.

> 'What is better than to sit by one's fireside in the evening with a book, while the wind beats against the window and the lamp is burning . . . One thinks of nothing . . . the hours slip by.'

> Thanks, I have to go

> Oh noooo. Are you 🥺 🫠 😳 Is it bc of the beating and burning????

> No. It's. great sentence. Say thanks to Clyde.

> Sure you're OK?

> I'm OK.

She sends a thumbs-up emoji. She uses dark thumbs.

I don't need to go at all, but I want to be alone so I can write the sentence in my journal and read it repeatedly. From the refuge of my wardrobe, I marvel that it contains freedom and choice. Relaxation and peace. To have a fireside, to have an evening, to enjoy a storm and have no one tell you to do something else, and to let hours slip contentedly by.

I'd been hoping for a happy one, but the sentence makes me cry.

This time, though, my tears progress from silent rolling drops to chest-squeezing sobs to deep, heaving chokes that go on for I don't know how long until I'm left weak and heavy with juddering lungs and a leaden, lurching longing for a life I can make my own.

Seeing as I'm feeling sad, every sad thing I've ever felt sad about or might ever feel sad about joins in to sadden me as well. My family. My ignorance about romantic love and the realization that I'll probably never be OK enough to experience it.

Falling off my bike and breaking my toe when I was eight and no one believing it hurt that much so I didn't get it X-rayed and now have a wonky pinkie. Grandma Tara, sick and in bed, alone, dying during lockdown, when I couldn't visit or read to her. Species dying out. War. Famine. Rape. Earthquakes. Babies unloved in cribs. This beautiful brutal world that makes no sense. My mother.

Other thoughts flash in my brain like strobes. Champ giving me a prancing piggyback across the lawn to cheer me up after a fat slug touched my five-year-old bare ankle, terrifying me and making me scream. The pained look on Becca's face when she's concerned about me, which is most of the time now. The line about Moses toeses being roses, which Dad sing-songed when I told him some of my favourite tongue-twisters last week. He didn't recall the rest, so he showed me the clip from *Singin' in the Rain* on YouTube. I loved it so much, I made him watch the whole film with me in snatched sections over the next few days.

Now when I clap my eyes on Moses's shoes I can't help but see bright blooms of flowers festooned at the forefront of his feet.

My mind rests like a stylus in the ditty groove of the 'Moses toeses roses' song and goes along with it in circles.

Wiping my wet eyes on my sleeve, I decide it's time to tell Champ my plan.

I just don't know how to do it.

18

A piece of paper has been placed on the table. The one at which I habitually sit in Period 3 on a Tuesday. I see it when I enter Room 4 for our scheduled English lesson: a third of an A4 sheet, torn with a ruler, with a sentence written in blue pen.

No one is paying it any heed. 'What's this?' I ask Sophia, who sits next to me in English. She shrugs and pulls her books out of her bag.

'Who put it here?'

'Dunno. There when I came in.'

Miss McLaughlin is connecting her screen to the board. 'Sit down, 10F,' she calls. 'Books out. Get in English-learning mode, please.'

'Did you. . . ?' I ask her, pointing at the piece of paper.

'In your bag, please, Jodie Jones. Don't read it. We're starting.'

I sit and read it. Obviously. I'm not going to put an unexpected sentence on an unexpected piece of paper sitting unexpectedly on my desk on an unexpected Tuesday into my bag without reading it. What kind of human does she take me for?

Behind the door of every contented, happy man there ought to be someone standing with a little hammer and continually reminding him with a knock that there are unhappy people, that however happy he may be, life will sooner or later show him its claws, and trouble will come to him – illness, poverty, losses, and then no one will see or hear him, just as now he neither sees nor hears others. But there is no man with a hammer. The happy man lives at his ease, faintly fluttered by small daily cares, like an aspen in the wind – and all is well.

Gooseberries, Anton Chekhov, 1898.

I look at Miss McLaughlin for clues. She's mid-flow, asking the class rapid fire questions about essay structure. There is no man with a hammer behind her, or behind me, because I turn to check. Facing forwards again, I wonder why these three sentences of all the sentences in all the books in the known world are the ones someone, presumably her, let's face it, has left lines from on my desk. Because who except an English teacher would quote Chekhov or even know who he is, and who except a professional text analyser would see how hammers and gooseberries have any connection at all?

They're not the types of sentences I usually like, but that doesn't mean I don't like them. The rhythm of the first sentence is hypnotic, the flow broken with the trinkety ditty of 'little hammer', and again with 'knock'. I love that life shows its 'claws' and the soft fricative sounds of 'fainty fluttered'. But this is a line with a moral, and although I can surmise what the moral is, I don't know why it's relevant to me, and why today, and why here.

'I said put it away,' Miss McLaughlin says sharply.

'There is no man with a hammer,' I reply. She frowns at me with her hands on her hips as the class erupts into sniggers and snorts.

'Bag. Now.'

She doesn't give me a detention, which is good because I've almost run out of days. Still, I put it in my bag, bemused. I wonder whether I should thank her. I mean, I should. I'm just not sure I will.

'I want to be an author,' I tell Becca when we leave the lesson.

'Might have to be,' she says. 'Not like you'll get any other job at thissch rate.' She slams her hands on her hips and stands in front of me, glaring, obstructing the traffic, her eyes bright and brimming with wetness. In the thronging corridor, people shout at us to move, but this is not something that ever bothers Becca.

'We're blocking the way.' I tug on her jumper, and we follow the uniformed hordes down the main staircase. 'As you might gather, being an author is not a permitted career route.'

Becca nods. She knows my mother's expectations are exceptionally high and our choices are extraordinarily limited. To me, the best job in the world would be forming sentences, or working in an industry that does, but my mother does not agree. It's acceptable to like books, words and reading – as long as you're a prodigy at Maths and Science and you uproot from your pitiful consciousness even the pithiest notion of pursuing an arts-based profession.

Becca is not one to worry about words prefixed with 'ex', pitiful consciousnesses or puny notions. I, on the other hand, micro-choose to say, 'uproot from your pitiful consciousness even the puniest notion of pursuing an arts-based profession' instead of 'forget about a career in the arts'. I enjoy doing this. No one can stop me thinking in plosive alliteration and this paltry freedom is epiphanic.

By now, we're crossing the playground with fine feathery rain flitting fitfully in our faces. We saunter under the overhang, but we are flitted on all the same.

On the football pitch, I can see Moses running for an airbound ball, his curls like ariels, and my brother waving at him, shouting for a pass.

Becca grins moronically and asks, 'What doessch Champ want to be?'

'An architect. My mother wants him to be a CEO, software engineer, futures trader or – lower rung – doctor.'

'How issch a doctor on a lower rung?'

I rub my fingers together implying moola is the answer and Becca grimaces. She knows my mother wants us to be top students and go to Oxford or Harvard, preferably both. 'Can't he do what he wantssch?'

'Of course. As long as he wants to do one of those things.'

'Poor, poor beautiful Champ,' Becca says in a tone mired in melodrama.

'Oh, do not feel sorr—'

'Lisschten to me, you,' she interrupts. 'I can't deal with you failing everything. You're sschmarter than everyone I know.'

'You don't know everyone.'

'Tut. What the hell, Jodie Jonessch. Do the damn work, will you?'

19

After Tuesday's boring, mundane, lacklustre, dreary, banal, tedious, wearisome, humdrum, monotonous detention, I return home to a surprise. The surprise is not that the long slow vowels in each of those adjectives make them especially onomatopoeic as they dolefully and drearily draw out the dour, dire, dull interminability of the prolonged, wronged and squandered time they so aptly describe.

No.

The surprise is that Moses is sitting in our stark kitchen on a counter stool, scrolling on his phone. Our kitchen comprises a sleek range of matching white-fronted wall and base units with a central island and breakfast-bar area, incorporating an inset sink unit, gas hob with overhead extractor, wall-mounted electric oven, and having further space for additional appliances after recently benefiting from having been refurbished to a high standard throughout.

Or at least, that's what it said in the brochure when we bought the house.

I dislike the way estate agents describe houses.

As Moses has his hair tied up, he is revealing a small, previously unseen mole on the top of his ear. He is consuming a clementine, segment by segment. Moses eats slowly. And that is both a sentence and a sentiment that I like.

'Oh,' he says, glancing up. His eyes are warm and brown and soft and gold and glowing. 'Hey.'

'Why are you surprised to see me? I'm the one that lives here.'

He laughs, shifts slightly as if to stand, then stops mid-movement, which is curious and sharpens my focus on him. He slips his phone into his side pocket, where it's likely to fall out because side pockets like that have no zip. That's what always happens to boys on buses who think side pockets are reliable and should know better because they never are, but not being his mother or his side-pocket guidance counsellor, I don't advise against it.

'Why are you here?' I ask, meaning, in our bleak anaemic kitchen. My mother must be out. She's not happy about any friends coming over, except sometimes Tavish, so Moses being here is risky. Champ and Tavish compete against each other in almost everything, which my mother likes because it means Champ works even harder than he would if she alone pushed and pressured him.

Moses lifts his hands, opens his palms and says, 'Pssh. I mean, honestly? Why are any of us here?'

Moses makes the world shift, lift and lighten. The small magical creature creeps in to the hollow and nestles once more in the sanctum of my chest. But I also feel anxious and uncomfortable because he's a boy, and I don't know how to navigate the whole boy thing.

'Ohhh,' he says. 'You don't mean existentially.'

I don't know what existentially means, but it's more or less got the word existence in it, so I can work it out. I remind myself to look it up later. 'I mean, literally,' I reply. 'In our uninviting, uninspiring, nothing-to-eat kitchen. When my brother is absent and there is nothing to indicate why any human would willingly want to spend time in this space.'

He laughs again 'Your brother's excused himself to use the facilities.'

'I see.' The most interesting things seem to happen when Champ is in the toilet. I remind myself to pay more attention to when he goes so I can open myself to further prospects of fun before he flushes and his post-flush return ends the reverie.

I open the cupboards to see what there is to eat. The usual. A clingfilm-wrapped half pack of Kallo rice cakes; a packet of dried porcini mushrooms; a stack of mackerel and sardines in fish coffin-tins; Yutaka rice vinegar, Lee Kum Kee soy sauce, vermicelli noodles, bags of jasmine rice, and tins of chickpeas. I don't know why I'm looking: even if there was something worth eating, I wouldn't be allowed to cook it in case I made a mess. And as I can't load the dishwasher correctly, I'm not allowed to try. I could smuggle out a rice cake, but it's hardly going to fill me up, and they're no doubt stale. They should package them in mini packs of five but either no one seems to have yet thought of this, or they have and we don't buy them. Perhaps a clementine, which I can eat mindfully to mimic Moses.

Clementine it is.

Moses says, 'Jodie?'

I pause and grimace, my hand over the fruit bowl. He hasn't said 'Jodie Jones' but I also don't want to ignore him outright because Moses is wearing a light blue jumper and indigo jeans, and this combination pleases me more than I wish to admit. I'm not sure how he changed so quickly out of his school uniform, where he's going, or why, but one gets used to not knowing the whole picture or even part of it when one is fifteen.

'It's . . . Jodie Jones,' I say, plopping a cool clementine onto my palm and turning to face him.

'Urrrrch.' He slaps his forehead. 'I know that, as well. Damn. Sorry.'

He seems genuinely contrite, but I'm still unsure as to why he's in here and talking to me, and not in Champ's room, or in a room with soft furnishings, at least, and for reasons I can't fathom, I find it hard to look him in the eye. I steady my gaze a little to his left where it rests on a green and white vase on a shelf where people who use their kitchens for cooking might store jars of flour with interesting clamp-down lids.

'Would you rather . . . be a lemon or a lummox?' he asks. 'Wait, what *is* a lummox?'

I'm distracted. The rhythms of 'clamp-down lid' echoes the sounds of closing one of those jars. Then I consider his question. Why would he ask me that? Perhaps he was reading something on his phone before I walked in, and he didn't have time to look it up.

'I think it's someone who's clumsy,' I reply. 'Or maybe dim.'

Moses smiles, his teeth a parade of white seafront houses, his curls a frolic of frisky coils, his eyes iconic. 'Like me?' he asks.

It's hard not to smile back. I wonder if smiling is infectious, the way yawning seems to be. 'Not like you.'

'Good to know.'

'More like Mr Fowler,' I add.

He chuckles. 'Except "lummox" has a connotation of

115

gangling, cloddish likability, and Fowler is quite simply a knob.'

I laugh, liking his use of 'gangling' and 'cloddish' and the phrasing at the end of the sentence. I wonder if I should say so, but my mouth decides that that would be strange. We stand a minute. A cat stalks with silent stealth across the garden wall. Planes rise high through thin cirrus clouds. Bananas ripen unnaturally and sadly in a white ceramic bowl. It's all very quotidian and unremarkable, or it would be if it weren't for Moses and his clothing.

I glance at his shoes and see a profusion of flowers where his toes should be. Will it always be this way?

In an attempt to be more like him and express something going through my mind, even though it's a more direct approach than I'm comfortable with, as a rule, I say, 'There's a line in *The Book Thief* about you.'

'Did I steal a book?'

'I don't know. Did you?'

'Not that I'm aware of. Am I Death? Do I think the souls of the recently deceased are soft and cold, like ice cream?'

'Do you want to hear the line or not?'

He laughs, wedging his fingertips into his pockets. 'Sure.'

I clear my throat. 'I don't remember it exactly, but it's something about liking people who don't just notice the colours, but talk in them.'

He seems pleased with that, judging by his reaction.

'So? Lemon or lummox?' he asks when he stops laughing.

'Why would I want to be either of those?'

'You wouldn't. That's the point.'

A flush flushing. A door opening and closing. Footsteps in the hall. Champ's arrival in the doorway. Champ's snigger and snort. These are all unwelcome intrusions.

To exit the room, I have to pass my brother who is now throwing an apple up like a ball and catching it. The air between us is static.

'Yeah, bye. Go away. Let's get out of here,' Champ says, but the last part is not to me. Moses squeezes past the stool with an apologetic smile, and as I leave, Champ says, slamming the apple down in the bowl, 'Tavish and Bear'll meet us there.'

There's a good rhythm and rhyme to 'Tavish and Bear'll meet us there' so I run it around my mind. I hear Moses say, 'Why're you mean to her, man? Don't be a dick,' as I saunter down the hall.

'Later, Jodie Jones,' Moses says, and I turn to face them as Champ opens the front door. He's wearing a grey jumper and blue jeans, which is dolefully lacklustre compared with Moses's ensemble.

'Don't you start,' Champ grunts, checking his hair in the mirror on his way out. 'That Jodie Jones shit does my head in. She's just looking for attention.'

My eyes flick quickly to Moses's and his to mine. He shakes his head slightly, as if to say, 'ignore him', and I wonder, after they close the front door, if I've imagined it, or if the head shake means something else. When something belongs to Moses, you say it's 'Moziziz'. I'm not overly fond of how that sounds. Like a bluebottle trapped in a blue bottle, or greenbottle trapped in a green one.

A siren outside screams in circular sounds. I'm glad I'm inside but my cortisol spikes all the same.

I'm sure my mother's taken clothes from my drawers. She often throws out the ones I like that she doesn't approve of, but now I have very few socks and pants, and I liked those green cords.

She's definitely trying to mess with my head.

20

That evening, when my mother comes home, she reminds us she's been running a company all day with employees who are idiots, and she is in no mood for further idiocy from her family members. She grumbles and gripes and utters a sky-full of unnecessary sounds and sentences that fill the otherwise peaceful house with everything other than peace.

This is a cue for us to gather round her, offer vocal condolences, reassure her and ensure none of our belongings are lying illegally around the house; that Daniela should re-clean the hall floor that is already clean enough to lie on in white clothing; that we should be present in the kitchen without being summoned; and that we should not even think about arguing when she takes out tonight's delights, which turn out to be more containers of salad in biodegradable boxes.

Champ and I sit submissively to eat the ones she has selected for us – without considering our preferences – using metal forks to save using the wooden ones they've come with, even though they're already in the takeaway bag and we'll end up throwing them away eventually so, really, what's the point?

I don't know what today's infraction is, but Dad doesn't merit a superfood salad. Or perhaps Champ and I don't merit anything other than superfood salad and Dad is extricated from its enforcement by being an adult and therefore able to choose his own meal.

The salad has protein in the form of grilled salmon, nuts and edamame; greenery in the form of varying leaves of overly large girth, interspersed with thin, wiggly strings of rocket; vitamins in the form of sunset-coloured mini tomatoes, brown quinoa, roasted fennel, asparagus tips, and a substance that might be alfalfa, but I'm baffled as to what alfalfa actually looks like. Again, the salad is coated in the lemongrassy, or whatever it is, dressing I dislike but still have to eat. We are allowed slices of brown sourdough this time, but it tastes of mouldy mushrooms to me so I'm not granting it entry to my mouth.

'Practised?' my mother asks Champ. A grain of quinoa is stuck between two of her bottom teeth and I'm glad of it. Champ nods, reaching with uncertainty for a slice of bread, and she narrows her cobra eyes. Her leaf-speared fork stops halfway to her mouth. 'How long?'

'Hour and a half,' he replies, his face impassive and open, the slice seized, buttered and bitten into. What a skilful liar he is. He knows and I know he's practised for less than twenty minutes. I contemplate mentioning this to the one among us who doesn't know this information, but I desist. My mother says, 'Another hour and a half,' which is punishment enough, I'd say. Not that he'll have time. Champ and Tavish have a national debating competition next week and need to go through their POCs, which in debating does not mean People of Colour, but Points of Clarification. Champ doesn't mention Tavish's imminent arrival to our house, so neither do I, even though it's unfair that Tavish is allowed to come here, yet my mother shoos Becca out on the rare occasions she makes it through the front door.

I'd prefer Moses to be Champ's debating partner so he'd be allowed in, but I have no choice in these things. Tavish has unspoken permission to study here because parliamentary debating is educational, looks good on a CV, and it's competitive: someone wins cups and trophies, and my mother wants that someone to be her son. Besides, this is Champ: different rules apply, which isn't fair but then life's not fair as Champ repeatedly points out. His exact words are, 'Suck it up, arse-wipe.' So the arse-wipe sucks it up.

'I emailed the head. About the spring concert,' my mother says, lancing some leaves. They aren't easy to lever into the mouth as they leave the leaves whole in their leafy superfood salad, but she makes the dribbly cram look easy. 'Dribbly cram' auto-repeats in my mind as she calls to Daniela to 'get some water'. Between the three of us, we have six legs, six arms and three brains able to coordinate movement so we could undertake this very simple task for ourselves.

Daniela says, 'Of coss.' She pauses the pointless floor recleaning, enters the kitchen with a circumspect smile, apologizes to my mother when she hasn't done anything wrong, removes the water bottle from the fridge, places it on the table, takes three highball glasses from the cupboard, puts one before each of us and carefully pours us each a glass of water with a nervous sniff.

I like Daniela. She has thin brown hair, dry eczema-y skin and slightly slanted dark brown eyes. She's studying a further pharmacy qualification to practise here, as her degree is from Romania, so I hope she'll be able to leave soon and do something better than clean our house in nervous silence and get told off repeatedly for not doing something properly by my mother. Daniela works hard to ensure our house upholds its appearance as a sterile clinic with no signs of human life: no letters on sideboards, no evidence of coffee cups or crumbs, no errant fluff on carpets or rugs, no fingerprints on light switches, no fleece blankets strewn on sofas after a family movie-night because there is no family movie night. There is no 'family' so there can't be, really. My mother loves giving me chores, especially as punishment, so I for one am happy we have a cleaner. Less to do.

Mortified, I glare at the table. Champ is engrossed in the tomato he's pronging. I'd gloat that he's still in her bad books, but then my mother glares at me while I'm attempting a dribbly cram myself with limited success. 'Perhaps you'd like to tell me why your form tutor emailed me today,' my mother says.

I place the forked leaves down and wipe my mouth. No, I wouldn't, thanks. I know why. My mother knows why. What reason would I have to tell her something she already knows? The detentions are at an almost record-breaking level. I didn't do my History prep on Paul Ehrlich and Sahachiro Hata because I enjoyed the sounds of 'Sahachiro Hata' so much, I spent an hour fribbling about on the web finding phrases in Japanese. *Mamori Tai. Chichicata. Shinrin-yoku.* My recent Biology test result was another 'cause for concern', and this line has been bandied about by at least three teachers this week.

'Are you deaf, or just rude?' my mother asks. 'Why did your form tutor email me?'

The second question isn't the same as the first, but she is agitated so it's not the time to point this out. I swallow a morsel of masticated edamame and reply, 'Because of the detentions.'

She jabs her fork in the direction of my eyes, the volume of her voice rising. 'Because you are failing,' she says, jabbing in rhythm, 'everything on purpose. You *want* to show me up. You *want* to make me look bad. What *I* want to know is why.'

Her rhythm is a little off and the fork jabbing stopped earlier than predicted. I'm eighty per cent certain her question is rhetorical, so I sit looking apologetic, which I don't feel, but then looking obstreperous, defiant and truculent doesn't seem a good idea.

She throws her fork on to the countertop, which would have been funny if it had been the wooden one, but it isn't so it isn't, and slaps her two palms down hard. Her gaze is fierce but I'm expected to keep my eyes on her. 'After all I do for you . . . this is the appreciation you show me? You make me look like a bad parent in front of these lowlife losers who aren't good enough to clean my toilet.'

'Twas brillig, I think, *and the slithy toves*
Did gyre and gimble in the wabe;

Champ's eyes lift and twinkle. He has renewed verve in manoeuvring that tomato to his mouth. These are our beloved teachers she's talking about: the ones I should respect and listen to, as should she, because they are educating us and because they are mainly hardworking, benevolent human beings, unlike her. Mr Fowler being the exception. But my mother has no respect for them. Designer labels, yes. People who have higher status and more money than us, yes. People who can organize internships in multinational conglomerates or Fortune 500 companies so that Champ and I can make more money than we currently have and buy even more designer labels, yes. For hardworking, benevolent human beings, not so much.

My mother is standing with her hands flat on the counter looking combative. Leaning forward. Her worked-out biceps tense and toned. Her lips thin and tight. Eyes cold. Should I eat? Should I wait? Which would make her more aggrieved? My fork remains pronged in the leaves for when I work this puzzle out. 'She wants another meeting on Tuesday morning. You think I have time for this? I'm running a successful business – which you can't understand, of course, because it's something you'll never be able to do.'

Wouldn't want to, I think breezily. And it's not so successful since you took it over.

'Your one and only friend might be dim but you're even dimmer than she is. She studies night and day and still gets second-rate grades. But you? You *choose* to stop studying and mess up your life. You *choose* to throw your future away. And you want me to waste *my* time going in to talk your teachers about it?'

I shouldn't say it, but I do. 'Dad could go.'

She slams the table with her hands. 'Don't talk back to me,' she screeches. 'Who asked you?'

You did, actually. Literally just now.

So. Much. Left. Unsaid.

Similarly left unsaid is that Dad can't possibly go to this meeting because she needs to be there herself to talk to my teachers in a derisive tone. Belittle them, show them who has the power in the room. Threaten and humiliate me in front of them to show she's parenting me correctly, unlike the 'yoga latte' mothers who have mediocre expectations of their mediocre children. A category I've now fallen into.

'I've found a solution,' I say, 'so you don't have to—'

'I SAID BE QUIET!' She's beside me, suddenly, her face inches from mine. 'Do you really want to provoke me?' she growls. 'Do you? I wouldn't, if I were you. You're this close to the line. Don't push me. I'm warning you.'

Beware the Jabberwock, my son!
The jaws that bite, the claws that catch!

I keep my eyes on my superfood salad. She is a hologram. A hot-air balloon. A beaker of bubble tea. She doesn't scare me.

She hisses, 'Get out of my sight,' which I'm happy about. The alternative is a tirade that will fill the air for hours with ugly words no one wants to hear. I'm hungry and I haven't finished eating the leaves, but I get up to leave, relieved.

Champ is chewing, even though I know he hates this salad as well.

I don't see Dad as I pass the study, but under my bedroom door, I find a piece of paper. It reads:

Woodshadows floated silently by through the morning peace from the stairhead seaward where he gazed. Inshore and farther out the mirror of water whitened, spurned by lightshod hurrying feet . . . Wavewhite wedded words shimmering on the dim tide. A cloud began to cover the sun slowly, wholly, shadowing the bay in deeper green.
(James Joyce, *Ulysses*)

The sentences confuse me, delight me, silence me. How slow the words and sentences are, how gentle the rhythm. The softness of 'floated silently by through the morning peace'; the marvel of what in the world 'stairhead seaward' means. The unusualness of 'he gazed' at the end of the sentence, even though it's lovely that way around. I don't know why the whitening mirror farther out has lightshod feet hurrying over it, or what 'woodshadows' or 'wavewhite wedded words' are, but they sound tender and mystical.

Enlighten me on his suitcase intentions it does not, but Dad does know how to lift my spirits.

In my wardrobe, I read the lines again and again. Big hot tears roll down my face and on to the water-whitened words, which is weirdly apt.

Despite the sentences being astonishingly beautiful, I realize my mother is the cloud covering the sun slowly and wholly, shadowing me in a much deeper, darker hue than green.

21

Becca wants the bee back but I don't know where it is.

I search the spots in the house where everyday useful things are stowed to give the appearance that no one lives here: the low cupboards in the dining room, the side drawers in the kitchen, the wooden chest on the landing. I'm wearing my uniform and have completed my usual Wednesday pre-school routine but this particular Wednesday morning, aside from bee-hunting, we have an appointment with Dr Kumar.

Today is also the day that Ambrosia Benedictine is visiting our school. I'm fretful we won't be back in time for her talk, even though our appointment ends at 10.45 a.m. and she's not speaking until 2 p.m. I'm determined to hear her talk and ask her about writing and writers, but also about 'phlegm' and 'inflammation', if time allows.

All manner of cataclysms could occur. My mind happily supplies me with modes of misfortune that might make me miss meeting her. Riverbanks flooding. A mechanical malfunction of our motor vehicle. A poorly passenger having a pulmonary embolism in the vehicle preceding ours. My mother derailing the day with an unscripted visit to Oxford University, where she is expecting both Champ and me to apply and attend. An atomic bomb falling with a mushrooming boom on the London Borough of Wandsworth.

Champ has already left for school. I have just enough time to open his bedroom door and scan his room for the bee – both highly illegal activities. There is no bee on his bed to bolster future Becca babies. No love gift from someone I love to someone I used to but now not so much, offering him a love he doesn't desire or deserve.

I hope he hasn't binned the bee.

My mother is dressed today in beige and cream, her hair shiny and slick, her eyelids peppered with pinkish glitter, her lips a coral red. I know she has pale-pink toes to match her pale pink nails. I also know that her matching Surname and Surname underwear costs more than Ambrose spends on trainers, and that's a lot, but these are not visible and I'm grateful for it. She has a scar across her belly from the Caesarean she had to have when I was born, but this isn't visible, either – at least not physically. I'm repeatedly reminded of it, so it might as well be on show; it's just another spectre of resentment hanging in the ghostly air.

She's waiting in the hall. Her waiting is noisy even though she's not saying anything. Her cashmere coat is on. Her Whatever and Who Cares Anyway handbag hangs in the crook of her arm. Her low-heeled shoes are chock-full of kittens. Her tasteful trousers are wide but her ass is pancake flat, and you can see her pants line half the time. The usual mask is displayed on her face, although there's no mask really, not if you know her. She's wearing her annoyed mask today, which she's probably worn since last night or maybe since she was born, and it has brewed on a low simmer ever since.

'I said be ready at nine,' she says, checking her make-up in the mirror.

'It's eight fifty-eight.'

It's a battle of wills, mine versus hers, and she wants to win. She pouts and wipes the dent of her upper lip. 'You are not wearing shoes or a jacket. Your school bag is open and in the kitchen, not zipped or on your back. I hope your water bottle's full, at least.' She turns and flicks the bolt that acts as a secure lock on our front door.

My water bottle isn't full, but there's a water dispenser at Dr Kumar's; failing that, I'll have to fill it at school. I slide on my shoes without opening the laces, but only because she's rummaging in her bag and doesn't see, then I scamper into the kitchen, zip and grab my backpack, run back and pull my puffer off the peg.

'Eight fifty-nine,' I pant.

'Not by my watch.'

Dad appears, looking scruffyish but dressed. He's holding his phone and glowering. 'I can . . . Shall I take her today, Monica? You're busy and you have that . . . Then you can get on with—'

'Oh, yessss, Elliot. Come and take over, why don't you. Be the man of the house and push the woman aside who has been doing everything around here. Take my authority away like you're the one in charge of this family when—'

'Didn't mean that. I just meant—'

'Annnnd now you interrupt me,' she snaps. She stands stock still, her eyes ablaze. 'Don't. Try. To. Speak. Close your gaping mouth, get back in there, pretend to work and leave the parenting to me. Like always.' She raises her face to the ceiling.

'Why oh why am I always surrounded by useless people?' she screeches at the top of her voice. 'Is it so much to ask to have support and encouragement? Argh!' she tips her head down and yells at us both, 'Stop looking at me like that. How about getting out of my face? You can see my mood. Read the room, Elliot.'

Dad regards me in a way that worries me. Is he afraid? Irate? Both? He's trying to tell me something, but before I can unpick it, he blinks slowly like a chameleon and walks back to the study.

'Unbelievable. Move it, Jodie,' my mother says in a too-loud volume for this small space. 'Thanks to you and your father we're now late.'

I want to say 'Jones' but I'm distracted. What was Dad trying to tell me?

My mother opens the door. Rain is falling sideways. It's harder than it looks from the sitting-room window, and the sunless sky is granite grey. My mother yells, 'Oh for crying out loud!' and takes off her coat. She has to move the other coats to find her hooded rain mac, locating it under Champ's huge down coat that is effectively a duvet with arms. Then she jabs a flimsy umbrella my way and picks up the long golfing one for herself. It's now 9.03 a.m. but it's not worth pointing this out.

I want to take my latest sentence back to my wardrobe and spend time with it, roll it around in the vault of my mind, play with the rhythms and sounds, and have a chat with James Joyce about what the words mean, but we have to leave. I zip it in my inner pocket to look at later.

Our umbrella-accessorized next-door neighbours are leaving their house, too. My mother's demeanour changes at a speed that is astonishing. Gone is the maddened mother. In her place is a charming woman, calm, cool and in control. As we close our front doors, I look at James, he looks at my mother, she looks at him, he looks at me, my mother looks at Minty, Minty looks at me, James looks at Minty, Minty looks at my mother, and my mother looks at me. It's a supremely loaded second.

My mother's mouth breaks into a warm beam of teeth. These are acceptable neighbours. Sort of.

James, my mother likes to tell us on repeat – presumably to promote our work-experience prospects and/or inspire us to higher heights – is a mergers and acquisitions lawyer at a firm called Surname, Surname, Surname and Surname. He is tall with thick greying hair, black wide-rimmed glasses and a stripy scarf. My mother is impressed with him for reasons I can't comprehend. Minty has thin blonde hair and a rounded body. She wears flat lace-up shoes and the kinds of dresses middle-aged females wear to English summer weddings, decorated with English summer flowers in English summer colours. Because of this and because she works for a charity, my mother thinks she's an imbecile. They have two sons, which miffs my mother because she'd rather have had two boys, given the choice, and she makes that clear whenever she can.

My mother trills as she walks down the steps, 'Jodie, say hello to Minty and James.'

I don't because a) she doesn't say Jodie Jones and b) I don't need prompting to say hello – I'm fifteen. I was going to, anyway, because that's what I've been programmed to do since I was old enough to speak, but now that I've been told to, I've lost the motivation. Even though the name 'Minty' is worth picking up on. Instead, I squint at James and Minty in a way that visibly states, I don't appreciate being made to say hello to you just because my mother wants me to, and if you have to talk to me at all, then at least use my full and proper name.

'Jodie.' My mother's voice is hard cold metal. She stops on the step, turns and glowers at me. She hates the rain and I enjoy making her stop and stand in it, even under a giant golfing umbrella. When I still don't repeat the desired phrase, she tuts, titters and tells them, 'I have a pride and I have a punishment. Three guesses which she is.'

James and Minty laugh, thinking it's a joke. I've heard it before and know it isn't. James says, 'Hello, Jodie.' He clearly hasn't understood my smile because he doesn't add the 'Jones' part, so I tell him, 'My name is Jodie Jones.'

James and Minty laugh again, thinking it's another joke. My mother says, 'Have to go. We're late for her psychiatric appointment,' which brings their laughing to an abrupt and awkward halt. As we scuttle, hunched, to our cars, the rain pattering on my legs and feet, Minty, just ahead, says to me, 'I keep forgetting to ask. I know Champ has a Chinese name, but do you? Not the best time to ask, I know! But do tell me next time I see you. I'd love to know.'

We're at the kerb by this point. As we're nearing our respective cars, late, in a rush, and getting wet, and standing here longer than necessary would be grating, vexatious and pestiferous, I decide it is indeed the best time to tell her the whole 21.69-second answer, so I stop walking and say, 'I do, yes. It's Jiāyì. The first character, jiā, means "good", "beautiful" and "auspicious" but it also means "home", "family"—'

'Jodie,' my mother says firmly as she unlocks the car. 'Not now.'

James and Minty shuffle uncomfortably, so I carry on a little louder. 'But it also means "home", "family", "excellent", "increase" and "add". I once asked my mother if "jiā" basically means "add more excellent and auspicious beauty to your increasing home and family", but she said it doesn't work like that and now refuses to engage when I ask her further questions.'

'Jodie,' my mother snaps. 'Get in the car.'

'The second character, "Yì", means "virtuous", "chaste" and "fine", but it also means "one", "justice", "righteousness", "decode", "translate", "interpret", "joy" and "harmony".'

'JODIE.'

James's gaze flits from me to my mother as he moves his umbrella handle to his other hand. Minty looks flustered, her expression blank, as if she's been freshly lobotomized.

'My name is Jodie Jones,' I say to my mother and turn back to Minty. 'I can't see a common thread between those words,' I continue, eyeing the heavy clouds, 'so I don't know the one single definition of "*Jiāyì*".'

James smiles at my mother, who is now in the driver's seat with the rain-speckled passenger window half open. His eyes sparkle. I'm taking this in when Minty laughs under her yellow umbrella and says, 'Goodness. That's just fascinating.' She bends to speak to my mother through the window. 'Running a successful company, a beautiful home, and bringing up gorgeous, brilliant children. Don't know how you do it, Monica. You make it look easy.'

My inner tube deflates. My mother lives for praise like this. Her achievements have to be enviable, the best, the most special, or the stuff that hits fans will hit fans. She'll find time now to answer no matter how late we are, and the fact we're still standing in the rain will cease to bother her.

'Not easy,' she says with a laugh. 'I work incredibly hard, Minty.' She presses the ignition button and tosses her head so her ink-slick hair flicks and falls in a flourish. I wonder if she's fooling them with this coquettishness. She seems to fool everyone else. 'Especially now they're teenagers.' She raises her neat, pencilled-in eyebrows, and they all chuckle together in complicit, tacit agreement.

She won't like the comment about Champ and me being beautiful and brilliant. Like Snow White's stepmother, my mother likes to be the beautiful, brilliant one. She adds, 'Although with this one, no one understands what I have to deal with.'

'James is right. You and Elliot must come in for drinks again,' Minty says. Her gaze flicks to me momentarily and after a doleful smile, back to my mother. 'It's been too long. I'll check my diary later. Getting wet!'

'Yes,' James says, 'what about Saturday?' His eyes are still glittering like disco balls.

'I'll send you some dates,' my mother says, 'might not be for a while. You know how it is. Busy busy. Not much me-time, and I very much need that.'

Pah. There is all and only 'me-time'.

'Get in Jodie,' she says, so I get in, sit on the now damp seat, and buckle my seatbelt. Once we've driven off, she turns back to the person we know her to be. 'What the hell? What's the matter with you? The state of you,' she says, her head turning my way but not enough to actually look at me. 'You look deranged and you act it as well.' She snaps closed her visor shade. '*Come in for drinks*,' she mimics in a mean voice. 'Joking, aren't you?'

I know my mother will never go in there again. Minty might not be as thin or well-dressed as my mother, but she's warm and kind, and she and James are very wealthy. Last time they invited us, my mother chatted, laughed, danced and sang – life of the party, as usual – until Minty mentioned the name of the designer she'd bought their statement sitting-room light from, and said James's big birthday present was 'just a little villa' on a private island called Mustique. My mother proceeded to knock red wine half on her and half on the floor, shouted at a waiter for bumping into her when he didn't, cried because her cream silk dress was ruined, and then made us all leave.

Later she said she'd never go there again because Minty has no idea about wine and serves oily, fatty food full of gluten. She told the neighbours across the road that Minty should 'have a modicum of self-respect' and lose weight, have a facelift or at least some Botox, and do everyone a favour and change caterers next time.

I don't know enough about adult relationships to know whether the wine and the comments are acts of revenge, but I wouldn't be surprised.

I also don't know if this is why, in the kitchen at that party, before the wine incident and when they thought no one was looking, James stood very, very close to my mother's back, whispered in her ear, and she threw her head back, slid her hand into his, and laughed.

In the car, my mother, gives me furious three-finger grief combined with double-handed steering-wheel thumping all the way to Dr Kumar's for deliberately embarrassing her, looking sad and making people think I have a miserable life. She doesn't care if I really am sad. Then I think that F. Scott Fitzgerald probably never used the phrase 'gives me grief' so I shouldn't, either.

There's a hole in my tights near the knee. My forefinger wants to waggle it but drawing attention to it would be unwise. Holes in tights, like other clothing infractions, are unauthorized. She'll stop at M&S to buy me a new pair when my sole aim is to avoid being confined in this small space with her a second longer than is necessary. There's a bookshop on the high street, which would make a stop bearable, but she won't book stop to book shop today. She glances at her phone. Again. She does it obsessively. And they say teens are addicted to screens.

I play with my latest sentence offering, adapting it to my current view.

Houseshadows heaved heavily by through the morning mizzle from the seathead streetward where she gazed.

It's not easy. 'Houseshadows'? Can they heave heavily through anything? Houses are inert. And 'seathead'? 'Stairhead' is actually a word. I think.

Outside and farther away the glimmer of water wettening, swamped by rainshod scurrying feet.

I like James Joyce. He had the same malady as me, it seems. Wordsounditis. I hope to be as skilled at it as he was when I get to be as old as he was when he wrote what he wrote. And that is a sentence he would never write.

I block out my mother's ongoing verbal noise by wondering how he might have phrased it. I can't come up with anything, so instead, my mind drifts back to the line in *The Great Gatsby* and I try to rework it to fit this moment.

There is malice in my mother's heart throughout the winter drive. In her dark garbling, threats and insults come and go like wraiths among the hissing and the disdain and the snarls.

'Snarls' isn't right.

At least it passes the time.

22

In Dr Kumar's waiting room sits a standard-looking push-button drinks machine with options. I'm mostly curious as to whether the nozzle is blocked and the dispensed drink misses the lip of the mug, but I don't have a mug or even a paper cup to check this and don't know if the machine will dispense one.

On the windowsill are interesting plants that turn out, on closer inspection, to be plastic. I like knowing that Poppy, the receptionist, has biscuits in a drawer, which she gave me last time to stop me asking every five minutes if there was anything to eat. The downside of the waiting room is that the TV is always on, broadcasting programmes with the sound off and awful subtitles that can't possibly be accurate. I don't know why it's on at all: it would be infinitely more pleasant in this waiting room if the TV were off.

My mother is in Dr Kumar's office for seventeen minutes and fifteen seconds, meaning from 9.45 a.m. to just past 10.02 a.m. I've noticed everything there is to notice about the waiting room so now I notice things about Poppy. Poppy is Caucasian, wide-hipped and wavy haired. She wears a white blouse and tight black trousers that look itchy. She has low gums and small teeth, and pale red roots under dyed brown hair. On the orange arm of her black glasses, it says 'Superdry'. When she answers the phone, she says, 'Putney Clinic. How can I help?' so fast that it sounds like, 'Putnik linik huck un a hup?'

Poppy tells me our appointment is until ten forty-five and then someone else has an appointment, so I'll stop badgering her for the time, asking whether Dr Kumar ever runs late and tapping my foot on the floor in anxious anticipation, which she says is distracting her from her work.

I don't find a decent sentence in any of the seven books I pick up because they are all on psychology and well-being, and those kinds of books are not renowned for their profoundly beautiful sentences. Poppy doesn't care as much as she should about the pointless, silent TV broadcast. Actually – and I explain this to her after I ask for a cup – it's worse than pointless because 'pointless' means something has no effect. Silent daytime TV with noticeably inaccurate subtitles has a negative effect.

'Not my decision, is it?' she says with a belligerent facial expression. 'Boss wants it on, so it stays on. Take a leaflet if you want one and stop fiddling with the rest of them. If you want a hot drink, the machine dispenses a cup along with the drink.'

I think about the boss/TV thing as I choose a drink called 'Mochacreme'. When we're adults, we're free to make our own decisions but if there's always a boss whose decisions override ours and who we have to smile at daily even if we don't feel like it, then how free are we ever, no matter how old we are?

The nozzles aren't skewwhiff on this coffee machine, so my beverage dribbles on-target into the cup. 'Mochacreme' is sweet, watery hot chocolate with a faint coffee scent, so that's disappointing, but not as disappointing as the thought that one day, through no choice of your own, you might have to wear itchy clothes and keep the TV on all day at your place of work when it has overly large and inaccurate green subtitles written in a horrible font.

Dr Kumar is wearing striped trousers today: blue and lighter blue. They're a little like pyjamas. I wonder if there's a psychiatrist's dress code, because even if there is, these can't be in it. His shirt doesn't really match the trousers, either. It's pale yellow with little green flowers: the kind of shirt a teacher would wear when everything else is in the wash.

I tell him an author is visiting my school today and therefore, very sorry, but I need to leave early and talk to him next time. I stand up to go but he asks me to please sit down again because we have ample time.

Our session today involves him talking to me without my mother in the room. I like this new development. I can kick my legs as much as I want, but when my mother's not here, I don't feel the same inner compulsion, so I sit relatively still and keep my eyes fixed on the clock. It's 10.04 – even-numbered time. The second hand is a continuous whirler, not a click-halt-clicker. As I clock watch, Dr Kumar asks about my maternal grandparents. Sometimes you need to mentally check the maternal-paternal thing, like some people have to check left and right. I refrain from answering until he tells me it's perfectly possible to speak as well as watch the clock.

We have forty-one minutes and I need to fill them somehow so I might as well tell him. 'My mother's father went to prison for fraud when she was two. Some Ponzi thing. She didn't . . . I never met him.'

Dr Kumar nods, nonjudgmentally, his long, clean hands splayed on the armrests of his chair.

'When she was four, her mother left her alone in the house and went away for the night with her dad's best friend. A neighbour heard her crying and called the police. My mother went to live with her aunt who . . . Well, she wasn't very nice.'

'Your mother mentioned that,' Dr Kumar says. '"Wasn't very nice" is a grave understatement, unfortunately.'

'She was put in care. When Archie – her father – got out of prison, he sent her to boarding school. Maybe he squirrelled enough of the money away for that, at least.'

'Hmm. And your paternal grandparents?' Dr Kumar asks.

It's 10.05. Still OK. 'Dad's father was Chinese. He's dead now. His name was Lei Ma Zhang but everyone called him Lenny Zed. Dad's mother, Grandma Tara, was my favourite grandparent but also my favourite person full stop.'

'Can you elaborate on them?' he asks. 'Your grandparents.' He waits for me to continue, knowing I will.

'They met in Hong Kong. He was a banker, but he was a quirky, fun and humble one.'

Dr Kumar grins so I'm guessing he grasps the subtext.

'He spoke in short sentences. Like, "Pah. Crazy world". And, "Funny! You get that from her!" He died when I was eight from an aneurism. He was at a Chelsea match at the time.'

I don't think this indicates much to Dr Kumar. To me it indicates that you shouldn't support Chelsea, but there are those who might argue with that line of reasoning.

'Go on,' he says, so I continue, my eyes still on the clock – 10.06. Time does go slowly when you watch it.

'Grandma Tara's sentences were long and full of commas.

She used to squeeze us and smother us in kisses. Her apple pies were buttery and melted in your mouth. We got covered in flour when we helped her bake, and her kitchen-cupboard handles were always sticky from her opening them with doughy hands. She read us bedtime stories and pointed out the names of birds and trees when we went on walks. She took us on trips and bought us interesting presents.'

'Can you give me an example?'

'She bought me an ornamental shoe when I was twelve to remind me that not everything in life is practical and some things are purely for fun. I love that shoe. One Christmas, she bought me a star so I could name it. I have the certificate. Guess what I called it?'

Dr Kumar contemplates this. 'I don't know . . . Tara?'

I shake my head.

'Tara means star,' he tells me.

'I'm aware of that, Dr Kumar. Guess again.'

'Um . . . Harry? Starry Star Face? I really have no id—'

My eyes leave the clock and alight on him. 'Starry Star Face?'

He laughs. 'Popped into my head.'

'Now I wish I'd called him Starry Star Face. No. It was Quasi-star-doh. Yours is better.'

Dr Kumar chuckles and places his left hand on his thigh. I'm not sure what the gesture means but he has the cleanest nails. He must scrub them hourly with soap and a little brush. 'Jodie Jones,' he says gently, 'I have a timer set. You'll be in very good time for the author visit.'

'There might be obstacles and hold-ups—'

'Even with a whole series of obstacles you'll make it back on time. Tell me more about Grandma Tara.'

I stop looking at the clock at 10.09. It's boring watching it. It's definitely not a job I want when I'm older, so at least I've ruled that one out. 'She lived in Surrey, but she loved travelling. Maybe *because* she lived in Surrey. Surrey is lacklustre. Sorry.'

'No need to be. I don't live in Surrey. Carry on.'

'She swam in reefs and hiked up fishtail mountains and fell in love with men with big moustaches and had a pet chameleon.'

'Big mousta—?'

'It was a phase. She had a ginger-hair phase, too. Heard of "Bannermans"?'

'The interior designers? Of course.'

'Her father was Conrad Bannerman.'

'Gosh. I see. Right.'

'She spent her childhood in Srinagar, Kowloon and . . . somewhere in Germany with a long name. Her father started the business, but she was the one who made it successful.'

'And your mother took it over?'

I nod. 'Dad's sister Jo is a geneticist. I don't know why Dad didn't do it. It either has to do with his position at the Department of Business and Trade or my mother's desire to run it herself.'

I'm not sure about the word 'geneticist' – it catches too much on the teeth. Genetics is OK, though. Nice vowels.

Dr Kumar says, 'How lovely. I love Bannermans. Beautiful things.' His smile is genuine, as is his interest. He's not writing anything down or looking over notes today. He's just listening, his hands interlocked on his lap. 'What kind of relationship did Grandma Tara have with your parents?'

'Dad worshipped her. My mother couldn't stand her.'

When I become quiet, Dr Kumar picks up on the thing I'm unsaying.

'What was . . . How did she die?' he asks.

I fiddle with my skirt hem to avoid ripping my tights completely. This is fragile eggshell ground. I'm silent until he says, 'Jodie Jones?'

'I think it's time to go.'

'Jodie Jones. It's important.'

Why is everything important so hard to say? I sigh, and through gritted teeth I mumble, 'She . . . she had a stroke. Quite a serious one. The winter before Covid hit. We visited her in hospital when she was recovering, and then every day when she was back home. I took . . . I used to take my schoolwork and do it at her kitchen table. She liked it when I read to her, so I sometimes read her Dr Seuss, sometimes from a novel. She liked Austen, Dickens, Tolstoy, Salman Rushdie, Rose Tremain, but I had to skip the sexy parts with those because I was deemed too young to know about lust.'

Dr Kumar's legs change from right over left to left over right. He could be smiling but it's hard to tell. His mouth is a montage of minuscule movements.

'I told her everything: about Becca learning to crochet, Champ hating the cello but playing it anyway, Dad making us walk around castles and stately homes in half-term to look at Bannermans' renovation work but only after my mother made us spend every morning doing workbooks and reading *Brave New World* and *1984*, which we didn't understand despite having a dystopia in our very own house.'

Dr Kumar scratches his cheek. He even does this slowly. He's a tortoise of a man, really. He doesn't pick up on the 'dystopia' comment, but he's a psychiatrist so he'll no doubt come back to it, and this time, he doesn't badger me to carry on. Why do we use the term 'badger'? When has a badger ever hassled anyone?

'Then we went into lockdown and couldn't visit her because she was vulnerable. We had to stand on the road and talk to her through the window. She had no one to take care of her, not properly. She was alone most of the time.' I pause because my throat thickens and the words get jammed. I try to stem the tears, but they spill out and roll down my cheeks.

Seconds pass.

'What . . . happened then?' he asks as soft as sifted flour.

'She got weaker. Confused. We don't know if she took her medication properly. Dad, Champ and I sat with her that day, two metres apart on her drive, but we had to leave after twenty minutes because my mother wanted us back.' I push the venom down. 'She died that afternoon.'

Dr Kumar hands me tissues but the mass of my emotion is stuck in a deep, wet cavern full of fat, cold snakes. The tree beyond his window ruffles to remind me that life goes on, but my heart doesn't care about motivational trees because it's withered with emptiness and pain. I study the carpet, my mouth a furious twist, and whisper, 'We wouldn't have left her. If we'd known. She was supposed to make a full recovery. Dad hasn't been the same since.'

I hope he gets the hint that I haven't, either.

And then I crumple, the cavern caving open, but only slightly because I will not and cannot open it entirely. He waits for me to let it all out, but it will never all come out. Never. This, I know, will stay with me forever.

'I'm so very sorry, Jodie Jones,' he says, and he means it. He folds in his lips, and asks, 'Do you need a moment?'

'The time,' I remind him.

'We have plenty. I want to go on if you're sure you're OK.'

I nod, so he says, 'How did your mother react?'

I wipe my eyes and tell myself to stay calm. 'Her face stayed blank.'

What I don't say, is that there is blank and there is blank.

'Mmm,' he says. It lingers in the air. 'How did things change . . . after that?'

'Dad and Aunt Jo sold Grandma Tara's house in Richmond, the one they grew up in. With our half, we bought a bigger house.' Win – win for my mother, I think. Lose – lose for my dad. 'She spent the money Grandma left me on renovations and took over the Bannermans business.'

Dr Kumar holds very still and squints. 'She spent your inheritance money?'

'Most of it,' I say, flatly.

'Did your father not—'

'Too late by the time he found out.'

'Hmm.' Kumar crosses his legs in the opposite way again. He does it gently, like his knees are made of meringue and he doesn't want to crush them into powder. 'Has there ever been . . .' he begins, rutted ridges rumpling his brow. 'Is your mother . . .' His words are meringue, too. Eggshells. Rice paper. The membrane around bubbles. 'Are you . . . in danger?' His eyes meet and lock on mine. 'Jodie Jones?'

I smile and shake my head.

'I want to be sure that you'd tell me if you weren't safe.'

'I'd tell you,' I lie. Because I don't remember the last time I felt safe with her.

Leaving Dr Kumar's office, my mother is in a better mood, possibly because she has had her say, and she has a lot to say. She doesn't berate me on the short walk to where the car is parked.

She doesn't make conversation, either. She is 'pointless' in a way, because she has no effect on me, positive or negative, and that's about the best one can hope for from her. I don't tell her this. Telling someone they're pointless is rarely going to come across in the positive way it's intended.

If Dad leaves, I've decided what I'll do.

Because I do have choices, after all.

23

The rear of the car is the best place to sit, but when I open the back door, my mother says, 'Does this look like an Uber?' She drives a Mercedes SUV, and as far as I'm aware, that's not the number-one model of Uber vehicle in London, but rather than say, no, actually, it doesn't, I clench my jaw and sit in the passenger seat. Her car smells of luxury claustrophobia and synthetic trees. She looks in the mirror then checks her phone, claiming it's because of business and profit margins, also known as things I would never care about in my brief and precious time on earth, when half the time she's posting things and checking likes and comments on social media. She smiles at something, attaches her phone to the magnetic phone holder, and says, 'Seatbelt.'

I've already reached for it, as she can see. She doesn't need to tell me to put it on at all, but she rules this car kingdom: she chooses the smells we smell (Armani perfume; artificial-pine car freshener); the temperature, direction and force of the heater (hot; legs; strong); the aural ambiances (Classic FM on louder than necessary to show her cultural superiority to other motorists); and the incessant verbal commentary (so I'm drawn into her orbit and can't for a single moment have space or peace for my own thoughts).

To try to stem the flow, I ask, 'Can we drive through Richmond Park?'

'Read the damn room, Jodie,' she yells. 'Does it look like I'm in the mood for route requests? Half the morning's gone.'

My guess is that she isn't, and I'll wager a further guess that she would not like to be reminded right now that my name is Jodie Jones. But driving back through the park is the bonus of this journey, not the drawback: the wild, coaxing openness and the prospect of deer surely outweigh any prospective delay. Especially on this miry, mizzling morning with its dwindling winter mist. It's tragic that I can't voice this objection, because now my admirable use of 'coaxing', 'prospective', 'miry' and 'mizzling' will go to waste – at least until I get home when I can write them down.

Instead, we drive through the heave, surge and lurch of the city, past shineless East Sheen and lifeless Mortlake, via the far less picturesque electric-lit windows of shops named after a face that is fat, a rose that won't wait, a drug that is super and an ox that is part of the fam. We can't drive past Deakin's, her rival and competitor, because she'll fly into a jealous fit, so we take a parallel road. I'd much prefer to see deer and misty trees, but no one asked what my preference might be.

Miraculously, I seem to have my phone with me. I search for sofa beds and send the best in a flurry of links to Dad. Then my phone pings so I check it. Becca has sent two messages and a TikTok.

> How was it at the doctor's?

> U comin in? Chemistry test was . . . 💩 😱

In the TikTok, Loretta Fogel, queen of pouts and fake eyelashes, is taking duck-lip selfies on a packed bus and Becca is rollicking like Beyoncé to the 'I woke up like this' part of 'Flawless' at her back. I grin. Becca and Loretta do not see eye to eye. It's not a height issue so I'm not sure of the origins of that phrase. I must look it up.

'Mute that,' my mother snaps. She hates noises from phone videos. It's finished, anyway. I search through the emojis and send Becca the Easter Island statue face with its pouty Loretta lips, the evil eye amulet (can't find eyelashes) and the cracking up smiley. Loretta Fogel is a burr in the shape of a girl – I don't like her, either. But I also don't see the point of TikTok. Copying dances. Filming yourself doing stupid stuff. Watching other people filming themselves doing stupid stuff. The inanity and vanity of modern-day humanity. Drives me to profanity. Maybe to insanity. I'll write that down when I get home as well, even though it sounds more like rap than a line by F. Scott Fitzgerald.

My mother calls the shop. Her tone is snappish and bossy. 'Beth, did you speak to Duncan?'

Beth did not speak to Duncan. Beth is going to wish she'd spoken to Duncan. *I* wish Beth had spoken to Duncan. Whoever Duncan is.

'Why not?' my mother snaps to Beth. She turns a sharp left into a road with nigglingly narrow speed bumps that make my neck bones knock. 'Not my problem if he's sick.'

Work talk makes my brain foam, froth and furdle. I can't escape the confines of the car, so I watch Becca's TikTok again on mute and wonder whether, peradventure, I don't get the whole social-media thing because my phone is never in my possession long enough to care.

Becca's messaged back.

> NEED TO SPEAK TO YOU! WHEN U IN?

> 5 minutes

It could be 4.8 minutes but Becca is not fond of exactitude, so these days I round it up. Before I lose this useful device, I look up 'eye to eye' (the *Bible*: Isaiah) and synonyms for freedom until my mother snaps, 'No wonder you're failing. You're always on your phone.'

'How can I be when you take it off me all the time?'

'Don't you dare get smart with me. You've missed the whole morning, and you can't afford to miss a second. What did you have?' She cuts in front of a red Fiesta and the driver beeps furiously. In the wing mirror I see him giving her the finger. I want to ask, wait, am I smart or can I not afford to miss school?

Instead, I reply, 'Chemistry test.'

'What? Last time you got C. We pay a fortune for that school. For Cs? I don't think so.'

I didn't get C. I got thirty-five per cent. But she doesn't know that.

'Every holiday I buy you workbooks and download past papers and you get a hundred per cent but in school you get C. You're playing games with me, but I can play games, too. Don't worry, I'll buy more workbooks and you'll keep doing them until you get an A plus.'

Words want to leave my mouth, but I close my lips so that they can't escape. Until she died, Grandma Tara paid for my school; since then, the money she put in trust for our education covers it. My mother has never paid a pound of it herself.

So much remains unsaid. A whole sky full of sentences and sentiments. But I kindly leave it free for cumulus dreams, Heathrow-bound aircraft and wide-open hope. I look up, inquiring if the sky is in any way grateful, but it doesn't give a hoot.

A hippo-shaped cloud chases a cat cloud. My mother starts telling me what kind of life I should be living and then asks, 'Are you listening to me?' I am not listening to her because there's a cat chase in the clouds and the hippo is gaining, but something must have gone in, because instead of opening the window and shouting, 'Run, cat, run!' I reply, 'I need to be less selfish.'

'And?'

'And I'm lucky you give me all this time and attention when you've given up your own dreams, have a business to run and so much else going on. I should be thankful, behave myself and get top grades.'

'Exactly.' As she fills the car with even more unnecessary sentences, I tune out and watch the smaller residents of the world. An unctuous fox stalks towards a green wheelie bin. Crows caw and whirl in the thin sky above. A toddler in ladybird wellies and a matching rain mac is poking a puddle with his plastic magic wand. I wait for it to rise in the hope he's Poseidon's half-god love child, but the puddle stays on the ground. Oh, well. Mortal kid. Must be hard.

From my mother's mouth floods sentence 478 since we entered

the vehicle, but as none of them are ones I wish to add to my collection, my ears fade them out. I block my nose and breathe through my mouth so she can't control what I smell, then place my coat over my legs so she isn't in charge of my leg temperature, either. The streets are bleached of colour, so whatever finicky little bit of it there is stands out. A woman in an orange coat and bright green shoes strides with a bouncy golden dog at her heels. The world's tallest man in a flat tweed cap and a dark tartan scarf holds hands with his absurdly short girlfriend, who's dressed in a red fleece onesie and black buckled wellies. With protracted lip movements, I enunciate, 'Black buckled wellies,' because the sounds are so satisfying.

'God's sake. Do you have to say every random word that comes into your head?'

I ignore her because I really don't. I say about a tenth of them. If that.

'He-*llo*? I'm talking to you. If those grades don't get better, there'll be serious repercussions. You have no idea of the work you create. And do you care? No. You don't care about anything except yourself.'

I wonder why saying 'wellies' means I only care about myself. I can't see a logical link. A memory floats in of being in Grandma Tara's kitchen. Someone – Dad? Grandma Tara? – lifting me on an arm to see a painting of a boy in a blue suit blowing bubbles. Her kitchen walls have yellow tiles. Bright flowers bloom in bold jugs on the windowsill. My mind reminds me of the taste of rusks, but I might be making that part up.

My mother moodily mentions as many of my mutinous misdemeanours as she can muster on the morose and maddening motor journey to school.

I imperiously ignore her and instead imbibe incoming impressions into my investigative eyes while inventing sentences imbued with as many identical initial letters as I can imaginably initiate without it sounding irritating.

Although I think I failed with the second of those.

24

It's 11.27 when we arrive at the school gates, hours before the author talk. This pleases me, so I sigh, forgetting, fleetingly, that I shouldn't give my mother the slightest indication of how I feel.

She uses it against me. Of course.

'Relax when you're top of the class again,' she says as I open the car door. She is looking not at me but forward, through the windscreen, so she could, in fact, be talking to the sparrow hopping on the bench near the entrance – I'm not really sure. I'd like to clarify that I don't have just one class, but I know she means all of them, so I don't bother answering.

She outlines the things I should do and be and then she turns the engine off. I'm nervous now. What's she doing?

'We are not like these people,' she reminds me. 'I expect my children to be the best.'

I want to ask, 'The best what?' but I keep my trap shut to save myself and the sky above from twenty-eight more unnecessary sentences. I look up and notice the hippopota-cloud has lost its mass, the cat cloud has escaped, and the blue dome has turned a graveyard grey. The breeze-block walls are equally grey. The pavement is grey. Not the most uplifting view.

'You go straight to school every day this week and come straight home,' she says. 'Phone.'

I slap it on her palm.

'Right. No more Instagram,' she said, deleting the entire app. 'What else? And don't think you're getting this back.'

'No. Please,' I plead, employing the eyes and the hands and the collapsed-body look. My acting skills are good. They'd have to be to get past my mother. She can't know that I don't care, or she'll find something else to punish me with. She insists – for our safety – that our locations are switched on so she can see where we are at all non-scheduled times, and – for our safety – links our devices regularly to her laptop so she can read our WhatsApp messages. I enjoy the thought that – for my safety – she's trying to work out the secret codes of my robot arms and brown circles when there aren't any. This invasion of privacy makes the confiscation of my phone a state of life I prefer. Usually.

'Good. Teach you a lesson.'

My phone has been forcibly removed from my possession as punishment purely for being myself. Again.

'One week,' she says, not looking at me. 'Longer if you don't get As in everything.'

'They don't give As,' I remind her. 'It's a different marking system.'

'You know what I mean! Whatever's equal to an A. And stop the crap, will you. I don't have time for your bullshit.'

She slips my phone into her bag. To the coo of some grumbling pigeons, also grey, I step out and brace myself for the onslaught of school. She normally drives off before my arms are through both straps of my backpack, but alas. Drive away, I think. Go. Go. Go. Turn the car back on.

She takes off her seatbelt and gets out of the car.

In rigid horror, I hear her door clunk closed.

Her walking in with me, like I'm five years old, is mortifying. Eyes glide sideways as she swishes through the front door. Lips twitch when I'm spotted shrunken and sullen beside her. She hasn't made an appointment, but this won't deter her. She loves turning up unannounced in her bougie brand-name clothing, sleek heels and vast dark sunglasses.

'He-lloooo,' my mother says, smiling at the receptionist, Miss Sweeney, whose eyes take in my mother's cream cashmere coat, her Whatever the Buck handbag, her air of royalty and her charm-inducing dimples.

'Helloo, Mrs Jones,' she says genially in her warm Irish accent. 'Looking fabulous as ever.'

'Ohhh, thank you.' My mother beams. She lives for this. 'Jodie had an appointment with her psychiatrist again. I hate that she misses school, but I assume you know her history. And now, with her current behaviour . . . all these detentions and low grades . . .' She shakes her head and sighs. 'It's so difficult for me. I honestly don't know what to do with a child like this. I'm used to high achievers.' She looks at me sadly, not caring for a moment that there are two Year 11s standing behind us trying not to laugh. 'Let me speak to the Head.'

'Oh, Mrs Jones. I'm sorry to hear that but unfortunately, the Head is away at a conference.'

'Then get her head of year.'

'Mr Fowler is teaching all day. The best thing to do, now, is to make an appointm—'

'I am a parent at this school,' she sternly reminds Miss Sweeney, which is irrelevant information because why else would we be here? 'I took time off from running a global business to speak to someone about my failing daughter. Call Mr Fowler and tell him I'm here.'

'Right you are . . . I understand . . . I do, so . . . and I'm really sorry, but you'll need an appointment for that. He can't just—'

'Yes, he can. Call him. I don't have time to waste. Someone can teach his class for him. I want to speak to him right now.'

'Oh, now that's . . . see, without an app . . . Oh, I have to get that. So sorry. Would you excuse me a moment?'

Miss Sweeney answers the phone. My mother shouts, 'I'm right here talking to you, in case you hadn't noticed, and I was here first! You do not answer the phone when you have a parent in front of you. It's very easy. They can wait!' but it's too late – Miss Sweeney's already picked it up and is looking terrified at my mother.

My mother is vexed. 'This is why you never deal with the little people,' she says to no one in particular. 'Hello?' She stops Mrs Levitt-Yeats, head of sixth form, who is signing in with her electronic lanyard, and barks at her to get Mr Fowler. Mrs Levitt-Yeats, eyes wide, face rankled, says, 'You'll have to go through Miss Sweeney for that.'

My mother, her body jerking with rage, yells, 'No wonder my daughter is getting Cs. This place is full of imbeciles!' And she bangs the green exit button and marches out, which I'm glad of.

I smile sweetly at a startled-looking Mrs Levitt-Yeats and watch my mother from the open window to make sure she really goes.

I see Pam, the lovely grey-haired lab technician, approaching my mother's car, and hear her say, 'Er . . . Hello? Excuse me?' Pam raps on my mother's window. My mother regards her but doesn't open it. Pam knocks again. 'Hi. Yes, hello,' Pam says. 'You seem to have . . . If you look down at the lines – you see, you've parked over two disabled spaces.' Pam's cheeriness is uncheerful. 'I had to park halfway over . . . down the road . . .' She points with her walking stick. 'Over there. And walking is hard because I have a hip—'

'Sorry?' my mother says. She never pays attention to street signs, restrictions, kerbs, lines on the road, or other people's exit requirements. If she gets a ticket she flies into a rage and blames it on someone else: sometimes Dad, sometimes the idiot issuing the tickets, which Dad said used to be called a traffic warden but is now, apparently, a civil enforcement officer. Which is also a CEO. How are you supposed to know which is which?

'Well . . .' Pam makes an indignant cough-laugh that's neither a cough nor a laugh. 'That's . . . I mean, that's just incredibly inconsiderate. These bays are for—'

I am so very glad I'm not in the car right now.

My mother says gratuitously loudly, 'My daughter has serious mental-health issues and needed to see her psychiatrist urgently. Some disabilities aren't visible, you know. How dare you!'

Oh boy. Great.

'Oh, I . . .' Pam stutters. 'Goodness, I'm so sor—'

'Are you. Do you *know* how hard it is to have a mentally ill child? No. You don't. You jump to judge me because you have to walk, what? Twenty more steps? People like you – my God. Unbelievable. Now move before I run you over.'

Pam's mouth opens, she steps aside, and my mother – fuming,

livid, disgraced and enraged – reverses out. I'm grateful I'm nowhere near her.

My mother will no doubt be splenetic and apoplectic now. In other words – although why would you need other words when those two are perfect – I bet she is she is angry as buck.

The relative silence of the main corridor is a welcome reprieve after my mother's noxious non-stop nagging. There are no malicious sentences firing through the air, so it feels spacious. Hollow. Unperturbed. A refuge for sore ears. Do I go to Geography and explain publicly that the reason for my late arrival is that I've had yet another psychiatry appointment? Or do I wait a fortuitous fifteen minutes, write my initial-letter sentences in my notebook in the toilets, and join the corridor traffic and head straight to lunch?

Some choices are easy.

A wave of noise signals the end of Period 3: decibels rise, and voices, footfall, banter and bruhaha fill the corridors and stairs. I don't like the rowdy, roary gap between lessons. The fire, thirst, lust and malice of a thousand teens; their energies, moods, histories, hostilities, hormones, gripes, pressures, stresses, messes, competitivenesses, anxieties, notorieties and body odours thundering, thrashing and rattling through the walls of the building. Exiting the toilet cubicle, I skip past Loretta Fogel, who nudges Lucy Lee. They snigger because skipping isn't an accepted method of movement in their fearful little world where everyone has to be and do and walk and think and dress the same as everyone else. Becca says they're jealous of me, but my more nuanced, educated guess is they're just vindictive buck-faced brats. I'll skip if I want to. Buck you.

'Cubicle' is an ugly word. I'm not aware of an alternative. 'Pubicle' is more apt.

Pinned on a display board in the English corridor are quotations printed on cream and blue card.

> *The difference between the **almost right** word and the **right** word is really a large matter . . .*
> Mark Twain

> *I am not afraid of storms, for I am learning how to sail my ship.*
> Louisa May Alcott, *Little Women*

> *I remembered that the real world was wide, and that a varied field of hopes and fears, of sensations and excitements, awaited those who had the courage to go forth into its expanse, to seek real knowledge of life amidst its perils.*
> Charlotte Brontë, *Jane Eyre*

I wonder who put these up. Miss McLaughlin? Is she getting into the finding-sentences mission or has the entire English department decided this is a fun task and asked the English prefects to come up with some new displays? Either way. The displays make my day. If days can be made. Which is debateable.

25

Becca is queuing with our year group on the stairs down to the dining hall. She's saved me a place by sticking her arm at an odd angle between herself and Eva Grigson. Eva Grigson isn't happy about it, her face tells me, but Becca Hitchin is cool and for some reason no one messes with cool girls. I'm not sure why cool gets to rule. 'Kind' would get to rule if I was leader, but as Becca benefits from the advantages of coolness, I do, too. Becca is even cool when Eva tries to block me out and Becca snaps, 'Hey. What the hell, Eva? I'm ssscchaving thisssch sssschpot – can't you sssschee my arm?' and then reaches into her mouth cavity and slots her spitty retainer into its purple plastic box.

Eva backs off and I slide into the space where the arm once was. Someone told Eva they liked her haircut last week and Eva said, 'Yeah, I'm really here for it,' which flummoxed me all day.

'I'll get you curry and rice,' Becca says, knowing I'm a fan of both. I like that Becca knows these things about me. She knows stuff no one else does. She knows I only shampoo once, deeming the twice thing to be entirely unnecessary and merely a ploy to sell more. She knows I tested Dad's brandy when I was ten by swigging it from the bottle and nearly spat it all over his desk. And she knows the length and texture of the socks I like, which is useful at Christmas.

She knows other things, of course. She knows my censorship of the f-word is not a prudish thing. It's because we have a richly populated, bounteous, profuse, lush, opulent, Brobdingnagian language and we fall back on the f-word far too often. I'd be the first to admit it's effective. The frustrated ferocity of that 'f'; the eruptive outburst of the 'uh'; the cranky, champing 'k'. The guttural clunk of those two staccato syllables. My go-to alternative is 'bucking', but it's nowhere near as satisfying.

Becca, being my closest and favourite-ever friend, knows there is another reason I don't use the f-word. It has associations. Of the negative variety. People shouting and swearing brings on unparalleled panic because it reminds me. But she kindly doesn't mention this.

In return, I know she always shampoos twice, despite my very valid argument. I know she kissed Jason Dror when we were in Year 8, and last summer, let Micha Von Schiffer's hand explore the inside of her shirt and let him do more than that the next time, but not the whole lot. I know she feels like the 'thicky of the family' (her words), and that there is, in fact, a stupid scale because we looked it up. The Urban Dictionary has one. Theirs goes from 1: Fool to 10: Bucking Dumbass. Except it doesn't say 'bucking'. It says the f-word. Which I could just say like everyone else, but I choose not to. And I know Becca wants to be a mum more than she wants to have a career, but she would never admit that to anyone except me.

'How was it?' Becca asks, lispless. She's genuinely interested in my appointment because she's Becca, and I want to tell her about bosses, TV and mochacreme, but I just shrug.

'How's The Dictator?'

'Dictatorial.'

'Clyde said he might have another sentence for you.'

'Why "might"?'

'He doesn't think it's up to your usual . . .' she waves her hand, '. . . high standard or whatever.'

'Found one in my schoolbag this morning,' I tell Becca. 'Had to be Dad. And I'm guessing the one in my shoe was from you.'

'Are you asking, or are you just making random rhymes?' Becca asks, and without waiting for an answer adds, 'How's the father of my children?'

'Hope you're not talking about my brother. You're making me feel sick.'

We both choose mac 'n' cheese 'n' salad, although the second 'n' isn't acceptable and the first one is, which raises all kinds of questions. The salad doesn't, thankfully, contain rocket or lemongrassy dressing.

As I'm packing my bag for the afternoon lessons, Moses walks past the Year 10 lockers. His presence inspires quiet contentment, even in this neurotic, chaotic, antagonistic, caustic, hectic, anaemic, despotic, bombastic, egotistic, toxic, unhygienic school environment where 'ic'-suffixed adjectives seem to represent its icky atmosphere most accurately of all.

'Hey,' he says, smiling, and by doing so, disregarding the teenage protocol of refusing to recognize the existence of anyone in the years below. 'How's it going?'

One side of his collar is slightly turned up and his hair is wilder than usual. 'Blair,' I reply.

'That good, huh?'

I pull a face. The world's greatest writers would never have their characters respond with a retching noise, especially one with the name of a former British prime minister that Dad once met and keeps going on about. But then characters in the world's greatest novels rarely have to deal with the situations I have to face. Namely school. But others, as well.

'Can't be that bad,' he says. He's blocking the way and causing corridor traffic but people just scowl and go around him because he's Moses Calvet and Moses is also cool. The power of personality amazes me. '*Something* good must have happened today,' he adds.

Grandma Tara used to say, 'Tell me the highlight and the lowlight of your day.' I don't like to be reminded of this, though, because her dying was the lowlight of my life. A nanoscopic shake of my head fails to dispel the memory.

'Yesterday?' Moses prompts. 'At some point in the last week?'

'Actually, yes,' I admit. 'I found some excellent words in French.'

Moses smiles warmly. 'Perfect. Which ones?' Most of the kids at school call him Moses 'Calvett' but Champ said his surname is pronounced 'Calvay', which sounds to me like a sunny cobblestone yard shaded by a cool canopy of leaves.

I pronounce the words in my best French accent. '*Coquillage. Chuchoter. Saperlipopette. Étoile.*'

He grins and rests his gaze on the floor, nodding and thinking. Then his eyes rise to mine and glimmer. The corridors are emptying. We're late for Period 7, but it doesn't seem to concern him.

'All to do with sound – to me, at least,' he says, leaning on the wall, in no apparent rush to leave. I like the way the ends of his shirt sleeves hover above his wrists but I couldn't explain why. '*Coquillage*. You know, when you put it against your ear, you get the sound of the sea.' As he mimes a shell, his fingertips touch the curls behind his ear. I have to look away for a second but then look back when he says, '*Chuchoter*. When you . . .' he leans forward, towards me, and lowers his voice to a whisper, 'don't want anyone to hear what you have to say.' He stands back, his eyes on mine. '*Saperlipopette*.' His voice rises to a regular volume. 'An expression you say when you're surprised – definitely the loudest on the list. Old-fashioned, that one – no one really says it any more. My grandma does, so I especially approve of that one.' He sits a thumb under his chin and rests an index finger across his upper lip, affecting a thoughtful pose. 'And . . . *étoile*.'

He's stuck, surely. His theory blown to smithereens. How can stars have anything to do with sound? I'm transfixed. The world recedes into a dim and distant mist. The only things that exist in the universe are Moses, me and the stars. The moment extends and expands infinitely, like travelling through space. He moves his fingers from his face, and says slowly, softly, magically, his two hands spreading outwards, 'The sound of . . . silence.'

There is no longer any desire in me to leave for my lesson, if in fact there ever was.

> *My heart is like a singing bird.*
>   *My heart is like a rainbow shell.*
>   *My heart is gladder than all these.*

Moses laughs. The lateness is pulling us towards our respective classrooms like we're being drawn by invisible strings. 'Gonna get detention,' he says. 'Come on.'

26

Period 7 is Chemistry, which is fine because the symbol abbreviations on the periodic table are curious, and our teacher, Mr Trussell, is from Manchester but supports Spurs, which bothers, more than you think it would, those who like football. He doesn't give me detention because when he asks why I'm late, I tell him the birthday of my life came to me in the corridor, and he laughs and says, 'Best excuse I've heard all week.'

To ward off the complaints of my classmates, he adds, 'Er . . . that's enough, thank you. I read that poem to my wife at our wedding. When you unexpectedly remind me of the joy of my wedding day, Campbell, you too can avoid detention for being late.'

As they learn about fractional distillation, I study the periodic table and decide I like the names 'Rubidium,' 'Beryllium' and 'Yttrium' best. 'Lawrencium', 'Einsteinium' and 'Californium' sound made up and therefore somewhat comical. There should be 'JodieJonesium', of course, but there are spaces for that.

Then we head to the hall for the talk. The way most of my

year group feels about the author talk is this: indifferent, blasé, nonchalant, apathetic, irked. I looked up the etymology of 'irked' once because it's unusual. The great oracle of the web said it might be from the Old Norse word, *yrkja*, meaning to work, and according to Dad, when you know that, you understand the link. This speaks volumes about his job and why being an author would be a better choice. For me, anyway.

I don't feel irked about the author talk. I feel eager, euphoric, exuberant, exhilarated, expectant, edgy. And those are just the 'e's.

Ambrosia Benedictine is wearing black trousers and a black top with a black furry gilet that she takes off when she realizes our school is overheated. I wonder if her colour comes out in her writing instead. I'm not familiar with her books, but columns of them are neatly piled on a table to her right, with some displayed forwards so we can see the covers. She seems to have written five.

She talks about her path into publishing, the inspiration for her books, which she holds up and talks about in turn, and the 'thrust' of the narrative. I get a little stuck on the word 'thrust' because it doesn't have the kinds of connotations I want to be thinking of at this moment or indeed any moment. It's also an ugly word that stays in the front of your mouth too long and makes your lips and teeth work in a way that is irksome.

I listen patiently for the part where she explains her collection of favourite words and sentences, hoping she'll share one exceptional one at least, but she doesn't mention it, which is displeasing. As her 'thrusts' are about spying, sleuthing, murder, unknown parents, righting wrongs and avenging honour, the rest of my year are somewhat more engaged than they were when they sat down, whereas I'm somewhat less.

At the end of the talk, she signs books. The queue is for those who have been seduced by her thrusts, which is not a pleasing thought. I wait in line and when I get to the front, I say to her, 'I don't want a book, thank you.'

Mr Gregorius, another of our librarians, looks embarrassed, which is strange because he has no reason to be – it's not his thrusts that are unappealing. 'Could you . . . can you stand aside, then, please,' he says, 'so we can get some of the others signed?'

'I'd like to ask Ambrosia Benedictine a question.'

'Might have to wait till the end. Only about ten more to go.'

I stand aside and wait. Becca's forgotten her calculator, so she says she'll meet me in the locker room.

'All good, Jodie?' Mr Gregorius asks quietly. After a split-second pause, he adds, 'Jones'. He has soft blue eyes, a large diamond earring in his left ear and wears what Becca calls 'retro' clothes. I call them tight orange trousers, shirts that look prickly, and brown and gold diamond-pattern sleeveless jumpers. He wears a rainbow badge to show anyone who is gay or questioning their sexuality or gender that he is a person they can talk to, even though you should be able to talk to anyone about that, badge or no badge. No one wears a badge of varying brown stripes to indicate you can talk to them about race, or a badge of books to show they're approachable for reading recommendations, but perhaps these are things I'd change if I were ever in charge of anything.

Ambrosia Benedictine carefully makes eye contact with the book-buyers in the line. Some buy her newest novel, which is about teenage podlings who solve the mystery of their cousin's death at the Notting Hill Carnival, but most buy the one set in a Walthamstow housing estate about a girl who discovers she was kidnapped from her front garden as a toddler, sparking a nationwide search. The author doesn't look like she's ever been to a Walthamstow housing estate – or the Notting Hill Carnival for that matter. Maybe she researched them online.

Sharpie in hand, she asks her future readers their names, then frowns awkwardly when they say, in turn, Caoimhe, Akachukwu and Khemkhaeng. She laughs nervously and asks them to spell that please. I happen to know that Khemkhaeng goes by her nickname, Nok, and that Nok is messing with Ambrosia by asking her to also dedicate the book to her siblings – Pongprom and Ngam-chit.

By the time Ambrosia Benedictine has signed books for Alchemy, Lettuce and Moon Unit, who we just call 'Mu' but Mu doesn't mention that, you can tell Ambrosia Benedictine had enough of this book signing and possibly school visits in general.

It's not great timing for her or for me by the time she's finished. She seems agitated, skittish and disconcerted, and I'm late for registration. 'Disconcerted' is not really the opposite of 'concerted', and I'm curious about the change in pronunciation: 'concerted' sounds like you've been to a concert and had your fill, but that's not what I ask her about because time is short.

'Could I see one of your journals of favourite sentences?' I ask. 'I mean, whichever one you have with you – you probably haven't brought them all. Just for a quick flick through.' I wonder whether F. Scott Fitzgerald would have used the phrase 'quick flick through' and decide he probably would if he'd been in this situation, meaning likely to get another detention for being late.

Ambrosia Benedictine replies, 'My?'

That flummoxes me. 'My' isn't a question but somehow it

works in this context, and that's not something I'd previously considered.

'Jodie Jones, you need to get going,' Mr Gregorius says, packing unsold books into a box, his eyes flicking to the clock and his movements a tad agitated for what the circumstances require.

I look back at Ambrosia Benedictine and wonder, for a moment, whether she also likes to be called her full name. 'Ambrosia Benedictine,' I say, just in case, 'you do write down the most appealing sentences you find, don't you?'

'No, but what a wonderful idea,' she replies. 'Where's the nearest loo?' I'm not sure whether she's offering one of her favourites or whether our conversation is now over. I assume it must be the latter, so I go to registration.

The author visit was not as satisfying as I had hoped.

When I get home, my mother barely looks at me. She barks, 'Take the washing out of the machine and hang it up, and not by the shoulders this time. Makes them dry funny. Then go up and study.'

Damp clothes are cold and gross, and I find it peculiar to hang up pants. Mine (not by choice) are floral and microfibre from a multi-pack; Dad's are mainly grey and have a strangely complicated frontal region; Champ's have wide elasticated waistbands advertising brand names and I'm always tempted to un-elasticate them, and my mother's are silky, lacy triangles. This is a level of familial intimacy I would rather not be privy to. I have no desire to picture them in their smalls when I'm talking to them but it's also a smidgeon amusing, especially when they're telling me off.

Dad always says there's nothing a cup of tea can't fix so when the pants are dangling and the jumpers suspended with acceptable, shoulder positioning, I take him a cup. He likes them with digestives or Hobnobs or, even better, buttered muffins or crumpets, but ours is a biscuitless, muffinless, crumpetless household. He's sniffing and sneezing under a blanket, the skin under his nose red and flaking, his voice growly. He asks me how the author visit was, and I tell him the truth. 'Not worth getting another detention for.'

Especially not when my mother reacts the way she does.

27

At school the next day, I go to ask the librarian, arrayed today in a cardigan of cornflower blue, a skirt that is short and flippy and black, and shoes in a style called 'Mary Janes', if the new titles I've requested have arrived. Her reply is, 'There isn't space in the library for all the books you request.'

I wish people wouldn't answer the questions they weren't asked, and instead answered the ones they were. I didn't ask if there was space in the library. I asked if the books I requested had arrived. I wait, wondering if she'll answer the question I have asked, but she doesn't. So I say, 'Is that a no?'

She flares her nostrils. 'Two'll arrive on Wednesday.'

I think about 'two'll' for far too long.

Eventually I move away from the desk. She's been stamping books for a few minutes now. She's an adequate if lacklustre librarian – she issues books efficiently enough and keeps the library shipshape, tidy and quiet – but my thinking is that stamping, cataloguing, replacing titles to their relevant locations, ordering, displaying, culling and shushing aren't the only jobs librarians should master. A further and crucial job requirement should be knowledge of where the best sentences can be found in every book in their care, but Ms Tiffany Frisk doesn't do that.

I'm aware her name shouldn't bother me, and yet, somehow, it does.

Later that day, the topic in PSHE is body image. Moses and I answer an inane quiz on how we feel about our bodies.

I respect my body . . .

- ○ Never
- ○ Seldom
- ○ Sometimes
- ○ Often
- ○ Always

Then Miss Slavin shows the slides.

'Question one. Have you ever wished your body looked different? If so, which parts.' Moses steals a look at me sideways. Gingerly. Peeping.

'Absolutely. Not my elbows, which are magnificent, as mentioned. But my ankles are an abomination. My ears. My nostrils. My butt. I wish mine was just like Kim's.'

He pulls on his fringe hair and says, shyly, quietly, mainly to the table, 'Don't need to change a thing. Perfect, just as you are.'

No one can hear us because they're all talking, too, but I still feel exposed. My surprised eyes rise to his and hot blood floods my flushing face. 'Me? Really not.'

'Really,' he says. 'Coolest girl in school. Maybe the UK. Don't know about the rest of the world.'

'Um. Wow. Thanks. But I need reasons.'

'Ohhh,' he says, 'You need reasons, do you?' He rubs his chin pensively and juts out his lips. After an aeon, meaning five seconds or so, he says 'You're super smart. You're a hundred per cent original. And you don't put up with any crap.'

I take this in for a further aeon and mutter, 'I'm also messed up.'

He semi-shrugs. 'Who isn't?'

I make a 'fair enough' face and our eyes briefly meet. 'You came up with those reasons too quickly,' I tell him. 'You've been thinking about this, haven't you?'

'Only for a few weeks.' He faces the front again, which is good because I surely resemble a cranberry by this point. Awkwardness arrives to sit between us like a creature with boundary issues. I am conscious of the passing seconds. They are, each lone one, astoundingly, preternaturally, uncharacteristically long. We retreat to our inner worlds, him with his fists sitting vertically on the tabletop and me wondering what I'm supposed to learn from this PSHE lesson that I don't know already. Except the bemusing news that Moses Calvet thinks I'm perfect.

Does that mean he likes me? Or does it just mean he thinks I'm perfect? Is there a difference? How can anyone tell? I think Moses is the bee's knees, as Grandma Tara used to say, but I'd never be brave enough to tell him that. I'm filled with admiration that he has the pluck, guts and bottle to speak his mind.

'Mosesssss! Jodieeee! Your answers to question one, please. Is there a body part you'd like to be different?'

Even if we did, does she really, honestly, think we'd tell each other, never mind everyone else?

Miss Slavin hasn't said my full name and I refuse to repeat the line about Kim's butt in front of the class because someone might think I mean it. I glance at Moses warily, and quickly he says, 'I said I want a tiny ski-jump nose,' making the class laugh. Miss Slavin reminds us to please take this lesson seriously and be mature. 'And Jodie?' she asks. 'What was your answer?'

'Her name is Jodie Jones,' Moses says. 'Why is that so hard to remember?'

When I walk out this time, it's not because I'm angry. It's because I can't stop smiling.

Later, I am withdrawn from my scheduled PE lesson to attend a meeting with my parents, Mr Fowler (my Head of Year), Madame Arnaud (my form tutor), Miss Slavin (the school SENCO) and Miss McLaughlin (my English teacher). My mother is agitated, but despite her head toss and brisk footsteps, she walks in nonchalantly. 'At last,' she says. 'My father always said it's rude to keep people waiting.'

They mutter apologies and she shrugs amiably, as if she is trying to forgive them but it's quite hard. She's wearing a cream jumper with pale pink trousers, her Big Name handbag on a chair beside her as if it's another member of the parent body. Her hair is sleek and blow-dried, her nails painted deep blood-red. My teachers seem wary of her, and I have no doubt that this is intentional on my mother's part. 'It seems my daughter's still playing games with you,' she says, 'but I'll tell you exactly how to deal with her.'

'Er ... actually, Mrs Jones,' says Mr Fowler, 'we're meeting today because we're past that stage, I'm afraid.' He looks tired today. Like he's been in the tumble dryer. He pulls his shirt sleeves back an inch for no reason. His watch looks expensive but it's the kind that wants you to think that.

'What are you talking about?' my mother asks.

'We'll come to that in due course.'

My ears hear only the sounds of those words. Duke horse. D'you coarse.

Dad, seated beside my mother, seems contained. Detached. A little bedraggled, even though he's wearing a grey suit and white shirt with a hedgehog tie I bought him last Christmas. The tie is dark green and the hedgehogs are pale green and facing in different directions as if it's a hedgehog free-for-all on hedgehog highway. Dad has worn the tie for me. To support me. Who'd have thought ties could be empathetic? But then, politicians wear them to show their leanings, and Chemistry-teaching football fans wear them to annoy those who think they should support their local team, so there's more to ties than meets the eye. And that's a phrase I like.

Their sentiments drift in and out of my ears. 'Not applying herself ... fourteen per cent in her recent Geography test ... unsustainable level of pastoral care ... setting a bad example ... fail her GCSEs ... need to manage your expectations ...'

If there is a school of tact and diplomacy, I don't think my mother passed the entrance test. 'Mediocre,' she says, turning to me. 'You wilfully choose to be unexceptional. I can't understand you.'

'Monica,' Dad says firmly. 'Stop talking to her like that.'

My mother's eyes widen and flare. 'Oh, criticizing me, are you? In front of these people. Instead of supporting me, fighting on my side, backing me up, being there for me. Thank you,

Elliot. How about criticizing your child who refuses to make the best of the few pluses she's got?'

There is a collective pause while eyes meet eyes across the table.

'Mrs Jones, I know this is a difficult conversation,' Miss Slavin says, warily, 'but if we could all just remain courteous.' She's clearly shocked. I don't know why: they've seen how my mother behaves at parents' evenings, although perhaps it comes across as academic concern.

Mr Fowler outlines all the extra work I create for them, but I've stopped paying attention. He doesn't mince his words. Whatever that means. Why would words need mincing? And how, logically, could one do that?

Dad looks at me with worry in his eyes. My mother's expression does not indicate worry.

I don't see how I'm doing anything wrong. I think of lines of a poem Grandma had in frame on her wall called 'Wild Geese' by Mary Oliver.

You do not have to be good.
You do not have to walk on your knees
for a hundred miles through the desert, repenting.
You only have to let the soft animal of your body
love what it loves.

'Jodie Jones?'

Madame Arnaud has said something, but I missed it. 'Sorry?'

'I said, "what do you think?"' She's French so she says 'sink'.

'About what?'

Another pause. Different eyes meeting eyes. Same people. Same table.

I want to say, 'It doesn't really matter, though, does it? What does any of it matter, when my favourite person died all on her own and my dad is leaving home and humans have the capacity and desire to do terrible things to each other and because of that my mind is a monstrous and menacing place a lot of the time and all I have to comfort me are the sounds of words and sentences.' But they're teachers – to them, education is all that matters. All that will ever matter.

'We've tried to keep you on track,' Miss Slavin explains, 'but right now, the interventions don't seem to be working.'

'Jodie,' Dad says. He doesn't say 'Jones', and this time, it grates me. It undermines me, and this is objectionable, so I ignore him and gaze at the ceiling. There's been a leak and one of the panels has a brown water mark in the shape of India. 'Just to be clear, they're considering your . . . er . . . removal,' he says, 'to a special unit.'

'It's a school,' Miss Slavin is quick to point out. 'For . . . for those unable to learn in a mainstream setting. If you apply the week before we break up for Easter, you could secure a place for September.'

'No,' I say.

'Listen, Jodie,' Mr Fowler, says, omitting the 'Jones' because Dad has now sanctioned it. 'Your attendance here relies on your cooperation. We do our part. Your part is to do the work, put in the effort, and get involved in the school community. Those things haven't been happening.'

In Xanadu did Kubla Khan
A stately pleasure-dome decree:

'You've been on report three times and you've got at least two detentions a day for the last two weeks – there are hardly enough days left this term to complete all your detentions.'

Where Alph, the sacred river, ran
Through caverns measureless to man
Down to a sunless sea.

Mr Fowler doesn't move his jaw or open his mouth much when he speaks, so his words go through a sort of wide, flat funnel. I think he's also chewing gum, which is against the school rules. Interesting that he is telling me off about the school rules whilst chewing gum. Maybe it's his micro-choice and he's micro-choosing it.

'You're doing zero work, you're falling behind, you're causing disruption in lessons, and you're making us loads of extra work in pastoral notes, meetings, emails . . . And you don't care, which is the worst part of it all. It can't go on.'

And all should cry, Beware! Beware!
His flashing eyes, his floating hair!

'No,' I say.
Eyes meet eyes and they ask me to wait outside.

While I'm sitting on one of three yellow chairs, students pass, the clock ticks, and Moses walks by. He has a book open, but he sees me and looks from me to the Head's study door.

'Are you . . . ?' He points to the door with the book.
I nod.

'What, parents, Slavin, Fowler?'

'Arnaud, McLaughlin . . .'

'Psshh. Whole war cabinet. Need anything?'

I twist my lips. 'Cabinet like cupboard or cabinet like government?'

'Both work.'

I grin. 'Seen Champ?'

'Not since reg. Would you rather . . . have crisps or not have crisps? I've only got half a pack and they're cheesy Wotsits. Not everyone's first choice.'

I'm hungry. I'm hungry a lot. I need more doughnuts and carrot cake than I'm currently being supplied with, and I'd eat the Wotsits happily any other time but right now. I decline with a head shake and a half-smile lip twist.

I didn't have him down for a cheesy Wotsits fan. As he's friends with Champ, I know stuff he hates: racism, internet trolls, clothing with labels and sport on TV. I know he loves walking up steep hills, playing ultimate Frisbee, talking about time and space and life, and drinking mint tea. Thanks to PSHE lessons, I discovered his middle name is Rufus, his mother is English and his father is French, and the people he loves best are his Senegalese grandma and French grandpa who live in southwest France. He thinks paying £4.80 for a sugary coffee-flavoured drink is 'criminal'; he reads *One Snowy Night* to his three-year-old sister every evening, even in summer, because it's her favourite book, and his earliest memory is crying as he watched a red helium balloon rise to the sky with his dummy tied on the end.

It's these details that tickle me. As yet, I have not learned how he prevents his curls from tangling, the toothpaste he'd go for if he were buying, although teens don't, usually, as a rule, or which kinds of sentences he likes. But I enjoy knowing what I do know. I think the book he'd give as a birthday gift would be a non-fiction book on the degeneration of mankind into the messed-up ignorant lamebrains we are today but maybe it would be something witty, playful and French, like *Asterix the Gaul*.

He is two seats away, sending my stomach on a sudden lurching lift drop. He's in hues of blues today and he's hard to look at because I might cry. I glance at the colourful cover of the book he's reading, and he holds it up to facilitate my prying eyes. It's called *The Namesake* by Jhumpa Lahiri.

'English,' he says, keeping his finger in the page as he waves it to secure his spot. He's in sixth form so this might be a text I'll study for A level. If I pass any GCSEs, that is.

'There's a train wreck in Chapter One so you probably won't . . .'

He knows the situation. If there's an accident, gunshots or a violent event in the reading choices, they choose something else so that I can study it, too. If there's violence in all of them, I'm not sure what they'd do.

'What's . . . it about?' he asks, meaning the meeting.

'If I can stay or need to go to a special school.'

'Daym.' He leans forward so his elbows are on his knees and the book is swinging downwards. 'That what you want?'

I shake my head. I need this place. I need to be near Becca and her humming, her retainer entertainment at break time, her arm keeping me a spot in the lunch queue for a dining room that I don't ever sit in because the noise bothers me, but I still queue with her and choose what to eat and Becca brings it out and eats with me in a classroom, which we're only allowed to do as long as we don't make a mess and clean the tables afterwards, and I need the library, lacking as it is. I need the humdrum sights of the stacked chairs in the corner of the hall and the broken, locker doors near the gym and the posters by the science labs of the most accomplished female scientists that have ever lived and the lopsided printouts, Blu-Tacked on the doors and walls, advertising bake sales, non-uniform days and lunch clubs. I need the cruel and cheerful jokes of the girls and the boys who like and hate each other and the overall familiarity of it all and the possibility that Moses might walk by as I sit outside a meeting to determine my educational future and offer me half a packet of cheesy Wotsits.

'So, let's tell them that,' Moses says, and I realize I must have said some if not all of those words aloud.

Tears sting my eyes. I blink them back, but they've given me away. My hands shake as I wipe the tears off my cheeks and I want to say, 'I can't,' but I won't permit words to come out of my mouth because I don't trust myself.

The door to the office opens. Mr Fowler glances from me to Moses to me again, then asks me to come back in. Mr Fowler's trousers are too short and he's wearing his pale blue socks with pink flamingos, some of which are standing in a way I'm not sure some flamingos can stand. I don't know what that says about him, but it says something.

'Hold up,' Moses says, stuffing the cheesy Wotsits back in his bag.

And he follows me into the office.

28

As the situation at school is spiralling out of control, Dr Kumar has recommended I spend more time doing what I enjoy and being with friends, so my mother has permitted me to go out for a certain time on certain days to certain places, and has given me my phone back with restricted access. The time slot given for my freedom is one hour on Tuesdays and Thursdays, and two hours per day on Saturdays and Sundays; the permitted places are the local library and Becca's; the restricted access, half an hour before and after the aforementioned freedom slots to allow for planning, transport apps, my safe arrival and any necessary post-visit messaging.

At Becca's, all I can do is lie on her bed and think of Moses. The calm and articulate way he spoke to my teachers and parents. His poise and certainty. His rational frankness. His curly hair.

'Rational Frank' would be a good name for a band.

I feel a career in band-naming might suit me well.

Becca is curled in a beanbag, her limbs too long for it, talking, singing, retainerless, 'You Belong With Me' by Taylor Swift and playing with Lyra's ears. I hear snippets of her ramblings but I'm not really listening. 'You know, in Crystal Palace... Seriously, Burger King and

Claire's Accessories, man. What was that all about? What was the guy in Juno called? Anyway . . . I wasn't scared. I swear, I wasn't scared . . . Just don't get why my mum's so invested in the plunger.'

At my seventh request, she's stopped showing me braiding tutorials on YouTube, influencers doing uninfluential activities, and more memes than I care to see. Her movements are far more interesting to me, and so is the space she takes up in the world. How does she find sleeves to fit to the wrist?

The Hitchins' dog is a lustrous grey lurcher called Lyra, and I like her. We are not allowed a dog because of a) dog hair, b) cost, c) its dependence on affection, d) its need for human participation on muddy walks, e) my mother is not an animal lover, even though we are, and, predominantly, f) it would receive lots of attention and she will not be superseded in that regard by a pet. It goes without saying that we aren't in unilateral agreement with a life that's hair-free, lacking in affection and devoid of muddy walks, and that even though three out of four family members saying 'aye' is a majority, my mother's 'nay' vote wins.

Lyra knows nothing of this. It's better that way.

Rain hits the house sideways. The love gift sits on Becca's shelf.

Bee-atrice was indeed in the bin, but I washed it in the bathroom sink with some blue Herbal Essences shampoo and left it on the radiator in my room to dry. I didn't tell Becca that, even when she sniffed it and said it smelled nice.

'I'm keeping her,' Becca says, slotting her retainer in, 'asscha a love token that will one day win your brotherschh heart.'

'He doesn't have a heart.'

'You're not putting me off.'

This afternoon, we're supposed to be studying Maths and Biology. I have an ultimatum, which is not a pleasant word.

It reminds me of neutralizing tablets for digestive complaints. Excessive burping? Take an ultimatum!

I also don't like the totalitarian command behind an ultimatum. Do this or else. The 'do this' being the schoolwork they have decreed necessary because I need to 'significantly improve' in my effort and achievement. The 'or else' part is that I won't be eligible to continue as a pupil at my school.

Although I can't face leaving, I don't care enough to work. Right now, I'm clinging to the edge of a precipice by my fingertips. I did not mention this predicament when the ultimatum was ultimated. I also refrained from mentioning that 'ultimatum' sounded like a burping remedy, which I'm pleased about because the timing was all wrong.

'Sch'posche it'sch time,' Becca says, rolling sideways on the beanbag and sucking on her sour jelly sweet too loudly for my liking. 'Schellsch or fractionsch?'

'Neither.'

'Gonna be one, sscho choossche.'

As if choosing between two things you don't want to do constitutes a choice. 'Cells, then,' I say. But only because I know what she's going to say next.

'Schellsch it isch.' She folds herself into a limb-like cat's cradle and rises from the beanbag. She does an excellent impression of one of those tubes they fill with air that waves and vacillates in a comically desperate way. Whenever I see them and have my phone on me, I send her videos of them so she can connect with her floppy friends.

We study cells. I know this unit already, but I go along with it because she always forgets what we've learned and has to work hard and repeatedly to meld it to her memory. I learn something once and it's there forevermore. I just don't feel like proving it to anyone. Especially not my mother.

When I walk through the kitchen to leave, Clyde and Francine – who this evening is somewhere to be seen, namely, in the kitchen peeling carrots – are listening to something funky. The air is replete with the smell of frying onions. I really do think their musical accompaniments are dish-related. Pausing nearby, I glance at the double page open on their recipe stand. Vegetarian moussaka with miso. It doesn't seem like a dish that requires funky but what do I know?

'What *is* this?' I ask. My musical education is still in Year 1. If that.

'"Low Rider",' Francine replies. 'Oldie but a goodie. We can share our playlist if you want.'

I nod enthusiastically. 'I'd love that.'

In my restricted-access slot, I figure I could just about play a couple of songs a day as I walk to Becca's or the library. But how will I ever learn the secrets of rhythm and cooking?

'How's things?' Clyde asks as he fries. He's wearing a pale green shirt printed with huge yellow leaves with gaps that remind me of missing teeth. I don't know how to answer his question and think a while. Then, he asks, 'How's your dad doing?'

'He's . . .' My eyes drop to the open page. 'I don't know.'

I do know. He's constantly on Rightmove and closes the tab when I catch him. He's looking smarter and going into the office lately, but I don't know why. He's not drinking any alcohol, which might mean he doesn't want to drink any alcohol at the moment. or might mean he has an alcohol problem, or maybe even that he's on medication for something that prohibits him from drinking, but I don't know how to tell the difference. He's arguing with my mother, standing up to her in a way he never did, and it's causing domestic warfare. He used to boost her morale, protect her from getting upset, answer every time she called and listen endlessly to her issues and dramas, even if he was in the middle of something else. He would never tell her he was reading files, writing reports, emailing or whatever, because she'd cry and become furious, and her fury is to be avoided. Always.

Once he was telling me about Baudelaire, Wagner and Manet; we were having one of those mind-on-fire conversations about darkness, art, writing, music, painting, creativity – the kind of conversation that doesn't happen very often. Her name flashed up on his phone. 'Don't answer it,' I said. 'Please, Dad.'

'Can't,' he said, wincing and picking his phone off the coffee table. 'Not worth the aggro.'

'Becca mentioned things might . . . not be so good at home,' Francine says, her blue eyes looking directly at me and then back at the aubergine she's now slicing, which is just as well because I'm concerned about her fingers. I think of Dad in the study, sleeping on a hard, buttony sofa, his blue suitcase by the door in preparation for the day he picks it up and steps out of our house into a new life and a new home, breaking me in fragments from which I will never fully reform.

'None of our business, of course,' Francine says with a kindly expression, 'but if you ever need it, we could put you up for a while. Your dad and Champ, as well. If it's longer term, my sister has an Airbnb in Acton. Just,' she wafts an aubergine-y hand in the air, 'putting it out there.'

I'm intrigued as to why Francine has left my mother out of this equation and how she seems know my mother is the issue.

People say you never know what happens behind closed doors, but either those doors are more transparent than you think, or they've been left a crack ajar.

'OK,' I say, fixing my gaze on an Ottolenghi book on the shelf called *Jerusalem*. I consider adding that my dad is leaving us so he might not be part of the equation, either, but I can't bear to voice it. Instead, I say to Becca, 'Air bee-n-bee sounds like two crocheted bees hanging by strings from a tree branch.'

'Bear it in mind,' Francine says, and swipes the ends and the carrot peelings into the small green compost bin. 'I'll text Elliot and let him know, too.'

'Text Elliot' sounds like 'Tex Stelliot'. Meanwhile, onions sizzle and hiss. The carrots await their carroty fate and the aubergines' oozing seems overly woozy. Clyde conducts the music of the pan with his wooden spatula. Funk does seem to go with this dish but who am I to make such judgements? The extractor fan is a suspended vacuum cleaner, sucking the thoughts from any brains near the hob, and the funk and sizzle sound infinitely better when he switches the fan off.

Becca looks uncomfortable and winces when I glance at her.

'Sschorry,' she mouths.

Later, when I leave, she says, 'I wassch worried about you, ssscho I told them about your dad sschleeping in the sschtudy. Didn't think they'd . . .'

I nod. ''S'fine.'

'I didn't tell them that so Champ could sschtay here, you know.'

'Liar.'

She grins but she looks sad. 'Jodie Jonessch,' she whines, her hand on the latch of the closed door. Her eyes are bright and wet and intense. 'I hate that you had to go through that. If I had three wisschesch, my firsscht would be go back in time and make sschure you were nowhere near it when it happened. But there's sschhomething elsche bothering you. I know you. Tell me what it issch. Pleassche.' She locks eyes with me. 'Issch it becaussche your dad might be . . .'

'Bye, Becca.'

She lets go of the latch but stays in front of the door, blocking my way. 'My schecond wisschh would be for you to have a different mother,' she says as I reach for the door handle.

I pause. 'You'd use two of your wishes on me?'

'I'd ussche all three. I'd do anything for you. I really would. Excsschept make you a bee becaussche you don't want one.'

'Anything? Like not have a crush on my brother?'

She tugs at the coats on the hooks by the door. She's battling the urge to cry, her welling eyes giving her away. 'Didn't mean for that to happen. It'ssch hard to be young and in love.'

I snort. 'I don't know what romantic love is, but it isn't that.'

'Fine. I herewith sschhall never sschpeak of him again. He'ssch nothing to me. Lessch than nothing.'

'Good to know. Can I go now?'

'No. Did I ussche "herewith" correctly?'

'No one says "herewith". People write it, but only lawyers. "Henceforth" is probably better but who knows what the difference is. Move, will you?'

She opens the door. 'Bye. Go.'

'Let bye gos be bye gos,' I reply as I step out. 'What would your third wish be if it wasn't to do with me?'

'To have Champ'ssch babiessch,' she says, and bursts out laughing.

I close the door with a click.

29

On Sunday, once my mother has left to do whatever she does on Sundays, Dad says, 'Monopoly?' and lets me win suspiciously quickly. This is peradventure because he and Champ want to watch the rugby.

While huge men battle it out in the mud for a little oval ball, I lie on my stomach and arrange the Monopoly money in colour order in a fan on the floor. Then we go for a roast in a local pub, and leave so stuffed that the three of us waddle home, groaning. It's the best day we've had in a long time. I wish it could always be like this – the three of us joking, laughing, eating, Champ relinquishing his knobishness and remembering I'm his sister and that he likes me sometimes; Dad gazing at us both with so much love and pride it hurts as we crunch through crispy roast potatoes, pick up Yorkshire puddings and eat them like they're toffee apples, and wipe gravy from our chins with our hands.

Our happiest times as a family are when my mother isn't there.

Don't leave don't leave, don't leave, don't leave I command Dad using my most advanced mind-control to date. It could be like this. We would make it so. Don't go. Please.

I'm not sure how successful my mind-control is, or has ever been.

All shall be revealed soon.

At our next appointment, Dr Kumar seems preoccupied and pensive. He is seeing us together first, and then individually.

My mother has ordered me not to slouch, not to ask for snacks like a beggar, and not to act like I've been lobotomized, so the first thing I do when we walk in is assume a gorilla pose and ask Poppy in a babyish voice if she has any 'bishkwits'. My mother tuts and says, 'Three out of three. Don't give her any.' I wink wickedly at Poppy, who now doesn't know whether to pull her hand out of the drawer with the biscuit pack, or let go and close it.

Dr Kumar arrives, saving Poppy from her Hobnob discombobulation. Would manufacturers sell less, more, or roughly the same number if they called them 'DisHobNobulations'? I'd certainly buy them.

Dr Kumar says to me, 'I'd like to start by getting to the bottom of your recent . . . er . . . change from your perspective.' He says it as 'recen terrr change'. 'I know you've stopped studying at school, you won't answer unless you're called by your full name and your focus is solely on one area. Aside from the sounds of words and sentences, what else are you enjoying at the moment?'

I stare at the shelf of lever-arch files, all white, to my right. Outside the window, a wind-whipped tree convulses under a low grey sky. The lone picture on the wall is an abstract – blue and green stripes on a white background. I don't understand abstracts. I wonder if anyone does. Are they fragments of thoughts on canvas? Noncommittal moods? Are they trying not to say something while sort of saying something? Why not just say something?

My legs kick up again. I'm not sure whether I'm doing it deliberately or whether they're doing it of their own accord, but off they go. The yellow armchair reminds me of something. 'What's your favourite Wes Anderson film?' I ask Dr Kumar.

'Er . . . ?' Dr Kumar says. I've distracted him from whatever is going on in his brain. 'Sorry?'

'Wes,' I repeat. 'Anderson.'

Dr Kumar eyes me enquiringly. 'I'm not sure I—'

'*Fantastic Mr Fox*, *Isle of Dogs*, *The Royal Tenenbaums*. *Asteroid City*, *Life Aqu*—'

'Yes. Of course. I know the . . . I think I know who you mean. I don't think I've seen them all, though. Why do you . . .' His eyes search mine, his pen whirling between his fingers in a skilful way I envy and wish to master. 'What makes you ask that?'

'The yellow chair.'

'The yellow . . .' He looks at it. 'Sorry?'

You don't always need to clarify why a chair has made you ask something, but this time I feel I do. 'There's something yellow in practically every frame he shoots. Often an item of furniture.'

'Ah.'

'Mine's probably *Grand Budapest Hotel* but *The Darjeeling Limited* and *Isle of Dogs* are—'

'Jodie!' My mother's voice is a snapped elastic band. 'This is not the time.'

'Mrs Jones, if you wouldn't mind.' It isn't her turn to speak, which is a challenge for her because she's a serial interrupter. She has to 'put in her penny's-worth' as Grandma Tara used to say. Grandma Tara also said 'a penny for your thoughts' and 'spend a penny' rather than 'go for a pee'. Did everything cost a penny when she was young? It seems odd that giving your opinion, sharing your concerns, and urinating cost the same amount when none of those should cost anything.

Dr Kumar turns to me. There is a riffling, pinprick pause. I enjoy it very much. My mother clears her throat belligerently. Neither of us pays her any heed.

'Why is it you... Why do you like those ones best?' Dr Kumar asks, his psychiatric spade doing a little surface digging.

I shrug, but I know exactly why. The breathtaking beauty of them is why. The wily witticism is why. The playfulness. The colours. The frames. The otherworldliness. Instead of outlining this, I reply, 'When Dad and I watch those ones in particular, we pause each frame and talk about it for ages. We don't get very far with the film but it's fun.'

'Ah. So ... nothing to do with the storyline being ... meaningful?'

Dr Kumar thinks I'm trying to send him subliminal messages in film codes. I wonder if I should have. I hate to disappoint him. 'No,' I respond, reminding myself to do this next time.

Dr Kumar carries on. 'I know you've seen a fair few trauma counsellors over the years, but things have altered in recent weeks, haven't they?'

I don't like the word 'trauma'. I find it traumatic. My mother's eyes spear me and the snakes on her head hiss, but I hold my mirrored shield up so she can't hurt me. Turn yourself to stone, She-Fiend. Don't hiss your hissy head at me.

'How's your sleep?' Dr Kumar asks.

'Erratic, episodic, periodic and sporadic,' I reply. I've already prepared this answer and used it once before. I like all those staccato 'ic' sounds. They're onomatopoeic, if you think about it, which is another word with a satisfying 'ic' ending.

Dr Kumar asks, 'By 'sporadic' do you mean you sleep well some nights and not others, or that you have restless sleep every night?'

I nod and say an emphatic 'Yes'.

He waits and I know I need to say something else in the pulsing pause. I don't sleep well, and I don't like to talk about it, so I say, 'I sleep like a baby.'

'Babies wake up all the time.'

I wink and click-point my finger at him. Bingo.

My mother's torso rears.

Dr Kumar asks, 'Are you experiencing any more dreams?'

He means the recurring ones. I kick a little slower.

'Would it help to see a bereavement counsellor again?'

My legs stop. They seem to have had expended their surplus verve for now. If I had a band, I think I'd call it 'Surplus Verve'.

'It would help very much, yes. If it brought her back,' I reply.

'Jodie.' My mother speaks softly but there is steel behind it. 'Stop it, will you. Cut it out.'

Dr Kumar shifts slightly and make a nanoscopic sound, like tiny bus braking to stop at a tiny set of traffic lights. He says, 'Please, Mrs Jones.'

My mother shushes, squeezing her fingernails into her palms until her knuckles go white. She draws in breath to remind us that she's in the room and she is not enjoying being excluded from this conversation. She shuffles on her seat, straightens the side locks of her hair with her hands, and places her manicured digits on her cream Prada handbag, pointing to the triangle bearing the brand name as if to signpost it for us, or for her, it's not clear which. The journey home is not going to be an enjoyable one. She doesn't like being ignored. Especially by a dependant she rules over and a professional she's paying to provide a service.

Dr Kumar then asks me a plethora of questions about my home life, my school life and my childhood. Given the choice, I much prefer 'superfluity' to 'plethora', but it sounds a bit stupid when you actually use it. 'Plethora' is a disgusting word because it sounds like 'placenta', which is the organ that comes out of a vagina after a baby's born. 'Vagina' isn't a delightful word, either, but I'd rather not think about those. Not in his office. Ideally not ever.

I shake such thoughts from my head.

When Dr Kumar asks me about my friends and Champ, I mention that Becca is well, but I don't tell him about the love gift or the babies, because my mother is in the room. I add that Champ is his usual self and hope he picks up on the nuance.

'And how is school?' he says. 'How are you getting on?'

I kick my legs again. My mother puts her hand out, near my knees, to indicate that I should stop. It's a little too déjà vu, if I'm honest.

'Perpendicular,' I say.

'Sorry?' His head docks in a way that makes it perpendicular, and I want to laugh. It's quite sweet, the way he does that. Earnest. I'd imagine it would get cloying and lose its earnestness quite quickly, but I don't see him often enough for that to happen.

'Quadrilateral. Obtuse. Axis.'

'I see,' Dr Kumar says. 'Is this what you're learning in Maths?'

I don't tell him what he should already know. Maths has lots of satisfying words, and now, this is the only aspect of it I enjoy, even though I used to be the best in my set if not the year, and could be again, but I don't want to give my mother the satisfaction.

'And how's Science?'

'Malleable,' I reply. 'Liquefaction.'

'Right. I see.' He smiles, but this time it's not as innocently earnest. 'Let's try it another way. Do you like your subjects? Doing well?'

I think about this. 'Your subjects' are the people you rule over if you're a monarch. It's strange that it's the same phrase for the topics a government makes the teenagers of its nation ingest and regurgitate under the guise of education. He's still waiting for an answer, so I say, 'I'm not exactly ruling over them,' to cover both possibilities. I think that's clever, myself. I don't answer the 'doing well' part of the question because does he mean academically? In life?

His gaze fixes on me more closely. He nods slowly. He's not a man for rapid movements, and that's commendable. I plan to tell Dad about this later. I feel my mother's eyes jabbing me, but I don't look at her. I can't help but wonder whether an additional déjà vu is a deja déjà vu or a déjà vu vu.

My mother turns her head to the side as if she's just been insulted and can't, for some reason, respond. The fact she's still managing to keep silent is both stupefying and intriguing, but then I suppose there is silence and there is silence. Her silence is preposterously loud. She radiates a fog of annoyance accompanied by a honking foghorn.

There's something about being here that makes me even less inclined than usual to be cooperative. Perhaps it's because, as my mother can't talk over me, I have free reign. An absolute monarchy. Perhaps it's because I always have to be a particular person and act a certain way, and I've had enough of it. I recite the line from 'The Schoolboy' by Blake because that sums it up precisely.

How can the bird that is born for joy,
Sit in a cage and sing?

Seeing as he's not getting not very far with me, Dr Kumar asks my mother to step out so he can talk to me alone.

'I hear your history class is visiting the Imperial War Museum this morning,' he begins, once she's gone.

I answer with a swallow. Meaning I swallow my saliva. I don't give him a bird.

'I can understand why that might be difficult for you,' he continues, 'always being on guard for danger, avoiding crowds. The fear of loud noises, weapons, people running, the sound of screaming, gun shots, and so on. But it's been a few years, and I was hoping you'd be a little closer to overcoming some of those difficulties. A museum is a relatively safe environment.'

Nowhere is a safe environment. Anything can happen anywhere at any time, and he's deluded if he thinks otherwise. I inspect the fluff on the floor.

'Do you still have flashbacks?'

I do, but no one knows when or how often because I keep them to myself. Instead, I say, 'flashback' because it sounds so ritzy.

He doesn't sigh with his mouth, but he does with his face. He likes it when I talk, and I'm not talking enough. He knows and I know we're heading towards treacherous ground.

I'm fully aware that he consults with other psychiatrists and psychologists, including ones who have seen me before, and he rereads my notes before meetings. He brings things up that he can't possibly know because doctors before him asked me those questions, and he can quote answers I gave years ago, word for word. All of these things I find invasive, creepy, perturbing, meddlesome, and like I'm famous and have a page on BrainyQuote of all the memorable things I've ever said.

He isn't getting any closer to unearthing what's changed lately, meaning in the last two months. I used to tick lots of their tick boxes, which made them happier than it made me. But I'm not ticking any of the boxes now. Do they rewrite the boxes when that happens? Is tick-box writing a career?

'You told Dr Haliki about the ... er ... about your experience.'

Dr Kumar is waiting for an answer, but I don't reply because it isn't a question, it's a statement. Also, I don't want to do this today. I don't want to do this ever again. But yet again, I have no choice. They think my mind is a locked-room mystery and they want to solve it. I'm not sure minds are solvable but maybe I'm wrong.

'How do you feel now?' he asks softly. 'When you see a bridge?'

I feel like a thousand
                i n s e c t s
                have
                swarmed
                into my body
                and are
                buzzing around
                furiously

I feel like I'm struggling to keep
            food
         in my stomach
        because the nausea is so
                sudden
              so intense
       it launches my insides
                            outside

I feel like something
        bad
        can happen
          at any moment
because humans
            are terrifying and   can't be trusted
    and this is
       every
       single
       time
            I go outdoors

I can't walk near a kerb
I   freeze   when I hear screaming or cars driving fast or engines revving or fireworks that sound like a gunshot
      Ipanicwhensomeoneshoutsandswears
  I can't listen to
      watch
        or read
  about violence   or stabbings
  or shootings or   worse
 so I avoid the news
    on TV
  the radio
     newspapers.

I take ear-defenders and earplugs everywhere I go
    My insides clamp
        shut
  if I hear an emergency siren
      especially when I'm on the street
        and I think
          I'm going to
        pass
          out

Fire extinguishers terrify me.
Men in riot gear terrify men.
People running terrifies me.
   And on
   and on
   and on.

I shrug and say, 'Not good.'

Dr Kumar nods slowly. 'Would you . . . tell me something . . . about that afternoon, Jodie Jones?'

I jut out my jaw. He knows this from my file. Every. Last. Detail. Still. He's never heard it from me.

He enunciates slowly, 'Your mother . . . she was taking you to a violin lesson before your audition for a . . . uh . . . for a music scholarship later that day.'

I'm silent, listening to the sounds he's making. 'Music' sounds less musical than 'scholarship', if you think about it, but the two together sound twitchy. He carries on. 'You came out of the tube station and walked towards the bridge.'

'I . . . can't.'

'Just . . . slowly. Can we try . . . Jodie Jones? You walked across the bridge together. Through the crowd, you saw a man with . . . He had blood . . . on . . . across his face and someone was running after him shouting. And you were scared. . . You were only ten, so of course you were . . . but what I'd like to know is . . .'

    My stomach

             flips   Skin

                          prickles

I n s e c t s   begin to throng

    Food rises.

           White light

        crushes

        my head.

    I will explode or combust.

'Jodie Jones, was your mother holding your hand?'

I retreat to the wardrobe of my mind and huddle there, my arms around my knees, the door closed. Except physically, I'm still sitting in front of him.

I close my eyes and kick my legs and say, 'Aspidistra. Profligate. Rumination.'

'You were together, weren't you, when . . .'

He pauses for a longish time between the words, giving them a space in the air. I consider how some pauses seem empty and others rich with suggestion.

'I have a theory, you see. About . . . what happened, Jodie Jones. And I'm wondering . . . if it's correct.'

He's a butterfly collector, tiptoeing up to a tiny fragile creature he wants to nab and pin in a frame. Except this is Dr Kumar and he's not like the others. He wants to help me because he's a kind person, the sort who isn't driven by money or status but by what he can do to help people heal, and I admire this about him. Except he could be driven by money just a little bit more and buy some non-pyjama trousers and a non-clashing shirt.

Dr Kumar is persistent. 'The . . . er . . . the events unfolded just as you were walking over the bridge. In the chaos and confusion, you were separated.'

A pause that is waiting for me to fill in a second part, like a dependent clause, which we learned about in English. 'Despite the rain, we . . .'; 'As I swam, I . . .'; 'Although we hate you, we'll . . .'

My palms are sweaty and I wonder what evolutionary advantage we gain by having slippery palms at exactly the moment we need to cling to the tree we're leaping up to escape from a sabre-toothed tiger.

'I'm going to go very slowly, Jodie Jones. These are the facts as I know them. I want to check them before I tell you what I think happened, or perhaps you'll tell me yourself. Which would be better.'

His eyes rest on me, but I don't let mine meet his. I let the sweat of my palms seep into this unexciting blue sofa and wonder if it's mingling with the sweat of former patients' palms and that is not a happy thought. I move my hands and wipe them on my school skirt.

He is speaking very deliberately and with surprising focus. His eyes remain on me.

'As they came out onto the bridge, people began screaming and running. Cars beeped their horns. There were sirens. Gunshots. Through the crowd you saw glimpses of the . . . of the men and you heard the shots . . . You and your mother were on the far side of the bridge, a hundred feet or so away.'

Slowly, carefully, he picks up a piece of paper and he hands it to me. On it, he has written down what he thinks happened that day.

More swarms swarm than ever before, more flips, more prickles until everything everywhere is noise and heat and interference and pain.

He knows. More or less.

He knows.

'Write it down, Jodie Jones,' he says to my panicking face. 'If that's easier.'

Somehow I do.

And the truth of it, bared like this, makes me implode and explode and unplode and replode.

'And then . . .' he says, after reading the words on the paper.

And.

Then.

I throw up on the carpet.

With that, today's session comes to a premature end.

My mother is supposed to have her turn but because of the word I dislike that means purging food from your stomach, she is taking the shaking mess that is me home. She rolls her eyes, hoping to elicit sympathy from Poppy the receptionist for my behaviour in general, and today in particular, and arranges a further appointment date. I drink the water they've provided once I stop retching, Poppy gives me two digestives and I look up some SAT vocabulary words on my phone. Those lists are long. Today's choices are: Harangue. Timorous. Harbingers. Nuzzle. Histrionic. Ensconce. Obdurate. Lachrymose. Enshroud. Repudiate. Laconic.

My mother won't let me use my noise-cancelling headphones or earplugs in the car, but I usually make myself invisible ones by blocking out what she says and rewriting sentences to fit my mood. But today I'm doing something else. I got the idea from Becca. On the front page of a journal she gave me for my birthday she wrote, 'Manure for your word bank.' She was alluding to an Evelyn Waugh line about our vocabulary needing regular fertilizing.

So I fertilize my vocabulary by making the SAT words into sentences.

My mother's obdurate and histrionic haranguing is a harbinger of a lachrymose mood later, so until I am ensconced and nuzzling a fleece in my wardrobe, I shall repudiate her by being laconic.

I couldn't make 'timorous' work.

I'm no longer timorous of her, and never will be again. My vocabulary will have to remain unfertilized with that particular adjective for now.

30

'She's getting worse. Like a small child. Where's Champ?' My mother closes the front door and removes her coat and shoes.

Dad appears from the study. When she comes home, we need to display our devotion by greeting her in the hallway (all of us), saying how lovely she looks (Dad), and commiserating on her dreadful day (all of us). Champ's absence from the welcoming committee is conspicuous. Dad, his fingers half jammed in his jeans pockets, which surely can't be comfortable but all males seem to do it, so what do I know, glances from me to her and says, 'Upstairs.'

My mother, typically upset by this maltreatment, this time says, 'He can stay there for now,' and Dad and I, surprised by the lack of outburst, follow her into the kitchen.

Dad sees my face and mouths, 'You OK?'

I nod because what else am I going to say? Then I hold up one finger behind my back to demonstrate to Dad the current level of my mother's annoyance. He does a low-down squeeze of my other hand. I'm here and I love you.

But you're not always, Dad. Are you? I think. *And you won't be for much longer.*

My mother scans the tiled floor and marble surfaces with hawkish eyes for an errant smear or crumb, and stands with her back to the steel magnetless fridge door. 'Her behaviour today takes the absolute biscuit,' she says with force. 'On top of that, she chucked up all over the place.'

'Oh no,' Dad asks me. 'What happened?'

I'm disturbed by the phrase 'chucked up' and it wasn't 'all over the place', because the whole world isn't covered in my puke, but I keep that to myself. And why are biscuits taken anywhere and why is that bad?

'She's fine, Elliot. Clearly. Making a massive deal out of nothing, as per usual. You might want to ask how I am. Jesus.'

I run 'I am Jesus' though my head because without that full stop, it changes everything. As we take a pew and Dad listens to today's psychiatry session from my mother's perspective, he frowns, scowls, smoulders, pouts, glowers, groans and other verbs with long, low, assonant vowels. Then he rubs his eyes and sighs. He does this a lot; his eyes are well-rubbed rounds with raw red rings.

'Stop bloody sighing,' my mother snaps, taking out a glass and filling it with filtered water from the fridge without offering us any. 'Does my head in. Sounds like a deadbeat bum.' She drinks, her eyes looking him up and down. 'Speaking of which. Is that what you wore today?'

Dad scans his clothes and nods.

'Christ's sake, Elliot. She's doing a good enough job of embarrassing me without you joining in,' she says, about me, her only daughter, light of her life and all that. She puts the glass in the dishwasher, closes it and remains standing. 'Please tell me you didn't humiliate me further and go out of the house in those clothes. You're losing your grip, you really are. Don't look at me like that. I'm not the only one who thinks it. The state of you. You look like complete crap. So, your mother died. She was old. It happens. Get a grip, will you?'

I regard my Dad. She has a point, but she doesn't have to be so blunt. He is tired-looking, unshaven, dressed in working-from-home clothes, which for him means dark jeans and a brown speckled cardigan over a green Save the Whale T-shirt he bought in Australia. My mother looks cuttingly corporate; he looks like he'd been for a ramble in the woods. I'm wearing my pale grey school uniform, which shows both my status as a minor and my lack of choice in what I wear for the majority of my days. I have a feeling that our current attire changes the dynamic between the three of us but there's no valid reason it should.

'It was years ago, Elliot. Time to grow a pair, wouldn't you say? Other people have it much worse than you, you know.'

Dad frowns. 'It's called grief, Monica. There's no time limit to it.'

'Bullshit. You've read that somewhere. Endless grief is not a thing. People move on. Adults move on. Meanwhile Coco Loco here is losing the plot and thanks to her, so am I.'

Dad looks riffled. Or is it ruffled? Maybe it's both. I'm considering this when he asks, 'Are you OK, Jodie Jones?'

I reply, 'I'm fine. When queried, Dr Kumar was unable to choose a favourite Wes Anderson film.'

Dad smiles. 'Not everyone has one.'

'Really? Why not?'

'Well . . .' Dad shrugs. 'Might be into Kubrick.'

'Can you shut up about films?' My mother's long fingers, tipped with pale pink fingernails, make her look daintier than she is. She is shorter now she's shoeless but she's tapping her rings on the countertop in an irritating way to remind us of who commands the attention in the room. I'd like to hold out a palm to still her, like she did with my kicking legs, but my mother is not one to be stilled.

Hers is the only perspective that counts, at least for now. In my mother's version of events, which she outlines in detail, I am a disgrace. Wilfully rude, deliberately impossible, unappreciative, selfish, unstable.

'She gets it from you,' she says to Dad, who is not any of those things.

Dad, in his defence, comes to my defence. 'Mon, she's been through such a lo—'

'Really. Has she.' She says it in a tone that is not a question. 'What about what I've been through? What I'm *going* through. All this . . .' she waves a dismissive hand, 'new crap she's doing? It's all on purpose, you know.'

She's not facing me, but she knows, clearly, that I'm there.

'And do you deal with any of it? No, Elliot. You do not. You leave her all up to me. Like you leave everything else to me – the house, their education, our pitiful social life, your family business, which I took on and run alone because the employees are all useless. The least you could do is make an effort.'

Dad's jaw is clenching. He shaves less regularly so his jaw-clenches aren't quite as noticeable as they were when his face was bald, but I see them. Apart from crying, which he does quite a lot, Dad shows emotion in infinitesimal movements, as if mustering the energy for anything more is too much for him.

He moves measuredly and morosely around the house, as if a weighted blanket is across his back. He doesn't socialize. He doesn't exercise. He's been this way since Grandma Tara died. Like a vacuum has scooped his insides out and only a flimsy frame remains.

My mother is wrong. I'm not selfish. I do appreciate things. Admittedly, I'm deliberately impossible and wilfully rude sometimes, but so is she, and not even sometimes.

She's still talking, and her words have a jagged rhythm I'm not fond of. 'Were you at the doctor's today? No. Did you witness the award-winning show she put on? No. Did she do everything she could to make *you* look like a bad parent? No.'

'Did you? Put on a show?' Dad asks me.

My mother shrieks, 'Do you think I'm making it up?'

'Monica, for God's sake. Stop all the—' Dad's sentence cuts off and he makes a noise like a lion with a lower-leg wound. I've never seen or heard a lion with a lower-leg wound so my analogy is merely conjecture. Dad's noise is short and roar-less, so maybe it isn't quite the same.

Which word did he omit? Stop all the what?

My mother is theatrically shocked. She's as surprised as I am that he's defied her, but I didn't go to drama school so my reaction is more subtle. 'How *dare* you! You don't get to interrupt me!' she howls. 'It's called parenting, Elliot. Try it sometime. Oh my God. After everything I do for you and for this family. I've given up everything for you and your bloody children!'

She means her freedom, her dreams and her future. Her career as an actor didn't happen – not because it's an uber competitive field and only a few make it, but because she married Dad and had us. She likes to remind us all of that. I count how many seconds until she starts crying and wailing this time. One ... two ... three ... four ... five ... six ... and she's off. Dad apologizes. As usual. Clouds lug sluggishly past. I watch their white lightness and try to think of sentences to bring me peace but only words appear in my mind. Collywobbles. Diaphanous. Bibble. Akimbo.

He doesn't pick up on 'your bloody children', even though there is much to say about this. In between sobs she says, 'You can't cope, and you make it my fault. You're the one who has no backbone. You're the one who walks around the house like a moody teenager – setting a terrible example to your children, I might add. And you're telling *me* how to behave? God, that's rich.'

Dad stands behind her and rubs her back until she shrugs him off and he sits down again, deflated. 'Come on, Mon. Don't be upset. I know you have a lot on. Did you make another appointment with Dr Kumar?'

'Next Thursday!' My mother is disgraced by my need to see yet another psychiatrist, and to have to return is a shambles. 'She's wasting my time! I've got important meetings with clients!'

This is probably true, but she would never let Dad take me to any appointments because despite the shame and disgust of having a child like me, she also needs the medical establishment and preferably the whole world to know what having a child like me is putting her through. Plus, Dad rarely leaves the house these days, anyway, unless he has to go into the office. She's as ashamed of him as she is of me. 'Unprofessional,' I've heard her say to him about his slipper-clad conference calls. 'Where's your self-respect?'

My mother checks my phone and sees the email about the seven Minor Penalties I've received this week for not handing in prep, not writing the answers in timed practice in lessons, not answering when I'm asked questions, being late for registration, turning up to lessons without books. I've also received two Majors for behaviour and attitude and I'm now on report. Again.

She roars. 'What the actual hell?'

'Monica,' Dad says wearily. 'Let's deal with that later.' He sighs, slaps his thighs and rises to fill the kettle and put teabags in mugs. 'Tea, Monica? Jodie Jones? Cuppa?'

'Don't you "Monica" me. You let her get away with this. I have high expectations for my children. The least she can do is to stop acting like a moron and do as she's told.'

'What are the detentions for, Jodie?' Dad asks.

'Jones,' I say.

'Everyone knows your stupid name!' My mother's shout picks up force and volume. Brewing bursts are moments away. Two-finger fury. Three. Will it be four? 'I'm warning you! Don't make me lose it.'

My eyes fix on the countertop that isn't a bar but has barstools. At that moment, Champ walks in and surveys the scene. 'Just getting . . .' He waves his water bottle, surely sensing my imminent roasting as he runs the tap.

'Where were you?' my mother asks. She means when she came home.

'Sorry. Didn't hear the door.'

'Right. I get it. Whatever you were doing was clearly more important than your mother.'

'Course not. I was studying. I had headphones on.'

I surreptitiously hold three fingers up behind my back and, being by the door, he sees them and says to me in a blunt tone,

'When you're done, I can show you how to answer that Haber question for Chemistry. I don't have long so it'll have to be soon.'

I slide off the stool with Dad's eyes on me. She doesn't stop me. He blinks as a nod, and because my mother's nearly in a four-finger rage now, yelling at Dad about how little respect we all give her. Her tantrum, like a child's, is a full-body experience of jerking and shuddering and hair and eyes and arms. Opportunity is banging on the door with its fists, so I exit the kitchen and follow Champ gratefully up the stairs. At the top, I whisper, 'Thanks for that.'

Champ forms an L on his forehead with his thumb and his forefinger to remind me I'm a loser. Do all sixteen-year-old boys act partly like they're five and partly like they're twenty-five? My guess is yes. And that's a sentence that I like.

Champ's navy sweater says 'Georgetown' across the front in white lettering and I swear his hair is lighter. 'You owe me,' he says. He isn't exuding the warmth or fluffiness his benevolent actions should suggest, so as he walks to his room flipping his water bottle like a juggling club, I say, 'I actually know about Haber but peradventure we could—'

'Obviously,' he says, without turning around. 'I wasn't serious.' Then he faces me. 'Did you actually just say "peradventure"? Please bucking please tell me you didn't.'

Champ uses the authentic version of the word, but I refuse to repeat it. He uses it regularly when he's out earshot of my mother.

'What?'

'Peradventure,' he repeats. 'What the buck.'

'No, but really. Why don't we say "peradventure" any more?'

'Because it's bucking stupid?'

'I like it,' I reply, and decide to 'peradventure' whenever

henceforth the chance of doing so fortuitously unfolds. And possibly to 'henceforth' and 'fortuitously' as well.

I don't say that. Instead I mumble, 'I . . . Champ?'

'What?' He looks annoyed. He doesn't look annoyed when he's with his friends. Maybe it's just me. I long for my big brother to be my big brother again and make us forts out of chairs and blankets (even though he left me alone in one for ages once, telling me he was going to fight rival knights when he was really watching *The Simpsons*). Champ might have thrown my favourite teddies out of a moving car window and left me in a maze crying when I was four (a lady took pity on me, but when I didn't know Dad's phone number, she said, 'I can't help you, then, can I?' and left) but my removal from the kitchen is a definite save and I am steeped in relief and appreciation.

Still, it's worth a try. 'Can you pretend you have magical powers and move small objects when I close my eyes?'

Peradventure this is not the best tactic because he tuts and says, 'How old are you?'

'You never grow out of—' but he's shut his door in my face by then.

'She nearly went into a five-fingered mood earlier,' I say through the wood. 'Just so you know.'

'Because you were doing what?'

'Being myself. As ever.'

He snorts. 'Right.'

'What's that supposed to mean?'

He snorts again.

'How is this my fault?' I ask him.

'Because you know what she's like. And I know what you're like.'

'I still don't see how this is my fault.'

Silence behind the door.

I ask, 'Want to play Monopoly?' I don't know why I'm asking. He always whips my hide at Cluedo, Monopoly – every board game we play because he's so competitive. I don't mind because I have no interest in winning. I prefer inventing new names for Professor Plum, Reverend Green and Colonel Mustard. Professor Purple Pants, Brethren Greenfly and Colonel Walrus Face are still my favourites, and that hasn't changed since I was seven.

'Got homework,' he says. We're still talking through a door, I would like to point out. 'Some of us care about our grades.'

'One game.'

'No. And cut out the crap at school. You're an embarrassment.'

'Please, Champ.'

'Go away.'

31

Later, in his study, Dad conveys that he is achingly concerned about what happened in today's session. It's not the first time it's happened, but he's always achingly concerned when it does. His achingly-concerned-face consists of pinched, pulled-in eyebrows, tense, trembling lips, a reddened neck, noisy breathing, rapid blinking, and downwards face rubs. He also crosses and uncrosses his arms over his chest, randomly runs a harried hand through his hair, and shakes his head as if he's saying no to himself again and again. Along with this, he speaks in a falsely upbeat tone to make me think everything is all right.

I look through the study window at the rain and explain that it's the usual reason, the usual stuff. Dad is frustrated that progress isn't being made, but I've told him more than once that progress doesn't mean life is spick and span and crisp and sweet and easy-breezy-lemon-squeezy. Sometimes, progress is managing to hold your head up all day, even if it's a day when you vomit on the carpet and partly on the suede shoes of a kindly psychiatric professional.

I am also achingly concerned. Maybe not 'achingly'. I'm not

sure what that even means, but when I see it on Dad, it does look like he's aching. My concern is about Dad's mood and what happened in the kitchen when I left. I heard the noises. But I don't mention them or the escalating conflict and the repercussions thereof in his relationship with the She-Beast. My concern is conveyed by repeatedly interrupting his frowning and thinking symposium by asking him seemingly random questions, then sitting on his lap, pulling his earlobes, and trying to get him to play Red Hands with me so I can slap his hands hard because I'm faster than he is.

He's not in a hand-slapping mood, so I say, 'Dad. What do these words mean?'

'Hmm?'

'I asked what these words mean.'

'Which words?'

'I haven't told you them yet.'

'Ah.' A pause. 'Go on, then.'

I open my journal and say, innocently, '"Erogenous", "missionary", "sapio", "metamor".'

'Mmm.' Colour rises to his face. He appears a little flapped. 'Flapped' isn't often used in everyday speech, but we do say 'unflappable' so I'd argue it should be, and more often. I'd imagine Dad would prefer it if I asked someone else about these words, but he knows I have no reasonable mother figure to guide me, so he gives it a go.

He explains 'erogenous', which is awkward for both of us, especially as he stutters a lot, rubs the back of his neck, and says, 'zones' and 'stimulate' more than is usual in the course of an evening. His explanation of 'missionary' in this context is quite enlightening and provokes further questions that make his ears redden and his eyes work hard not to meet mine. He isn't sure about 'sapio', so I have to add the second part of the word, which is 'sexual', and this makes him blink more times than I can count. If his definition is correct and it means someone attracted to intelligence, then I think I will probably be sapiosexual, if I'm sexual at all. He has to look the last one up on his laptop. I'm hoping he'll pick up on the subtext, which is my mother's likely infidelity, but I'm not sure Dad has ever been all that skilled at picking up subtle hints.

'What exactly are you reading that has these words in it?' he asks, plainly sweating.

'Historical novel. Bit of a saucy one, it turns out.'

He tilts his head. 'Which era?'

Oops. There is no historical novel. 'Can't recall. Why do you ask?'

'Not sure they'd have mentioned "erogenous", "sapiosexual" or "metamor" in any period of the past. Not sure those words existed.'

I've been rumbled. I know it. He knows it. I just have to come out with it.

'I have a strong suspicion that your wife is not being faithful.'

'Ah,' he says. 'So those words were just—'

'Clues. Yes.'

'It could have been a forthright comment from the start and saved me the . . .' He waves his hand.

'I know but I learned a lot, so thank you.'

'Well, I appreciate your honesty, but our marriage is between the two of us.'

'Infidelity is never just between two people. That's the point, Dad.'

'Jodie Jones,' he says, 'if that's the case, I will deal with it. It doesn't concern you and you don't have to worry about it.'

'Course I do.'

'No, you don't. It's going to be OK. I have a plan,' he says. 'I can't tell you what it is, but I'm working on it.'

Yes, Dad. That's what I'm worried about, I tell him with my eyes. If you're working on it in the same way you're 'working from home', not much is going to get done.

'Weird TV shows?' I suggest. 'I can start. People cooking competitively. People dancing competitively. Seriously, why do people watch that stuff? Dad.'

'Hmm?'

'You're staring into space.' I prompt him again.

'Fine,' he says. 'Celebrities eating bugs in a jungle.'

'Couples buying and renovating houses.'

'Murde—' he stops and winces, aware of what he was about to say. 'All reality TV is weird. All TV, really.'

'What are you watching at the moment?'

He grins. 'You wouldn't like it.'

I get up, kiss his stubbly cheek and leave him to his Scandi noir.

32

On the bus to school, I eye-spy my brother once I've established what else is in view. Headphoned folk face forwards. Pensioners window-gaze. Mothers in low-rise jeans scroll on phones beside infants in wheel-locked buggies. Chinwaggers natter, shaking their heads at the woes of the world. A man in mock-croc trainers and a faux fur coat twists the ends of his well-waxed moustache. School kids' PE kits are strewn in string-handled bags that will no doubt be forgotten on the floor between the seats when we get off. I stay near the door, just in case. Watchful. Alert. As always.

To distract myself from the nauseating terror of being in a busy public place, I ease my mind by rereading my latest offering, found in the front pocket of my rucksack.

> *She walks in beauty, like the night*
> *Of cloudless climes and starry skies;*
> *And all that's best of dark and bright*
> *Meet in her aspect and her eyes;*
>
> Lord Byron

At least I know where this one has come from. Byron is Dad's favourite poet. He's read his poems to me a few times before, but I'd forgotten about this delight. I want to take it to my wardrobe and be alone with it: roll it around in the vault of my mind, play with the rhythms and sounds of 'cloudless climes' and 'starry skies' and wonder what the best parts of dark and bright might be.

The windows are wet: fat droplets of rain on the outside, foggy condensation in the inside, panes of glass between the two forms of water. A middle-aged man with stubble and a denim jacket boards the bus looking waspish. Belligerent. Dangerous. My stomach clenches. I watch him carefully and try to distract myself. 'Aspect'? A strange choice of word. But with Byron's exactitude, I presume it's no mistake.

Two stops later, Wasp Man gets off and I relax somewhat. The bus lurches and hisses; its doors open and close. It sounds weary. Apathetic. Disillusioned. Buses are not the most motivational method of motion in the grey, cold tedium of a winter that refuses to turn into spring. No one looks happy on this vehicle except Champ, who's laughing hysterically with Tavish about something on Tavish's phone. I haven't spoken to Champ yet, but he doesn't make conversation-starting easy.

I don't know if it bothers him when he hears the shouts and thuds of our parents fighting, but it must.

I don't know if he knows about the suitcase, but he must.

I don't know if he cares about the looming bleakness of our lives once Dad leaves, but he must.

He won't know I have a plan to put an end to all of this, but know it he must. We've held up five-finger warnings to each other far too often recently.

Plan A was underway, but then Dad's move to the study and the suitcase were unexpected, unwelcome and unforeseen obstacles that are now sabotaging the timeline of Plan A. This is why I now need to speak to my brother, and increasingly urgently.

Over half the bus consists of pupils from my school; at our stop, we exit en masse in a surge of verve and the bus seems to sigh. Perhaps it's the collective sigh of the passengers on board now the teenage rabble are getting off, the sigh of the suspension or brakes, or just the sigh of life on a London bus in March.

I like 'surge of verve'. I'd name my cat that but call him 'Serge' for short.

'Verve' is a great all-rounder, really.

Mr Fowler is standing in the corridor, greeting our year group as we enter the main doors.

'Morning, Robbie. On time for once? Wonders will never cease. Morning, Tyra. Er. Earrings? The school rules apply to you as well, you know. Stand there and take them out, please.'

There's no way to avoid him. I keep my head down and hope someone else with a uniform infraction distracts him.

'We're going to have a better day today, aren't we, Miss Jones?'

He says 'we' to speak about me, as if he's a part of me, an organ, or an undeveloped, unborn twin. Why the 'we'? Are *his* days bad as well? I'm grappling with this and the formality of 'Miss Jones', when he does something even odder: he replies to himself as if he's me as well.

'Yes, Mr Fowler. We are.'

This is exceptionally confusing. I know the meaning behind it: I haven't answered in the time frame he considers appropriate so he's answering for me. But I'm perplexed as to why this has become common parlance in English. Why is speaking to yourself as if you're someone else considered normal, yet saying 'dodecahedron' to yourself a few times in class is not?

'This is where you give me a sign you're awake,' he says.

I'm not a fan of a sardonic man. He's growing a beard for charity, and it looks like a wire brush is stuck on his face. 'I'm awake.'

'Good to know. I don't want to see a single detention coming into my inbox today. Got that?'

I find it intriguing that a detention could come into his inbox at all, when it's an hour of sitting in Room 3 and therefore not emailable. There's something else I'd like further clarification on, too. 'For anyone or just for me?'

'Don't be clever.'

Isn't being clever a desired trait in an educational establishment, and indeed what they're all hoping for? I'd ask this, but I've had my fill of this conversation and have the feeling that mentioning that will only make the situation worse.

I decide to dodge detentions today to desist from any further discourse with him. He is unaware that this decision is being detailed in my mind in dental alliteration and this delights me. He's a dick and everyone can detect that. Even him.

Our form room is an ICT room. I can see Becca's head, curls tied high, behind a computer monitor. On closer inspection, she's studying for this morning's quiz on cells from homemade flashcards. 'Tescht me,' she says, thrusting them at me before I even sit down. I will miss this lisp when her retainer accomplishes its tooth-straightening mission.

I test her until the start of Period 1 and wish her luck. Her

Biology set has been over this content in class, and we have – she and I – at her house. She also no doubt revised it until late last night because, unlike me, she cares about doing well. In our last Biology test on genetic inheritance and evolution, I wrote the lyrics to 'Brown Skinned Girl' by Beyoncé across the page because it was apt, but as my intention today is to avoid unnecessary interactions with Mr Fowler, when the time comes, I answer the questions instead. It's an easy test, but I only complete half because this is the micro-choice I present to my freedom-loving spirit today. An act of charity to myself. A sliver of emancipation cut from the gigantic cake of control.

Becca watches me as I put down the pen halfway through the test and lie with my head on the desk. I can feel her eyes scorching my back. Schhe's schhouting at me schilently to schtep up and finisch the damn tescht but schhe's also feeling inexpresschably schad becausche sche thinksch I'm heading schomewhere dark and dangerousch. And sche could well be right.

33

The end of term always feels scattered. No one can concentrate because we're thinking about the holidays, we need a break, and we're weary. We're actually far more than 'weary' but 'we're weary' sounds nice. People with interesting 'r's would say 'wew weawy', which is even better, or 'wew weally weawy', which I'm desperate for an interesting 'r' sayer to say to me. Repeat 'wew weally weawy' rapidly on a loop and you get closer to saying 'we're willy' than you'd ever like to be.

I don't know if I'll make it to July in this place, but I should be here after Easter, at least. Maybe I shouldn't try 'wew weally weawy' out on my teachers, though, or perhaps I won't be.

At break, Champ is horsing around in the sixth form common room with Bear and Tavish. I spy with my little eye them through the doors, laughing and punching each other on the arm – it can't be because it's the first of the month and for that inexplicable reason they feel compelled to bruise each other, so I'm not sure of their motive. I'm trying to decide which is the best place to approach my brother: home isn't ideal, but school isn't either. Only sixth formers are allowed in the sixth form common room. I don't spot Moses so I can't ask him to call Champ for me.

Now is not the time.

Instead, it's the perfect time to consider why horses are the animals chosen to describe people frolicking. Why not dolphins? Perhaps purely because 'Champ is dolphining around' is just too tongue-dancing to say.

On the shelf where everyone leaves lost property, mainly refillable water bottles, I see a yellow Post-it note and pick it up. On it is written, in lurid green pen:

The lights begin to twinkle from the rocks:
The long day wanes; the slow moon climbs: the deep
Moans round with many voices. Come, my friends
'Tis not too late to seek a newer world.

Ulysses, by Alfred, Lord Tennyson

I love it, but what it's doing there is a mystery. No one in a school will pay the slightest attention to a piece of paper with something written on it: the place is full of them. So I decide to make it mine, and pick it up. The line runs through my mind repeatedly, and the sounds and the idea of a new world stick with me.

At lunch, in the refuge of our under-stair spot, Becca is testy with me about the test. I point out that I've completed half of it and will therefore likely pass. Becca leans in to whisper, even though it's just the two of us sitting here. 'Have you got your period or schomething What's up with you?'

'I don't have periods, remember?'

Her body jolts backwards. 'Sschtill? Tsk. HOW ISCH THAT FAIR?'

'It's not a good thing, Becca. You're supposed to have them. Biologically.'

'Muscht be amazsching not to, though. Sschaves a ton on vag plugsch.'

'Gross.'

She lowers her chin and glowers at me. 'Jodie Joneschhh. I mean it. Tell me what'sch going on.' Her eyes act as searchlights, ones with an aggressively interrogative edge.

I want to tell her because she's Becca and she should know, but I can't tell her because she's Becca. She'll get emotional and concerned and talk to people about it whom I'd rather didn't know.

'Nowt,' I say, because I like that word. 'Don't fret, lass.' My Yorkshire accent is accurate, I think.

But the lass frets, nonetheless.

I spy with my little eye again for Champ before afternoon registration, but my little eye doesn't spy him anywhere. I'm aware he has clubs, music lessons and sports fixtures, but having never having had the slightest interest in his life before, I am not familiar with the specifics of his timetable.

He passes me in the corridor between lessons, but only because I follow him, hide behind a wall and then walk the other way to ensure it happens. He's talking to Bear and doesn't even see me.

At the end of the day, meaning literally at the end of the day, not in the football manager 'at the end of the day, it was a tough game and the lads done well' kind of sense, Madame Arnaud asks to speak to me. She asks how my day went, how I'm feeling, and praises me for my increased efforts over the last two days. 'Much better, Jodie Jones. Keep it up.'

She assumes talks like these are motivational, rather than understanding that my motivations are purely fuelled by the need to speak to my podling, but I revel in the fact that a) I know something she doesn't and b) my inner voice has exchanged the word 'sibling' for 'podling', which she wouldn't understand because I made the word up.

Moses sticks his head in the room and says, 'Oh, sorry. Thought no one was in here.'

Madame Arnaud says, once he's ducked out again, 'He's so good. He goes all around after school turning the lights and screens off.'

I ask her if I can leave now, please.

When the day comes that I can leave a place where I don't want to be without asking permission first, it'll be a day worth celebrating.

34

On the way home, Moses saunters past my bus stop. Not being a thought but a real person, I can't pretend he's a bus and watch him pass by. Especially as he stops and leans on the shelter, chewing on the end of a pen like he does this kind of thing all the time.

'This isn't your bus,' I say to a Fiat 500 driving by.

'It's the bus shelter I like to lean on when certain thoughts need thinking,' he replies to a van with *You've Been Dumped* written on the side.

Obviously, being an overthinker, I now think of which thoughts might need thinking at this bus stop, whether they are different thoughts to the thoughts that need thinking against other bus stops or at other times, and whether my thoughts would be better thought at different bus stops around the city – a thought about thoughts I hadn't thought of before.

'Those thoughts being?' I ask.

'Would you rather,' he begins, pausing and then resuming, 'eat the same meal every day for the rest of your life, or constantly have a small hair at the back of your throat?'

I think about that but not for long. I'm mainly thinking that this is a weird thought for anyone to have and even weirder to share so someone else then has to think about it.

'Neither, thanks.'

'No,' he says, removing the pen, checking it's not leaking, and then slotting it back in his mouth again, 'but if you had to choose one.'

'I don't, though. Why is 'would you rather' always a choice between two terrible things? Why can't it be two great things?'

'Because that's boring: either choice would be great. It has to be two bad— Your bus is coming. Throat hair or same meal every day?'

'Bye, Moses.'

He remains leaning on the bus shelter, chewing the pen.

As I board, I say, 'Same meal.'

'Really?' he says. 'What if it was like soggy chips with mushy peas or, like, overcooked—'

'Bye, Moses.'

'Would you rather be a centipede or a scented bead?' he asks as the door hisses closed. As I walk to the back of the bus, he says, 'A dinosaur or a diner's sore?'

Or at least that's what I think he said.

Champ's not on the bus, probably because I left school late, and this, I realize, is an added benefit of not being in trouble or detention: the bus is one more opportunity to catch him. I decide to avoid detention tomorrow, too, to maximize the possibility of talking to him, even if it is on a bus.

The other challenge, of course, is getting him to listen.

Avoiding detention the next day is more tricky than predicted. I have to do the following:

- Deal with a question directed at me personally in PSHE on why FGM is illegal in the UK when I'd rather not think of the long version of the name, never mind the act of it, but I answer in brief when I would otherwise have left the room.
- Complete a worksheet on Lagos that I found uninspiring, unchallenging and uninteresting, not to mention sorely wanting in words and phrases with pleasing sounds.
- Give Miss McLaughlin the English essay she demanded, but on Tuesday rather than Monday, and at 11 a.m. instead of 9 a.m., to endow and empower myself with another micro-choice.
- Actually do some Maths rather than repeat mathematical phrases that sound obtuse, cuboid and hypotenuse, although I calculate in my variable estimation that in all probability, these expressions will recur and multiply in my mind and my mouth in symmetrical sequences and at irrational rotations of constant frequency at an infinite rate, eternally.

Somehow, yet again, I manage to miss Champ, and wonder how he can slip out of school so surreptitiously. When I get home, his shoes are on the rack and his coat is on the hook. The house is quiet. On the slim shelf in the hall is a note in my mother's handwriting saying she'll be back at 5.15 p.m., but she's going out again at 6.30 p.m. It's now 4.45, which is perfect: I have thirty minutes to speak to Champ before my mother gets back.

On the kitchen countertop I see noodles and dumplings for us to warm up, which is a vast improvement on yet another night of superfood salad, but despite being hungry, I only have a finite time to speak to Champ, so I scamper swiftly upstairs.

I pause momentarily outside his room. If I knock on his door, he'll tell me to eff off. If I shout at him through the door, he'll also tell me to eff off. I want him to listen to me for once, so casting niceties aside, I push his door open forcefully and say, 'Champ, I really need to—' then halt abruptly and gasp. I see bodies. On the bed. Champ and Tavish locked together, mouths fused, shirts pulled up, legs spayed wide, hands grasping at body parts down open trouser-fronts.

They jump in a panic. Champ yells, 'WHAT THE BUCK!' although he uses the non-b version and that exact phrase, give or take a key initial letter, is precisely what's going through my head, too, because I don't have time to think of something that F. Scott Fitzgerald might say. I do a swift 180 and fix my rattled eyes on the hall ceiling as I hear frenzied shuffles, grunty curses and creaking bedsprings as they leap up. I realize, a tad too late, that what I need to do is leave the room and close the door behind me, so I try to do exactly that, but Champ swings me around and grabs me by the armpit so I can't help but see his red and raging face, and hisses, 'What the buck are you doing barging into my—?' And then he stops, his eyes wide, his jaw dropping slack. When I twist to see what he's looking at, my eyes and jaw do the same. Our mother is standing at the top of the stairs, expressionless. I'm aware her view is one of a tangle of bedclothes through an open door and Champ and Tavish, hair tousled, eyes wild, frantically zipping their flies.

I'm just relieved I don't see any pee nibs.

Then I wonder. Why is she here? Did she lie when she said she was out, or did she come back early? Either way, it must have been a ruse to catch us doing something. She just didn't think it would be this.

Tavish, smelling of a really quite lovely grapefruit cologne, darts awkwardly past me and my ice-cold, rigid, mother. He stumbles and nearly falls down the stairs in his haste to get out of the house. When the front door clicks closed, I glance at her. She is steel, impassive. But I know her masks well; this expressionless expression she's wearing is one of disgust but also shock because this, I am sure, she did not see coming. The shock is directly related to her golden boy's unanticipated gayness, but it's not just that: it's the secretiveness, the lettingherdownness of what she's just experienced. She is a particular kind of parent and she no doubt has plans for him that include extraordinary success and wealth, marriage to an extraordinarily successful and wealthy wife, preferably an heiress, and then high-achieving grandchildren who will achieve extraordinary success and wealth, marriages to extraordinarily successful and wealthy spouses, preferably also heirs and heiresses, and high-achieving great grandchildren who will, et cetera et cetera.

Champ slumps and sits at the foot of his bed. His face falls to his hands. I have turned into a pillar: I am there, yet not there, standing in the landing, unsure of what to do with myself. I've seen people kissing before but never two boys, one of them being my brother, kissing each other with adventuring hands on a bed in my house. I had no idea that my brother was anything other than in love with himself.

Tavish? Really?

My mother does not accept apologies, so Champ does not attempt to make one. She expects us to know without explanation what we have done wrong, and even in a situation like this, where he has crossed a boundary of deceit as wide as a ravine, saying sorry would make no difference. She never apologizes herself, of course. If anything, she'll give an unapology, an anti-apology: I'm sorry if you're offended by the truth. I'm sorry you're so deluded. I'm sorry if you're not smart/well/strong enough to deal with the reality of life. I'm sorry you think anyone's to blame except you.

The tick of the hall clock is the only sound I process. It marks time in taps as it punctures the still air. My mother, nostrils flared, is riled and rankled, but she's also cold, composed and calm. The worst combination.

'I expected great things of you,' she sneers to Champ with a slow and fatal head shake. She semi-snort-laughs and adds, 'But you don't exist for me any more. Not you, pathetic little pussy boy, and not your waste of space sister.' She walks away, which is a weapon, probably the best she has in her armoury for a moment like this, not that there have ever been moments like this before in our household.

I hate my mother. I know it's wrong to hate a parent, but whoever made up the rules of right and wrong didn't have in mind a mother like her.

Left behind is air static with drama: fresh, exposed, unclad – like recently sea-dipped legs on a January day at the beach. Obviously, I have no issue with Champ being gay, although it is a surprise. Obviously, I have no issue with Tavish being the one he likes, although I'm glad it's not Moses. The sole issue I have is what will happen next, because there's nothing obvious about that.

Then my brother does something I haven't seen him do since he was about nine, which is cry.

35

When I wake in my bed in the cold and the dark of the night, I remember something significant has happened.

It was bad enough before, but the situation is now irrevocable, a word that sounds like a mix of 'irie', 'revelling' and 'vocal' and should therefore be used to describe jaunty outdoor events like New Year's Eve fireworks with jerk chicken roasting in steel drums. Instead, its five syllables descend in pitch like stairs to a deep dark place, and that's where my family is heading. Dad is leaving. My mother will turn on Champ the way she turned on me, now that he's dishonoured and disappointed her. Champ is humiliated because his outing – meaning his enforced coming out rather than his trip to the local fruit farm – was purely my fault. I did not have the decorum to knock on his door, and because of this, but also because of other things, I am descending irrevocably myself, and there is no floor or foundation to stop me free falling off the edge indefinitely.

I lie, alarmed, in the darkness observing the shapes and shadows of my room. Listening to the wind whipping untethered objects about outside and the irregular rhythm of the rain pit-a-patting on the windowpanes and the corrugated shed roof, wondering if my plan will work now that the hitches and glitches and twists and turns have messed up my mind-map of how things will develop.

This is bad this is bad this is bad, I think, and pull the duvet up to my nose. The lights are never on in our house at night: it's dark and silent. We have to be in our rooms at nine with the lights off. I've almost tripped and fallen down the stairs a few times on my way to get water. The safest place is under this duvet.

Grandma Tara's face appears in my mind's eye.

'One has a conundrum,' I whisper to her. She used to say 'one' instead of 'you' to show she was speaking in general terms rather than direct, specific ones. I found it odd as a child, and harbour no surprise that the practice is politely being retired from the English language. We use 'one' mainly in the numerical sense these days: if one kept track of the many 'one's one used daily, one would be one-d out in no time and no one would be surprised. Still, it's fun to 'one', and it has its uses, specifically the one Grandma Tara used it for.

Namely.

When one's phone has been confiscated once more for purposes of control and coercion, one is forced to rely on one's other devices for one's information, one of them being a mini torch and one being an alarm clock. I pick up my mini torch and point it at my alarm clock, which doesn't read one a.m., although that would be fun, but 5.48 a.m., which in March in England is not a time anyone should be awake. And that is why, when one hears footsteps padding, one by one, down one's creaky staircase, one's curiosity is piqued. Perhaps one or two prior sounds roused one in the first place.

One listens hard, if one can listen hard, which one can. Then one rises silently in the darkness, dresses in the closest garments to hand and, one by one, inserts one's newly socked feet into one's snow-boot footwear, all the while listening hard. When one hears the front door close, one picks up one's mini torch, unhooks one's fake beard from the nail on one's wardrobe, and creeps down the stairs wishing one did, in fact, have a phone because ideally one should not walk around on dark streets on one's own, especially if one is a female, and that is a state that everyone in one's country and one's world should address with the utmost urgency.

One has to be quick: one doesn't want to lose one's mystery escapee and, more to the point, one wants to see where one's family member is going at this unacceptably early hour. Fortunately, the citizens of one's land are aware that 5.48 a.m. in winter in England – well, 6.01 a.m. now – is not a time anyone should be awake, so the figure one sees walking up one's road is undoubtedly the one that has departed recently from one's house. Its head is hooded, which is an indication it might be Champ, but then again one's Dad could have borrowed Champ's hoodie or indeed purchased one of his own, and one's mother could have too, if one is keeping her in the equation, which one is. The only one I know for sure that it isn't is this particular one, meaning me.

'One' gets tedious after a while. How did one keep it up all those years ago?

I pursue the silhouette. It's carrying a holdall-shaped object that must be a holdall or why would it be holdall shaped? The figure passes lampposts that permit me to see that it can't possibly be my mother due to its pace and gait and height. It is male. I further perceive that it's not my dad, because it's progressing with a boyish bounce that Dad does not possess. His is more a middle-aged lurch.

Champ.

I halt near some wheelie bins. What if he's having a crisis meeting with Tavish? I can't barge in on their private world again. Champ, nearing the corner shop, is hunched into himself, head down, crumpled, defeated, and that raises hackles because Champ is an entitled and arrogant arse. I doubt Tavish would leave his warm bed at this hour to meet him when he lives in Wimbledon, and we live in Putney, but what do I know of love and pain and train timetables?

Necessity compels me to continue.

I adjust my fake beard, pull my hat over my eyebrows, and follow. Champ turns left on to the main road. He passes a homeless person lying on flattened boxes in a doorway, their sleeping bag zipped over their head. He passes a weally weawy man raising the shutters of a shop with fingerless gloves and stops at the traffic lights to cross, despite there being no cars coming, probably because road safety is so ingrained and routine, but maybe because he's unfocused and not feeling his usually mutinous *I'm-crossing-regardless* self.

Although I'm in spy mode, he doesn't look round, so my extra precautions in subterfuge, which is a word I like very much but is far too hard to say in the normal flow of a sentence, are uncalled for. Plus, one would hope the beard would do its job and from this distance in the dark, he won't be able to see it's me, even though I'm wearing his old down coat, which isn't old, but he has a new jacket he likes better.

The streets are surprisingly interesting at six a.m. There are more cars are on the road than I expected. People are jogging. Jogging? In the dark? In short, tight Lycra? In the cold?

The idea of it is staggering. Fortunately, the joggers are not.

Those not jogging, meaning those wearing jackets suitable for the season and warm trousers of a sensible length, walk like automata or huddle at bus stops, scrolling, their faces blue from the glow of their phones. Darkness hangs hefty as fog. Lights from shops and lampposts dot and pepper the murk and reflect like fairy lights in puddles left by the rain.

Champ is nearing East Putney station. My stomach clenches.

He's leaving, too.

Gasping, I start to sprint.

36

He's through the barrier by the time I race in, shouting, 'Champ! Stop!'

Spinning around, he frowns at the frantic girl he recognizes despite the strap-on beard, and snaps, 'What the buck.'

He says it as a statement rather than a question but even as a question it's not really a question. Surely it should be followed by the verb 'to be', as in 'What the buck is that beard doing on your face?' 'Why the buck are you here?' 'What the buck were you thinking?' Not just the first part. Maybe he's saving himself some superfluous syllables. This is not the time to consider the grammar of swear words, even though when is, if not when it comes to mind?

'What are ... Where are you going?' I ask, winded. We're talking over the ticket barrier and the London Underground employee in the routine blue uniform is eyeing us. I didn't even know tube stations were open at 6.07 a.m.

'What's it to you?' Champ asks. On a scale of one to brotherly, his tone is around a two.

'Champ, please. Don't go.' The fake beard, I appreciate, must make me look a tad unhinged, so I pull it off. The uniformed man does a short, jumpy body gesture that means, 'Oh!'

It's distracting because that 'Oh!' might mean 'Oh! You're a girl.' Or, 'Oh! Unstrapping mine would be so much easier than having to shave.' Or, 'Oh! That's a little dramatic for a Tuesday; I haven't even had my porridge yet.' Or, 'Oh! relationship dramas – my favourite. Let me get my tea.'

I try to ignore him, because my big brother, whom I love more than he deserves because he's been unpleasant to me for years, who once played kings and queens with me and let me stab his plastic breastplate with my rubber sword, who gave me a leg up when I wanted to climb a tree and left me up there though that's not the point, who let me skid down a slope on his friend's skateboard and I fell off and gashed both my knees and he kissed them better even though they had little stones stuck in them and fresh red-blood dribbles, which did nothing to make them better but it was sweet of him and made his lips a bit bloody, who spoke to me in an Australian accent for months because I found it comical, but who now cannot entertain the idea that I'm someone worth talking to or spending time with, is going to get on a train this morning and leave, and it's more than I can bear.

'Look,' says the man in the uniform, 'either you go in or you come out, but you can't have this . . . whatever it is . . . going on over the ticket barrier.'

'But I've—' Champ waves his bank card. He's tapped in. I can't believe he's worried about his tube fare at this juncture, but the man says, 'I'll tap you out and in again – just get out of the way, mate. It's about to get busy.'

It doesn't look like it's about to get busy, but I don't say so. He taps Champ out. Champ leaves the station with me and we stand near the entrance, me holding the beard elastic and him leaning on the wall of a locked florist's shop. The wind spins the leaves in a twister then scatters the smatterings into the road. Society says it's spring, but nature is not one to abide by societal rules.

Champ's face is fury and hate. 'What do you want?'

'Don't leave me with her. Please. Please.'

'Why are you wearing my coat?'

'What?' It seems the least relevant detail when I'm in distress. 'Less rustling. Easiest to get off the hook.'

'Tsk. Put it straight back when you get in. Why are you following me? Why are you even up?'

'There were . . . I heard someone – I heard *you* going downstairs. She's . . . Champ, she's not . . . She's more than . . .' my eyes are doing the talking but Champ doesn't speak Eye. He doesn't even know the basics.

'Are you talking about Mum?' he asks.

I make the universal facial expression that says, 'of course I'm talking about her, you fatuous blobhead – who else would I be talking about?' To my surprise, he doesn't say, 'She's the last person I want to talk about' or 'Not in the mood for this right now'. Instead, for the first time in his life (probably) he's being a good listener and not walking off irritably whenever I verbalize a thought. More than anything, I want my family together and near me – meaning, Dad and Champ – but the She-Beast, She-Fiend, She-Devil, has driven them both away.

'I need to tell you something important,' I say.

His body unstiffens, and although he's not exactly being cordial, amiable, affable or the world's most prototypical podling, he replies, 'So tell me.'

37

We sit on the steps of the florist's with members of the workforce walking not especially forcefully towards the station arches on their way to work. Pigeons warble and woo. The breeze reeks of wee. Miles high in the sky, lights on a distant plane flare red. It's somewhat surreal. Not the place to explain something serious and meaningful. Not with announcements in the background reminding customers that all folded and unfolded e-scooters and e-unicycles are prohibited on all London Underground services and step-free access is not available at this station; or to our right, cyclists dismounting and de-helmeting with clinks and grunts near the disorderly row of bikes.

'That day. When we were on the bridge,' I begin. He knows which day and which bridge. Some topics need no elucidation. But that's as far as I can go for now. I pause and breathe deeply in the hope it will prevent my stomach erupting. One breath leads to another. I focus only and entirely on taking air in and blowing it out slowly through a thin mouth funnel.

Champ shivers his shoulders and rubs his hand down his

face. Although he is unbearably sad and deflated, he says, 'What happened, Jodie?'

'Jones.'

'Don't. Just don't start that—' He stands up in a huff.

'It was her fault we were late for the lesson,' I say quickly. 'She was philandering with some businessman in Caffè Nero.'

'*Philandering?*' Champ sits down again.

'Talking. Laughing. That kind of stuff.'

'Oh. Flirting. Jesus Chr— It's called flirting. Go on.'

'When she realized we were late, she blamed me – she said I should have reminded her we were in a rush. She flew into a four-finger rage. She walked out of the tube station so fast I had to run to keep up with her. She didn't wait for me. She was weaving in and out of the crowd and I thought I'd lose her and get lost, so I started running. I tripped on a paving stone and fell over hard.'

'Your knee scars.'

'My knee scars. Exactly. I started crying because it really hurt and I wailed at her to slow down and wait for me. She spun around, yanked me up hard by the arm, making that hurt as well, and hissed, 'Stop being a baby. I swear, if you don't get that scholarship, I'll really give you something to cry about.'

Champ's eyes flicker. 'Standard,' he mutters because this is typical parent behaviour. Our parent, anyway. We both know that when she's in a mood like that, we need to calm her down. Don't criticize her. Don't argue. Don't do anything that will make her lose her temper.

'I was hurt, and she didn't care. She didn't wait for me. And she was being horrible to me. So . . . I . . . so . . .'

'Buck.' Champ frowns. 'What did you do?'

'I told her I didn't want to do the stupid scholarship interview, I didn't want to go to that school and I never wanted to play the violin again.'

Champ whistles inwards. I'm astonished he's still sitting here. This is the most time we've spent together, just the two of us, in ages. 'Bad,' he says. 'Very bad. What did she do? Because she'll have done something after that.'

I press my palms to my mouth. Buzzing fills my brain and my limbs are dead weights. Panic builds, tsunami-like, in my chest. I dart to the road and retch in the gutter, but nothing comes up.

Champ, beside me in an instant, opens his backpack, unscrews his water bottle and hands it to me, saying, 'Drink'. I don't want to because of mouth germs but I do want water and I figure sometimes different rules apply and this is one of those times.

When I sit down again, Champ sits next to me and leans his shoulder against mine. He hasn't touched me willingly for as long as I can remember and he's being surprisingly kind.

'You OK?' he asks.

I gaze at the lightening sky. 'Need a minute.'

Still leaning on my arm he says, 'Take your time.'

A minute passes. Three. Maybe more. I don't know if I can tell him what happened. Will he believe me? Will anyone?

Champ closes his eyes. 'What did she do, Jodie? She did something, didn't she?'

I wait. Maybe the wave will subside. Maybe he will add 'Jones'. I'm hoping he will. After a while, I shake my head. 'I can't . . .'

Champ wraps his arm around me, nods and asks, 'Does Dad know?'

'No.'

'Well, you need to tell him. And me. Today.'

'We have an appointment with Dr Kumar at four. Just you, me and Dad. It might be a bit . . . hairy. If things go to plan.'

'What d'you mean?' He takes out a buzzing phone and gets distracted, but so do I. The phone in his hand has a blue case. His phone has a transparent case.

'Whose is that?' I ask.

'Mine. It's my other phone. So she can't . . .' He looks at me. 'What, you don't have a second phone?'

'What? No. With what money?'

'With your secret stash from your birthd— Oh, little sis. I assumed . . .' He sighs. 'You leave your official phone at the place where she thinks you are, and you take your other phone. Then you can go wherever you want, send whatever messages you want.'

I gawp at him. How did I not know this?

'So clever,' Champ says, 'yet so impractical.'

'Why didn't you tell me this?'

'Obvious. Well, maybe not to you. What do you mean, "hairy"?'

'Just come to Dr Kumar's. Please. Give me one of your phones and I'll type in the address.'

He grins. As I do it, he says, 'Listen, I'm going to stay with Tavish, and it might be for a while, but I promise I'll see you later.'

I hold on to his phone in both hands. 'Don't. Champ, please.'

'I promise you, I'll be there at four.' Champ stands, wipes the tears off my cheeks, kisses my forehead, takes the phone off me, picks up his bag and walks into the station. It's devastating to see the people you love leaving you, even if your brother is only going to stay with his boyfriend in Wimbledon for a while. I feel increasingly sick as he moves further and further away.

The uniformed man was right. It does get busy.

I watch the station entrance, numb and dazed. Then I see Champ again. 'Had to tap out,' he explains.

'What?'

'I'm walking you home. Just to the end of the road.'

The sky is lighter when we walk back so I don't strap on the beard, although wearing one is strangely liberating.

When we reach our street, he stands on the corner. 'Go,' he says, rubbing the top of my arm. 'I'll see you later.'

Even though I walk very slowly, there's only so slowly you can go. I reach our front door, and he waves at me, and leaves.

My guts are tight as Champ walks away. I consider, standing there, that the word 'guts' is one I wish to remove from my lexicon because I've yet to come across a beautiful sentence that contains it or a great writer who uses it, and as staccato and accurately onomatopoeic as 'my guts are tight' sounds with those four monosyllables and those harsh 'g' and 't' sounds, there must be a better way to phrase it.

Then I realize I don't have my key. The sole advantage of my dad sleeping in the study is that I can knock on the window in varying rhythms – from the beat of the England football chant to Beethoven's *Symphony No. 5*, which he's unlikely to get from the accuracy of my knocks, in all fairness – until he finally realizes what that infernal rapping is, gets up and lets me in.

38

The morning Champ leaves, I go back to bed and lie there shaking, crying, refusing to eat. Dad calls school to tell them I'm sick and I wail to my mother again and again that I have to see Dr Kumar. She makes a huge, noisy deal about cancelling meetings, but she books an emergency appointment with him at two-thirty that afternoon. It's not because she's worried about me; it's because she can't wait to show him my current behaviour and how exasperating it is, and that suits me fine.

My ornamental shoe is missing. The one Grandma Tara gave me. I loved that more than anything. I knew I should have hidden it.

I go back to sleep for a while and when I wake up, Dad helps me out of bed and we go down to the kitchen, where he microwaves some porridge because my mother won't let him cook oats in a pan, as he'd like. Then he makes me hot chocolate from a sachet that he seems to have secretly stashed in his study. 'Drink it quick. Before she comes back. I'll wash the cup and put it away. It's not hot – I added milk.'

He makes himself a coffee. Coffee smells of earthy, caramel caves but it tastes of putrid cat poo. Beer is a fizzy, fermenting, sour-sock drink. I know because I once had a sip of Dad's. I wonder if I'll like either of them when I'm an adult. Dad told me he trained himself to like them when he was at university. The idea of training yourself to like the taste of something that makes you gag, initially, is puzzling. Imagine the many, many times you'd have to drink it, loathing every mouthful, until your tastebuds surrender, die, and decide to accept it.

He's only drinking one of those two putrid beverages this morning. He brews his coffee in a filter jug, which he's only allowed to do if there's no trace of a single coffee ground on the counter, so he wipes it about four times, and waits a while before pushing the filter down so the jug doesn't spurt. When he does push it, he does it slowly, his hairy knuckles resembling large fleshy spiders.

There is a system, process, procedure and technique to it that I enjoy watching and when I mention this, he says, 'Ach, wait till you see espresso machines. Works of art. And delicious coffee.'

'Why don't you have one?'

He makes a face and I gather he's not permitted. The Dictator. Who's she to say what Dad can and can't have in his own home? Mind you, he had no say in the decorative and furnishing choices, either, despite hailing from a family of wallpaper designers, curtain makers and upholsterers.

'I'll go halves with Champ for your birthday,' I say, handing him the empty hot chocolate mug.

As he washes it he says, 'The one I like costs five-hundred pounds.'

'We definitely won't then.'

He laughs. 'Understandable.'

'Maybe we can contribute a fiver each and you pay the rest.'

Dad chuckles, dries the mug and says, 'Tell me about this morning. Where's my son?'

He drinks his coffee and I eat my porridge and I tell him about Champ leaving practically in the middle of the night. 'I followed him in the dark to the station.'

'You should have woken me, Jodie. That's dangerou—'

'Jones. I wore a strap-on beard.'

'This part of London is—'

'But it's already happened, so there's no point in telling me off now.'

He admits defeat with a lip twist and takes another sip. I mentioned the footsteps on the stairs, the easier coat to unhook, the hoodie and holdall identification process, the streets, the man in the station and the strap-on beard removal, Champ's conundrum of tapping in, and the crucially important element, which is that Champ has gone to Tavish's for a while. I leave out the part about the bridge, the retching and my mother.

I've finished the porridge and Dad washes and dries up the bowl, even though we have a dishwasher. He doesn't load it right, so she doesn't let him use it. I don't know where she is, and I don't ask because I don't want to know.

Dad is now wearing his achingly concerned face for Champ. He calls him, but Champ doesn't answer so he leaves him a message and a voice note. I want to mention Champ's other phone, but this might come in useful for me later so it remains a secret. Dad is uncharacteristically restless. This new development has rankled him. Is he worried about leaving now because he knows it'll just be me and her if he does? I hope so, because that's causing me some hysteria. Or is he worried that his only son, who is almost seventeen and therefore a minor and currently in the middle of his A levels, has gone to stay with a friend, who is also a minor, indefinitely?

Dad can see I'm upset. The tears and sobbing are surely a clue. To cheer me up, he says he's found a sentence he thinks I'll like, and he manoeuvres me by the shoulders into the study.

'When I was younger,' he says as he sits me down, 'I loved Jeeves and Wooster.'

I blow my nose on the tissue he offers me. 'Were they your cats?'

'No, they're—'

'Dogs.'

'No, no. They're—'

'Men. Are you also gay? Is that what you're telling me?'

'How about letting me finish my sentence.'

'Sorry.'

'They're books. Written by P. G. Wodehouse about a wealthy fop called Bertie Wooster. He's a bit dim but he has a clever and eloquent butler called Jeeves, who Bertie calls his "man".'

'Is *he* gay?'

'No one's gay as far as I know. "My man" was a way of saying "my butler" or "my manservant".'

'*Manservant?* What's a fop?'

'A dandy.'

'What's a "dandy"?'

'Do you want to read the sentence or not?'

'Yes. Did you have to train yourself to like Jeeves and Wooster as well, or did you like them right away?'

Dad chuckles. 'Always found them funny. Picking them up again to find you a funny part has cheered me up no end. Here, I wrote one down.'

He puts his large fleshy spider into his jeans pocket and hands me a piece of paper. There are quite a few sentences, not just one.

'Which is the sentence you like?'

'You'll work it out. Or perhaps you'll like a different one.'

'OK.'

I start reading.

I had left the old two-seater in the road, and I could just see the top part of it. And at this moment the summer stillness was broken by the tooting of its horn, and I buzzed to the gate with all possible speed for fear some fiend in human shape was scratching my paint. Arriving at my destination, I found a small boy in the front seat, pensively squeezing the bulb, and was about to administer one on the side of the head when I recognized Chuffy's cousin, Seabury, and stayed the hand.

'Hallo,' he said.

'What ho,' I replied.

My manner was reserved. The memory of that lizard in my bed still lingered. I don't know if you have ever leaped between the sheets, all ready for a spot of sleep, and received an unforeseen lizard up the left pyjama leg? It is an experience that puts its stamp on a man.

I laugh and Dad laughs, too.

'What d'you think?' Dad asks.

'Why is he squeezing a "bulb"?'

'Car horn.'

'Ah.'

I tell him I enjoy the sibilant calm of 'summer stillness', the pace speeding up and the comic formality of 'administer one on the side of the head'. I like the long 'a' vowel sounds of 'stayed the hand'. But I especially like the energy of the verb and the 'e's in 'leaped between the sheets', and the clipped sibilance of 'a spot of sleep', neither of which sounds like sleep is about to happen any time soon. I like the lightness of the 'e's in 'received' and 'unforeseen', and then the jolly, liquid alliteration, definite article and unexpectedness of 'a lizard up the left pyjama leg.' The aristocratic poshness should make it seem conventional, stiff, old-fashioned, prim, stately and a smidgeon Downton Abbey, I continue, but it's really quite disarming.

'Blimey,' Dad says. 'I just like the lizard line. I couldn't even articulate why. You're really quite discerning with your appreciation of sentences.'

'Thank you.' I fold the piece of paper and slip it into my hoodie pocket next to the strap-on beard. It's not what I'd have chosen but it's great all the same. 'I was hoping for one that made me smile next.'

'Wodehouse is just the ticket,' he said. 'Don't worry about Champ. I'll talk to him. It'll be fine.'

It won't be fine, and we know it. 'Don't tell her I followed him, or about the strap-on beard'.

'I'll tell her he left early this morning but that he's safe.' He kisses me on the side of the head and says, 'I need to check there's no coffee grains.'

We hear the door. My mother is back so we walk to the hall

for the usual welcome rigmarole. She's wearing work clothes and doesn't say hello; instead, she mutters, 'This is the worst day of my entire life. I've been crying since I woke up and no one gives a monkey's. Where is he? What? Why are you looking at me like that?'

Dad is being unusually firm. He stands in the hall looking at her. He doesn't mention the relevance of monkeys, but I would have. There's a pause before he says, 'Did you really post about it, Monica?'

'Don't provoke me, Elliot. Everyone knows you overreact to the slightest—'

'Answer the question. Did you post about Champ and Tavish?'

'Oh, what if I did? It's true, isn't it? More importantly, did you see the comments people wrote? Unbelievable! My life has fallen apart and they're criticizing *me*? Where's *my* sympathy?'

Dad frowns. She drops her head into her hands and cries, 'Someone save me from all the idiots I'm surrounded by. All the sacrifices I make, and do I get the slightest recognition? I might as well be invisible.'

'Monica—'

'Don't "Monica" me! My life has upended.' She moans and wails and says a hundred sentences that the sky didn't need, and I turn my mind off and imagine an empty dome of silent birds. 'Go and get ready,' she says to me, eventually, even though we don't need to leave for an hour and a half. 'And don't show me up by wearing a hoodie or stupid clips in your hair. Be down here at two.'

I roll my eyes behind her back. Fine. I'd rather wear my pjs. It's what Dr Kumar tends to wear anyway.

As she rummages in her handbag, she says to Dad, 'Those comments. They've knocked me sideways, they really have. People are so heartless. Call Champ and tell him to take a taxi home. I'll deal with him after I unfriend all the trolls I thought were my friends.'

I leave Dad to tell my mother Champ isn't coming home, especially not after her public outing of him on social media. I climb the stairs to chat with P.G. Wodehouse in my wardrobe, cry in private about Champ and wait for the next stage of my plan.

38

'Jodie Jones,' Dr Kumar says, as if speaking to a tiny lemon-yellow moth resting on a wilting, pink pansy petal, 'I hear you haven't been feeling well.'

'I'm fine,' I say, causing my mother to glare at me with headlight eyes, which I pretend not to see. Dr Kumar's trousers are fawn-coloured, his jumper pistachio and V-necked. He seems to have invested in some appropriate psychiatrist's workwear from a Psychiatrist's Workwear Catalogue. I wonder what prompted the change.

'Oh,' he said. 'I was under the impression you—'

'I'm better now.'

'Re-ally,' my mother says, smoke seeping from her nostrils. 'This morning you couldn't move, your life over because your brother went on a tube across London, blah, blah blah; and now you're completely fine?'

'Yes.'

She is displeased and this pleases me, but there's a long way to go before I feel pleased overall. My Part A ruse has worked to get us here. Now I need to make Part B happen.

'Right. Er ... Well, in that case,' Dr Kumar says, looking from her to me, 'let's talk about Champ.'

My mother tells Dr Kumar that Champ's a sneaky liar and she's always known it: he's lazy, ungrateful and spoilt, and that I am, too, and worse. Dr Kumar asks my mother how she feels about Champ being gay and she says, 'He's not gay. He's looking for attention because Jodie gets it all.'

I notice a subtle change in his eyes, but Dr Kumar doesn't rise to it. Instead, he clasps his hands and holds his knee with them. 'I see,' he says. 'That's worth exploring. I'd like a better picture of your childhoods. Jodie Jones, could you tell me some early memories?'

I keep my part brief and show zero emotion. 'I don't remember being a small child.' I want to add one of my favourite lines from *Alice in Wonderland*: 'It's no use going back to yesterday, because I was a different person then', but I'm aware I'm in a psychotherapist's office and he'd have things to say about that.

'Mrs Jones,' he says, turning to her. 'Would you mind filling me in?'

My mother visibly grows now she's been given the supremacy to speak. She laughs a tinkling laugh, and says, 'Horrific pregnancy. Very complicated birth. She managed to wind the cord around her neck. They had to carve my stomach in half to get her out because she wouldn't just come out like everyone else.'

As if I did it deliberately. And it's called a caesarean. Lots of women have them. *Carve my stomach in half?* Really?

'Difficult from the start,' she adds. And after a resentful head-shake, 'Their character is there from the very beginning, isn't it? You should know, being a psychiatrist.' And she snide-laughs again.

I wonder what he makes of her. People consider her

impressive, beautiful, charming, a force to be reckoned with, a fireball, if a little strict. But he's hard to assess.

'When I took her out in the buggy, people would stop to look at her, jealous I had such a pretty baby. And she was clever – much cleverer than other babies her age. Aware, and doing things way ahead of the curve. She barely stopped crying, though, constantly bothered about something. Extremely irritating baby. And when she got bigger, she made my life hell. Every day she'd pull all the books off the lowest shelf and every night I had to get Elliot to put them back. In the end, I told the cleaner to move them up a shelf or two so she couldn't reach.'

'Made my life hell' is not an agreeable phrase, and it's not true, either. Some people experience gruesome, macabre, unspeakable, sickening, horrific, atrocious ordeals in their lives. Ordering your husband and your paid help to reshelve books in your warm, safe living room is an unacceptable comparison.

'D'you know, she used to sit in the middle of the pile and hold a book up to her face, pretending to read,' my mother says with a derisive laugh.

'I *was* reading.'

She snorts, as if I'm all of these things: asinine, imbecilic, fatuous, doltish, cretinous, inane and ignominious, which is a word that means disgraceful and undignified. She doesn't say 'ignominious' though. Probably because saying 'ignominious' aloud, mid-sentence, is a challenge for anyone with a normally functioning mouth. Still, 'ignominious' is more precise.

Dr Kumar observes us like an ornithologist, which is someone who studies birds. Why 'orni' and not 'birdi-thologist'? I remind myself to look it up. I want to tell Dr Kumar that Dad was the one who read to me; he would do it until he'd had enough, even though I hadn't and was still asking for more.

'And her primary-school years?' Dr Kumar asks.

'Obedient, back then. Sweet when she put her mind to it. She was good at ballet until she was seven, but I stopped taking her because she couldn't be bothered to do it properly.'

Interestingly, she doesn't mention the violin.

So I do.

'She forced me to do ballet,' I say, my face displaying none of the emotions erupting across my torso, 'and I hated it. She forced me to play the violin, too.'

'Rubbish,' she says. 'You loved them both. You can't remember anything at all, so you fabricate an entirely new past. One in which I am the baddie. Your brain's a blur . . . a total fog.'

'I hated them both and you know it. Especially the violin.'

'I'm worried about her, Doctor,' she says. 'I really am. She has no concept of reality She makes things up all the time. No, she does. Can't you tell? You're the psychiatrist. Thought you'd be more perceptive than this.'

'Mrs Jones, would you mind . . . ?' Dr Kumar says, delightfully lightly, considering. His eyeballs move more than is customary, like he's calculating a mental maths question in his parietal lobe, which I think is the region of the brain where numbers are calculated. I wonder in which part of the brain my thinking about thinking happens. It's pleasing to think of where my thinking might be happening, and to think I might be thinking about how I think in a different region to where the initial thinking happens, depending on what I'm thinking.

The atmosphere in the room is electrically charged. Dr Kumar is serious now. 'Mrs Jones, would you tell me yourself what happened on the bridge that day?'

A crack of panic.

My stomach
        heaves.

    Blood
    floods
    from
    my
     head.

'I've already told Dr Haliki and ten doctors before her. Maybe you should do your job properly and check your notes.'

'I have checked my notes, but I'd like to hear it from you.'

'You *know* what happened. Everyone knows what happened. We were late for a very important violin lesson to prepare for a music scholarship audition at St Paul's. All the . . . It all kicked off, and in the chaos, we got separated. But do you know what? She didn't get hurt, I found her within the hour, it was four years ago, and it's over. We are all fine. This ongoing drama she's creat—'

'No,' I grunt, holding my abdomen. 'That's not what happened.' But I can't say more than that. The nausea is intense.

The i n s e c t s
                swarm back
                  into my body
                buzzing pounding seething
                  wings beating
                    savage ferocious
                    incensed

I bend double in the chair and try to breathe.

'We've been doing some work, lately,' Dr Kumar tells my mother, 'Jodie Jones and me. I'm going to read you the account she managed to write down in our last session.' Dr Kumar picks up the sheet of paper. My eyes clang wide and I bolt upright. I want to leave the room. I need to leave the room. I know what's coming. I feel sick. I can't do this. My eyes tell him that in very clear nonwords.

His eyes meet mine and say, you can. Stay with me, Jodie Jones.

He clears his throat and I swallow hard.

    My palms sweat.   I'm itchy.

        Myneckfeelstight.

'This is what Jodie Jones has written. *We were late for the audition and my mother blamed me. She said I should have reminded her we were in a rush. She marched out of the tube station and I had to run to keep up with her. I thought I'd lose her, so I started running, tripped over and hurt my knees.*'

My mother sneers, shaking her head. 'Not true, for a start.'

'If you could ... let me read on,' Dr Kumar says with a frown. '*It really hurt and I was crying. She spun around, yanked me up, hurting my arm, and said she'd really give me something to cry about if I didn't get the scholarship.*'

My mother is shaking her head in disbelief, and smiling. 'I did nothing of the kind. Of *course* I waited for her. Do you really think I would—'

I want him to stop because this is the hardest thing I've ever done, but I also need him to carry on so I take forced breaths and try to keep calm.

'I told her I didn't want to do the audition and I never wanted to play the violin again. Then we heard shouting. People started running in panic out of the building on the other side of the bridge. The people in front of us turned in fear and ran the other way, past me, back towards the tube station. I didn't understand was happening. She disappeared and I froze. She didn't come back for me, and I couldn't see her in the crowd. Cars and buses screeched and braked. Horns were blaring. Then I heard screaming.'

It's strange to hear my words coming from his mouth. I feel detached from it. Like it happened to someone else. So why is my body convulsing?

'Utter tosh,' my mother says, incredulous. 'What's amazing is that you believe her. None of that happened.'

'All of that happened,' I say, my voice small, my mouth tense.

'I'll read on, if I may.' Dr Kumar doesn't look at her. *'There were sirens. I heard shouting, swearing, then gunshots. I didn't know what to do. I wanted my mum, but I couldn't see her. Then I saw her up ahead. I gasped and ran towards her, shouting, "Mummy! Mummy!" I grabbed hold of her arm and said, "Mummy, help. I'm scared. I'm scared. Mummy. What's happening?" She said, "Get off me," and wrenched my hands off her arm. Then she walked away and left me standing there on my own.'*

The   i n s e c t s
               hiss andhorde
My head crackles and splits
       from my ears to crown
       Bile
       rises.

My mouth
    fills   with   fluid
        Think
I'm going to be sick.

> *Aurora,* I think.
> *Flibbertigibbet.*
> *Propinquity.*
> *I slit the sheet, the sheet I slit, and*
>   *on the slitted sheet I sit.*

My mother turns to me and hisses, 'Liar. We were together the entire time. That never happened and you—'

Dr Kumar speaks over her: '*A man shouted, "Get that girl out of here!" And a huge policeman all in black with a helmet, a mask and a machine gun across his chest grabbed me by the waist and ran with me in the other direction. Over his shoulder I could see the man they'd shot lying on the ground. The policeman put me down, held me by the shoulders facing the other way and said, "It's OK, love. Look at me. It's OK. I've got you. Who were you with? Your mum? Were you with your mum?" I nodded and he said, "We'll find her," and he took me to a police station with the siren blaring.*'

My mother is unnervingly still. Unblinking.

I, on the other hand, find it hard to keep my legs from shaking. I snatch at lines to keep me steady.

> *My name is Ozymandias, King of Kings;*
> *Look on my Works, ye Mighty, and despair!*

Dr Kumar says, 'That's not the end of the story, though. Is it, Mrs Jones?'

'What are you talking about?' she asks. 'More lies? What else has she made up?'

Dr Kumar continues: '*It felt like hours later when she picked me up from the police station. She ran in, thanking them, crying, acting as though she was so relieved to see me.*' Dr Kumar keeps reading, '*When she hugged me, she whispered in my ear, "You'll pay for this." Then she smiled and thanked them, and I had to walk out of there holding her hand.*'

I feel the implosion inside and slam my hand over my mouth. I've managed not to chuck, but I don't know how long I can keep it down. Come on. Come on. Breathe. Think of a poem.

I wandered lonely as a cloud . . .

'Oh. My. GOD. Of course I didn't do that,' my mother shouts, and then she laughs, as if it's the most ludicrous idea ever voiced. 'Why do you believe her? This is insane. She's mentally ill and you believe her over me! I'd be careful if I were y—'

'What I think,' Dr Kumar says, 'is that Jodie Jones angered you, and because of that you left her alone in the middle of a violent and dangerous terror attack—'

'How *dare* you?' she says innocently but there is menace beneath. 'I did *nothing* of the kind.'

She's so good at this. What if he believes her? What then?

That floats on high o'er vales and hills,

'She was a child, Mrs Jones. Your daughter was ten years old. She was vulnerable, she was terrified, and she needed you.'

My stomach
    spasms.
    Eyeballs   throb.
Saliva   oozes   in   my mouth.

Something something *milky way* . . . something
  Something something *sprightly dance.*
And then my heart with pleasure fills,
And dances with the daffodils.

'Oh, please,' she says. 'What do you know about parenting?'

'Mothers protect their young, even at the risk of their own lives. Her trauma doesn't only stem from witnessing the attack. You abandoned your child when she needed you most. She could have been killed, and you walked away and left her there alone. That is the root of Jodie's trauma.'

My skin bursts into flames.

'It was her fault!' my mother screams. 'I wouldn't have done it if she'd—'

Dr Kumar's eyes meet mine. He knew this is what happened. He guessed, more or less, what she did on the bridge. He wrote it down, handed it to me to read, and even though he'd got some details wrong, I burst into tears. He gave me time and nodded and handed me a pen and I rewrote it accurately, even though it was so, so hard and the pen broke the paper twice. Then I threw up and we left.

'Oh, Jodie Jones,' Dr Kumar says quietly.

His eyes are infinitely kind. All I can think is, some parents love their children more than anything. My mother loves anything more than she loves me.

'"Oh, Jodie Jones" what?' My mother's screech is derisive. She pushes her shoulders back, her eyes wild, her mouth hard, her nostrils flaring. 'You don't know what I have to deal with!' She is talking to him, presumably, but she's looking at me.

She's close. Just a little further. My mind reminds itself of a line from Mary Shelley's *Frankenstein*: 'Beware; for I am fearless, and therefore powerful.'

Fearlessness is what's needed. I hold on to the arm of the sofa and say, 'Why don't you tell him you bully, and belittle, and humiliate me? Tell him you control every aspect of my life because your main concern is how I make you look.'

'Liar!' She grabs my metal water bottle from the table and launches it me. It hits the wall near my head and bounces off, making a loud thunk. I was expecting her to shout and scream but I was not expecting that. I'm pleased to note my bottle is remarkably robust.

'Hey! Hey! Stop that!' Dr Kumar, shocked, staggered, slams his papers on the table. 'Mrs Jones, calm down.'

She shifts to the front of her chair, her lips thin and white and taut. 'She has twisted the facts, as always,' she breathes. 'How dare you accuse me of abandoning my child. There is no better mother alive than me. I do everything for my children. I gave up my life for them. No one will ever care about them as much as I do.'

Nearly there.

'You?' I say, a crash of chaos of my head, my voice shaking but clear, 'You are cruel and abusive, and you've only ever cared about yourself.'

And then she blows.

She bolts off her chair and lunges at me. I leap up and throw my arms across my face to block her. Dr Kumar is on his feet but she's faster than he is. She grabs my right arm, slamming it across my neck and pinning me to the wall. 'Abusive? I'll show you abusive. How DARE you?' She slams me hard against the wall, winding me. 'You owe me everything, you ungrateful— You're mental. How DARE you spread lies about me?'

Dr Kumar wrenches her hand off my arm, pushes her backwards and stands in front of me with his arms out wide. She doesn't even see him. He's nothing to her. She springs forward again, lashing out, trying to hit me as Dr Kumar bats his arms around. She mainly hits him, but through his arms she grabs and yanks my hair, pulling my head hard to one side. 'OW!' I wail.

'Sectioned! That's what you should be,' she screams, pulling harder. 'Sectioned!'

Dr Kumar grabs her wrist and shouts, 'Mrs Jones. Let go of her! NOW!' But my mother pulls harder until I'm sideways, my scalp on fire. I can't believe this. I knew she'd roar. I didn't think she'd go for me.

Poppy arrives at the door, wide eyed. 'I've called security,' she shouts and then barks into the phone at her ear, 'get the police!' She runs in, helps Dr Kumar prise my mother's fingers from my hair and pushes my mother back so hard, she falls on the floor. All the while, Poppy's still on the 999-call stating the address and situation, and through her bent arm, I see Dr Kumar, palms out, blocking me from my mother who is getting up and screaming at him and Poppy, 'I'll sue you for assault. I'll finish you. You wait. You have no idea who you're dealing with! As for you,' she says, lunging forward to me again. Poppy jumps in front of me, and so does Dr Kumar. I stand still and silent behind them, gazing at the mayhem. At least I don't feel sick any more.

'Jodie!' Dr Kumar barks with urgency. 'Jodie!'

'My name is Jodie Jones.'

'Out! Get out of here. Quickly!'

My mother goes for me again, shrieking, 'Everyone thinks you're so clever. I'm the genius! You're nothing!' Saliva sparks out of her mouth, and her shirt is out of her skirt and skewed to one side. She's the one who looks deranged. Poppy, phone in hand, is acting as a human shield and kungfu windmill, her arms flailing up and down to protect me from my mother's vicious lashing hands. 'How dare you shame me?' my mother yells. 'No one behaves like this with me and gets away with it. I should have aborted you when I had the chance!'

She is a poltergeist. She is potatoes diced. She is a comma splice.

'Mrs Jones! Stop it!' Dr Kumar shouts. 'Stop!'

As I back towards the door, my mother starts shouting obscenities. I clap my hands over my ears so as not to hear.

The Jabberwock, with eyes of flame,
Came whiffling through the tulgey wood...

Dr Kumar shouts at her to calm down and Poppy shouts at me to wait outside.

'I would love to wait outside,' I reply, and duck out with my hands over my ears, avoiding the swinging arms, and stagger as far from the office door as I physically can. Something crashes in the room and Poppy bolts out to stand in front of me, as does Dr Kumar, as my mother, bag swinging, storms out, hissing, 'You wait! You just wait! You've seen nothing yet. Nobody does this to me.'

A security man arrives, panting, saying the police are on their way.

My mother shoves past him and she's gone.

After giving me a glass of lemon barley water and two wafers from his drawer, which I wasn't aware he had or I'd have bugged him for them earlier for sure, Dr Kumar calls my dad and suggests he and Champ come a little earlier than planned.

40

It's strange to be in Dr Kumar's office with Dad and Champ instead of my mother. Champ is wearing a jumper that must belong to Tavish: dark blue, woolly, round necked. It's amusing that he has a boyfriend and he's wearing his clothes – not because he has a boyfriend and not a girlfriend, but because another human being (aside from Becca) is attracted to Champ, and for the longest time, I've only thought of him as a fatuous gnat and not romance material. More importantly, he's making a micro-choice – or is it a macro-choice – by choosing what he wants to wear for once, and I like that.

Dr Kumar has calmed down. He was ruffled for a long while. I think the third cup of tea helped, and my insistence on testing him on the capitals of the world. Always takes your mind off things, in my experience.

'Great to meet you,' Dad says, shaking his hand. 'Elliot Zhang. This is my son, Champ.'

'Charlie,' Champ corrects him as he shakes Dr Kumar's hand and sits down. 'Don't want to be Champ any more.'

'Oh . . . right,' Dad replies. 'OK. Sure. Might take me a while to get that in my, you know,' he points to his temple, 'but I'll get there.'

'I'm still Jodie Jones,' I point out. 'In case anyone's wondering.'

Dad's eyes smile but it's a sad shocked kind of smile, which is a thing, I now realize. He's sitting on an unexciting sofa beside me, and Champ – Charlie – is on the other. Dr Kumar, perched on his yellow chair, crosses his legs and his hands rest on his knees, like butterflies landing on a flower. The butterflies are little more skittish than usual and the flower is not quite as still as other knee blooms have been.

'Good to finally meet you both,' he says, and clears his throat. I wonder whether he will mention that I called my brother a noxious rectum boil, but I hope that in the spirit of patient confidentiality, he'll hold back.

As Dr Kumar explains what has just happened, Dad's face buckles with emotion and his head falls into his hands. Charlie stares at the wall, his knuckles white. Dr Kumar lets my dad and Charlie ask the many questions they need to ask and then he gets to the crux of it all.

'As you know,' Dr Kumar says, 'I've been meeting with Jodie Jones, here, and with Mrs Jones, for a few weeks now.' I'm grateful he says my full name and I soften in my seat.

'Yes,' Dad says, sitting forwards on the sofa. 'Jodie's always been, well, Jodie, really. I mean, the . . . er . . . the incident,' he clears his throat, 'didn't *cause* her to behave differently, obviously, but she's definitely developed certain behaviours since then, presumably to cope with the trauma. It would be good to hear more about that, if . . . er . . . if this is the right time.'

'Dad. My name is Jodie Jones.'

'Sorry,' Dad says, and squashes his face into a sorry-really-sorry scrunch. He glances at Dr Kumar and says, 'But I interrupted you. Please go on.'

'No problem,' Dr Kumar says. 'We'll come to the coping mechanisms in good time, but first off, I should say that I have no hesitation in giving a positive diagnosis, especially after what happened this afternoon, and that's what I've invited you here to discuss.'

Champ-now-Charlie lifts his eyes to mine, but Dad's remain on Dr Kumar's face. I know what Dad's thinking. He's aware his second child is not neurotypical and has PTSD and possibly something more, but he'd like to know what the 'possibly something more' might be that's causing her strange and troubling behaviour.

'A positive diagnosis? Of what?' Dad asks.

'Oh ... sorry. I specialise in NPD. I thought ... you ... were aware ... ?' Dr Kumar notes the blank faces of Dad and Charlie, and adds, 'Narcissistic Personality Disorder.'

Dad frowns at me, perplexed. 'Really? Gosh.' He turns to Dr Kumar. 'I mean, I wouldn't say Jodie has—'

'Sorry,' Dr Kumar says, stopping him there with a raised hand. 'Not Jodie. Your wife.'

Dad stares at him. 'Sorry?' He looks from me to Dr Kumar to Charlie and back to Dr Kumar, his head jerking like a harried bird's. 'I'm ... you've lost me. You've been seeing Jodie, not Monica.'

'I *have* been seeing Jodie—'

'Jones,' I cry loudly, because they all seem to have forgotten.

'I have been seeing Jodie Jones, but only because she had concerns about her mother.'

Dad is unambiguously confused.

'Jodie Jones,' Dr Kumar says. 'Perhaps you'd like to elucidate?'

Yes, actually, I would like to elucidate because 'elucidate' is an enchanting word and because seeing the bewilderment on my dad's face is torturous. 'A few months ago,' I begin, 'I realized that it couldn't be normal, how she behaved on the bridge. How she behaves every day, with you, with us, with everyone else. I know there's not really such thing as "normal" but I know a normal-ish mother wouldn't act like that. So, when I had my phone one afternoon, I searched online for mental-health disorders, personality disorders, behavioural disorders, that kind of thing. I thought she might be a psychopath, but when I read about the traits, it didn't match.'

Dad shakes his head, perplexed. I'll admit, 'I thought my mother was a psychopath' is not a sentence one usually says in a tone of neutral frankness, so I appreciate his disbelief. Charlie's eyes don't leave mine but there's alarm in the way he holds himself. I continue, because it's not as if I can stop now, micro-choice or no micro-choice. 'I looked up sociopath but that wasn't her, either. I kept reading and searching, and eventually, I read something and thought, this is it. This is her. Definitely.'

I pause, because Dad has to digest it thus far. I'm not sure about 'thus'. I like it and it seems very Jane Austen, but it's also a tad knobby in this century. I must read more Jane Austen books to see if she actually wrote it, or I just think she did. I carry on. 'I looked up therapists that specialise in that disorder but not exclusively.'

'I'm a general psychiatrist,' Dr Kumar adds helpfully, 'but I specialise in NPD.'

'I don't . . . understand,' Dad says, looking from Dr Kumar to me and back again.

'People with Narcissistic Personality Disorder rarely seek therapy,' Dr Kumar says. 'They either don't know they have it, or if they do, they won't accept it and don't notice or care about the effect their conduct has on others.'

Dad's head is shaking slowly, and his hands span out to face the ceiling in a gesture of helpless discombobulation.

Charlie figures it out, though. 'So . . . you played up at school and invented an obsession with words to annoy Mum so much that she'd make appointments for you to see Dr Kumar. When all the time, you were bringing her to see him. To find out if she has it.'

'Precisely, Charlie,' Dr Kumar says, nodding vigorously.

I fight the urge to say it's not an invented obsession, thank you, because that's not the important part of today.

'Hang on. Hang on. Wait. Let me get this straight,' Dad's hands make a clearing in front of him. It's quite visual, really. '*You* were bringing *Mum* to see Dr Kumar?' Dad asks.

For an intelligent person he takes a while. 'Yes, Dad.'

Dad is blinking more times than is biologically natural. He is still shaking his head. It's a lot to take in, to be fair. 'Blimey. That's quite astonishing. And . . . has she?' he asks Dr Kumar. 'Got it?'

'Well, there are diagnostic criteria for NPD, and she would need to fulfil five from the list, but from what I've seen I would have no doubt in saying she does. At least five. If not all of them.'

Dad sits back and blows air from his cheeks. 'Whoa. I . . . I don't know much about it. Isn't it just, you know, a big ego? Could you . . . I mean, what is it exactly?'

Dr Kumar nods. 'Well, it's a spectrum so not everyone behaves in the same way, but people with NPD tend to be excessively absorbed with their own needs. Their relationships are usually superficial – to gain admiration, mainly. They feed off what we call a "supply" of attention, and to get that, they often neglect the needs of those who depend on them.'

Dad lapses into shocked silence. Champ – Charlie – is staring at the floor. Dr Kumar is leaning forward. The whole scene has a filmic, thriller dimension. The kind of film with dramatic music and camera angles that change direction too quickly.

'They tend to have fantasies of success, power, or fame,' Dr Kumar goes on, 'and a strong sense of entitlement. They envy other people and their achievements and think other people should envy them. They might believe they are special or unique; they lack empathy, can't take criticism well, if at all, and don't take responsibility for their behaviour.'

Dad's hand covers his mouth.

'I'm sorry,' Dr Kumar says. 'This is hard to hear. Can I get you—'

'No, no,' Dad mumbles. 'Please go on.'

'Well, they find it hard to show genuine emotion, so as your wife, any affection she may have shown you would mainly have been driven by her own need for adoration. She may have bombarded you with love early on but then ignored and devalued you. As a parent, she violated boundaries, and showed love when Champ – sorry, Charlie – and Jodie Jones did things to please her, but then withdrew it when they didn't.'

'God,' Dad says, after a short while. 'That's her to a T.' He smiles but it's not a happy smile. He looks like he might cry as well.

'Would you like me to . . . Shall I stop for a minute to let you process that?' Dr Kumar asks softly.

Dad sits forward, clears his throat and rubs his thighs. 'No, no. Please go on.'

'Narcissism in mothers is my specific field of research, actually, which is why Jodie Jones wanted to bring Monica to see me.'

Dad pushes his hand through his hair and leaves it there, like it's stuck. I'm not sure if he's blinked for the last five minutes. Dr Kumar, on the other hand, is using his long eyelashes almost artistically. Having only really been half alive for the last two years, Dad seems strangely energised by this discovery. 'This is . . . I mean . . . Bloody hell.'

Charlie regards me in a way that, if I didn't know him better, conveys admiration.

'Jodie Jones developed scenarios in our sessions to try to showcase her mother's heated behaviour and unkind comments towards her. Some aspects of narcissism tend to be predictable, you see. I'd more or less confirmed it, to my mind, anyway, and then Jodie Jones constructed a situation earlier this afternoon to make Mrs Jones angry so I could see an outburst for myself. It went far beyond what either of us expected and got violent, unfortunately. It was very upsetting, I'm afraid.' He pauses and adds, 'Your wife was physically abusive, and said things no mother should ever say to her child. I'm desperately sorry for that.'

He really is. I wonder if he'll get struck off or whatever, but I hope not.

'From what I can gather,' he says, 'your wife has been mentally and emotionally abusing Jodie Jones for a long while. And if I'm not mistaken, both of you as well. Possibly physically, too, towards you, Elliot.'

The air in the room is electric. I've never known what that meant until now but it's a thing, I can confirm. Dr Kumar gives Dad time to compose himself and hands him a box of tissues.

'So . . . like,' Charlie says, his lips colourless. 'What happens now?'

'For an official diagnosis I'd need to work with your mother further to carry out tests and procedures, but after today, I doubt she'd agree to that. My main concern, though, is to get the right help for you. You've suffered abuse. You and your father, and especially Jodie.' After a micro-pause, he adds, 'Jones.' Which I'm indebted to him for. 'And with abuse inevitably comes trauma. Especially after what your wife did on the bridge.'

'Wait . . .' Dad says in alarm. 'What do you mean? What did she do on the bridge?'

Dr Kumar's sessions are usually an hour, but I have a feeling this one might be longer. I'm not convinced Dad should know this right now, or ever, but Dr Kumar evidently thinks he should because he asks Poppy to make Dad a cup of tea, gives me some noise-cancelling headphones to wear, and then tells him and shows him my written account.

Dad is crying quite dramatically by the time Dr Kumar has finished. His hands are over his eyes and he's sobbing vast hard breaths.

I take the headphones off and lay them on the table. Charlie gets up and stretches. I get worried he's about to leave, but instead he walks over to me and sits on the edge of my chair. He puts his arm around me, pulls me close and says, 'I've been such a bastard to you.'

'You have.'

He laughs. 'I really have.'

I don't realize my hands are balled into fists until Champ reaches over and unfurls them. He holds my fingers in his, and although they're cold and clammy, I don't pull away.

Minutes, maybe hours later, Charlie shakes his head and says, 'No wonder.' He doesn't say what the 'no wonder' relates to. My mind runs riot through passageways of possibility. No wonder what?

Unhooking his arm from my shoulders, he links his left arm through my right and says, 'Jodie Jones?'

Finally, he's used both names. Finally. Halleluiah. 'What?'

'I wish I'd been there,' he says. 'To protect you. I'd have done everything I could to get you away from there.'

'Me too,' says Dad, his face a crumpled mess. 'Me too.'

For as long as I can remember, I have not publicly shown emotion about the incident, what my mother did to me or how she's treated me since. My wardrobe knows, and once, two years ago, I let my guard down at Becca's. But now, in Dr Kumar's office, seeing the pain in Dad's eyes, with Charlie's arm in mine, and with the truth aired and exposed and freed, I feel a hinge unclick, and finally let go.

I know it's not a crying competition with Dad, but if it was, I would have won.

Once she's had oceans of tea, spoken to the police and reported today's earlier events for the umpteenth time, Poppy seems quite lively, which I suppose a soap-opera drama in your place of work can do to someone; especially someone who, it turns out, is an unexpected superhero. She's curiously charming, even flirtatious, with Dad and it makes me look at him as a man instead of as my dad, and I see that he is nice-looking. Kind eyes. A sweet smile. He's a bit crinkled, a smidgeon old, and a tad deflated and depressed. But who wouldn't be after all those years with my mother?

Maybe it's waking up from the drifty dream of all that love might bring that's depressing. I wouldn't know. I probably won't ever know. And maybe that's just as well if it means you'll marry someone like her and one day turn up at a psychiatrist's office in a checked shirt that needs ironing only to be told that in the face of life-threatening danger, instead of sweeping your ten-year-old daughter in her arms, holding her as close as she could and running her to safety, your wife threw her hand off, walked away and left her alone when she needed her most. And now, after years of maltreatment, she has violently assaulted that same daughter, aged fifteen and, yet again, walked away from her as if she means nothing.

41

At the Hitchins' kitchen table, from left to right, sit Becca, Charlie, Dad, Francine and Clyde. Ambrose is out, and Amaryllis has band practice: she's a vocalist, which is a singer, but it's unclear why the same role has two different names.

Charlie is comparing the sugar levels on three jam labels, probably just to have something to look at, but he does tend to packet-check as a hobby. Becca, fiddling with my food hair clips, these ones being mini pretzels and gummy bears, is stoically coming to terms with my brother's gayness and the blistering reality that she will never mother his babies.

Becca's mother, Francine, is somewhere to be seen, namely standing now beside the boiling kettle in green dungarees dropping triangular teabags into an eclectic array of empty mugs. Clyde, in a collarless shirt and his stripy canvas slippers, is slicing a loaf of crusty sourdough he's baked and slotting slices in the toaster.

Maybe that would make a good tongue-twister. I toy with it for a while. Six-foot man in stripy slippers slices crusty sourdough and slots the slices in toaster slots. My tongue fumbles in two places. I end up with 'slipey strippers' and 'slike is clusty'. The rest isn't too tricky.

It's not that easy to make tongue-twisters.

That might be my new hobby.

There are lots of reasons I'm enjoying sitting here today, but can I just say that I'm gaining so much pleasure from my clothing? One of the quotations I have on my wall is by Ralph Waldo Emerson, who wrote, *To be yourself in a world that is constantly trying to make you something else is the greatest accomplishment.*

So today I'm wearing blue and white dotted flares under an orange and purple crocheted dress, a red velvet waistcoat with big yellow pom-poms, sunset-coloured platform trainers, and some red, fluffy smiley-face earmuffs and a neon elephant necklace that Becca found for me online. I haven't yet dyed my hair pink or green, because, you know, school, but I've cut it shorter and made some watermelon and banana hair clips to wear in it at weekends. The first day I was free to chose my own outfit, Dad said, 'You look great, Jodie Jones. Are you going to a fancy-dress party?' I told him it's Japanese street fashion from Harajuku in Tokyo, and he'd better get used to it.

The emancipation of these macro-choices (it does mean large-scale: I looked it up) makes me feel extraordinarily contented indeed. Not everyone can carry off this look, but I feel I am all of these things: motley, many-layered, eye-catching, kaleidoscopic, quirky, colourful and comfy. I can almost understand my mother now with her cashmere whatevers, her Thingy Whatsit handbags and her Doo-Dah shoes made of maimed and massacred kittens. Wearing garments you choose for yourself and that make you feel good equals all kinds of happy.

Becca asks Charlie if he'll play cards with her and to my astonishment he agrees. Becca invites me to join them, meaning she pulls repeatedly at my sleeve saying, 'Come. Come. Come. Come on-nah.' But I shake my head and bat her hand off me with a dessert spoon. I'd rather sit here and listen to the conversation. Besides, I think it's sweet that those two play cards together on the sofa, seeing as Charlie is still skittish about Bee-atrice and Becca is still gutted he's gay. But even a verisimilitude of a friendship between them is heart-warming.

'Verisimilitude'. What a word.

Reminds me of a very silly millipede called Jude.

But that's just me.

I have a feeling Dad will speak more freely now they've gone. Without much of a prompt, except that it's the topic of the day, I guess, Dad says, 'She adored me once. She flattered me, lavished me with love – or what I thought was love. Then she belittled me, criticized the way I looked, my job, my salary, the way I walked, my parenting. She'd insist conversations that happened didn't happen and I was losing my mind. Then she'd say she loved me, lavish me again and say I was over-sensitive and making it up.'

Francine leaves the teabag only moments in the hot water. Clyde butters toast with a scraping gliding sweep. In an infinitesimal spot in an immeasurable universe, the planet rotates slowly on its axis in a vast and tiny milky smudge of stars. I study the shape of my fingernails and think two things.

The first is that Clyde's toasted homemade sourdough bread bedaubed in butter is one of the most pengalicious dishes a mortal can devour. The other is that you don't know the details of your parents' relationship when you're a kid. You only see what they want you to see, and even then you don't care because you only care about yourself. Now, sitting here, a window is opening on how bad it's been for Dad, and I don't know why the vigour of the wind is the highlight of this metaphor, but it hasn't been a breeze.

I need a pee but I don't want to miss anything, so I sit schtum, my bulging bladder a bit of a bother.

'I'm not great at confrontation,' Dad says.

I want to shout HAH because that's an understatement. He's rubbish. He always gives in and opts for an easy life.

'In the last three years, Monica definitely got stricter with Jodie—'

'Jones,' I whisper under my breath.

'—but other things were going on: Covid changed the world, my mother died, I had a breakdown.' He pulls his face downwards from the cheeks with both hands, making his eyes stretch unattractively. I wish he wouldn't do that: it makes him look unhinged and he isn't. He's upset and devastated and harassed and those feelings are perfectly valid. 'Jodie got more and more difficult once her hormones kicked in – at least, that's what we thought it was. The more stubborn and difficult she got, the harsher Monica disciplined her. I thought it was just Monica's way of parenting. Teenage girls aren't easy.'

Francine nods as she places a mug of tea in front of him, and the movement and stretch of her mouth convey compassion. She lets him talk, and I'm grateful to her for this.

'All marriages have their ups and downs, don't they?' Dad says. 'I always try to see the good in people, and it wasn't Monica's fault – I felt sorry for her. She had a terrible childhood. Not that that excused her behaviour.'

Dad sips his tea. It's watery: I can tell just by looking at it. Dad likes his strong, Yorkshire and orange; he expertly squeezes liquor from his teabags against the lips of mugs. But he drinks it without making a moue, even though I know his tastebuds must be crestfallen. If they have crests that can fall. They're mountainous looking in close-up, so they probably have.

'We met at uni. I'd had a few girlfriends before Monica, but she was something else.'

I make a moue myself. Dad had girlfriends? This is fascinating and I will drill him relentlessly at a later date for more on this.

Francine offers me tea. I don't drink tea. In fact, I made up an anti-tea protest song:

What do we not want?
Hot tea!
When do we not want it?
Never!

But I don't sing it because I don't think anyone desires to hear it at this precise moment. Another time for sure.

Dad is still talking, so I shake my head in the universally accepted gesture that means 'no, thanks'. I wonder if it really is universal or if 'no, thanks' is a nod or a salute or a tongue poke in other parts of the world.

I realize I've drifted and turn my mind back to Dad.

'She was impressive. Beautiful, clever, confident. Incredibly well-dressed, even as a student. I'd never met anyone like her.'

Clyde is handing us holey toast on plates and Francine is now sitting and listening in a way that is heart-wrenchingly kind. For once, there is no music playing. Perhaps, so they can give him their undivided time and attention, or perhaps because there is no perfectly corresponding deep-conversation-with-tea-and-toast music. I wish I could ask. Either way, they know which is apt – music or no music, and which music when – and for this and many other reasons, they're my favourite people on earth. Well, aside from Dad, Becca, Moses and, on a good day, Charlie.

'Lots of people have difficult childhoods but they don't behave like that, do they?' Dad goes on. 'I started to realize a few years ago that it didn't add up. My mother died and I went into a fug. But then I started standing up to Monica. The arguments that that caused – I mean, unbelievable. I moved into the study. Monica said she missed me, but when I wouldn't move back to our room or fall into the same patterns as before, she said I'd never been good enough for her. She said she had a friend who was a lawyer, and that raised my hackles.'

None of this is surprising, but it's all news to me. Outside, the wind blows in bouts of blistering ferocity. Inside, we're warm and safe, and it's quiet enough to hear the mass mastication of toasted bread, the subtle sipping of insufficiently strong tea, and the inning and outing of breath in between.

'She's always controlled the finances – I transferred my salary to our joint account every month – but I wanted to control my own money again. I didn't want her to know what I was up to, so I got a consultancy job she didn't know about, opened a separate account and started saving.'

I've finished my toast and want some more but I don't want to interrupt his flow. Not when I'm learning all kinds of new information.

'It was exhausting, working two jobs. Spending half the day in joggers, trying to nap in between meetings. She didn't like that, of course. She called me a slob and a loser, but she didn't twig why I was so tired.'

My bulging bladder bobs like a buoyant balloon.

Being an adult sounds complicated.

I wonder if I can just stay this age forever.

42

'Marmalade?' Francine asks.

Dad says, 'Please.'

I wonder at which point a bladder might burst. I get up because I think I'm nearing that point, and walk slowly to the toilet, listening hard. When I'm in the hall, I hear Dad say in a low voice, 'She started flirting with our neighbour, James. He's the lawyer. She didn't even try to hide it: she wanted me to be jealous. Then she threatened to ruin my career, destroy us financially, tell the police I harmed the children so I wouldn't get to see them. She got violent. That's when I thought, no. I had to get the kids away from her and out of that house, but I had to do it carefully. My mother always said, 'When your hand is in the lion's mouth, you take it out slowly.' I didn't know what she meant until now. You know, I barely drink any alcohol – the odd beer sometimes – but I stopped completely. I stopped doing anything she might use as a weapon against me in court.'

Damn. Why do you always need the toilet at crucial moments?

When I return, Dad, Francine and Clyde are musing over

half-empty teacups. I've missed something, I can tell. A car drives by with 80s disco playing, which doesn't match the mood inside but that's another element of life you have no choice over. Dad and Francine are quiet. I feel a little awkward, so I try to balance a spoon on my nose with limited success and it clatters on the table.

'More toast, Jodie Jones?' Clyde asks.

'Yes, please.'

As Clyde rises to supply me with a supplementary slice of his baked delight, he's humming a ditty that makes my mouth twitch up. Perchance that is the reason the spoon will not stay put. I leave Dad with Francine and walk over to the toasting station.

'Clyde,' I say, putting the spoon down. 'Did you know that poured drinks "guggle" from a bottle?'

'I did not.'

'Nobody says "guggle" any more, but I wish they did. Can I ask you something.'

'Always.'

I realize I've asked an unrhetorical, pointless question but it's too late now. I just have to carry on. 'It might not be an easy question to answer.'

He nods sagely. 'Some questions are like that. I've faced many of those in my fifty-five years on this planet. G'wan and ask. I'll do my best.' He says 'arks' instead of 'ask'. Then he pauses and adds in a Jamaican accent, 'C'yan promise you nuttin, though.'

I take a deep, slow breath.

He looks at me.

I look at him.

Frowning, to show him the gravity of the question, I ask, 'Which book would you give someone for their birthday?'

Clyde is in a state of insensate uncertainty, which manifests itself in a hard blank glare. It's as if a part of him has gone on holiday yet his face and body are standing in front of me.

'That's it?' he asks. 'That's your question?'

'Yes.'

'The one you think isn't an easy one to answer?'

'Yes. I've been wondering about it for a long time.'

'I see.' He places the plate of toast down in front of me, his eyes, twinkling.

I pick up the knife and take a corner off the butter. 'I'm not expecting you to answer it right away. You probably need time to think about it. It's just that I can usually guess but I can't with you.'

'Who am I giving this book to?'

'Would the choice change depending on the person?'

'Course.'

I nod sagely and smooth the butter over my toast, imagining my knife is an ice skater with white boots and a sparkly dress. 'Say . . . someone my age.'

'Mmm-hmm.'

'Say, I don't know, someone like me.'

'Mmm-hmm.' He rests his huge frying pan hands together, forming a steeple, taps his fingertips, and lets his fingers fall between each other. 'Tell you what,' he says, 'why not wait till your next birthday and you can find out?'

'That's not till November.'

'And you need to know before that, do you?' He peers at me, his eyes soft and brown with green flecked rims.

I hesitate. Twitch my lips. Think it through. 'I suppose I could wait till then, but I'd rather not have to.'

He nods, smiling. I like his translucent, pale green glasses. They sort of nod with him. 'What date?'

'Tenth. But because that's ages away, can you give me a hint?'

'Best you wait. You want honey?'

'Please.' I twist my lips and squint. 'Clyde. That won't be easy.'

He hands me the honey, his eyes smiling. 'How 'bout this,' he says, folding his arms and tucking his hands under his armpits. 'I'll probably know you always. Is that fair to say?'

'I hope so.'

'Me too. Which means I'll probably be giving you a book for your birthday every year, no?'

'Oh. Really?'

'Don't see why not. And I will choose that book with a great deal of thought. So you don't need to wonder which one I'd hypothetically give you, because it won't just be one and it won't be hypothetical. You catch my drift?'

This pleases me no end, especially because he says 'juss' instead of 'just' and 'driff' instead of drift.

'No Kant please.'

He laughs loudly. 'No Kant.'

'Clyde?'

'Yes.'

'Can you please, please just tell me what you'll give me this year?'

'No.'

We sit back down at the table. He looks from my dad to Francine, trying to catch up with the conversation, and once he figures it out, he listens for a bit, but he's still grinning. I'm not sure which part of our interaction he finds amusing. I wonder if I'll ever know, but this isn't a question I'm going to ask him now. Maybe at some stage. But not now.

'Is she still in the house?' Francine asks. She means my mother.

'For the time being,' Dad says with a sigh. 'Until we sell it.'

Francine reaches out to touch the arm of my dad sitting beside her. She says, 'I'm so sorry, Elliott.'

'I shouldn't have let it go on for so long, but I wanted Jodie to have some stability after the . . . you know. Course, I didn't know Monica had done that to her. How could any parent do that to their child?'

Francine takes her hand off his arm and looks at Clyde. Neither of them would behave like that with their children, that's for sure. I know it's an emotional time and everything, but it's interesting to me that my dad is talking about me like I'm not here. I suppose he needs to talk to other adults about it, and I wonder if I should leave. I don't want to because I'm finding out all kinds of things that I didn't know, so I stay where I am and chew quietly. Even though Dad's telling this to Clyde and Francine, he's telling me, too, I'm sure of it. He wants me to know.

'Charlie and Jodie are the most important people in my life. They always have been. I should have protected them.'

The magical creature leaves my chest and the hollow expands into an ache.

Some parents love their children more than anything. My dad is one of them.

Still, his smile is all of these: regretful, chagrined, penitent, hangdog, lugubrious and crestfallen. 'I can't believe I—' he starts. 'I should have known better. I should have . . .' And he trails off, shaking his head. 'I let them down.'

Adults talk in a completely different way to each other than to their children. The language they use, the hand gestures, the unsaid things they all seem to get and I don't. They aren't doing the usual eye rolls and making the don't you have homework to do? comments aimed at getting rid of me, either. It's fascinating.

'Is Monica getting any help?' Clyde asks. He leaves an empty room for Dad to walk into, and I love Clyde for that. For lots of things, actually.

Dad says no and rubs his eyes. 'Picking my wars. Dr Kumar said the devaluing, control and sabotage are typical of the personality disorder, and she won't change – in fact, she feeds off creating pain. And now she knows she has something specific and it's called Narcissistic Personality Disorder, she refuses to be held accountable for her actions. You know, now she says she can't help it – she has a "disorder".'

Francine sighs. The wooden floor has a spot where the plank has turned grey from a nail. I stare at it numbly. I realize I rarely left space like an empty room for my dad to wander into. Partly because I didn't want to tell him the truth about what my mother did to me that day, and partly because I didn't understand what he was going through.

'And now she's trying to win sympathy . . . from doctors, from James – from anyone she can. James will be lavished with attention and adoration. The whole cycle will just start again.'

Dad doesn't say how long he has known about my mother and James. Did he learn about it from me? Or did he know before and that's why he moved to the study? Did Minty get minty about her husband's affair with my mother? It's not the kind of thing you can ask, and the timing is definitely off to ask it now. Illicit affairs seem far-fetched in British sitting rooms when everyone's drinking a nice weak cup of tea, the clocks have just gone forward and the bin collectors are clanking and whirring along the tidy, geranium-lined avenue outside. It seems so unlikely that furtive romantic liaisons could happen in this setting, never mind murderous crimes, but they clearly do.

Dad has given his notice at work and will be taking over at Bannermans. My mother has been removed as CEO and I'm going to work there in the holidays. Apparently, I can wear what I like because 'designers like quirkiness and creativity'.

He might regret saying that.

Once we're out of the rental flat and have a permanent home of our own, Dad said I can choose my own bed or at least a blind with clouds on it so I can say 'nice sky' whenever I see it, and won't have to hide my books, and for supper I can eat something other than grilled protein and salad in a box that someone else has chosen for me. I'll have a whole row of cereal boxes in the kitchen, half of them sugary. I'll eat Nutella slowly from the back of a spoon, leave the cap open on the toothpaste, and say, 'I'm in the mood for pancakes' and I'll be able to make them for once. I'll go for walks (with no time limits) to stalk deer in the park and I'll ask Becca to sleepovers; I'll lie on a rug and read on a rainy afternoon, and pages and pages later, stretch idly and yawn and think, milk and a biscuit, I think, and open a tin containing a selection of the country's most moreish cookies. Charlie, film nerd, will choose our Sunday night movie, Tavish will hang out with us without it being educationally related and maybe they'll invite Moses, or maybe I will. Dad will have a new green study, or perhaps this time he'd like a blue or lemon one, with high ceilings because thoughts need height, and we'll have long conversations, he and I. We'll leave spaces for each other like empty rooms, and we'll laugh and we'll hurt and we'll cry until the tears stop spilling out, if they ever do, which I doubt, but who knows, and hopefully, little by little, we'll start to heal.

43

When I go back to school, the air feels different, the chairs feel different, the stares feel different. I can't quite grasp the hows or the whys of it, as Dad might say, but the school atmosphere feels broader, brighter, brasher and less mired in static.

It's a Wednesday, the first in the summer term, the first after the break that brings us one holiday closer to the end-of-year exams. Everyone else in my form has spent the three weeks of Easter revising; I spent them on the internet researching NPD and its repercussions in more depth, reading about effective eye-movement treatments for PTSD, searching for outrageous clothes and the type of home furnishings I'd actually want to have in my new room, and going for long walks with Dad on wind-clad cliffs in colourful cagoules. The rental flat is sufficiently small for us to want to flee it quite frequently, so flee it we did. We met Charlie and Tavish on Box Hill, and drove them to Devil's Dyke and Beachy Head, walking and walking until we felt cold and clear and battered by the blustery April elements. Revise, I did not. But that's understandable.

When we first moved into the rental flat, Francine gave Becca a note to give me that said:

For everything there is a season, and a time for every matter under heaven . . .
a time to weep, and a time to laugh;
a time to mourn, and a time to dance;

Ecclesiastes

From that, I gleaned that revising could wait. That's perhaps not how King Solomon intended his writings to be interpreted, but he was famously wise so perchance it is.

In form time, Lucy Lee sees me, whispers and smirks at her cronies. The lowlight, I surmise, is that Lucy *et al.* are still spiteful buck-faced brats. School is still school is still school, and why we repeat phrases thrice and don't say 'thrice' much any more are both mysteries to me.

Another lowlight, although it could also be a highlight or maybe a midlight is that Becca barely leaves me be: she has reassigned her romantic fixation to Rosario Tondo and is crocheting him a cat, which she badgers me for help with, which is weirdly more acceptable than crocheting him a badger and catting me for help with. She buys me baked goods at break when I don't want them, then eats them herself, and abandons Makery Club at lunch so she can cling to my arm like I'm a helium balloon tugging towards a wide-open sky, which might not be far from the truth. I know she means well, but it's a little suffocating and when I tell her to stop treating me like a five-year-old, she says, 'I wasch going for schix, acshully,' so I know she has her retainer in.

The highlight is that Charlie is not only acknowledging me in school, winking and mouthing, 'You OK?' and stopping momentarily as he passes me in the corridor to see if I really am, he also joins us for lunch in the allocated classroom. When the cheese-and-potato pie has been demolished, I tell him how much I appreciate his company, and he says, 'Not doing this every day so don't get used to it.' Then he gives me a hug and goes back to the sixth form common room.

In PSHE, which this week is about credit ratings, personal finances and opening a bank account, Moses turns to face me. 'I don't give a toss about this,' he says. 'I made Champ tell me . . . I know more or less what's been going on. Not in detail, but . . . how are you doing?'

I shrug. 'I'm a work in progress.'

'Best people are.'

We sit for a minute, and I revel in sitting next to a human who is humane. After a pause, he adds, 'Can I do anything?'

'Not really. But thanks. I mean . . . cheesy Wotsits, if anything.'

'All out,' he says with a flinch. 'Next time.'

We chat about this and that, definitely not about finances. When Miss Slavin chooses us to give feedback, Moses says to her, 'We didn't talk about that, actually. We talked about other stuff.'

I wait for the imminent detention but instead of telling us off, Miss Slavin surprises us by replying, 'Well, I'm sure you had your reasons, and verbal communication and listening are also important life skills.' Then she asks another pair about interest rates, which makes us wonder whether we shouldn't have just ignored the brief all along.

In English, we study *The World's Wife* by Carol Ann Duffy. Her poems are astonishing, brilliant, thought-provoking, but 'Medusa', the one we are set as a timed unseen, stuns me. For me it's not unseen because I've seen it, meaning I took the anthology out of the library and read the poems over and over lying on the rug in my new room. I neglect to mention this, because reading to enjoy and reading to analyse are different ways of reading.

I decide that Duffy and 'Medusa' deserve considerably more veneration than some of the others in my class are likely to bestow in forty-five minutes, so I micro-choose to venerate them. Miss McLaughlin does that teachery glance over the shoulder as she walks around the silent room, standing behind me for longer than propriety dictates, and after the allotted time plus extra time for the extra timers, reads parts of mine aloud, which I don't mind on this occasion because Miss McLaughlin seems overly animated and Becca dissolves in tears. I want to remind Miss McLaughlin that there is more to life than an analytic paragraph on poetry but I'm not sure an English teacher would agree.

44

The first thing Dad bought in the rental flat was an espresso machine. The pleasure he gets from that is well worth five-hundred quid.

When he unzipped his blue suitcase, the one that had sat in the study causing me stomach-squeezing panic, inside were my missing hairbrush, socks and underwear and clothes, a new pair of pyjamas, packs of spare toothbrushes, Oswald, my cuddly, toy owl, and the old-fashioned shoe ornament Grandma Tara gave me. There was also a cardboard folder containing the newspapers published the days and weeks after the incident at London Bridge.

I did not like to look at them. 'Why have you got those?' I asked. Shuddering. Feeling sick.

'Your mother wanted to destroy them.'

'I don't want reminders, Dad.'

'They helped me to . . . I just wanted to understand and process what you'd been through.'

I realized that because I never wanted to talk about it, he'd never been able to talk about it. I didn't occur to me that he might need to.

He hadn't packed many of his own belongings in that case. Most of them were ours. He'd been preparing our exit for months but just couldn't manage to do it. He'd collated screenshotted evidence of her threats, and photos of his injuries, kept a diary, had meetings with lawyers, changed legal documents, and searched for a rental flat. Knowing that, made me happy and sad at the same time. Happy because he'd had a plan to get us away from her, and sad because he didn't realize the truth about her years ago and get us out of there sooner.

'How are you so . . . I don't know . . . resilient?' he asked, watching me take my belongings out of the case and place them on the shelf in my temporary new room. 'After all she— After all you've been through?'

'I'm not really, Dad. I've just been doing my best because I don't know what else to do.'

He hugged me, stroked my head, and said, 'I can't tell you how sorry I am. About everything. I wasn't there. I haven't been there for you since Grandma died. I fell in a hole and I couldn't get out of it but I should have found a way because you needed me.'

'You were doing your best as well. You didn't know what to do, either.'

'True.' Dad was smiling but he had tears rolling down his cheeks, which is quite a skill. 'Something else, you are,' he said. 'Can I . . . D'you mind if I ask you a personal question? Unrelated.'

'Course.'

'Are you . . . you know . . .' He paused.

'Am I what?'

'Gay. As well?'

'Because I like *words*?'

'Because you don't like boys. To my knowledge.'

'I do like some boys. I might like girls as well – I don't know yet. I don't think so. I just like words more.'

He chuckled and wiped his eyes. 'Is that going to be enough?'

'Do I have to choose?'

'Course not. I just . . . I want you to be happy. I hope she hasn't ruined your ability to . . .' He made a face.

'To?'

'Love. Be loved. I just . . . You deserve it, you really do.' Then he said in a Yorkshire accent, 'Any road, I'll ne'r forgive mesel.'

I blame *Happy Valley*. He's been watching it on repeat.

I like the phrase 'any road'. It means the same as 'anyway' but it's more visual and seems loaded with possibility. This road? That road? Which road is best? Is there ever a best road?

'Road' sounds weird when you say it too much.

He cried again so I held his hand. We were silent for a while. Then I let go because it felt weird.

'But . . . I had you, Dad,' I said. 'And you loved me.'

'Love you,' he corrected. 'Present tense.'

'Yes. Love. Present tense. And that's why I think I'll be fine. Was it . . . I think it was Oscar Wilde who said, "With freedom, flowers, books and the moon, who could not be happy"?'

He squeezed my hand. 'You and books, eh?'

'Me and books.'

I did my best to explain, in layperson's terms, that oscillations and susurrations of sound made me feel I could make it through another onerous day. That's what buoyed and balanced me: seeing a slew of beauty in the ruins, and that slew was usually in the form of sentence rhythms. Their resplendence and transcendence calmed me.

I'm not sure Dad dug it, but he grinned all the same. He had a deep furrow across his forehead, and it made me wonder about wrinkles and how you can nearly always tell how old someone is, which is mysterious. Like life sits on us the same way even though we're all so different.

'Slew of beauty in the ruins?' he repeated, long after. Do ageing brains really work that slowly? I was thinking about this when, about three decades later, he added, 'Is that one of yours?'

I admitted that it was.

'Hope you've written that one down.'

'I write all of them down. Listen to these.' I opened the book Clyde said I could keep, called *To a Mountain in Tibet* by a travel writer called Colin Thubron. I read aloud some of the words and phrases I'd highlighted. Dad listened, his eyes full of love. Or maybe confusion. But it seemed like confusion of a loving variety. He sniffed a short sniff, in the universal or maybe not universal expression of being impressed.

'You'll be a writer one day, mark my words,' he said. 'But you know, it's not just about the sounds.'

'What's not?'

'Literature. Writing . . . you know. Stories.'

Mystified, my head lopped in a tilt.

'It's about the meaning,' he said.

'Meaning?'

He laughed. '*Meaning*, literature shines a light on the human condition. Pain, love, despair, compassion, boredom, confusion, longing. All the big stuff.'

I needed to think about this, but Dad was on a roll.

'It's hard to know how to live a good life when the world's unfair, people are suffering, people do bad stuff, you have a million decisions to make about what you believe in and value, and nothing makes much sense.'

This deserved some space around it, so I gave it some.

'If the sentences sound good, all the better. But there's beauty in even the simplest things when they reflect the complexity and richness and suffering and joy and love and, I don't know, profound depth of life and being human.'

Although he was wearing an itchy jumper that smelt of old washing machines, I hugged him and said, 'I'm very fond of Clyde, but I am extraordinarily lucky to have you as my dad.'

'Likewise,' he said in a wobbly voice. I'm not his dad so 'likewise' didn't work in that context, and I told him that. One really needs to mention what goes through one's mind from time to time. Too much not-saying is bad for one.

'Still, I think it helps if you find your thing, Dad. Whatever it is that makes your heart feel calm. For me it's words and sentences. Maybe I need to pay more attention to the meaning and the human condition and complexity and so forth but having a thing is the thing.'

His expression was puzzled, reflective. 'Having a thing is the thing?'

'It is. I think I know what your thing is,' I added. 'And yes. I will.'

'Yes you will, what?'

'Yes, I'll visit castles with you.' He hadn't dragged us around any since Grandma Tara died. They were closed during the pandemic, but they'd been open again for a while, so Charlie and I bought him a new National Trust subscription for his birthday. Well, we bought it with our birthday money, which he gave us when it was our birthdays, so he really bought it for himself, but we didn't tell him that.

'You sure? Thought you didn't enjoy it.'

Because the situation sometimes calls for it, I lied through my teeth, which is a strange expression because you're not going to lie through your kneecaps, are you? 'Course I enjoy it. Unless you make me do a morning of workbooks first.'

'Never wanted you to in the first place.'

'In that case, whenever you're ready.'

45

Moses is leaning against a lamppost at the corner of Becca's road, between an Audi and a Ford Focus. He's wearing a red T-shirt with yellow writing under an orange puffer jacket, and bright blue cords. He smells of laundry just taken in from the line on a mid-to-warm cloudy day in May and looks a bit like a Refreshers sweet. At least to an outsider. To me he's a sonnet in human form.

In the gutter beside him is the plastic arm of a very small doll and the doll, the fresh clothing smell and the sweetie-colours distract me.

'Would you rather . . .' he begins.

'The customary greeting in these parts is "hello",' I explain. He ignores me and I wonder what kind of fresh horror he'll make me choose between this time.

'. . . eat an entire wet loaf of bread or drink a pint of tiny slugs?'

'Why forty-two?' I ask, pointing to his T-shirt as he unleans from the lamppost.

'Douglas Adams,' he replies. When my face effectively displays a blank screen, he adds, 'I'm guessing you haven't read any of his books.'

I shake my head.

'Pshh. In for a treat,' he says. 'I mean, you may not like them – some don't – fair enough, whatever, but they're great and the word play is . . .' He can see I'm not following so he adds, 'According to him, the number forty-two is the answer to life, the universe and everything— Watch out.' He sticks his arm in front of me, saving me being crushed by the Audi, now reversing out of the parking space. 'Don't you look before you cross the road, Jodie Jones?'

'I do when I'm not distracted by slugs and the number forty-two.'

'Forty-two won't save you from being run over. Hello, by the way. So, what'll it be? Wet bread or slugs?'

'What's the bread soaked in?'

'Water. Tap. Cold.'

'How small are the slugs?'

'Like skinny grey prawns.'

'I detest both options.'

'That's the point. Nice beanie. Won't lose you in a crowd. How you doing?'

We take the train to Barnes and walk to Barnes Green. I like his idea of a walk in the park, even though it isn't an idiomatic walk in the park for me because I'm nervous of being outside and even more nervous of walking around in public with him and would really prefer to dash indoors and stay there. Moses makes me feel notably better by telling me that his name in French would be 'Moise', which rhymes with 'noise' and as he's not a fan, his grandparents in France call him *mon loulou*. I'm so enamoured by this, the nerves subside and I start to enjoy taking in the flat, short lawn, the quivering leaves on the tentative trees, and being immersed in green that I've read is called forest-bathing.

After a while, I stop looking behind and around me, and instead I remember that my feet are padding on the surface of a planet. I imagine the round globe like a ball in space and little me walking over the top of it, my feet pushing gently against the cool earth.

'Play any instruments?' Moses asks me. His lace is loose on his left shoe and his stride is more of a rhythmic spring. I shake my head. My chest tightens. I hope he doesn't ask more questions about this because I don't want to explain or even think about instruments, especially violins.

'Took me a while to settle on the guitar,' he says, not probing, which I'm grateful for. 'I tried a few out. I suck at the sax, and that is the wrong direction for the air to be going. No. The guitar's the one for me. I still think I'm better at the spoons, but I'm working on my chords. Give me six months and I'll be Jimi Hendrix.'

I don't know who Jimi Hendrix is, which he works out in no time, so he fills me in. The sounds of him expounding excitedly about left-handed, upside-down guitar-playing wash over me, and I notice an alarming sense of calm. The breeze is warm and the sky is more blue than white now that spring is tentatively turning into summer. No one is taking their jacket off just yet, but signs of something better are in the air.

Pondside, Moses pulls a Tupperware box from his pocket, pares open the lid and stoops by the edge near the gathering ducks.

'What's on today's ducky menu?' I ask.

'Grapes. Cut in half, obvs. And some not-so-frozen-any-more peas.'

'Why grapes and peas?'

He's looked it up, he tells me. Bread and crackers are bad. Oats, rice, lettuce and the contents of his tub are apparently fine.

'Do you . . . want to . . . ?' he offers me the tub.

I decline and remain a foot away from the bank, my hands in my pockets, watching him. 'They like *you*,' I say. 'There's a vibe. I'd hate to break the . . .' I wave my hands, 'bond.'

'Course they like me,' he says with a wry smile. 'I'm providing them with round, green foods they'd never find in the wild. Why grapes and peas? Now I'm wondering.'

I let him wonder. Wondering is good. We all could do with more wondering time. I wonder things myself. Some of them I voice. 'Why are you friends with my brother,' I ask as he lobs half a grape towards a bashful mallard further back.

'He used to be less of a knob,' he replies, not looking at me. 'He's way too worried about what people think of him. Like most people, I guess. You don't seem to have that malady.' He turns and smiles at me. 'Quite the opposite, in fact. You defy the unspoken teenage rule of never standing out. That's bothered him, especially lately.'

'You do that as well,' I point out.

'Yeah, but I also do my schoolwork. I don't repeat nice sounding words aloud in class. And I'm not his little sister.' The ducks are arguing so he turns back and says, 'Hey. Hey. Scuse me. None of that, thank you. Be nice.' He talks to them like they're small children, telling them off for being greedy and not sharing with the others. He throws a pea or two at the timid mallard and adds, 'He's not that bad. Hopefully, things'll be better for him now. It's been tough for him as well. Your mother was . . .'

He doesn't finish that sentence, but he doesn't need to. He stands up again with a knee click I wasn't expecting in one so young, and turns to me, closing the lid on the box. 'If I'm being completely honest, I stayed friends with him mainly as an excuse to hang out with you.'

The ducks kick off, but the box is empty. He turns around to tell them that.

Warmth. Pauses. Blank air. These surround me. I feel the need to fill the pauses, to be more open and direct myself. It's scary, but what the hell. 'You know what I think? I think I'm lucky to know you, Moses Calvet,' I admit to his back.

His lungs rise as he draws in a deep breath. I shouldn't have said it and, mortified, I look skyward. A flock of long-winged, long-necked bird flies by in a V shape. Are they geese?

'I can do better than that,' he says quietly, and he turns, stands in front of me, and catches my eye. 'I'm lucky to know you, Jodie Jones.'

I can't keep his gaze, so I shift it to the ducks. My insides squeeze in shame and joy and annoyance. He's using words better than I am, and he's right. Saying 'I think' is irrelevant – it's just padding to mask what I really want to say. I'm both delighted with his reply and irritated with myself.

'Hungry?' he asks. 'I'm all out of grapes and peas now, but there's a café on the other side of the park.' It takes me a while to decide because that's complicated. I've had enough of listening to noisy ducks, though, so I agree.

The café is quiet, which I'm glad of because I'm not a fan of café noise, either. Some people listen to recordings of it to help them sleep, which I find bewildering. It would do the very opposite to me. The barista has a sleeve of tattoos and a short, orange fringe. Her eyes are bright blue and she's strikingly pretty. He could be with someone like her, I think. Someone who lives with friends and puts out her own recycling. Someone who knows what a mercado is. Someone who doesn't think that ordering something she has chosen for herself in a café is a rare and profound freedom.

'Hey, guys. What can I get you?' she asks.

'Could you please wait a moment?' I say, and turn to Moses. 'I would like to pay for my food and drink myself, regardless of kind offers or chivalrous insistence or bill-grabbing arguments, because I've felt immensely stressed about who's going to pay for what since we left the pond and I don't want to continue to feel stressed all the way through my avocado toast.'

Moses laughs, a wide-pan yawn, showing his teeth off to the cosmos. 'I get that. I really do. Man, you should see the bill-paying arguments in my family.' He hasn't looked at the menu board yet and I've already decided on my drink and food option, but maybe he's been to this café before and tasted everything on offer so he already knows what he wants. 'It's no biggie, really,' he says. 'I'm really happy to get this, you know. But if you feel more comfortable paying for yourself, then that's honestly all I want.'

'I would feel more comfortable paying for myself. Or paying for me and for you. I just want to know, either way. Actually, can we just split it, so I don't feel weird about it?'

'Course. But will you let me get it another time?' he asks with a grin.

'Who says there'll be another time?'

He laughs again, casts his eyes over the tables and points

at one in the corner at the back. 'Where shall we sit? That one OK?' He still hasn't scrutinized the menu board.

'Sorry. Do you know the menu by heart?'

'Er . . . no,' he replies. 'I can learn it if you want?'

The barista is looking from him to me, amused. She probably wouldn't be quite as amused if there was a line of agitated customers behind us.

'That won't be necessary,' I say to him. And to her I say, 'Avocado toast and apple juice, please.'

Moses orders a flat white and eggs Benedict, which I would never, ever have had him down for but it just goes to show that predicting someone's beverage and breakfast of choice can be tricky, nodulous, reticular, mazy, hazy, Martin Scorsese, and downright blinking hard.

We swap numbers before we leave the café. That evening, he sends me a message for the first time. It's a good, if unusual, start to a teen-message exchange.

> Do you like seeing plays?

> > I like seeing Shakespeare plays. For the word play, the sound play, the rhythms. So many relevant lines – 'That one may smile and smile and be a villain.'

> Let me guess. Fowler?

> > I had someone closer to home in mind, but that works, too. This one's also apt: 'Look like the innocent flower but be the serpent under't.'

My money's still on Fowler.

> If I send you a brown circle will you know I'm smiling? I'm not sure I'm a smiley face person.

I will now . . . Been to the Globe? I'm a fan. I saw Much Ado set in revolutionary Mexico last year. So good. We could go to something. If you want. Together, I mean, obviously, not to different shows on different days. Unless you'd prefer that.

> I would not prefer that. I'd prefer to go with you.

Yay!

> I don't know the normal response to yay so I'm going to bed now.

OK. Night, Jodie Jones. Sweet dreams.

> Wet loaf of bread.

Noted. I'll remember that when I invite you to dinner.

> But obviously neither.

Obviously. You didn't say you wouldn't come to dinner though. No wet bread or tiny slugs. Not for main course anyway. Hey, Jodie Jones?

> What?

I enjoyed spending time with you in the park today. Let's do it again. If you want. That reminds me. Becca told me you're collecting sentences. I've got one for you. Want to hear it?

> Yes.

'O, she doth teach the torches to burn bright! . . . Did my heart (like) til now? forswear it, sight! For I ne'er saw true beauty till this night.'

(PS: This may or may not relate to you and the way you eat avocado toast in a specific crust-first order.)

(PPS: I exchanged a word. I didn't want to freak you out.)

(PPPS: I know it was the day and not the night but it doesn't rhyme).

> Ok. Bye.

I put my phone down. I know the line: it was our Year 9 Shakespeare text. Romeo says it when he first sees Juliet at the Capulet ball. Most of my class only loved it because in the Baz Luhrmann version, Leonardo di Caprio 'looked at them' from the screen, and was 'so pretty'. Not sure how many liked the poetry. I know the word Moses has substituted is 'love' and I'm relieved he can't see my face smiling, blushing, cringing.

Running through my brain is:

Raise me a dais of silk and down;
　Hang it with vair and purple dyes;
　　Carve it in doves and pomegranates,
　　　And peacocks with a hundred eyes.

46

Dad's been called in for yet another meeting at school. We're sitting around the same table in the same office with more or less the same people, except on a cellular level, they're different. They have different food in their stomachs creating different bodily reactions, different clothes and haircuts, and different moods caused by whatever is happening to them lately in their lives beyond school that's preoccupying their thoughts – and that depends, of course, on whether their minds are untrained and get on every thought bus that passes or whether they're aware of the thoughts popping up and can remain sitting at the bus stop watching them pass by.

It's amazing that people think anyone is the same from one day to the next.

Mr Fowler definitely isn't because he's off sick, and the chair where he sat in the last meeting is being used as a resting spot for what looks like a witch's cloak in a carrier bag but could, I suppose, be a graduation gown. It's not Halloween, but one would like to believe one could dress as a witch any day of the year and it's not limited to when the rest of the world decides it's an acceptable form of attire. Plus, our teachers have to wear graduation gowns to prize-giving and prize-giving is tonight, so it would make more sense if it were a graduation gown, but it still makes no sense why our teachers wear graduation gowns to prize-giving.

They are preparing for the meeting. They shuffle papers, find files and look for previously shared psychiatric reports online. I'm not sure what they're thinking of, or what concerns them beyond that, and that pleases me. We all have a rich inner world and that's fascinating.

Miss Slavin grins through red-lipsticked lips; she's wearing her tight, royal blue jumper today and her leopardskin shoes with the tie at the back. She does have trousers on as well – she's not just wearing a jumper and shoes – although that omission would be curious to see at a high school. Her trousers are boring and black, so they don't require or deserve any focus: the lips, the jumper and the shoes, on the other hand, are just asking to be talked about.

My mother is not present. No one has mentioned her or asked why, so my guess is that they know some if not all of what my psychiatrists and psychologists have promised is confidential information, which is concerning. Or perhaps my dad has told them, which is less concerning but also somewhat concerning.

Dad is seated beside Miss Slavin. He's wearing a pale blue shirt with a tie I bought him for Christmas when I was twelve. The tie is a dark blue with small yellow rubber ducks on it. I can't believe he's worn it at all, never mind to a meeting at my school. But he's supporting me, and if I had a tie of support, I'd wear mine at appropriately supportive occasions, too. My current tie suggests I'm supporting Newton, my school house, but I don't care about Newton in the slightest, so I'm now considering the micro-choice of upgrading to a more truthful tie.

As I ponder the possibilities of supportive ties, I hear the phrases, 'remarkable improvement . . . commendable progress . . . still some work to do but . . . considering the circumstances . . . options now wide open.'

Dad glances at me with love and damp eyes. I hope he doesn't cry because that image combined with the rubber duck tie would not be my favourite memory to cherish.

'Jodie Jones?'

'Hmm? Sorry?'

Madame Arnaud is smiling with her lips but her eyes express frustration at my fecklessness.

'I said, "What do you sink"?' she repeats.

'What do I think about what?'

There is a collective pause while eyes meet eyes across the table.

'The suggestion is that you redo this year,' Dad explains gingerly. 'Start Year 10 again in September.'

'What? Why?'

'Because this has been a challenging year for you. You've missed so much work. There's no way you'll be prepared to sit your GCSEs this time next year,' Miss Slavin explains. 'The best option is for you to redo Year 10.'

Another pause. More eyes meeting eyes. Mainly theirs meeting mine this time.

I want to say, 'Yeah, but it doesn't really matter, though, does it?' But they're teachers – to them, this is all that matters, and it's all that will ever matter. And maybe they're right. Maybe it matters because if I do have to spend seven long years in this place and my brain can easily process the stuff they want me to absorb and regurgitate, I might as well absorb and regurgitate it well and leave waving those pieces of paper that open doors to gaining more pieces of paper, which open more doors to gaining more pieces of paper, and those might ultimately lead to the pieces of paper, plastic-coated or virtual, that you can buy things with, like spaces to live in with furniture of your choosing and kitchens to cook in with gadgets and little somethings to nibble on and music that perhaps randomly and perhaps logically accompanies the preparation of specific dishes, which is the kind of kitchen I'd like to create with my personal pieces of paper when I grow up.

'Is it really necessary?' Dad asks Miss Slavin. 'Seems excessive. Jodie can catch up. Can't she? You can, can't you, Jodie?'

I don't answer. He doesn't say 'Jones' and it annoys me.

'It would give her the very best chance to reach her potential,' Miss Slavin is quick to point out. She means in my GCSEs, because that's the only potential she thinks is worth reaching, whereas I know for certain I have other potentials worth reaching.

'No,' I say.

'Jodie Jones,' Miss McLaughlin says, 'you're not . . .' She hesitates and makes a face. 'How can I put this? Catching up on what you've missed this year will be incredibly hard. It's a huge amount of wor—'

'No,' I say.

They eye each other and Miss Slavin asks me to wait outside.

I push back my chair, the metal legs of which make a coarse scraping sound on the linoleum floor. Dad clears his throat and addresses my teachers, deliberately, I'm assuming, before I leave the room. 'Jodie's the most intelligent person I know. She's the one who worked out the truth about her mother. She looked up a psychiatrist specializing in her mother's disorder, one who conducts research specifically in that field, and she managed to get her mother to take her there, thinking the sessions were about Jodie. Dr Kumar recognized the signs in my wife without hesitation.'

I turn to leave.

'She saved us,' Dad says quietly, his voice wavering. 'She saved me.'

The next pause has a different feel. I'm not sure how. Weightier. Charged. *Verklempt*. If that's really a word.

I hope Dad *is* crying if he feels like it, because men should cry when they feel like it and not be ashamed to do it in front of people, but even so, I'm not sure I want to see it myself when he's in my school milieu wearing a rubber-duckie tie.

'We understand that, Mr Zhang. We do,' Miss Slavin says gently, speaking as if the teachers all share one head. 'Jodie deserves enormous praise for her initiative and her bravery.' She turns to me. I'm still standing behind the chair at this point. 'But you do know you didn't have to go to those elaborate lengths, Jodie Jones. All you had to do was tell an adult you could trust. Domestic abuse is a crime. So is neglect, so is emotional and psychological abuse, and so is coercive control. Do you know what coercive control is?'

Course I do. I've looked this stuff up for months. I don't reply.

'I wish you'd just told one of us,' she says. 'Or Becca, or her parents. Someone.'

I keep my eyes fixed on the radiator. I guess I could have done that. I didn't think of it, actually. I just wanted to know if I was right about her. Maybe I got a little fixated on that. Like the unnamed narrator in *Rebecca*, I didn't communicate, which would, you'd think, have been the most obvious and simple course of action.

'In *The Lord of the Rings* . . .' Dad begins, and I wonder where this is going. Is my mother Sauron? Is Charlie Gollum? Is Dad Bilbo? Because in my head this is and has always been the case. 'Elrond says a great line. Something about the task being for Frodo alone and if he can't find a way to do it, no one can.'

We all sit wondering what to say about that, or at least I do.

'Jodie Jones found a way,' Dad clarifies, 'when no one else could.'

'No child should be tasked with a job like that, Mr Zhang,' Miss Slavin says.

I want to say 'No Hobbit, either' but keep my mouth shut.

'Oh, that wasn't the part I meant,' Dad explains but his point is lost.

'We have no doubts about her intelligence and capability,' Miss Slavin says, 'but she needs to have built up a solid foundation of knowledge in Year 10. She needs to have had essay practice and lab practice, passed topic tests. And she hasn't.'

As I walk out of the room, I pause by the door and say, 'Miss McLaughlin. Can I speak to you, please? In private?'

'Um . . . I . . . OK, sure,' Miss McLaughlin says, standing up. 'But just so you know, being exceptional at English isn't going to cut it.'

I wonder about the etymology of that phrase as she follows me out.

'What is it?' she asks, standing in a way that shows me she's pressingly ready to leave again, like an invisible magnet is pulling her back to the office.

'Your foundation stops in an abrupt and jagged orange line under your chin.'

Her eyes blaze and her hand reaches to her jaw. 'I'm . . . sorry?'

'We can all see it because we sit lower down than you. They make fun of you. It's bad enough when people make fun of you over something you can't change but if you can change it . . . I just wanted you to know.'

She's shocked and isn't sure whether to tell me off or not. Then she says, quietly, 'I put make-up on in the dark so I don't wake my partner . . .' She grins. 'I can't believe no one's ever mentioned it. I'm so glad you told me. Thank you, Jodie.'

'Jones.'

'Right. Jodie Jones. Sorry. I'm . . . Gosh. How embarrassing.' With her hand sitting under her chin, she says, 'On the back of that, though . . .'

She's about to tell me off, I think. For being blunt or rude or talking to teachers in a way that's unacceptable because it has to do with their private lives. Instead, she adds, 'It's bad enough when people make fun of you over something you can't change but if you can change it . . .'

'Touché,' I say with a nod. I don't know what it means but someone once said it in a film and it sounded cool.

She eyes me wisely, smiles and heads to the staff toilets before returning to the office with a faintly wet neck.

47

While I'm sitting on one of the yellow chairs, students pass, the clock ticks, and Becca approaches. She's rummaging in her cloth bookshop bag and nearly doesn't see me. She looks from me to the Head's study door.

'Issch that the meeting to . . . ?'

I nod. The coincidence that she should walk past, just like Moses did the last time I was sitting here, is uncanny. Unless it isn't uncanny, but I don't know what the opposite to uncanny is. Uncanny means unearthly, preternatural, freakish. Canny means shrewd and circumspect. The two don't seem related enough to be opposites. Although perhaps there's more canniness about these chance meetings than uncanniness, so there is an oppositeness going on after all.

'What're they schhaying?' Becca asks, removing her rummaging hand from her bag.

'That I should start Year 10 again.'

She puts her now free hand on her hip in a belligerent manner. 'What? That'sch crazschy. Isch scchat what you want?'

I shake my head and blink a few times. For no logical reason – it just happens. The blinking, I mean.

Miss Slavin opens the door and indicates, merely by standing there, that the time has come for me to reenter.

'Wait,' Becca says, and follows me into the office, despite Miss Slavin's protestations to the contrary.

Although Becca doesn't match my now rather high cheesy Wotsits standards, she tells rather than asks the teachers who are overseeing our educational development that she will lend me her notes so I can catch up and she'll be happy to help me study but they should know that the helping never happens that way around because it's me who helps her, always, and if they do put me down a year then they'll have to make two spaces in the year below because she'll be going back down to Year 10 with me, and no, sorry, she won't leave the room now, because do they have the slightest idea what I've been through, not only because I happened to be on London Bridge when a terror attack happened, but because of my mother and the way she's treated me every single day since, and it's a miracle that I'm as together as I am and how dare they, how DARE they, punish rather than reward and support me for that?

I stand still and silent, but my eyes are popping. It's startlingly rude and disrespectful to talk to teachers like that, but I don't say so. Becca wipes away her angry, stubborn tears and links my arm in hers, hard, adding, 'Whatever you decsschide for her, you decsschide for me, too. And I mean that.'

Although she says it with her retainer in, which makes her sound gloriously amusing, they take her seriously, and after much harrumphing, which is a delightful word, and a few more eye conversations to which we are both privy and yet not privy, they permit me, hesitantly, to continue to Year 11 in September but with 'close monitoring and subsequent meetings if need be'.

'The need won't be,' I say quietly. Becca echoes me more loudly and firmly, and so does my Dad, straightening his rubber-duck tie, so we ultimately say that strange sentence not just once but three times.

When we exit the office, I politely request that Becca please release my arm now, which she does to my great relief, but instead of returning her arm to her own personal space, as is required, she uses it to place her Daunt's bag on a yellow chair and then embraces me tightly using both of her upper limbs, which makes me feel all of these things: restricted, confined, asphyxiated, edgy, consoled, fortified, safe, loved, ineffably grateful and somewhat teary.

I quite like the sound of 'Becca echoes'.

It sounds like an echo in itself.

I turn to walk away, relieved, and turn back when I hear my name. All of it. Which is another relief. Miss Slavin, Madame Arnaud and Miss McLaughlin have come out of the office and they stop in front of me, their arms cradling folders. I wonder what they want now. They seem wistful. Slow. Ponderous. I stare at them because something's going on and I can't work it out. Miss McLaughlin smiles and says, 'You think all we care about is how well you do. Academically. Don't you?'

My silence is a yes. So is Becca's. Miss McLaughlin can definitely speak Silent because she seems to understand.

'But it's not, I promise you,' Miss McLaughlin says, her eyes sad for reasons I can't comprehend. 'We care about you so much, Jodie Jones. We see how creative you are, how individual, how special. You too, Becca. What an amazing friend you are.' Miss Slavin's eyes are welling up, and Madame Arnaud is smiling the kind of smile you smile at the end of watching *Titanic*.

'We've got your back,' Miss McLaughlin says. 'Might not seem that way, but we always have had, and we always will. We'll do anything to help you. All you have to do is talk to us.'

I see my chance and I grab it. 'Does that mean I don't have to do any homework?' I ask.

'Nice try,' Miss McLaughlin says, and the three of them laugh and walk away when I wasn't actually joking. Becca is talking a hundred miles an hour about the meeting but I'm not listening because through my head runs:

And hast thou slain the Jabberwock?
Come to my arms, my beamish boy!
O frabjous day! Callooh! Callay!
He chortled in his joy.

'Twas brillig and the slithy toves
Did gyre and gimble in the wabe;
All mimsy were the borogoves,
And the mome raths outgrabe.

48

Moses is parting the red blanket. It's not quite the Red Sea but the gesture is benevolent nonetheless. He's sitting on the checked sofa in our temporary home, 'a stylish, conveniently located, luxury urban oasis with stunning views of the park whilst moments away from train routes into central London and while being in easy reach of local amenities.'

No one seems as bothered as I am with the 'whilst', the 'while' or the 'being'.

Moses waits for me to place down the tray of Hobnobs and Ribena, blanket back, offering me sofa space and some of the fleece. He's not wearing the orange T-shirt/burgundy jeans combo today, but that would have been something against the scarlet throw.

'Too soon?' he asks, regarding the space he's made for me.

I stand up and nod.

'Only because it's chilly.'

'Mmm.'

'Not meaning anything snuggly by it.'

'Mmm.'

'Maybe a bit.'

I fight the urge to smile and, feeling awkward, turn around, as if looking at something curious and compelling behind me when we both know there's nothing there except a door and it's closed. I don't know why humans do this: make odd gestures when we're embarrassed. Turn around and look at nothing. Sniff. Look to the side. I guess it's a subconscious thing. When I turn back, Moses's eyes are on me, the remote is in his hand, and the blanket is off his legs as if he's about to get up. 'I can turn it off.'

'What is it?'

'*The Office*. US version. There's nothing . . . you know. Not in this episode. Not in any, I don't think.'

He means nothing disturbing: no car chases, armed police, shootings, stabbings, screaming, swearing, shouting, fear, panic, blood, sirens, vehicles screeching to a stop. No auditory or visual reminders that humans can be inhumane to each other and, far too often, are. I will never be able to watch things like that, but I don't mind. As long as I have a houseful of books, people and food of my choosing, why would I want to?

I hand him a mug that's slightly overfilled and therefore is a little chancy with this sofa, but he takes it with skill, and I sit down, not right beside him but not at the other end of the sofa, either. He takes an immediate sip, which is the correct action under the circumstances, wipes the side of the mug with his hand to ensure a dribble-free freedom of mind, and straightens the blanket over his legs.

A glance at the TV. The characters are funny. A fat-cheeked man with a domed bald head and a gormless look. A middle-aged woman with hair clips and glasses. A good-looking man and woman who appear to be a couple. Now and then they talk about each other or their job directly to the camera.

'Is this a documentary?' I ask. They seem too caricatured to be real.

'Spoof.'

'Ah.'

'Never seen it?'

'I tend to watch things in pockets. The latest being Wes Anderson movies.'

He likes this. I can tell by the fiesta his curls are now dancing in. He asks, 'Favourite?'

'Well, it was *The Darjeeling Limited*—'

'Top film.'

'Agreed. But now I'm leaning towards *The Grand Budapest Hotel* or *Isle of Dogs*.'

He sucks air in through his lips, which have a pinky tinge. 'Close call. Not *Asteroid City*? That's underrated. Like taking an eye bath in colours.'

I grin and have to un-grin before I sip my Ribena. I've made it a bit weak, but he doesn't mention it, which is kind, so I won't either, and instead offer him the plate of biscuits. I wonder how many he's going to take, because two seems right: one for immediate consumption and one as a back-up because you're going to eat a second anyway, so why be coy? But he only takes one, which is interesting, but I don't know why I find this interesting. I wonder what 'society' says but this reminds me of Mr Fowler, and he is not someone I wish to be reminded of.

I put the plate of biscuits on the coffee table, wondering why it's called a coffee table when it could equally be a tea or Ribena table or, if you're an adult, wine table, and consider what they called a table like this before coffee arrived in the country. An ale table? Did they even have small convenient tables for drinks in days of yore?

My mind is rampaging, I notice. I try to focus on the programme in case he's sending subliminal messages through TV codes. Moses laughs at something the hair-clipped lady says but I find it confusing. 'I don't . . . What's going on?'

'There's backstory and character development and stuff. I guess you can't really get it from one episode. It is funny . . .'

A cold draught sweeps across my legs. I understand the blanket now. I cross my arms for something to do, and then, when that feels rude, uncross them again. They sit on my lap looking languid. What do I usually do with my arms?

'Which one's your favourite?' he asks, putting the biscuit back on the plate. I don't feel like eating mine, either. Too much crunchy-crunchy followed by sugary gunk stuck in your teeth that you need to poke at for ages afterwards with your tongue. I put mine back, too.

My eyes flick up at the TV and from character to character. 'I don't know them well enough to—'

'Of the sentences.'

I turn and gaze at him. It goes on for a while. 'What do you mean? Wait. You did that?'

He grins.

'What? All of them?'

'I dunno. I think so. Unless someone else has been leaving sentences around for you as well.'

'But . . . the Joyce one under my bedroom door? The Chekhov on my desk?'

'The Byron in your backpack. *The Road* on the table in the hall. The Post-its around school; the displays in the English corridor. There are more – you haven't come across them all yet. You'll find them. Checked your inner coat pocket recently?'

I shake my head and laugh. 'I'm ... But I've been finding them for a while. How did you ...'

'Becca.' His expression seems all of these things: sheepish, mischievous, coy, klutzy, hangdog, wry.

I'm perceptive. How did I not see this. How did I not work it out? 'That's the nicest thing anyone has ever done. For anyone. Ever,' I decide.

'Nah. People hid families in Nazi Germany. Saved their lives. That stratum of humanity is right up there for me.'

He's right. I wish he wouldn't make comments like that, though. They make me like him even more.

'And your favourite?' His lips twist and his eyes smile.

'The Joyce. If I had to choose. But honestly, I like them all.'

'Good-good.' He's exuding calm but he's euphoric – I can tell from the way his body has inflated and his cheeks are twitching skywards. 'Who did you think was giving them to you?'

'I don't know. Everyone. My dad. Miss McLaughlin. Clyde. Becca ...'

'Even the ones about love?'

'Well, yes, but, you know. To give me hope. So I wouldn't write it off. As a possibility.'

The screen is a distraction but somehow it helps. I keep my eyes on it, grateful for something to look at.

'Have you?' he asks. 'Written it off?' I feel too warm, suddenly and my blink reflex seems to have malfunctioned. 'Because I was hoping myself,' he adds.

That makes me look at him. 'Hoping myself, what? That isn't a sentence.'

He laughs. 'Hoping you hadn't written it off. Hoping you might like me as much as I like you.'

My foot taps on the floor and I bite my bottom lip. My eyes delight in the brightness of my shoes: orange and yellow bubble platforms with toxic green stripes. 'I don't know how much you like me so I wouldn't know if I like you the same amount.'

'Fair.' He sniffs and grins. 'Do you . . . like me at all?' He says it quickly, so the words roll in to one another. Likemeadall.

'Sitting here with you, aren't I? In an indoor room. Half watching TV. I wouldn't do that if I didn't likeyouadall.'

'Good to know. Shall I . . .?' He points at the slightly open window. 'Bit draughty.' He closes it and sits down again. 'Do you like me because I'm Champ's friend?'

I shake my head. 'Charlie. Not Champ.'

'Charlie.' He nods. 'Right.'

'He's not here so that's surely eliminated.'

'Is it . . . because I wear a combination of hues you find visually appealing?'

'No. But that helps.'

'Is it . . . because I find you sentences?'

'I wasn't aware it was you.'

'OK. Well . . . as you aren't being particularly forthcoming with your feelings and forthcoming is called for, I'm going to be the most vulnerable I've ever been in my sixteen-and-a-quarter-year existence. OK?'

The air in the room is a thrummed guitar string. I focus on the screen and move my head in the affirmative.

'I think about you with affection almost all my waking

hours.' He pauses, his red-socked feet crossing over each other like they're hugging, presumably so I take that in, but maybe also because he's nervous.

'I look forward to Thursdays because I get to sit next to you in PSHE. I meticulously engineer risky visits to your house and chance meetings, both in school and outside, so I'll bump in to you. And when you do move to a permanent place, just say the word and I'll build walls of bookshelves in your room. I've got no carpentry experience and the YouTube videos I'm watching are unlikely to equip me with professional-level DIY skills, but I'll do my best.'

I am at a loss as to why he's telling me this. I don't fill a bra the size of twin baseball caps; I don't have short skorts, long legs and netball skills; I'm not top in every subject except Physics any more, even though my grades are better, I need to see psychologists and psychiatrists regularly because I was walking across a bridge at the wrong time when I was ten years old and in the midst of the violence and chaos, I learned something about my mother that I should never have learned and I don't know if I'll ever get over it.

'I'm not worth it,' I whisper. I mean not worth the time it would take for me to heal enough to be normal, if I ever will be, which I probably won't. But also, I'm not worth him because he's the best example of an under-forty-year-old human male I've ever met. I don't tell him that Clyde might be the best example of an *over*-forty-year-old human male I've ever met, because I don't mean it how it sounds, and he might take it the wrong way.

Moses turns off the TV, which I'm glad of because the credits are rolling and the names are distracting. 'You're very very worth it,' he says. He reaches into his jeans pocket, pulls something out, balls his fists, and hides both hands behind his back.

'Pick one,' he says.

I choose left and he hands me a folded square of lined yellow paper. On it, he has written:

> *What is this terror? what is this ecstasy? he thought to himself. What is it that fills me with this extraordinary excitement?*
>
> *It is ~~Clarissa~~, Jodie Jones he said.*
>
> *For there she was.*
>
> *Mrs Dalloway by Virginia Woolf*

'I know. Pick another one,' he says, putting his hands behind his back again.

I laugh and choose the right. On that piece of paper, he's written:

> *She is beautiful without knowing it, and possesses charms that she's not even aware of . . . Anyone who has seen her smile has known perfection.*
>
> *Cyrano de Bergerac by Edmond Rostand*

'That's not me. That's like, I don't know, Lalisa Manoban.'

'That's you,' he says. 'OK, maybe perfection's pushing it, but your smile's definitely a nine out of ten.'

We laugh and I stare at the pieces of paper. They relax me. He relaxes me. So why do I feel as if my skin has been pared off?

'I don't know how to do this,' I tell him, meaning relationships and romance and love dramas and late-night messaging and staring at my phone while I wait for his dots-in-progess to turn into words, and laughing, and replying, and the urgency of feelings and moody window-gazing and the sharing of secrets and the fact that everyone else will rapidly know about our quiet, private interest in each other, and kissing and whatever comes after the kissing that I can't do until I'm sixteen but which might someday involve the exploration and touching of body parts, which makes me recoil and shudder but which must be affectionate and enjoyable or why would anyone do it?

And now there's also another worry, of blood and hormones, and boys knowing about your cycle and potentially, optimistically, rubbing your feet when you're teary and crying about nothing much at first, and then about every sad thing that's ever happened to any human and creature on the planet, like I was last week when my cycle came back with a vengeance after two years. But also, and before any of those other things, I don't know how to do this. Sit in a room with a boy who is excellent in every way – well, maybe not every way but then, realistically, who is? – and have a conversation with him about how excellent I think he is and how electrified and petrified that makes me feel.

'I mean, me neither?' he says. His tone rises like a question.

I feel it deserves a semblance of an answer, but I can't speak. I keep my eyes down, so he won't see my expression.

He falters, then. 'It doesn't have to be ... you know. Romantic. Unless you want that.'

My silence says, I do want that. I really, really want that. I just don't know if I can. Probably not, realistically. Or at least not for a long while and a mountain of money on therapy. Even then.

He adds, 'Maybe we can just ... you know, go slow. See how it goes ... Or if you're not into ... I mean, if you don't want to ... that's fine, too. Obviously.'

I scratch my ankle and bite the inner skin on my cheek. At least I don't turn and look at the door again.

'Like, I'm in. Completely. But I'm happy just to be here with you and be your friend. Any which way. Promise. I just want to be in your life. If you want me to be.'

My fingers fiddle with the hem of my jumper and he lifts his hand, as if he wants to touch mine, but he holds back because he's unsure. I'm so moved by this unassuming, tentative gesture of respect that I stop fiddling, reach up and take his hand. It feels warm and soft.

I'm as surprised as he is that I've done this. I don't like hand holding as a rule.

Through the thrum of the room in the stark and the cold of the day, I'd reached out to touch the boy sitting beside me.

I could feel through his hand the warm familiarity of Moses, his mild good-natured stillness, his tender concern, his wide and open heart.

A ghost of a smile is on his lips, his face shy. 'You sure ... this is all right? Jodie Jones?' he almost whispers. Hopeful. Uncertain. Exposed.

I shake my head. I'm not sure of anything, least of all this.

'You can call me Jodie,' I quietly reply. 'But only you.'

He bursts out laughing and inadvertently squeezes my hand. 'Uh-uh. Your name is Jodie Jones. It would feel strange to call you only a part of that. Unless you utterly insist.'

'I mainly did it to annoy my mother,' I admit. 'And that mission has been accomplished. I've got used to it now, though. I'll have to think about it.'

'You do that.'

I let go of his hand and make a sorry but it's weird face. 'I can't . . .'

He breaks into a broad and beaming grin and says, 'It's OK. Don't need to. It's all good.'

But then, because he's so sweet about it, I take his hand again.

Belying the casualness of this, of us sitting fake-nonchalantly holding hands and talking about my name, is the force of how it feels. Electrically charged. Extraordinarily intense. Ardent, fierce, perfervid. If perfervid is even a word. I may be sitting stock-still, inert, but a flood of blood is surging furiously through me in a foaming, frothing fizz. I sense the manic motor of my heart, the throbbing tingle in my hand, my surprised unblinking eyes. The vim, pep, zip, zing and oomph of life itself. I sense depth and meaning, whatever that means. This sole, lone moment transforms into one that's bigger, wider, fuller and more momentous than any other moment I have known, and I feel a swelling bubble inside me that might pop into a laugh, a cheer or an explosion of tears, and it takes all the might and force I have to keep it in.

Whereas once, the mere thought of Moses holding my hand would cause me to feel all of these things: terrified, anxious, roused, intoxicated, rhapsodic, entranced, exultant, jubilant and Panglossian, I realize for the first time in my short and eventful life that there are moments and situations in which words are neither suitable nor necessary. Which is a revelation to me.

Dad's right. There's beauty in even the simplest things if they reflect the complexity and richness and suffering and joy and love and profound depth, and whatever else he said, about life and being human.

As we sit there, Moses's hand in mine, I feel all of these things:

And that feels fine.

Acknowledgements

My agent, Jessica Hare, loved Jodie Jones from her first read of the half-formed thing I sent her one January morning, and she has supported it and me always, so my first thanks is to her. Anthony Hinton and the team at DFB are a dream to work with; I'm honoured to be published by them. Thank you all for making the process so positive, fun and seamless, and particularly for your presentation pitch to lure me your way, which was honestly the most heart-warming and humbling hour of my authorly life.

I'm indebted to therapists Anne Thompson and Carol Rawlence for reading the manuscript to check the Dr Kumar sections. The writer, Colin Grant, was (loosely) the inspiration for Clyde Hitchin, but poetic license and imagination means they are not one and the same, and Sheena Wilkinson (tutoring on that same magical Arvon trip) encouraged me to continue the first two chapters I'd written years and years before. Thank you all.

My colleagues are superlative and I'm grateful every day to work with them. Well, most days. Well, some. When the weather's bad and there's nothing good on telly. Some have cameoed in my other novels; in this one, Martine Arnaud, Josh Clements, Matt Trussell and Shivani Vyas generously let me include them, and The Greatest Department (English, obvs) suggested writers and sentences when I needed to make quotation changes. One morning, on different trains to work, I sent my colleague, Fredric Calvet, Head of MFL, a message with the four words in French to check their meaning and usage; he replied to say that, to him, they all related to sound, and told me why. For that delight on an otherwise humdrum commute, and for letting me use your message almost verbatim, Fred, I have given Moses your surname.

I'm profoundly grateful for my friends, especially Jem and Clare (bighearted, encouraging, lifesaving), Joe K (benevolent, witty, entirely dependable), Emma Cabrera (droll, chauffeur-like when I break limbs, the world's most talented florist), and my cinema, reading, writing, and thinking buddies. Most of all, thanks to my mother (unconventional, uproarious, wise), who has always had my back and cheered me on, my cousins, aunts, uncles and sisters around the globe, and my growing brood who are my greatest joys. Some mothers love their children more than anything. Your mother is one of them.

The incident on the bridge is based on the London Bridge attack 29th November 2019.

Monica Jones was hard to write; I had to research her and her condition, but the experience of growing up in a home and environment where you do not feel safe is not fiction and, unfortunately, is the reality for many children and teens. If this is you or someone you know, please talk to someone you trust, and/or get in touch with the organisations on the following page.

Support

If any of the issues raised in *My Name is Jodie Jones* are directly relatable, here are some organisations in the UK that may be able to help you.

Childline: 0800 1111 | childline.org.uk
Free, confidential 24-hour support for under 19s for any problem, large or small. Via the website, you can also have a 1-2-1 chat with a counsellor online, play on-screen games, and read info and advice.
SHOUT: text 'SHOUT' to 85258
Free, confidential, 24-hour messaging service for anyone of any age struggling to cope.
Samaritans: 116 123 | Samaritans.org
Free helpline for those of any age having a difficult time or are worried about someone else. You can talk about relationships, family, grief, finances, study or work stress, loneliness, depression, illness, substance and alcohol use, thoughts of suicide.

Papyrus: 0800 068 4141 or text 88247 | Papyrus-uk.org
Prevention of young suicide, and the promotion of positive mental health and emotional wellbeing in young people.
Switchboard: 0800 0119 100 | switchboard.lgbt
National LGBTQIA+ support helpline, and chat via the website.
Young Minds: youngminds.org.uk
Online advice via their website on a range of situations and feelings, including grief.
The Mix: 0808 808 4994 | themix.org.uk
Offering support for young people under 25 through an online community; social media; a free, confidential helpline and counselling service. Offers help for any challenge – from mental health to money, from homelessness to finding a job, from break-ups to drugs.
Kooth: kooth.com
Online platform with forums and mental health professionals available to chat to via messaging for anyone 13+ who needs help with their mental health.
Winston's Wish: 08088 020021 (8am–8pm weekdays) | winstonswish.org
Live online chat, helpline, text or email support for those aged 25 and under who are affected by grief and loss.

In an emergency, dial 999 or ask someone you trust to do it for you.

For those outside the UK, please search 'support for young people' to find services in your part of the world.

Permissions

We are grateful to the following publishers and estates for their kind permission to reproduce copyright material used within this book:

Truman Capote quotation from "'Go Right Ahead and Ask Me Anything' (And So She Did): An Interview with Truman Capote", Gloria Steinem / 1967. From *McCall's 95* (November 1967), 76-77, 148-152. 154. Copyright © 1967 by Gloria Steinem. Included in *Truman Capote: Conversations* (University Press of Mississippi). Reprinted by permission of the Truman Capote Literary Trust and the Office of Gloria Steinem.

Charles Frazier, *Cold Mountain* (Grove Press 1997). Used by permission of Grove/Atlantic, Inc.

Daphne du Maurier, *Rebecca* (Victor Gollancz Ltd/Orion Publishing 1938). Reprinted with permission of Curtis Brown Ltd, London, on behalf of The Chichester Partnership. Copyright © 1938 The Chichester Partnership.

Cormac McCarthy, *The Road* (Alfred A. Knopf/Penguin Random House 2006). Reprinted by permission of Pan MacMillan.

Mary Oliver, *Wild Geese*, from *Dream Work* copyright © 1986 by Mary Oliver. Used by permission of Grove/Atlantic, Inc.

Mary Oliver, *The Summer Day*, from *House of Light* (Beacon Press 1990). Reprinted by the permission of The Charlotte Sheedy Literary Agency as agent for the author. Copyright © 1990, 2006, 2008, 2017 by Mary Oliver with permission of Bill Reichblum.

PG Wodehouse, *Thank You, Jeeves* (Herbert Jenkins/Penguin Random House 1934). Reprinted by permission of RCW Literary Agency, on behalf of the PG Wodehouse Estate.

Although every effort has been made to trace and contact all copyright holders, if notified, the publisher will rectify any errors or omissions at the earliest opportunity.

Credits

We also acknowledge the following writers whose work is cited in the book:

Louisa May Alcott, *Little Women* (1868)

William Blake, *The Schoolboy* (1789)

Charlotte Brontë, *Jane Eyre* (1847)

Emily Brontë, *Wuthering Heights* (1847)

Lord Byron, *She Walks in Beauty Like the Night* (1814)

Lewis Carroll, *Alice in Wonderland* (1865)

Lewis Carroll, *Jabberwocky* (1871)

Anton Chekov, *Gooseberries* (1898)

Samuel Taylor Coleridge, *Kubla Khan* (1816)

Ralph Waldo Emerson, *Essays* (1841)

F. Scott Fitzgerald, *The Great Gatsby* (1925)

Gustave Flaubert, *Madame Bovary* (1857)

James Joyce, *Ulysses* (1918)

Immanuel Kant, *The Critique of Pure Reason* (1781)

Christina Rossetti, *A Birthday* (1861)

Edmond Rostand, *Cyrano de Bergerac* (1897)

William Shakespeare, *Romeo and Juliet* (1597), *Macbeth* (1606)

Mary Shelley, *Frankenstein; or, The Modern Prometheus* (1818)

Percy Bysshe Shelley, *Ozymandius* (1818)

King Solomon, *Ecclesiastes* (approx. 450 BCE)

Alfred Lord Tennyson, *Ulysses* (1842)

Mark Twain, *Letter to George Bainton* (1838)

Oscar Wilde, *De Profundis* (1905)

Virginia Woolf, *Mrs Dalloway* (1925)

William Wordsworth, *I Wandered Lonely as a Cloud* (1802)

About the Author

Author photograph: Alexander O'Neal

Emma Shevah is half-Thai and half-Irish. She was born and raised in London, but has lived and travelled in lots of countries.

Emma has a BA Hons in English and Philosophy, and an MA in Creative and Professional Writing. As well as being an author and creative writing teacher, she is Director of Literacy and Oracy, an English teacher, and a learning support teacher at a central London school, where she works with students, some of whom are neurodivergent, and all of whom are delightful.

Hailing from a neurodiverse family herself, she has four children and has written middle-grade novels and books for younger readers.

My Name is Jodie Jones is her YA debut.